THE DISCIPLE

Steven Dunne has written for fun since attending Kent University in the late seventies when he first became interested in writing and performing. His primary focus was comedy. He wrote and performed sketches as well as dipping his toe into the terrifying world of stand-up comedy. He is now a full-time English teacher in Derby.

To find out more about Steven visit his website at www.the-reaper.com

By the same author:
The Reaper

STEVEN DUNNE

The Disciple

AVON

AVON

A division of HarperCollins*Publishers*
77–85 Fulham Palace Road,
London W6 8JB

www.harpercollins.co.uk

A Paperback Original 2010

A catalogue record for this book is
available from the British Library

ISBN: 978-1-84756-164-0

Set in Minion by Palimpsest Book Production Limited,
Falkirk, Stirlingshire

Printed and bound in Great Britain by
Clays Ltd, St Ives plc

Mixed Sources

Product group from well-managed
forests and other controlled sources
www.fsc.org Cert no. SW-COC-001806
© 1996 Forest Stewardship Council

FSC

FSC is a non-profit international organisation established to promote the responsible
management of the world's forests. Products carrying the FSC label are independently certified
to assure consumers that they come from forests that are managed to meet the social,
economic and ecological needs of present and future generations.

Find out more about HarperCollins and the environment at
www.harpercollins.co.uk/green

Thanks go again to Jeff Fountain for his continuing practical support and encouragement.

I'd also like to thank all members of my informal support team who have continued to promote *The Reaper* series, especially my wife Carmel and my wonderful sister Susan Dunne – thanks for pestering me to finish *The Disciple*. Also thanks to Dennis and Geraldine Lee, unstinting in their support and leaders of *The Reaper*'s second front in the South of France.

Thanks to fellow Weekenders cricketer Joseph McDonald for taking the trouble to produce thoughtful and expert input on police procedures.

A big thank you again to Waterstone's for putting up with me in-store on more than one occasion – particularly Sean Heavens in Derby and Glenys Cooper in Burton-on-Trent.

And once more I'm grateful to HarperCollins for the opportunity to reach a wider audience and their belief in *The Reaper* series. Thanks to Claire Bord, Maxine Hitchcock, now departed to pastures new and, of course, Sammia Rafique for her thoughtful input.

Finally thank you to David Grossman, my agent, for taking me on as a client and providing his expert guidance.

In loving memory
Jean Robertshaw
(1930 – 2009)

Chapter One

The man eased the door closed, guiding it gently onto the latch. When he heard the lock click he sucked in a lungful of the sharp salty air to clear his head. He could hear the occasional gull in the distance but it was a lonely note, the early birds not yet on the wing, the light insufficient to make out the pickings left by the receding tide.

He looked at the sky, dark and damp, no hint yet of the grey dawn peeping over the horizon, then hitched his jogging bottoms higher and retied the strings. He smiled as he rearranged his genitalia, feeling the tacky moisture of recent sex along his groin – even at the age of forty-three, the thrill of illicit conquest still bestowed a childish buzz – then stepped onto the wet road and crossed to the far pavement.

He turned to see the girl in the first-floor bay of the guest-house, barely covered by a worn curtain that had doubtless shrouded hundreds of copulating lovers from the eyes of the world. He grinned but motioned her away from the window in mock censure. She, in response, let the curtain slip to show him a breast, then let the curtain fall completely and stood before him naked.

The man put his hands on his hips in feigned disgust, then looked around and pointed down the road, as though someone else would be walking around at this ungodly hour.

The girl shrugged her shoulders and laughed. She turned her back, bent over and pressed her buttocks against the window.

1

The man shook his head and turned to jog away, realising that his departure was the only way to end the cabaret. Kids today!

As he turned onto King's Road, jogging gently towards the burnt-out skeleton of the West Pier, Tony Harvey-Ellis glanced at the grey-black ocean, wondering whether to risk a dip after his run. The water would still be mild even in late autumn.

He pulled in a huge breath and looked around in vain for another soul. He loved this time of day when he could have Brighton to himself. The early hours were the best time to venture out onto the streets. The throngs of tourists had eased after the hot months but Brighton still drew frenzied hordes of hens and stags all year round, carousing long into the night – enough to deter most residents at the weekends.

This was *his* time, time to think; increasingly his only time since his life had become so complicated. With all the new accounts needing his attention and the constant juggling of the demands of his wife and stepdaughter, he had become unused to solitude. At least Terri's age was one less problem to concern him – she was legal now. Her real father would find it difficult to pin anything on him after so long . . . assuming he still cared.

Harvey-Ellis paused briefly, stretching his upper torso and flexing his knees. The sweat was beginning to dot his forehead and his knees felt ready for some real work. He checked his watch – it was five o'clock – and prepared to set the stopwatch on his chunky Tag Heuer.

A noise that was neither the sea nor a car made him turn. A figure, indistinct in a tracksuit and baseball cap, was jogging along the promenade a couple of hundred metres behind him, feet slapping at the ground, breath steaming in the sharp air.

Annoyed at having his solitude contaminated, Harvey-Ellis consoled himself with the thought that at least he'd have a spectator to impress. He started his stopwatch then struck away powerfully from the jogger.

As he ran, Harvey-Ellis practised shifting an imaginary ball to

2

his left and then right. He felt good as he bounced lightly across the tarmac. Maybe this would be his last season. He loved his rugby, loved the physicality of it, the sense of brotherhood, the union of wildly differing human physiques melded into one team, one purpose. But he didn't love it enough to move from his position on the wing to a berth with the forwards, as his pace dwindled. He'd seen enough human battering rams with beetroot noses and cauliflower ears to want to risk his good looks.

He slowed and half-turned to see the other runner almost upon him. A natural competitor, Harvey-Ellis lifted his pace again. For a few seconds, he listened for the receding sound of the other runner's footfall, but instead it seemed to be drawing nearer.

Okay, thought Harvey-Ellis, time to put on the burners, show you a sight all too familiar to the fullbacks of the Southern and District League. He picked up his pace to a sprint, lifting his knees, pumping his arms straight and blowing his cheeks rhythmically to take the necessary shallow breaths.

For nearly a minute, he maintained this pace and tried to block out all movement in his peripheral vision. But his ears could not block the sound of the second runner closing in and his eyes could now see the shadow thrown over his own by the jaundiced glow of streetlights. His lungs could take it no more. He threw up his head and slowed through the gears to a stop. He put his hands on his knees and sucked air urgently into his lungs, turning to grin at his pursuer. He didn't see the clenched fist, or the small needle protruding from it.

'You win,' he panted.

*

Jason Donovan Wallis was alone except for Bianca, his tiny sister snoring gently in her room. His aunt was on nights again and the bitch had left him in charge. Dread. Not that he wanted to go out in this weather but her draughty old house in Borrowash, a few miles to the east of Derby, chilled him to the bone. No heating, no light. Storm damage, they'd said on the radio; the whole area was under blackout. Despite this, the heavy curtains were drawn across the windows, blocking out any hint of the faint moonlight, and Jason was not in the least tempted to change that.

He'd had a text from Banger chatting that the rest of the crew were 'Gonna make the most of it, smoke some peng, do some cars, whatever.' Did Jason want to 'stop being a gay and come and hang. LOL.'

Yeah, right. Walk around in the dark like a skank – with that killer still out there. No way. He weren't going nowhere on his own. That copper Brook had warned him about The Reaper after his mum, dad and sister were cut up. 'The Reaper's out there waiting, watching,' he goes, 'waiting to finish the job.' Jason was well gone at the time. Booze, drugs maybe, he couldn't remember. Brook had threatened him, tried to make him cough to that old biddy's murder. 'You're next, Jason – you're next.'

Jason eased into a secret smile. The Reaper had forgotten him. Jason was a survivor. And he'd sorted Brook out – no messing. Trashed his place and mashed his cat's brains in. *Feds who fuck with me get fucked up double.*

He pulled the blanket tighter around his shoulders, squinting at the single flickering candle he'd managed to root out from under the stairs. He listened to the wind howling and stared out of habit at the inert TV screen.

The noise of the front gate creaking on its rusty hinges made his head turn. Jason waited, not moving, aware of the rising tide of fear washing through him. But no one knocked at the door. No one banged on the window. Only the sound of the gate assaulted his ears, pounding against the wall under the weight of the wind.

'Bollocks!' he spat. Now he'd have to go out and refasten it or it would be hammering all night. Trust his aunt to be on nights, leaving him on his own to babysit. He listened for the sound of the gate, dreading its explosion, beckoning him off the couch, out of the sanctuary of the house.

4

But it didn't come. Outside the wind raged still, whipping sodden leaves and soupy litter into a drunken dance, but the gate refused to complain under the assault. Gradually Jason's annoyance turned to puzzlement . . . then dread began to seep into him. Now he longed to hear the crash of the gate, telling him it was only the weather out there messing with his head.

He tiptoed to the window to look out through a crack in the curtain into the wildness. A dark figure stood by the gate, perfectly still, perfectly calm against nature. Though Jason could see only blackness where the face should have been, he sensed that whoever was standing there was staring straight back at him.

He hurtled out of the living room. With the door opened, the draught sucked the life from the small candle but Jason didn't return to relight it. Instead, sprinting up the stairs three at a time, he bundled into his bedroom to look out of the window at the garden below. He could make out nothing, until a flash of lightning illuminated the scene. The figure had gone.

Jason's heartbeat was beginning to slow when a single bang on the door quickened it once more. He could feel panic rising within him like bile and was unable to keep his limbs still. Frantic, he looked round for his mobile, his only umbilical cord to the rest of humanity, then realised, a wave of nausea crashing over him, that he'd left it downstairs.

Another bang on the door, but it wasn't a friendly sound – rather a booming rhythmic knell.

After the third knock, silence returned. Even the wind whistling up from the Trent seemed to take a time out.

Jason held his breath. Eventually he plucked up the courage to tiptoe back down the stairs. He pulled open the tatty curtain that served to block the draught from the front door and peered through the condensation on the mottled glass. No one there. He heaved a sigh of relief and then fumbled in his pocket for his lighter so he could relight the candle. When he looked up once more, it was to see a figure filling the doorway. He leapt backwards in shock, pulling the curtain back across the door.

Jason shrank back to the foot of the stairs, cowering on the bottom step.

'I'm sorry about the old woman,' he said, almost to himself. Then he spoke more loudly, directing his words towards the door. 'We didn't mean to kill her. I told Brook. He knows. Didn't he tell you? Is it the cat? That was Banger's idea. I didn't want none of it. It weren't me . . .'

Jason began to whimper quietly but stopped at the sound of tinny music leaking out of the front room. He leapt to pick up his mobile and looked at the display. He had a text from an unknown number. Jason pressed a key and read the text.

You're next.

Jason let his hand fall and began to sob again. Then he lifted his phone once more and dialled the source of the text. It was picked up on the first ring. No one spoke.

'I said I'm sorry. Okay? I'm sorry. What do you want from me?' No answer. Then the noise of breaking glass in stereo. In his right ear on the phone. In his left ear from the kitchen at the back of the house. Jason lowered the phone and turned towards the gloom of the hallway. He bolted to the stairs and sprinted back up them, not daring to glance towards the dark kitchen.

At the top of the stairs, he turned and ran towards his bedroom again. It flashed through his mind that perhaps he should grab little Bianca to keep her safe, but he decided he didn't have time. She'd have to take her chances.

Jason shut the bedroom door and pulled a chest of drawers across it. He yanked back the curtains and opened the window. Immediately the cool spray of rain hit his face, soothing him. He looked down into the gloom of the overgrown front garden, at the billowing privet hedge that his aunt had been nagging him to trim, glad now that she'd refused to pay him and it had been left untended. If necessary, if he had to jump, Jason was confident it

6

would break his fall. Now all he could do was wait. He clutched his phone and pondered ringing the police but, before he could decide, the handle of the bedroom door turned. After a couple of increasingly urgent turns, it began to reverberate under the shoulder of the intruder.

Jason took a huge gulp of air and balanced himself on the sill. The door crashed again and the chest of drawers began to shift. His eyes closed, Jason launched himself into the void.

A couple of seconds later, he felt the breath leave his body as he hit the privet. He could feel his skin begin to tear from dozens of tiny scratches but felt himself come to a near stop, cushioned by the hedge's volume. Under Jason's weight, the hedge began to topple but he was able to cling on by grabbing a few flailing branches. He used their movement to land his feet on the pavement of Station Road.

Jason quickly righted himself. He looked down at his right hand. Incredibly his mobile was still in his palm. The display was lit. Another message.

Behind you.

Before Jason could turn he felt a hand grab his damp hair and pull back his head. Out of the corner of his eye, he saw the glint of a blade lifting towards his left ear, then a short, sharp pain as a hand pulled heavily across his throat . . .

*

Detective Sergeant Laura Grant walked unsteadily across the beach. A combination of the shifting shingle and the need to hold the two Styrofoam cups of coffee steady caused her to stumble as she picked her way towards the small huddle gathered around the tarpaulin-covered body spreadeagled by the sea's edge.

Scene of Crime Officers swarmed around the body, working with uncommon haste before the elements returned to launder the evidence. Some took pictures, some dug in the sand with

7

trowels looking for non-existent artefacts, others combed hair and bagged hands.

Grant rubbed her eyes as she walked. She'd only just returned to work after her sick leave, and though she felt the unscheduled bout of exercise was beneficial, the unexpected glare of the low sun certainly wasn't.

Trying not to stare ghoulishly towards the tarpaulin, she reached the hastily erected police tape and bobbed under with some difficulty as Dr Hubbard, the most senior forensic pathologist in Sussex, re-covered the body and rose from his haunches to speak to Detective Chief Inspector Joshua Hudson.

'White male, forty-ish. He's been dead no more than eight hours and no less than six, I'd say.'

Hudson looked at his watch. 'Which would mean he drowned between four and six this morning,' he said, sweeping back his thick grey hair with a tobacco-stained hand. 'Early bird, eh?'

'Or very late, Chief Inspector. Depends on your point of view. It is the weekend. And please don't pre-empt my findings on COD.'

'He didn't drown?'

'It's difficult to say definitively at this moment, Chief Inspector. I like to keep an open mind.'

'Fine. He *probably* drowned,' prompted Hudson, lighting up a cigarette and ignoring the reproachful glance of one of the SOCOs.

'Probably. But it's not exactly Cape Horn round here,' observed Hubbard, surveying the calm sea. 'And he's wearing boxers, not swimming shorts, so he wasn't planning a dip.'

'A lot of them aren't, Doc, until they've had a dozen Breezers and God knows how many tequila slammers.'

Laura Grant held out a cup of white froth towards Hudson.

'True. But he's fit for his age. Powerful legs – though not from swimming.'

There was a hint of smugness at that and Grant squinted up at the doctor for further explanation.

Hudson, however, had missed it. 'These things happen to the

8

fittest people, Doc,' he said and took his coffee with a brief wink at Grant and a quick 'Cheers, darlin''. Grant glanced up at the two uniformed officers on crowd control. PCs Wong and West both gave her a sly grin to provoke a reaction to her first 'luv', 'sweetie' or 'darlin'' of the day but Grant maintained the face of a stoic.

'Still . . .'

'Look, doc, he's got shorts on. He went in the water and I'm ruling out a shark attack,' said Hudson. Grant and the two uniformed officers exchanged an amused glance. Even one of the normally taciturn SOCOs managed a smile. 'So just tell me he went for a swim and drowned so we can all go home.'

'There is some trauma to the head,' replied Hubbard.

'Probably from a boat.'

'Even so, I'll need to examine the wound to find traces of boat.'

'What about his watch?' asked Grant, deciding it was time to pretend she was a functioning police officer. They all looked at the dead man's wrist.

'What about it?'

'Looks expensive, guv. If it's waterproof he might have gone for a dip voluntarily. But if it's not he would have taken it off. Unless . . .' she said with a tilt of her head for emphasis.

'. . . unless he was murdered,' nodded Hudson, kneeling to look at it. '12.05. Sorry, luv – waterproof.'

Grant shrugged her shoulders. 'Doesn't mean he didn't commit suicide, guv.'

'Suicide? How about it, Doc?'

'I'll say it again, I'm ruling nothing out. If you found his clothes . . .'

Hudson looked at Grant. 'We're on it,' she said. 'We've got uniform following the tide back. Maybe he left his ID . . .'

'A suicide note would be better,' added Hudson. 'You'll do a tox kit on him?' he asked Hubbard, who rolled his eyes. 'Bloody tourists. Why can't they die at home?'

'Oh, he's not a tourist, Inspector!' the doctor interjected.

Grant and Hudson turned to him, impressed.

'How can you tell that?' asked Grant, half-expecting some labyrinthine Sherlock Holmes monograph on 'The Identification of Tourists'.

The good doctor permitted himself a satisfied smirk at the sudden attention. 'Because I know who he is.' Hudson pulled back the cover and gazed at the black and blue face on the sand. 'That's Tony Harvey-Ellis. I've met him a couple of times. Rotary Club, you know. And maybe even a rugby club do, I can't be sure. But I know he used to play to quite a good standard. He's a fairly big cheese in Brighton.'

'Are we talking Dairylea triangle big? Or Christmas Stilton?' asked Hudson, now dismayed that his workload on the case was suddenly threatening to escalate.

'Stilton definitely – he's one of the partners in Hall Gordon Public Relations. They've got that large building on the front – pretty successful by all accounts, though I've always considered him to be a bit of a prat. Really fancied himself, if you ask me.'

Hudson reached again for his cigarettes. 'Great. That's all we need.'

*

Jason Donovan Wallis woke clutching his throat, panting for his last breath, trying to staunch the blood from a wound inflicted many times before. His gasps slowed as recognition dawned and he became aware of his surroundings. His heart rate levelled but with relief came the tears, slow and unwelcome but above all silent. All signs of weakness were ruthlessly mocked in White Oaks, so inmates cried with the mute button on.

Jason lay back on his bunk. His T-shirt was soaked with sweat so he tore it off, wiped it around his tear tracks and slung it on the floor. He sat up on his bunk and tried to calm himself by taking deep breaths, as softly as he could manage so as not to wake his roommate.

The sun slammed in through the grimy curtain-free window,

flat like a searchlight in a watchtower across the quadrangle. He shielded his eyes. Was this it? His life. Every morning, waking up in a fug of moisturised panic, remembering the old woman begging for mercy, or the sheet-covered trolleys of his butchered family, or, worst of all, the faceless psycho chasing him, killing him. What was it Father Donetti had told him after Sunday Service? *Cowards die many times.* How many times, he hadn't seen fit to mention. Jason hoped it wasn't too many more.

At least here the only danger was from other inmates, young offenders keen to seek out those weaker than themselves so they could pass on abuse from further up the hierarchy. So far he'd managed to keep his head down and hang tough in all the right places.

Jason stood and pulled his blanket over his pillow and tiptoed over to his bag, already packed for his release. He pulled out a fresh T-shirt, dragged it over his head and crept to the window to look out at the chill of the morning. It was early but he still had to screen his eyes from the low sun. He looked over the grounds, which were covered in a light frost, down the drive to the main gate, and then across at the outbuildings, which housed most of the workshops where the day staff tried to teach some of the inmates a trade.

For the first time since his sentence began, Jason was invaded by a pang for freedom, a yearning to get out of the block and wander round the site. He could have it to himself. He could even walk down the drive to the gates and peer at the world outside. If he really wanted, he could open the gate and walk out. If he wanted . . .

*

Hudson and Grant stood either side of the sheet-covered steel trolley. The two women were huddled in position, the younger slightly behind the elder, holding onto her arm with both hands. Hudson nodded to the mortuary technician, who peeled the sheet back from the corpse.

The older woman screamed and collapsed to the floor, the

younger woman's flimsy grip on her arm insufficient to keep her upright. Hudson managed to grab her and haul her up. The young girl ignored her plight and stared open-mouthed at the body of Tony Harvey-Ellis.

'Oh God, no,' she said, tears streaming down her face, her breath coming in short hard bursts. 'Oh God. Oh God.'

A second later the girl seemed to become aware of her surroundings. Her arms sought her mother and gathered her into an embrace, each wedging their tear-stained face onto the shoulder of the other.

Grant nodded at the technician, who re-covered the body with appropriate solemnity.

Hudson posed the superfluous question. 'Is that your husband's body, Mrs Harvey-Ellis?'

*

'I don't understand.' Amy Harvey-Ellis wrung the damp handkerchief around her fingers and stared at the untouched coffee that she'd accepted on her arrival, without understanding any part of the transaction. The tears began to well again. 'I don't understand. He shouldn't even have been here.'

Her daughter Terri grabbed her forearm and wrapped it in hers. 'Mum,' she said, for no reason other than to remind her she was there. 'Mum.' And as always, whenever comfort is offered to the tearful, the dam burst and Amy Harvey-Ellis began to shake with anguish once more.

Seated on the other side of the interview room, DCI Hudson and DS Grant lowered their eyes in a well-oiled show of respect for distress.

'Why shouldn't he be here, Mrs Harvey-Ellis?' ventured Grant, after an appropriate pause.

Amy looked up at Laura Grant with a desperate look in her eye. 'He wasn't supposed to be in Brighton. He should have been at a conference in London until tomorrow night.'

As discreetly as they could manage, the two detectives exchanged a knowing glance. 'Can you think of any reason why your husband would come back to Brighton early?' Hudson asked, fighting to keep an inquiring note in his voice.

'And why he might want to conceal his return from you?' added Grant.

Terri stopped consoling her mother and looked hard at Grant, tears beginning to gather in her own eyes. 'Can't this wait? We've just lost somebody we loved. We've just had to identify his body.' Without waiting for an answer, Terri gestured her mother to stand and led her to the door. Hudson made a show of getting out of his chair to usher them out. Grant didn't move.

At the door, Amy lifted her face away from her hands and spat out, 'My husband would never kill himself. Never! It's absurd. He loved us.'

'Please sit down, Mrs Harvey-Ellis. I know this is difficult,' said Grant. After a momentary pause, Amy Harvey-Ellis returned to her seat, accompanied reluctantly by her daughter.

'It's procedure. We have to explore all possibilities until we can rule them out,' added Hudson. 'I mean, there was no note with his clothing so the chances are it's an accidental drowning. He goes for an early morning jog, works up a sweat and fancies a swim. Something goes wrong, he gets into difficulties . . .'

'Did he have any health problems at all? Maybe a bad heart?' Grant spoke softly, probing gently as all the grief counsellors had advised.

'Nothing like that. He played rugby, for Christ's sake.'

'Okay,' murmured Grant. 'And you can't think of anyone he might have been staying with near the spot where we found his running gear?'

This time it was Terri who answered. 'We've told you, we don't know anyone who lives near there.'

'Okay, Miss Harvey-Ellis, I think that's all for now. Take your mother home,' said Hudson.

'Brook. My name is Terri Brook. Tony was my stepfather.'

'So you weren't blood relations?' asked Grant.

'Can I take my mother home now?'

'How old are you, Terri?' asked Grant.

Terri Brook looked at her, a puzzled frown creasing her forehead. Even Hudson raised an eyebrow. 'I'm seventeen, whatever that's got to do with anything.'

'Just for the records,' nodded Grant, taking a note.

'Now can we go home?'

Hudson turned to Amy. 'One more thing, Mrs Harvey-Ellis – how did your husband travel up to London?'

*

Jason Wallis stood and accepted the hand offered by the grey-haired priest, whose intense blue eyes fixed Jason as they shook hands.

'Cheers for our talks, Father Donetti. They were a big help.'

'A pleasure, my son. And I hope you'll remember what we said. No more shoplifting. I don't want to see you back in here.'

Jason smiled. 'No probs. And I'll try to go to church every Sunday, Father.'

The priest laughed. 'No, you won't, lad. But the Almighty is everywhere. Just ask him for help wherever you are. He'll answer you.'

Jason picked up his bag and turned to the large doors that would lead him to the drive and the gates beyond.

He walked down the drive, enjoying the crunch of the gravel underfoot. As he walked he could feel eyes on him, watching his progress. Without stopping, he turned to look. He couldn't see anyone, but that didn't mean some of his new acquaintances weren't following his exit, wishing they were in his place. He looked back at the buildings with something approaching affection. The dreams had stopped for a while. But now being spat out back into the world that had chewed him up, the dreams had started again.

He reached the gates, hoping there'd be no one there to greet him. He'd told his aunt not to bother – it was a long traipse with a toddler. He turned one last time to face the buildings that had offered him sanctuary these past months and then stepped outside the gates.

'Yo! Jace! MoFo. Over here, blood.' Three young men standing beside a cream-coloured stretch limo shouted in unison at him from across the highway. All were dressed for sport – baseball caps, sweatshirts, trainers. Only the jeans would betray them on the field of dreams, slung low as they were to flaunt grubby Calvins. The Stella cans they all carried were drained, crushed and discarded on the pavement with a sly look at the limo driver, in the hope of catching an expression of disgust.

Jason tried to look pleased to see them but the old fear started gnawing at him. He'd been warned by Brook.

Grass up his crew or face The Reaper.

He now adjusted his posture and his walk, showing he was dangerous, aggressive, best avoided. He shook out a cigarette and lit it with a macho pull. To finish his repertoire, he spat on the ground as if he hadn't a care in the world and rolled over to knuckle-tap his crew, a battle-hardened grimace glued to his face.

'Grets, Banger, Stinger. Gimme some skin. S'guarnin, blood?'

'Same old, same old. Smokin' the peng, dodgin' the leng. How was it?'

Jason grinned, taking in another massive drag of tobacco. 'Piece of piss, fam. I can do the time standin' on mi head.'

'Fucking holiday camp, yeah?' grinned Banger.

'We was gonna bring you a squeeze in case you'd turned fag,' said Grets, laughing.

'You keep your booty zipped, man?' joked Banger.

'What you chattin'?' laughed Jason in mock outrage. 'I only saw one guy who was blatant fag,' he shouted. 'He tries to gimme a tea-bagging and I tear him a new one.'

''Cept he probly enjoy it,' cackled Stinger. 'You shoulda sun-flowered his ass, blood. That'd learn him.'

15

'I hear that.'

The telephoto lens gazed steadily from the bushes a few hundred yards down the road, whirring rhythmically as the posse's likenesses were stored. It was lowered once the boys had ducked into the stretch, Jason bobbing in after a final nervous look around as if he expected someone else to be there.

*

'Poisoned? Are you sure, Doc?'

'There's no mistake,' said Dr Hubbard, sitting back in his cramped office and contemplating Grant and Hudson with his hands behind his head.

'So he was dead before he went in the water?'

'No, he wasn't. That's the clever bit. His lungs were full of water. He drowned. Without a post-mortem it looks like an accidental death. But I'll be telling the coroner murder.'

'We're listening,' said DS Grant.

'Scopolamine.' The doctor beamed at them as though expecting Hudson and Grant to slap their foreheads in recognition. 'Also called hyoscine. Dr Crippen was a big fan. Killed his wife with it.' When their expressions remained vacant, he ploughed on. 'It's in the *Pharmacopoeia*. It's a cerebral sedative which was used to treat epilepsy and other manias – I'm talking over a hundred years ago. Then around 1900 it was combined with morphine to create an anaesthetic which was used in the Great War. It brings on a condition called "Twilight Sleep" in which the patient is conscious but effectively paralysed and has no response to, or memory of pain. Very dodgy stuff though.'

'And was there morphine in Harvey-Ellis as well?'

'There was, Sergeant.' The doctor pulled a photograph from a pile on his disorganised desk. 'This is the victim's neck.' They peered at the picture. 'You see that pinprick? That's a puncture wound. He was injected.'

'Injected?' asked Hudson.

'Could it have been self-administered?' ventured Grant.

'Good lord, no. Even if he'd had the pharmaceutical knowledge, which is unlikely in his line of work, it's the angle. Somebody stuck a hypodermic into him, as though standing above him. Like this.' The doctor demonstrated the angle of the injection.

'So Harvey-Ellis may have been sitting on a bench on the seafront when he was attacked?' mused Hudson.

'Perhaps.'

'If he was out jogging he could have been tying a shoelace or getting his breath back, guv,' added Grant.

'Also possible,' nodded Hubbard. 'And the effects would have been very fast acting, particularly with his pulse and heart rate elevated. Harvey-Ellis would have begun to feel groggy almost immediately. Depending on dosage, he might even have been hallucinatory. Either way he's easily handled physically and mentally. It wouldn't take much to lead him down to the water and help him off with his clothes.'

'And in the unlikely event there are other people around at that time of day, the killer can make it look like they're a couple of drunks, guv.'

Hudson eyed Hubbard. 'So we're looking for a medical man between the ages of 130 and 160 years old?'

Dr Hubbard stared back at Hudson in blank incomprehension. A sudden explosion startled the two officers as Hubbard guffawed and nodded with genuine appreciation.

'Very good, Inspector. I'll have to remember that one for the dinner party circuit.' Hudson darted a quick glance at Grant. They waited for the mirth to subside. 'Well. It's difficult. I mean, older medical men, and particularly chemists, might be familiar with the narcotic qualities of these two drugs to some extent. Scopolamine is a derivative of the nightshade family so anywhere that you find those plants could be a source. My research tells me that the drug is used a lot in Colombia, some tree over there contains it, but it's not recreational like cocaine. It's used in rapes

17

and abductions, stuff like that. And it's colourless and odourless so very difficult to detect.'

'Are the two drugs used in combination for legitimate medical purposes?' asked Grant.

'I can't think of a single medical circumstance these days,' said Hubbard. 'Separately, yes. Morphine is used in the relief of severe pain as you'll know, and scopolamine in minute doses is used to treat things like motion sickness. Combined? No. No reputable physician would prescribe it. It was last used in the sixties during childbirth but sometimes there were complications when patients were unable to feel and report pain.'

'Which means any mention in the profiling database will definitely be worth a follow-up, guv,' nodded Grant.

Hudson sighed. 'Okay. It's a murder inquiry. Thanks a lot, Doc.'

Hubbard grinned, shaking his head again as they left. 'A 160-year-old doctor,' he chuckled. 'Very good.'

*

Jason woke with a start and ran his hand over his throat as he sat up panting. He took several deep breaths to calm himself, darting an eye to his bedroom door to be sure the chest of drawers was still in place. Jason threw back his duvet and padded to the window, tearing off his soaking T-shirt and throwing it down on the floor.

He pulled the curtain aside as minutely as he could and flicked a glance up and down Station Road. A light wind was blowing and the brown and withering leaves of the trees were shedding as the seasons waged their inexorable campaign. Branches swayed with gentle eroticism against the backdrop of the streetlamps. Nothing else moved.

He moved the chest of drawers away from the door and tiptoed to the bathroom. He drank from the tap to counter the dry stickiness of too many WKDs, downed with his crew to celebrate his release. Returning to his room, he fancied he heard a noise so he lifted the chest of drawers back into place as quietly as he could manage.

He flicked at his mobile. It was four in the morning. He pulled the curtain further back, opened his window and took a long pull of chilled air, faintly scented with decay and the sharp promise of winter.

He heard the creak of a floorboard and froze. His eyes darted around the room, at the dark shadows of the wardrobe, the blackness of an alcove. He could imagine The Reaper hiding there, waiting to strike. He flung himself back into the still damp bed and pulled the duvet over his head.

Finally, he poked his head out from his cocoon and heaved a timorous sigh.

'Oh my days.'

Was this all he had to look forward to – cowering in this gloomy old house, waiting to die? Waiting for The Reaper to spring from his hiding place and cut him to pieces?

He was invaded by an urge for the outdoors and dressed quickly. He padded downstairs to the kitchen to pull on his Nikes. He took a pinch of the barely eaten welcome-home cake baked by his aunt and crunched down on the icing. Kicking aside one of the three deflating balloons mustered for his homecoming, he tiptoed softly to the door. A minute later he was out on Station Road, hunching himself against the breeze in his too thin jacket, heading towards the bridges – one for the river and one for the railway that no longer stopped in Borrowash. He crossed the road that fed traffic across to the scrubby flood plains of the Trent and beyond, heading towards the path from which he'd occasionally fished as a young boy, and further on to the grounds of Elvaston Castle, dilapidated and long since abandoned to its fate by the council.

As he approached the railway bridge, Jason was halted in his tracks by a noise, which might have been a car door slamming. He turned to face the line of parked cars resting beside the pavement from their daily labours. Nothing moved. No one stood outside their car ready to disappear into their home and no engine was started by a driver making an early start.

Jason stood back against a hedge, completely still apart from his eyes, which flicked frantically around in the gloom. Then he spotted the cat wandering down the pavement towards him, bobbing along, not a care in the world. He breathed more easily but wondered whether leaving the safety of the house was a good idea. The Reaper could be out here, waiting for his chance. But that was exactly why he had to get out. In the open air he could see all comers. In bed, death lurked behind every curtain, every door.

He turned to resume his walk but before he could take another step the cat, now just a few yards away, swerved away from a gate and froze, staring at something behind a hedge. Jason tried to follow the cat's gaze but could see nothing. He crossed the road as stealthily as he could manage and continued to stare after the creature.

Jason's heart rate, already accelerated, missed a long beat when he saw the shoe glistening black against the streetlight. He could see a leg now, also dressed in black, and further up to what might have been a gloved hand. He looked around for an escape route, peering back up the road to his aunt's house, wondering whether to make a run for it. But to do so would take him closer to the figure hiding in the neighbouring garden. Before Jason could separate reason from panic, the figure stepped out of the garden and faced him in a manner he knew only too well from his dreams.

In the split second before he ran down Station Road towards the river beyond, Jason's feverish mind managed to register the black balaclava, black overalls and black sport shoes. Black . . . to hide the blood.

*

Chief Inspector Hudson lit a cigarette and watched idly as the Scientific Support Team unloaded their equipment and prepared to do their work on the sleek black Mercedes nestling in the parking bay of Preston Street NCP. A uniformed officer looked round, then took out a set of keys at Hudson's signal. He approached the driver's door then hesitated. He reached out a gloved hand and opened the door.

'Not locked, sir,' he said then stood back.

'Thanks.' Hudson discarded his cigarette and approached. DS Grant reached the top of the stairwell at that moment, panting heavily, and walked with some difficulty over to the hub of activity.

Hudson kept his eyes on the car as Grant joined him. 'It's four floors up, girl. Don't you think you should be taking the lift?'

'Good for me,' she grinned by way of explanation, though Hudson knew all about her claustrophobia.

'Face it, luv. You'll never see twenty-nine again. It's downhill all the way.'

'So I see,' panted Grant, giving Hudson the once over.

Hudson laughed, then turned his eyes from the interior of the vehicle to the uniformed officer and nodded at the boot.

'Okay, Jimmy.'

The officer popped the boot and Hudson and Grant moved to take a look. Inside was a soft brown leather suitcase which, to judge from its shape, appeared full. On top of the suitcase a dark blue suit covered in cellophane had been hastily tossed in. Next to the case was a set of car keys. The officer examined the suit and pulled a piece of paper from the pocket of the jacket. He handed it to Grant, who'd just finished snapping on latex gloves.

'Double room. Paid in cash,' said Grant. 'It's an invoice from the Duchess Hotel. I know it. It's a dive on Waterloo Street.' Hudson flashed an inquiring glance. 'A tom I know got beaten up there by her client.'

'So Harvey-Ellis did come back early for a bit on the side. Our big cheese has got himself a tasty cracker.'

Laura Grant smiled indulgently. 'Well, he was alone when he parked the car, guv, I've just seen the footage. The car arrived at 14.07 hours on Saturday . . .'

21

'14.07 hours,' said Hudson. 'This is National Car Parks, darlin', not the SAS.'

'That's what it says on the computer, guv. But I can put "Saturday lunchtime" in the report if you prefer?'

Hudson chuckled, then gestured at the suited technicians waiting to examine the car. They approached the vehicle and set to work combing, sifting and collecting.

*

Keep running. Keep thinking. Keep running. Keep thinking. Jason was used to neither but still he ran and tried to think, attempting to block out the vision of a vengeful hunter gaining on him. He'd set off into the murk of the fields, picking up the path that hugged the deceptively idle river.

But his tar-lined lungs wouldn't let him run and he had to stop to suck in much-needed oxygen. He wheeled round unsteadily, ready for an attack, but there was no one behind him. He coughed then sucked in a few hard breaths and tried to focus back down the path, but sweat stung his pupils. He wiped it away and a few seconds later he saw the figure, maybe a hundred yards away, striding relentlessly towards him. Jason turned and struck out again, trying to tamp down the fear that was constricting his lungs even more than the tar.

When he slowed again, he could hear the steady rhythm of his pursuer. Eventually Jason had to rest again but this time his rapid pull for oxygen couldn't ease the stabbing pains in his chest. He faced back down the river, trying to see, but again the sweat salted his vision. Although there was no artificial light to soothe him, a fine moon ensured good visibility and, as his breathing became easier, he was able to distinguish a dark figure rounding the bend of the path.

As he scrambled along, Jason began to sob soundlessly as he'd learned to in White Oaks. A part of his brain urged him to stop to face his fate: anything was better than this torment, day and night. But he didn't. Something basic, something primal inside kept him going.

When he stopped again, Jason realised he was at a fork in the path. The main path continued to follow the river back towards Derby, but the left fork wound its way round to Elvaston Castle and its dark tree-lined grounds.

He turned down the path towards Elvaston. After hobbling round a couple of ninety-degree bends, he staggered onto the overgrown bank of a stream. He settled into the undergrowth with a view of the path and tried to regain the rhythm of his breathing as quietly as he could.

Several minutes elapsed but nobody came down the path. Jason began to shiver and, worse, started to get cramp. He'd crouched in as near a position of readiness as he could manage but it soon began to hurt. After ten minutes of this, Jason finally had to swivel into a seated position and wait, eyes darting, ears pricked, every sense on heightened alert.

*

Hudson and Grant stepped into the gloom of the dingy lobby onto a threadbare carpet, feeling the tacky pull of ancient spillage on their shoes. The noxious odour of cheap disinfectant assaulted their noses and the tobacco-stained walls did the same for their eyes.

The man behind a cramped bureau gave Grant an unsubtle stare of approval as she approached, then turned to Hudson with an over-friendly grin. He was short, slightly overweight, and had long straggly hair that disguised his early baldness as ineffectively as the grin hid his yellowing teeth.

'It's thirty for the hour or sixty-five for the night and we don't do breakfast . . .' Grant's warrant card silenced the man and his manner became defensive. 'Oh yes, Sergeant. What can I do for you?'

'I'm DS Grant, this is Chief Inspector Hudson. We're inquiring after a guest who stayed here on Saturday night,' said Grant, brandishing a photograph of Tony Harvey-Ellis under the man's nose. 'Are you the proprietor, sir?' she asked as he took the picture from her.

He looked up at her and back at the photograph. After a moment's hesitation he nodded. 'I am.'

'Your name, sir?' asked Hudson, swinging around, preparing to take an interest for the first time.

'Sowerby. Dave Sowerby.'

'Do you recognise the man, Mr Sowerby?' asked Grant.

Sowerby concentrated fiercely on the photograph. 'No,' he said after a few moments of unconvincing deliberation. He handed back the photograph, returning his attention to the reception desk and fiddling with some papers as if to imply a heavy workload.

'Mmmm.' Hudson wandered off to the front door but neither he nor Grant made any attempt to leave. After a minute, Hudson ambled back to the desk, picked up the local newspaper from under a stack of documents and jabbed a finger at the picture of Tony Harvey-Ellis, smiling on the front page. 'Perhaps this is a better likeness, Mr Sowerby?'

'Is that the guy?' said Sowerby, hardly bothering to look.

'That's him,' said Hudson. 'His name is Tony Harvey-Ellis. But then you knew that because he stayed here Saturday night. Mr Harvey-Ellis drowned in the early hours of Sunday morning. The picture we showed you was taken at the mortuary.'

'Most people who see a picture of a dead body tend to react in some way,' added Grant, smiling coldly.

'You, on the other hand, didn't react at all, sir. Now why might that be?'

Sowerby tried to look Hudson in the eye but couldn't hold on. 'I didn't realise . . .'

'You didn't realise how important my time is, did you?'

'I . . . I . . .'

'You didn't realise that I get very pissed off when someone *wastes* my time when I'm investigating a suspicious death . . .'

24

His words had the desired effect and Sowerby's eyes widened. 'Suspicious!' he said, agitated. 'It doesn't say anything in the papers about suspicious. It says he drowned.'

'You calling me a liar now, sonny?' said Hudson, fixing Sowerby with a cruel glare.

'No, no.' Sowerby raised his hands in pacification.

'Cuff him, Sergeant. I don't like this dump. We'll do this at the station . . .' Hudson turned and began to saunter away. Grant made no attempt to reach for the handcuffs.

'Wait! Just hang on . . .' pleaded Sowerby to Hudson's retreating back. 'I've got a business to run.'

'Guv,' said Grant. 'Give him a minute. I think Mr Sowerby wants to help.' She turned back to Sowerby. 'Don't you, sir?'

'I do. I didn't realise . . .'

Hudson stopped at the front door but didn't turn around. There was a brief silence as Grant considered how best to continue. 'Maybe Mr Sowerby was just trying to protect a valued client.'

Sowerby looked from Hudson to Grant and nodded eagerly. 'That's it, a valued client – a regular.'

'I mean, we can understand that, can't we, guv?' continued Grant. 'He was just being . . . discreet.' Sowerby continued to nod eagerly and looked with hope towards Hudson's back. 'I mean, we'd want the same discretion if we stayed at a hotel, guv. Wouldn't we?'

Hudson turned now, his lips pursed. 'I suppose,' he conceded eventually and padded back towards the bureau. 'All right, we're listening.'

Grant nodded and smiled encouragement at Sowerby, who wasted no further time. 'Mr H is . . . was,' he corrected himself, 'a regular. He had an understanding that we'd turn a blind eye. You know . . .' He looked encouragingly at Grant.

'Discretion,' she obliged.

'That's it. Discretion. He was married, see . . .'

'No?' said Grant.

'He was. But he had a right eye for a pretty girl. And he always

25

paid cash, you know,' added Sowerby enthusiastically, before suddenly realising he'd said the wrong thing. 'Not that I don't . . .'

Hudson held up his hand. 'Any particular pretty girl this last time?'

'Well, he had more than one but this weekend it was the usual.'

'Usual?'

'Yeah, the one he'd brought here a few times. Very pretty. Brown hair. Slim but not . . .' Sowerby darted a glance at Grant, who raised an eyebrow '. . . not flat.' Hudson now had to douse down a smirk. 'And, of course . . .' Sowerby now stopped himself, beginning to look uncomfortable.

'Go on,' prompted Hudson.

'. . . young,' said Sowerby quietly. 'They were always very young.' Hudson and Grant faced Sowerby in silence, well-versed in tightening the screw. 'Not that I had any reason to think they were . . . you know . . . illegal.' He stared down at the floor to see how far he'd dug himself in.

'Then why think they might be?'

'The usual one. The first time he brung her in was a couple of years ago . . .' Sowerby stalled over the words. Hudson and Grant waited, knowing it would come '. . . And she'd tried to dress up normal but I could see . . .'

'See what?'

'She had one of those sweatshirts on.'

'Sweatshirts?'

'You know. You see them all over town. It was one of them from the posh school. Part of their uniform. Badge and all.'

*

Jason's limbs were screaming in pain. He decided he couldn't sit it out any longer. His pursuer had either given up or taken the wrong path. So, with daylight beginning to creep across the horizon, Jason clambered back onto the path, standing as upright as he could manage. He rubbed his back until the noise of a breaking twig froze his entire frame. Slowly Jason turned. The man was standing ten yards away, facing him, perfectly still, perfectly unruffled. Jason tried to see his face but it was completely obscured by the balaclava. Through the hot tears distorting his vision, Jason could see the man's breath as it hit the morning air. But unlike Jason, he wasn't panting with fear or looking round for help.

A second later the man moved towards Jason. In a black, gloved hand, raised to catch the dawn light, Jason fancied he saw the glint of a blade through his tears. He began to sob violently and his shoulders shook. He looked around to plot his escape but, instead of turning to flee, Jason's legs crumpled and his knees hit the ground. Wailing, he curled himself into a ball as the man walked towards him and inclined his head to look down at him.

'I told you. I'm sorry we did the old woman,' he wailed. 'I'm sorry about the cat.' The figure bent down on one knee to examine Jason. 'I'm sorry about everything. Please don't kill me. Please. I'll remember. I can be good. Please . . .' Jason's voice became a high-pitched whine as his emotions and any semblance of physical control disintegrated.

*

Jason had no idea how long he'd been unconscious but by the time he woke dawn had turned into a bright chill morning. Birds were singing and the low sun was beginning to burn off the dew. He lifted himself onto one elbow and looked around. The man had gone. Jason stood, grimacing at the squelch of excrement and urine in his trousers, and turned to waddle home, eyes lowered to the ground in misery.

Chapter Two

Hudson rolled his greasy fish-and-chip paper into a tight ball and threw it at the bin next to their bench. It fell short and a couple of seagulls standing guard on the seawall railing glided down to investigate. Hudson stood to pick up the offending litter then jammed it into the bin – to loud dismay from the gulls – and sat back down, squinting into the pale sun. He pulled out his cigarettes and threw one in his mouth. After taking a man-sized pull he exhaled into a Styrofoam cup, taking a large gulp of coffee before returning it to the bench.

Laura Grant had long since finished her tortilla wrap and now had her pen poised over a notebook, listing the tasks that Hudson deemed fit for the two DCs, Rimmer and Crouch, assigned to help them with the legwork, now that Tony Harvey-Ellis's death was being treated as murder.

'Anything else, guv?'

'I guess we pay a call to Hall Gordon PR. Find out if Harvey-Ellis had any enemies they'd know about. Put that at the top of our list.'

Grant raised her eyebrows and fixed him with her cool blue eyes.

'You honestly think it's possible?' asked Hudson. 'The daughter?'

'Stepdaughter,' said Grant. 'Harvey-Ellis wasn't her real dad.'

'But he was married to her real mum.'

'Remember what she said when we first broke the news, guv. Someone *we* loved. It jarred at the time.'

'She fits the description, I suppose. Right age, right hair,' conceded Hudson.

'And Tony and Amy had only been married four years.'

'Is that significant?'

'Well, let's assume Tony and Amy knew each other for at least a year before they married. That means Terri's known him for about five years. Terri is seventeen now which makes her around twelve when Tony and Amy first meet, thirteen when they get hitched.'

'So?'

'You've got two grown-up kids, guv. What were the most difficult years? Early teens, right?'

'By a country mile.'

'Right. Terri's a seventeen-year-old girl who's known her stepfather – the man who replaced her real father – since she was a teenager, before even. Now I don't know how many people you know with stepmums and dads . . .'

'Not many. Different generation. We had to grin and bear it.'

'Well, I know three. Two of them hated their stepparent with a vengeance. I mean, *hated*. Enough to wish they would just die for breaking up the cosy family unit.'

'And the third?'

'They had an affair,' said Grant. Hudson pulled a face. 'There are no half measures with this sort of thing, guv.'

'It's a bit of a reach, Laura. But it's easy enough to check all the same. Crouchy's on the car park cameras to see if it was the girlfriend who dumped Tony's luggage. So get Rimmer to sniff out a picture of Terri for that lowlife Sowerby to take a peek at, see if she's "the usual". Better yet, have him get a picture of her from school.' Hudson smiled. 'She might be wearing the same school uniform he saw her in.'

'Will do.'

'If this pans out and the girl has been having it off with her stepfather, it opens up all sorts of avenues. With Harvey-Ellis porking his wife *and* daughter,' he said, with a glance at Grant to see if she was offended, 'it brings the mother into the equation.'

'Hell hath no fury,' nodded Grant, ignoring her colleague's choice of language. She knew from experience that he enjoyed proving female coppers were oversensitive. She thought for a moment. 'Or maybe the mother knows and doesn't mind.'

'How could the mother not mind?' said Hudson.

'Maybe she knows but she doesn't know. Knowing tears her life apart. She loses husband *and* daughter. But if she blinds herself, she's a happily married mother – if that makes sense.'

'Female logic?' Now it was Grant's turn to pull a face and Hudson, with a guilty laugh, held up his hand. 'Okay, I know what you mean. She blocks it out.' He squirrelled a glance at her. 'Thank God you're not one of those lesbian ballbreakers they've got up in the smoke, Laura.'

'How do you know I'm not?'

Hudson laughed. 'Because you're a top girl, Laura. A top girl.' Grant raised a cautionary eyebrow, but couldn't resist a smile and Hudson laughed. 'Roll on next year, when I can collect my pension and piss off to Jurassic Park with all the other dinosaurs, eh?'

'Amen to that, guv.'

*

Jason Wallis lay on his bed and stared up at the ceiling, seeing nothing, hearing nothing, feeling only the dry distortion of old tear tracks on his cheeks. He'd woken up a couple of hours previously but hadn't moved at all.

The house was quiet now. His aunt was in bed resting before her next shift and baby Bianca had finally fallen asleep after her lunch of chips and beans. Thankfully his aunt hadn't returned until half an hour after Jason had waddled home, soiled and scarred by his ordeal. He'd had time to bung his fouled clothing into the washer and set it going before showering and retreating to his room in shame and terror, once more pulling the chest of drawers across his door for safety. He'd collapsed into bed and lost consciousness almost at once – to call it sleep would have implied rest – and had woken with a start some time later, a film of sweat covering every millimetre of his skin. He'd sobbed quietly for the rest of the afternoon before finally succumbing to something approaching sleep.

When he woke again, he was surprised to discover waking didn't involve panting and clutching at his throat. He merely opened his eyes gently and looked towards the window. The sun was beginning to set and Jason's tight belly had begun to growl. Footsteps approached his door, followed by a soft knocking.

'Jason?' his aunt asked. 'You in there?' She knocked again. Still no answer from Jason who continued to lay mute, eyes burning into the ceiling. Finally his aunt tried the door but the chest of drawers prevented entry. 'What are you doing, Jason? You better not be taking drugs, you little shit!' She rattled the door but couldn't shift the chest. 'Let me in.'

Jason sat up. Necessity required a response. 'I'm not. Don't worry, Auntie. I'm all right.'

'You sure you're not doing drugs?'

'You're doing my head in. I'm okay, I tell you. What is it?'

His aunt hesitated, then, no doubt mindful of the time, said, 'I'm off to work. There's a chicken pie in the microwave for you and I've put your washing on the radiators.'

'Cheers.'

'If Bianca wakes up, let her watch cartoons. But make sure you put her to bed before seven. Got that?' No reply. 'Got that?' she repeated.

'I've got it,' Jason replied, trying to keep the irritation out of his voice.

31

'You sure you're all right, Jason?'

'Oh my days, I'm all right.' Jason's aunt's grunted and her footsteps receded along the landing. A moment later the stairs began to complain under the assault from her hefty frame. The front door slammed, her car coughed into life and Jason heaved a sigh of relief. He closed his eyes and a tear squeezed onto his cheek.

'I'm all right,' he muttered. 'I'm all right.'

*

Hudson prepared a sly cigarette as Grant fired up the computer. Although she disapproved of him flouting the smoking ban so brazenly, she was disinclined to make an issue out of it.

There was a knock on the door and DCs Jimmy Crouch and Phil Rimmer came in without waiting for an answer. Hudson's cigarette hand moved from behind his back and returned to his mouth when he saw it wasn't the Chief Super. 'Take a seat.'

Rimmer, a tall and well-muscled thirty-year-old with short blond hair and handsome features, and Crouch, a smaller and broader man with thickset features and wavy black hair, pulled up chairs. Both were holding large envelopes.

Hudson moved over to a board where a large close-up of the late Tony Harvey-Ellis, face slackened and eyes closed, was pinned.

'Let's get started.' He pulled out his notebook from a pile of papers on the desk and flipped it open. 'This is our victim. Tony Harvey-Ellis, wealthy local businessman and ladies' man. As you know, Harvey-Ellis died in the early hours of Sunday morning sometime between 4 and 6 am, having left the Duchess Hotel to go for a run. His running shoes and kit were found on the beach, just past the West Pier. His body, however, was carried nearly a mile further down the seafront and was washed ashore just off Madeira Drive.

'According to the pathologist he drowned after being drugged or, more accurately, poisoned, with a mixture of . . .' Hudson broke off to peer at the preliminary forensic report pinned under Tony's face '. . . scopolamine and morphine. The assailant injected Tony with the drugs, rendering him incapable of defending himself. He was completely docile within minutes and unable to resist when the killer helped him out of his clothes and into the sea where, suffering from muscular paralysis, he drowned. Laura.'

The two detective constables switched their gaze to DS Grant, who took up the reins. 'As you know, his car was found in Preston Street NCP unlocked and with his luggage inside. It seems Tony had driven back to Brighton from London where he'd been at a conference and parked in Preston Street on Saturday around lunchtime . . .'

'14.07,' beamed Hudson.

'14.07,' echoed Grant, with barely a glance at him. 'At this point he was alone so it's reasonable to assume that the girl he was meeting is from the local area, although it's possible he might have already dropped her off at the hotel in nearby Waterloo Street. Either way he's booked a double room . . .'

'I thought he lived locally,' said Rimmer.

'He lives locally with his *wife*, Phil,' interjected Hudson. 'Out near Falmer. But Tony is what we used to call a shagger.'

The two DCs smiled and nodded; Grant shook her head in mock disapproval. 'Or a "ladies' man" to anyone under sixty, although his taste seems to run to young girls,' she continued, addressing Rimmer and Crouch. 'Not *very* young,' she added, 'but borderline legal.'

Rimmer took this as his cue. 'Theresa Brook goes to Roedean. She's in sixth form now studying English and Media Studies – very bright apparently. The school won't give us a picture though. Not without written authority from the Chief Super. They're afraid of paedos.'

'We may not need it, guv,' interrupted Crouch. He pulled a black and white A4 photocopy from his envelope. It was divided into four smaller squares each containing a distinct image. 'This is from the NCP on Sunday morning. The girl in this picture carried a case identical to the one we found in the car.' He passed it round. 'See, she's even got a suit wrapped in plastic over her arm. Now we haven't got her putting the case and suit in the car, but Forensics have lifted two sets of prints from the car and the case. One set belongs to the victim. Likely the other belongs to her.'

Hudson gazed at the picture of Terri Brook struggling under the weight of the luggage and nodded at Grant. 'You were right, Laura.'

'Is this our killer, guv?' asked Crouch eagerly.

'Not yet,' replied Hudson. 'For now she's just someone with something to hide.'

'Like what, guv?' asked Rimmer.

'This is Terri Brook, the victim's stepdaughter,' said Grant. The two DCs nodded with the gravity of it all but still risked a ribald glance at one another. 'We can now surmise that Harvey-Ellis spent the night with his seventeen-year-old stepdaughter. Jimmy, show this picture to the landlord at the Duchess, a Mr Sowerby, to confirm.' Crouch made a note.

Hudson crushed his lit cigarette between his yellowed fingers, sending sparks to the floor, then placed the tab in a drawer and strolled over to the window. 'Terri Brook was probably the last person to see the victim alive and now, seen cleaning up after the fact, she has to be a viable suspect.' Hudson's voice trailed off and he put his hand to his chin and tapped it with his fingers, a mannerism Grant recognised as a sign that he was perplexed by something.

'Guv?'

Hudson roused himself and turned to face Rimmer and Crouch. 'What else have you got, fellas?'

'Forensics are looking at the victim's running gear from the beach,' said Rimmer. 'They found traces of fresh semen on his tracksuit so it looks like the victim had sex before he went for his run. It's possible his partner's DNA will be present. They're following it up asap.'

'Jimmy?'

'Preliminary findings on the victim's room at The Duchess aren't good. The room was cleaned and another couple had already stayed there. The techs aren't hopeful. Anything they find is likely to be compromised.'

'All right. This is what I want. Continue chasing up appropriate CCTV if there is any. Concentrate on where Tony's clothes were found. That's where he was attacked. That's the one place we know his killer was. On that basis, organise as much uniform as you can and go door to door around that area. I want witnesses, whether they saw or just heard something. Why aren't you writing this down?' Rimmer hastily started scribbling.

'Anything else, guv?' he asked a moment later.

'Yeah. Parking tickets. You can't stand still in roller skates without getting one on the sea front so check details for the week before within a half-mile radius of the Duchess. Our killer seems to know his way about.'

'He?' asked Grant with a raised eyebrow.

'Figure of speech,' answered Hudson, not looking at her.

'Should I follow up on the school picture, guv?' ventured Rimmer.

'No. Forget it.' Hudson inclined his head. Crouch and Rimmer took the hint, stood up and left.

After a suitable pause spent watching Hudson pace the room, Grant returned her attention to the computer, keying in her ID when prompted. While she waited for recognition she looked up.

'Guv?'

'It's all wrong, Laura.'

'What is?'

'We've got two halves of a crime that don't fit together. This girl Terri . . .'

'Are we bringing her in?'

Hudson turned to her. 'Tell me why we should.'

'We have it from Sowerby and the CCTV. She cleared out the room she and Tony were staying in. Guilty conscience right there.'

'She's having an affair with her stepfather, maybe since she was fifteen. Anything else?'

'There isn't anything else, guv. That's why we should bring her in.'

Hudson paused, seeking the right words. His face cleared when he found them. 'Did she kill her stepfather?'

Now it was Grant's turn to think. 'Poisoning is a woman's crime,' she said. Hudson waited. 'There may be a motive we don't know about,' she ploughed on. 'She may have found out there were other girls.' Hudson said nothing. 'Okay, guv. Honestly, I can't see her as the killer.'

'Why not?'

'She'd need sophisticated medical or pharmaceutical know-ledge for a start.'

Hudson smiled at her. 'As opposed to English and Media Studies.'

'But she's a bright girl, guv. She may have made the effort. There's always the internet.'

'It's just the way Harvey-Ellis was killed, Laura. It was so cold and . . .'

'And professional?' Grant ventured.

'Exactly. I've seen a lot of domestics, I'm sure you have. And I saw Terri and her mother. They were in pieces. If either of them had killed Tony, it would have been a crime of passion. If someone had shot him six times in bed, I'd be looking at them. If someone had taken a baseball bat to him while he slept, I'd be looking at them. If someone had chopped off his knackers . . .'

'All right, guv, I get it.'

'And if Terri had done any of those things I could accept that

36

in the heat of the moment she might get her prints all over the evidence and her mugshot on camera. But someone managed to get the better of Harvey-Ellis while he was pumped up with adrenaline – a fit rugby-playing forty-three-year-old. Someone was waiting for him. And when they got the chance there was no hesitation. This was planned and executed by somebody far more ruthless than a seventeen-year-old schoolgirl.'

'So what now?' asked Grant, breaking off to answer a prompt from the computer. She hit the return key, typed in the words 'scopolamine' and 'morphine' from her notebook and returned her attention to Hudson.

'We speak to her to sign off on the details, but we treat her as a witness. Maybe she saw something; maybe she knows who might have wanted Tony dead. Unlikely, I know. Also, if we're treating the murder as professional then first we go to his profession . . .'

'Oh Jesus!' exclaimed Grant, staring intently at the monitor.

'What?'

Grant flipped the monitor round. 'The MO, guv. It's The Reaper.'

*

Laura Grant drove up the shady, tree-lined drive to a large white-washed house. She parked outside what looked like the main entrance and killed the engine.

Chief Inspector Hudson got out of the passenger seat, coolly taking in the surroundings. Mature trees, outbuildings, manicured paths leading off in all directions. There was an old-fashioned Victorian greenhouse to the rear of the property and he could see a large conservatory on the back of the house.

Grant, being half Hudson's age and never in touch with a time when houses could be bought for a few hundred pounds, was unmoved by such a show of wealth. She glanced over at Hudson, who seemed to be minutely shaking his head.

'Christ!' he said. 'No wonder this country's in the shit when

37

people who produce nothing but hot air can afford a house like this. Public relations, my arse. Did you know, when my mum and dad got married, they bought a terraced house in Balham for £800?'

Grant smiled. 'Yes, guv. I did know that.'

Hudson finally broke away from his surveillance and caught her eye. Then, with an exaggerated cockney accent, he added, 'In my day . . .'

Grant nodded towards the entrance as Terri Brook walked towards them. She looked stunning, though her eyes still betrayed the telltale residue of tears. She appeared much older than her seventeen years, dressed in figure-hugging black trousers and a ribbed polo neck. Her make-up was discreet, her mid-length brown hair lightly tinted and swept back and delicate pieces of gold adorned her ears.

'Hello, you found it then?'

Hudson nodded. 'Eventually. It's not often we get out to Falmer.'

'Really? What about the university?'

'Not so many murders and armed robberies on campus these days, miss.'

'Yes, sorry. Stolen bikes and soft drugs not your thing, I suppose. I'm sorry, I've forgotten your names?'

'I'm DCI Hudson, Miss Harvey-Ellis, this is DS Grant. Nice place you've got here.'

'It keeps the rain off. And I'm Theresa Brook, okay, but I prefer Terri.'

'Brook. Of course,' said Hudson, exchanging a glance with Grant.

Terri escorted them through the entrance portico into an enormous modern kitchen and through into an even bigger conservatory, furnished with sturdy cream sofas. She gestured for them to sit, then at a coffee pot and poured for both officers when they nodded.

'Where's your mother, Miss Brook?' asked Grant.

She looked a little sheepish and raised melancholy eyes to Hudson. 'Call me Terri. I'm afraid I owe you an apology, Chief Inspector. Mum's asleep. She's still not up to it. She's been sedated. I'm sorry. Perhaps if you came back later . . .'

Hudson paused for a few moments, then smiled in sympathy. 'Please don't apologise, Terri. We quite understand.' Grant raised an eyebrow at her superior. He wasn't usually so understanding when suspects tried to mess him around.

A pause from Terri. Then, 'I'm sorry you've had a wasted journey.'

'Terri, do you think I could have a glass of water?' asked Hudson.

'Of course.' She left to fetch the water after a brief pause.

'Guv?' said Grant once Terri was out of earshot.

'I think we should take a run at Terri while she's on her own.'

'She's only seventeen; she should have a parent with her.'

'How much less awkward would it be without her mother present? Christ, we're talking about an affair between Terri and her mum's husband.'

'I know but I'd feel a lot . . .'

Terri returned with a glass of water and handed it to Hudson, who took a token sip before placing it on the table.

'Terri. Perhaps *you* can help us with some things,' said Hudson in an easy manner.

'I . . . I don't know what I can tell you.'

'We just need some background, really,' said Grant.

'For instance, can you tell us about any enemies your father might have had?' asked Hudson.

'Enemies? What's that got to do with him drowning?' Grant and Hudson said nothing. 'Are you implying Tony was murdered?'

'We're not implying anything, Terri . . .'

'You are, aren't you?' Terri was incredulous, disbelieving. She seemed to be shaking. Hudson and Grant studied her carefully and couldn't detect any artifice.

39

'At the moment we're looking at all angles,' said Grant.

'Then you're making a mistake. Tony was a popular guy. Everybody liked him. Everybody. I can't believe anyone would want to murder him.' She stared into the distance and Grant fancied a sliver of doubt deformed her features for a second.

'Nobody had a grudge or wished to harm him in any way? Think back. We could be talking about a couple of years ago.'

Terri shook her head, now unable to meet their gaze. 'No one, I'm telling you.'

'We'll come back to that one,' said Hudson quietly. 'Do you know where your stepfather was staying in Brighton the night before he died?' Again Terri shook her head. Hudson hunched down over his notebook as if checking a detail. 'It was in a hotel in Waterloo Street. The Duchess. Bit of a pigsty actually. Not really your stepfather's sort of place I would've said. Do you know it?'

He looked back up at her as she shook her head. Her colour was darkening slightly, but otherwise she retained her composure.

'Any idea why he might check into that hotel under a false name?' asked Grant. 'Gordon Hall.' She continued to look at Terri. 'Actually the register says Mr and Mrs Gordon Hall. Did you know your stepfather had a lady friend?'

Terri's lips were becoming tighter and tighter and the ability to speak had deserted her. She shook her head again.

Hudson had some sympathy but he also knew that the more he tightened the screw, the more detailed the confession when it came. 'You see what he did there. That's a play on the name of his company, you know. Hall Gordon Public Relations,' he pointed out helpfully.

'Any idea who Mrs Hall might have been?' asked Grant.

'No!' croaked Terri, clearing her throat. 'Can I have one of those cigarettes please?'

'Of course.' Hudson took two cigarettes from the packet,

40

handing one to Terri and putting one in his mouth. He lit hers then his own.

'Whoever she is, I'm afraid it's now almost certain she was having a sexual relationship with your stepfather. I'm sorry to have to tell you that.'

After several long drags, Terri finally broke the silence. 'How do you know?' she croaked.

Not, *I don't believe it,* Grant noted. 'We found fresh semen on his jogging pants.'

'And traces of female DNA. The lab's working them up now. The semen is his, obviously. The other . . . well, it should help when we find out who she is.' Terri nodded dumbly, tears welling up in her eyes

'And the girl was quite young, according to the landlord. Maybe underage,' added Grant.

'It must be upsetting to discover what kind of man your stepfather was,' said Hudson.

Terri bowed her head and now began to sob. Hudson felt guilty. He remembered how his own teenage daughter regressed when the adopted habits of adulthood bit too deep.

'This must be difficult,' said Grant, moving to sit next to the girl to offer some comfort.

Hudson quietly pulled out the CCTV image from the car park and placed it on the table in front of Terri. She barely glanced at it but the violence of her sobbing increased, and her head sought refuge and bobbed up and down in Grant's arms.

Eventually a measure of calm returned and Terri was able to blow her nose and wipe her eyes. 'I loved him,' she said simply.

'I believe you,' answered Hudson, resisting the urge to be judgemental. 'Tell us what happened at the weekend.'

Terri found such a simple question difficult, embarrassed to be discussing the sex life she had hidden from the world. 'We . . . were together, you know, Saturday night. We were awake . . . most of the night.' She glanced up at the two detectives to see if they'd cracked her simple code. Their expressions were unaltered. 'Tone plays rugby . . . played rugby . . . and he wanted to go for a run. It was really early. Five o'clock.'

'You didn't go with him?'

'God no! He was only going to be an hour, he said. I saw him walk to the seafront and turn towards the old pier and I never saw him again.'

Her lip began to wobble so Hudson piled in with the next question to keep her mind busy. 'Did you see anyone else on the road?'

'No one.'

'Any cars pull away at the same time?'

'Not that I noticed.'

Hudson nodded. 'Go on.'

'I went back to bed and woke up at about nine and Tone wasn't back. I didn't think anything of it. I showered and went out to get a coffee, thinking he'd be back when I got back, but he wasn't. By half eleven I was frantic. I went for a walk along the front but I couldn't see anything. I thought maybe he'd had an accident and was in hospital. So I packed up his stuff and took it to the car park, threw it all in the boot. I hung onto his wallet. I was going to drive the car but thought it might be better to leave it for Tone. The only problem was if I wanted to leave the car keys I couldn't lock up. So I threw them in the boot. I figured it wouldn't be a problem. Unless someone randomly tried the door, most people would assume it was locked. Then I came home.'

'Was your mother here when you got back?' asked Grant.

Terri nodded.

'How long had your affair been going on?' asked Hudson.

Terri bit her lip, recognising the relevance of the question. 'Not long,' she replied.

It was an obvious lie but Hudson decided there was little to gain by challenging it. The victim wasn't pressing charges, the criminal was dead.

'I loved him,' she repeated in the softest whisper.

'This is very important, Terri,' said Grant. 'Who else knew you were going to be at that hotel?'

Terri stared off into space to think. She shook her head. 'Apart from the guy at the hotel, no one.'

'Mr Sowerby?'

'Mr Sowerby, yes.'

'Would Tony have told anyone?'

'I don't think so. Why?' She answered her own question immediately. 'You think someone planned this. You think someone was waiting near the hotel, to kill him.'

'It seems likely. Does your mother know about the affair?' asked Hudson.

She looked down. When she looked up she had more moisture in her eyes. She blinked it away and shook her head.

'As far as you know.'

'As far as I know,' she echoed into her lap. She lifted her head suddenly. 'You're not suggesting . . . ?'

'Hell hath no fury like a woman losing her husband to her daughter,' observed Hudson with more cruelty than he'd intended.

'Forget it,' spat Terri. 'My mother couldn't hurt a fly.'

'What about your father?'

'My father?'

'Your *real* father.'

Terri seemed momentarily nonplussed by the question. 'He . . . I don't know. I mean, of course not. Besides, he lives in Derbyshire.'

'That's not what we call an alibi, Miss Brook.'

'Do you know if your father ever visited your stepfather at his place of work?' asked Grant, as casually as possible.

Terri looked at her as if she'd been slapped. 'I'm not sure.' She bowed her head and cried some more.

Grant looked at her notebook. 'Would it surprise you to hear that a couple of years ago your father, Damen Brook, Detective

Inspector Damen Brook of Derby CID, paid a visit to Tony at Hall Gordon Public Relations? This is according to Mr Gordon, the company director. During his visit he assaulted your stepfather and threatened to have him arrested for molesting his daughter. Apparently he went to great pains to humiliate your stepfather in front of his colleagues. It caused a huge stink at the firm.'

'And your mother had to go in to assure the directors that all the allegations were groundless. Do you still say your mother knew nothing of your relationship?' Hudson and Grant waited.

'But she didn't believe it,' croaked Terri eventually, unable to look at them.

'Well, I'm afraid she'll have to believe it now.'

Terri looked up at them in alarm. 'You're not going to tell her?'

Hudson stood and motioned at Grant to follow suit. 'Of course we're not going to tell her, Terri. But do you honestly think this thing can stay under wraps?'

'I think what Chief Inspector Hudson means is that sooner or later she's going to find out.' Grant patted Terri on the arm and made to leave. 'And, all things considered, Terri, it would be better coming from you.' Grant followed Hudson out but turned back at the door. 'If it's any consolation, according to Sowerby, you were one of many.'

*

Laura Grant kicked open the door, holding two coffees. Hudson, phone cradled under his chin, saw it was her and removed the hand that was holding the cigarette from behind his back.

'Any luck, guv?'

Hudson made to answer then returned his attention to the receiver. 'Hello. Derby HQ? This is DCI Joshua Hudson from Sussex CID. Who am I speaking to? Sergeant Hendrickson, I wonder if you can help me. I'm going to be in Derbyshire on leave this weekend and I was wondering about looking up an old colleague, name of DI Damen Brook . . . well, no, I wouldn't really say he was a friend. Like I said, he used to be a colleague, only I wouldn't like him to find out I'd been in the neighbourhood and not looked him up. So I was wondering what shift he was on over the weekend so I could drop in . . . oh really? Next Monday. What a shame. Do you know where? Well, yes, he always was a bit like that, now you mention it.' Hudson listened to the monologue at the other end of the line. Finally he was able to get a word in. 'Well, thanks very much for your help, Sergeant.'

'There's one enemy DI Brook's made,' said Hudson, putting the phone down. A sombre expression invaded his features. He turned to Grant and took his coffee from her, taking a noisy draught. 'Bad news.'

'He's got an alibi?'

Hudson stubbed out his cigarette and ran his fingers through his grey hair. 'Far from it. He's on two weeks' leave until next week. There's some book coming out about The Reaper case so he decided to get away from the hoo-hah.'

'Where is he?'

'No one knows. Apparently he never sees fit to tell anyone. He could be out of the country for all they know.'

'So he could've been stalking Harvey-Ellis, waiting for his chance.' Grant couldn't conceal her excitement. 'He's our guy, guv. I can smell it.'

Hudson nodded. 'Maybe.'

'*Maybe?* This was your idea, guv.'

'I know, but I don't like it, Laura.'

'Why?'

'I don't know. I've got a daughter. And if I'd found out someone . . . well, I wouldn't wait a couple of years before I did something about it. If Brook was going to kill Harvey-Ellis, why didn't he do it as soon as he found out about the affair?'

'He assaulted him, in front of witnesses, he knew he couldn't kill him. So he decided to wait.'

Hudson nodded. 'Maybe. But the least he could do was have Harvey-Ellis arrested for raping his daughter. Why not take that option?'

'Why? Because he *wants* to kill him, guv. And maybe he wants to avoid a trial, avoid putting Terri and his ex-wife through the ringer.'

'Then it's the same problem we had with Terri and the mum. This murder was cold and calculated. If it's revenge for his daughter there's got to be some passion somewhere, even after two years. I don't see any.'

'Maybe he's a cold fish.'

'He's still one of us, Laura, the thin blue. Let's not lose sight of that. And you're talking about one of the smartest detectives in the country, by all accounts. He deserves any benefit we can give him.'

'If he's so good, why hasn't he caught The Reaper, guv? He's had several cracks at it.'

'Just the same, we don't want to be going off half-cocked. We've got nothing on him.'

'So what do we do?'

'Get everything we've got on all The Reaper murders so we can get a handle on what Brook's been up against – see how he thinks.'

'And then?'

'Pack a bag.'

Chapter Three

September 1995, Northern California

The vehicle swept into the gas station and drew to a halt next to a pump. Sensored floodlights banished the gathering gloom and cast the surrounding woods into surly shadow and a multitude of insects came to life at the sudden warmth of the lights. A powerfully built young man in oily dungarees, with unkempt straw for hair, half-ran, half-walked from the flat slab of a building towards the pump. He arrived and stood waiting for the driver, looking intently over the vehicle, wiping his mouth with a napkin extracted from his grimy shirt pocket.

The driver stepped out, pulling his map from under a sealed plastic wallet full of deep red rose petals on the passenger seat. He stared at it for a moment then tossed it back into the vehicle to cover the small box of bullets on the back seat.

'Fill her up, sir?' asked the attendant, his mouth still half-full of food. It had stained his chin with a film of grease. The man nodded and strolled towards the building, stretching and flexing his frame as he went. He'd been driving all day and could feel the tingling in his legs as blood reintroduced itself to his muscles.

He walked into the shabby prefab and let the fly screen clatter behind him. The man heard the nightly news report of the latest from the OJ Simpson murder trial being chewed over by the commentators. There was no escape from the story, even in this remote corner of Northern California.

His dark eyes flicked around the squalor, adjusting to the strip lighting that buzzed and flickered overhead. A water cooler burped its welcome somewhere in the back and insects glided towards his eyes and ears. The fetid atmosphere was almost tangible, unperturbed by the ancient fan struggling to push the treacly air around the room.

A man dressed in a soiled, sweat-stained, sleeveless vest, which must once have been as white as his arms, leaned forward across his desk. The reflected glow of a small TV danced around his three-day stubble.

'Evening, sir. Welcome to Alpine County,' beamed a middle-aged version of the young man filling his car. 'Caleb Ashwell's the name. That there's my boy Billy.' He turned off the TV and stood to greet his customer.

'Evening,' replied the man, declining to throw his own name into the mix. 'Am I on the right road for Markleeville?'

'Yes, sir. You're on 89 – ten miles out of Markleeville. That where you're headed, Mr . . . ?'

The man looked up at Ashwell and, after a pause, answered. 'Brook. No, I'm headed for South Lake Tahoe.'

A slow yellow grin filled Ashwell's features. 'Not far to go, sir. Maybe thirty, forty miles,' he said. 'You English, Mr Brook?'

'You could say that,' answered Brook distractedly.

'I knew it,' exclaimed Ashwell, slapping the counter. 'Just love that accent. Welcome to California, Mr Brook. God's own country. After Texas, 'course.' He held out his hand for Brook who kept his hands behind his back but, when Ashwell wouldn't be denied, he placed his thin hand into the American's rough paw and shook as firmly as he could.

If Ashwell noted Brook's discomfort at the contact, it didn't seem to have registered. 'And we all sure loved your

Mrs Thatcher over here. The Iron Lady. Mighty fine. Mighty fine. And your Princess Di? Well now, sir she's a real beaut, yes indeed.' Ashwell's face cracked into the professional smile of the salesman. 'Is that a Dodge Ram 250 you got out there, sir?' he said, marching to the grimy window to look out. 'Didn't know you could rent that model any longer?' He turned to Brook expectantly, waiting for his answer.

Brook gazed back, his own smile starting to function. 'I didn't, I bought it second hand in Los Angeles.'

'A '92?' The smile was broad but the eyes were probing. Clearly there weren't abundant opportunities for conversation on this lonely stretch of highway.

'No, 1991 – it's already clocked over a hundred thousand though,' replied Brook.

Ashwell seemed satisfied with that. 'In four years? Ain't a lot for the 250, sir. She's just getting started. Mighty fine vehicle – a real workhorse. You must be touring round a lot. You been to Yosemite yet?'

Brook nodded and fixed his interrogator with his dark eyes. 'I drove through yesterday. It was magnificent.'

'Ain't it? One of the Lord's finest day's work right there.' Brook shrugged. Ashwell pressed on. 'And you're gonna love Tahoe.'

Brook noticed a camera on the back wall, stared at the red light for a few seconds, then looked back at Ashwell with a half-smile.

Ashwell must have seen him looking because, unsolicited, he said, 'Had a couple of robberies last year. Goddamn bikers.' He looked around for somewhere to spit but then evidently thought better of it.

'You can never be too careful,' agreed Brook.

The young man came through the door, rubbing his hands with a cloth. 'Billy. This gentleman's from England.'

'They got a queen, Pop.'

'That's right, son. Whyn't you pour Mr Brook here a cup of coffee to take with him?' He turned to Brook. 'On the house, you understand. Freshly brewed. You ain't got far to go but you need to stay alert on these roads and a cup of hot Joe always does the job. It's awful dark out there when the sun dips.'

Brook smiled. 'Thank you for your kindness. What do I owe you?'

Billy returned with a lidded paper cup and handed it to Brook. 'Ten bucks even.'

Brook pulled a credit card from his wallet, thought for a second, then slid it back in. He then pulled out a large wad of notes, methodically looking for the right denomination, before pulling out a ten-dollar bill. 'Pity they didn't make these easier to use,' said Brook, apologetically. 'They all look the same.'

'Just like niggers,' chortled Billy, until his father's hand caught him hard round the head.

'Don't you talk your foolishness round real people,' shouted Ashwell. 'Get on up the house.' Billy's head sagged onto his chest and, close to tears, he slumped away. 'Sorry about Billy, Mr Brook. He ain't bright but he ain't usually that stupid.'

'No need to apologise – must be hard out in this wilderness for a boy his age. Your wife too,' said Brook, suddenly keen to make conversation.

'It sure is a lonely stretch of blacktop, sir, no word of a lie – but beautiful too. 'Specially in the winter when the snow's on the hills. Got a cabin up on the bluff,' said Ashwell, indicating behind him with a flick of his head. 'Momma's gone. There's just Billy and me.'

Brook nodded. 'I see.' He stared back at Ashwell but seemed lost in thought. He smiled. 'I don't suppose you sell corkscrews; lost mine last night at the campsite.'

'No problem, sir.' Ashwell slapped a penknife on the counter, which had various attachments including the corkscrew Brook was looking for. 'Five bucks.'

This time Brook counted out five ones. 'Well. Thanks again for the coffee.'

'Don't mention it, Mr Brook. Now you drink it while it's hot. And we'll hope to see you again soon,' he called to Brook's receding frame. Ashwell stood motionless, watching the Dodge pull away as the deathly quiet slowly engulfed the station again.

A moment later the silence was shattered as the sound of another engine signalled a different vehicle encroaching on the California night.

*

'I still don't see how you can rule out the wife and daughter.' Chief Superintendent Donald Maddy stroked his beard as was his custom when ruminating over matters of detection. It didn't help his deductive powers at all – he didn't have any – but, whenever matters outside his comfort zone were presented to him, he subconsciously reached for his facial hair to mask his unease. Grant had read the textbooks and knew that psychologists attributed this kind of mannerism to a desire for concealment based on inadequacy. She also knew that had she, Hudson and the Chief Super been discussing community policing or traffic management, Maddy would have opened himself up by putting his hands behind his head, inviting contradiction so he could show off his in-depth knowledge of the subject.

She looked over at Hudson who nodded. He always encouraged Grant to take the reins in the Chief Super's office, because he was too easily exasperated when those he dubbed 'pencil necks' didn't accept his superior expertise.

'It's the way he was murdered, sir,' answered Grant. 'He was

51

killed by someone who knew what they were doing. The wife and daughter wouldn't have had a clue.'

'They might have hired someone to do it,' observed Maddy.

Hudson's features began to darken but, before he could speak, he heard Grant say, 'Good point, sir. We'll certainly keep that in mind.'

Maddy seemed pleased that his impressions were of some value and attempted to gild the lily. 'What was that drug again?'

'Scopolamine mixed with traces of morphine.'

'Ah yes,' he said as though in recognition.

'It induces a condition known as Twilight Sleep,' said Grant. 'It's why Harvey-Ellis was so compliant with his killer, sir. We've got no material evidence here in Brighton apart from those drugs. Whoever did this has come and gone without a trace.'

'No witnesses, nothing on CCTV?'

'Not yet, sir.'

'What about this Sowerby?'

'A weasel, sir, and we're not ruling him out. However, we're dubious he could plan something this slick. And motive is weak – Harvey-Ellis was a good customer. There's always money but Sowerby swears blind he didn't sell him out. For the moment we believe him.'

'And he didn't notice anyone who might have been setting this up?' asked Maddy.

'No one.'

'Which leaves only the wife and daughter,' nodded Maddy. 'As I said.'

'Not quite true, sir,' said Grant. 'But this is where it gets tricky. The ex-husband also has motive and, what's more, he has professional criminal know-how.'

'Opportunity?'

'We're not sure yet. He lives in Derby. But he does know Brighton. Two years ago he found out his daughter and stepfather

52

were lovers and marched into Harvey-Ellis's office where he assaulted him and threatened him with arrest.'

'Sounds promising.'

'Yes, sir. But he's a serving DI in Derby CID. Damen Brook.'

Maddy made eye contact for the first time. '*The* Damen Brook? Of Reaper fame?'

'The same.'

Maddy took a minute to process the information, then shrugged. 'We must root out all bad apples, Detectives. That's our job. Do what you have to do.' He nodded at them both, clearly expecting this to be the end of the meeting. When they showed no sign of moving, he held out his hands. 'Something else?'

'We ran the combination of drugs through the database,' said Hudson, deciding it was time to contribute. 'The only recent incidence of those two drugs being used in a crime was during the last Reaper killings in Derby.'

'What are you saying?' asked Maddy, this time unashamed to have it spelt out for him.

Hudson paused for a second to be certain there would be no misunderstanding. 'We're working on the theory that Brook learns about the drugs while working the Reaper murders and then puts the same drugs to use when he kills Tony Harvey-Ellis.'

'Sounds reasonable. What's the problem?'

'If we clear Brook, it means Brighton may have had its first Reaper killing.'

*

The man listened to the music over the quietly chugging engine. He checked his map one more time then turned off the headlights to enjoy the music in the dark. Fauré's Requiem seemed appropriate to the grandeur of the landscape, not that he could see much of it now, tucked away as he was in a side road that had been cut into the terrain

to allow the US Forest Service to do its work in the thick woodland.

He ejected the tape, turned off the engine and stepped out of the car. He left the door open and allowed the light to illuminate his work as well as the thousands of excited insects heading for its unexpected balm. He produced a flashlight from a small rucksack and tucked it into his black boiler suit. Other items had already been carefully packed but the man extracted one and examined it. The 9mm M9 semiautomatic pistol was not his tool of choice – brutish and unsubtle things, guns – but when spur of the moment work raised its head, he would have to put it to use. He'd bought it from a pawn shop in LA last year but had never intended to fire it. Now that it was to be pressed into service, the man had to be sure he knew how to use it. He checked the safety lever again as the pawn shop owner had shown him and made sure that a bullet from its 15-round magazine was in the chamber.

When he was ready, he placed the gun back in the rucksack and pulled the bag over his shoulder. He reached back into the car to pick up the drink from the cup holder and closed the door quickly to extinguish the light.

In the dark he gazed at the cloudless heavens. All unnatural illumination now extinguished, the man marvelled at the *son et lumière* around him – the stars blinking like traffic lights and the Milky Way cradling all these celestial bodies in its opaque arms.

When he could bear to close his eyes to the majesty above him, his ears were invaded by nature's symphony. Insects, crickets and cicadas set the rhythm, accompanied by the birds who hunted them. The hoot of owls was familiar, watching for the scurry of rodents. Other calls, cries, warnings and death rattles he didn't recognise but the performance filled him with awe nonetheless – the cacophony of the forest as it lived and died. And all the time the damp smell of the timber filled his lungs, with an aroma unsurpassed by the sweetest perfumes as the ageless woodland exhaled all around him.

He wasn't sure how long he stood there in the night, composing himself for the task ahead, but it was difficult to pull away.

Eventually he flicked on his flashlight and started his walk to the forest at the edge of the tarmac. He could have driven onto the dirt track that wound its way through the trees but he couldn't chance being heard. And if the ground was soft he would have run the risk of leaving an impression of his tyres. As usual he'd thought of everything.

As he set off, a pair of eyes shone back at him, but the animal wasn't curious enough to stare for long and skittered away through the undergrowth. The distinctive three-note whistle of the Mountain Chickadee sounded nearby as it prepared to dip and dive for flying insects, but the man was now oblivious to all but the work in hand.

He walked steadily with the flashlight in one hand, drink in the other. It wasn't the city terrain he was accustomed to and he found it hard going at first until he hit his stride. Twenty minutes of steady progress along the track brought the man to a clearing at the top of a small rise from which he could see a building next to the highway, bathed in moonlight below. He doused his light. The track he stood on wound back into the forest and took a leisurely and sinuous course that would eventually bring it out behind the main road. Before that though, the man could see a light from a house set back from the road – this was his destination.

Having recovered his breath, he made for the light. A few yards further on, however, he stopped. Another track, overgrown and near undetectable, wound its way off into the trees and would have been of no interest had the man not spotted a dark patch a few yards further along it. He edged closer and bent over the stain, flicked his flashlight on and touched it with his fingers. It was oil. He peered down the track as best he could. As his eyes adjusted to the blackness, he fancied he could make out two lines on the ground that might have been flatter than the rest of the vegetation. He hesitated briefly, then crept along the track into the darkness.

A few moments later the track widened out into a flat and well-tended clearing, completely surrounded by high walls of rock and dense foliage. It was deathly quiet in this sheltered bowl and unnaturally hot. The man's recently shaved head began to itch in the heat. He guessed that this might once have been a disused quarry or part of an opencast mine. But interesting though the geography might be, what drew the man's immediate attention was the line of vehicles parked along the far rock wall. There were eight different vehicles in various stages of decay, from vaguely roadworthy down to rusted hulks, and, from what he could see, all were some kind of motor home. The newest he recognised – a bright yellow VW camper – and its tyre tracks were still visible across the well turned soil.

The man closed his eyes and took a deep breath. Something brushed his cheek and he opened his eyes at once. He shivered now, despite the heat. Maybe it had been a flying insect or a bird's wing because no foliage hung nearby. Maybe. What he couldn't explain was the sensation he'd felt, like the scrunch of long fingernails dragging across his day-old beard and, more, the distant scent of a woman's perfume hanging on the still air.

He turned the light back on and moved closer to the line of vehicles, stopping at the VW camper. His flashlight followed a line of five faint scratches along the side of the bodywork, travelling from the door handle back towards the rear door. The man shone his light quickly at the spot on the ground where the marks ended, cupping his hand over the beam to limit its visibility. A long painted fingernail, twisted and torn from its digit, lay on the ground – and beside it were more scratchings in the ground. He stared intently at the earth, which was firmer here.

'HELP,' he read. After a few minutes, he turned and made his way back to the main track.

Chapter Four

'A new book released today offers a chilling insight into the horrifying events of two years ago when the serial killer known as The Reaper struck in the Derby suburb of Drayfin. The family of Robert Wallis were subjected to a brutal attack in their home which left both parents and their eleven-year-old daughter, Kylie, dead. All the victims had been drugged and their throats cut. The only survivors were teenage son Jason, who was out of the house that night, and baby daughter Bianca, who was there but was spared.

'Brian Burton, crime correspondent at the *Derby Telegraph*, covered the case extensively and hopes to throw new light on the events of that night. Rose Atkins went along to his book launch to speak to him for *East Midlands Today*.'

'*In Search of The Reaper* by Brian Burton chronicles the terrible events of the night almost two years ago when Derby became the latest city after London and Leeds to be visited by the notorious serial killer, The Reaper. After he left, three people, including an eleven-year-old girl, were dead and two other children orphaned. I asked the author why he felt compelled to write this book.'

'I covered this case from the start, Rose, and I felt it was important to share with the people of Derbyshire, and hopefully beyond, some of the reasons why this terrifying killer struck in our city and also to highlight some of the mistakes that have allowed this butcher to remain at large.'

'In your book, Brian, you're very critical of Derbyshire CID. Can you tell us why?'

'I don't think there's been nearly enough analysis of what went wrong during the Wallis investigation and I hope the book sheds new light onto what more could have been done.'

'You're talking about the roles played by Detective Inspector Damen Brook and Chief Superintendent Evelyn McMaster.'

'It's no secret that I've been critical, particularly about Inspector Brook, whose competence for the investigation I questioned at the time. I think Superintendent McMaster's main failing was not realising that DI Brook's capacity to catch The Reaper was seriously in question. Her subsequent failure to remove him from the investigation showed a profound lack of judgement. But at least Evelyn McMaster paid the penalty for her failings and has since left her post. One of the most galling aspects of this case, in my opinion, is that the chief architect of the police's dismal inability to catch, or even identify a suspect, is still in the Force.'

'Why do you say DI Brook was unfit to run The Reaper investigation?'

'Well, you have to go back to the history of The Reaper, which I cover in the book. The first documented Reaper killing was in 1990 in North London. The family of Sammy Elphick were murdered in their home in Harlesden. The killings were highly ritualistic, with messages written in blood on the wall, something that is a distinctive characteristic of all the Reaper killings. Again both parents and a young child were slaughtered. And perhaps even more startling was that, once again, DI Brook was on the case.'

'To be fair, he was only a Detective Sergeant at the time though, wasn't he, Brian?'

'That's true. But as you'll see in the book, my research shows his superior, DI Charlie Rowlands, left the day-to-day running of the investigation to Brook. And in Harlesden, just as in Derby, no witnesses were found and no suspects were identified. Not one, even though DS Brook was on the case for more than a year, by which time a second family had also been killed – Floyd Wrigley, a petty but violent offender and heroin addict, his common-law wife and his young daughter Tamara. This time the killings took place in Brixton in South London and all three had their throats slashed.'

'Returning to your book, Brian, you also allege that a mental breakdown suffered by Brook shortly after the Brixton murders in 1991 was no more than a smokescreen for removing him from the case.'

'That's right. By then I think the penny must have dropped and Brook was axed from the inquiry. And what many in the Derbyshire constabulary have personally complained to me about is that an officer who was patently unfit for duty in London should then be transferred to Derby. To me, and others, that sends the message that Derbyshire's a second-class county. And, of course, what better place for The Reaper to strike than a city policed by a man who has already failed to catch him twice? And that's exactly what happened. The Drayfin killings in Derby remain unsolved and The Reaper remains at large.'

'But DI Brook was removed from that investigation at an early stage.'

'Too late, in my opinion, Rose. By the time a local detective, Inspector Robert Greatorix, had been assigned to the case, valuable time had been wasted and the trail had gone cold. To this day, nearly two years later, not a single suspect has been identified. Sound familiar?'

'Thank you, Brian, for taking time out from your book launch to talk to us. *In Search of The Reaper* is available from today. This is Rose Atkins for *East Midlands Today*.'

'Rose Atkins, with Brian Burton there. I should say that *East Midlands Today* contacted the Derbyshire constabulary prior to recording that interview and both Chief Superintendent

Charlton and Detective Inspector Brook were unavailable for comment.

'On a related matter, troubled teenager Jason Wallis was released from a young offenders' institution yesterday. Jason had served three months of a six-month sentence for shoplifting at White Oaks near Lichfield. Seventeen-year-old Jason survived the murder of his family by The Reaper two years ago, because he was out drinking with friends, and has been in trouble from a young age. This film of Jason was taken at the time of the Wallis family's appeal against Jason's permanent exclusion from Drayfin Community School after he allegedly assaulted a female teacher. Just a few weeks later, Jason's family were brutally slain by The Reaper in their home. Before Jason Wallis was released, we sent Calum French to speak to John Ottoman, husband of the teacher involved.'

'I'm standing outside the home of John and Denise Ottoman. Twenty-two months ago, Denise Ottoman, an English teacher for nearly thirty years, was teaching a group of Year 10 GCSE students when she was allegedly assaulted by Jason Wallis, one of her pupils. The assault, while never proven, led to Jason's suspension from Drayfin Community School, though he was later reinstated after the death of members of his family in Derby's first Reaper murders.

'Denise Ottoman meanwhile has not returned to work and was granted early retirement on health grounds almost a year ago, at the age of fifty-one. I asked her husband about his re-action to news that Jason Wallis would soon be free.'

'Appalled but resigned would be my reaction.'

'Why do you say that, Mr Ottoman?'

'Without wishing to personalise this and relive the events surrounding the assault on my wife, I should say that Jason Wallis has been a blight on this neighbourhood almost since he was old enough to shout an obscenity. He has been a violent and disorderly individual for much of his life and has shown scant regard for the feelings and welfare of anyone but himself.'

'Surely his early release is a sign that the young man has turned his life around?'

'More likely a case of the society we live in bending over backwards to accommodate anti-social elements. It's no surprise to my wife and I that the authorities have seen fit to release him, but what I find upsetting is that Jason Wallis can walk away from his sentence after three months while my wife Denise has not been able to set foot outside our house since the assault – she's a prisoner in her own home.'

'What do you say to those who believe that Jason's offending has its roots in his family's murder and that he's suffered enough?'

'Simply that Jason's anti-social behaviour started many years before the death of his family. His father and mother weren't the most functional parents and seemed to keep Jason on a very loose leash, which only encouraged him to greater heights of unpleasantness. The tragedy is, I taught Jason's sister Kylie at Drayfin Primary and I was as upset as her classmates that such a lovely girl should have been taken from this world so suddenly and so violently.'

'So you're suggesting it might have been better if The Reaper had murdered Jason instead of his sister Kylie?'

John Ottoman glared at the reporter. 'That's your interpretation of what I said, not what I actually said. I need to get back to my wife.'

'Just one more question, Mr Ottoman. If you could speak to Jason now, what would you say?'

Ottoman turned back and faced the camera. 'I'd remind him that The Reaper is still at large and to change his ways while he still can.'

*

Caleb Ashwell glowered at his son who stared sulkily at the neck of his Coca-Cola bottle, avoiding his gaze.

'Send a boy to do a man's work,' growled Ashwell. 'No word of a lie. Maybe you ain't no boy. Maybe you a girl.

How about it, Billy? You a bitch, Billy? Got too much of your whore momma in you? That true, boy?'

Billy's face darkened, his mouth opening, but he knew better than to reply and kept his counsel, continuing to stare anywhere but at his father.

A noise from the next room broke the tension and Caleb looked up at Billy who was finally able to look back.

'Go fix that, boy!'

Billy jumped up and went to the next room and Caleb stood to stretch his legs. He flung open the front door and stepped onto the stoop to roll a cigarette.

Billy came back to stand behind his father and eyed the tobacco tin. 'Can I have one of them, Pop?'

'These is for men, not boys, nor no cissies neither.'

'I ain't no cissy, Pop. I'm sixteen. Seventeen next month.'

'What you say?'

'I ain't no cissy. It ain't my fault Mr Brook don't stop. He just kept right on going, Pop. I followed all the way to Echo Lake and he don't stop. Just kept on going.'

Ashwell eyed his son with one final sneer of disdain then relented. He tossed over the tobacco tin. 'Well, maybe I didn't put enough sleep in the coffee. Pity we didn't get an address.' He struck a match and held it to his cigarette. 'Probably flat out on his porch sleeping like a baby . . .' He stopped when the flame illuminated a pale paper cup outside on the deck table. 'What the hell?'

Billy turned and they both approached the coffee cup as though it were a landmine. Billy picked it up gingerly. 'It's full.'

Caleb's realisation came a second too late – the baton was already travelling towards his head. As he turned to run into the cabin for a weapon, the tip crashed down on the front of his head, and he slumped onto the deck like an unsupported scarecrow.

Billy stooped to check his father, then looked up at his attacker as he stepped out of the shadows. 'Mr Brook?'

'Pick him up and get him inside.' Brook held the baton in his right hand and a gun in the left. He gestured with it.

The boy dragged his father up into the sparsely furnished cabin as best he could manage and Brook followed. There wasn't much to see inside – a blackened stove in the corner, a small dog-eared sofa and an old rocking chair with wooden spokes for a backrest. They faced the cold stove and an old TV, mounted atop a wooden crate. There was a rickety dining table and four matching chairs in another corner.

'Over there,' nodded Brook. Billy walked the staggering Caleb over to the old rocking chair and sat him down in it. Brook pulled a pair of cuffs from his belt and threw them at Billy. 'Pull his hands through the back then put those on his wrists.'

Billy hesitated for a moment, then stepped behind his father and pulled his arms together before clicking the cuffs into place. Brook ordered Billy to sit on the floor before slapping Ashwell's face to revive him.

Ashwell moaned and opened his eyes. He tried to rub his head with his cuffed hands, not yet registering the restraints.

'What the fuck?' He pulled urgently at the cuffs and tried to stand, but Brook raised the gun once more.

'Better relax, Mr Ashwell. It'll go easier that way.'

Ashwell looked up at Brook and shook his head to clear his vision. 'Mr Brook. What the hell you think you're doing?'

'Apologies for the crude attack, Mr Ashwell. It's not my usual style.' Brook swung his rucksack down to his feet and started to rummage around in it. After a few seconds, he extracted the penknife he'd bought a few hours earlier at the gas station below. From his rucksack he also removed a half-bottle of red wine and, using his recent purchase, opened the bottle. 'Needs to breathe,' he said to Caleb with a grin.

'You ain't answered my question, you sick son of a bitch. What the fuck you think you're doing? This is kidnapping. You can get twenty years for that in California.'

Brook smiled at him. 'You've researched it, have you?' Ashwell didn't answer. Brook pulled out a CD of Fauré's Requiem and looked over at Ashwell with a look of regret on his face. 'I don't suppose you have a CD player?'

'A CD player? That what this is about, you bastard? No, we ain't got no CD player.'

'Pity. Then again, you're a few notches up from my usual clients. The things you've done . . . maybe you don't deserve beauty.'

'Beauty. What the fuck?'

'I could always hum it for you.'

'Hum it to me? Fuck you, there's a TV there. Help your goddamn self. You want the key for the gas station? There's maybe two hundred dollars in the till. That's yours but that's all we have. Sooner you get what you want, sooner we can all get on with our lives. But do me a favour, leave the keys to these goddamn bracelets in the station so I can get my hands moving again, will ya?'

Brook eyed the overweight Ashwell. He'd certainly belied first impressions. The man was smart. His tone had changed now, was almost friendly as he tried to normalise the situation, tried to present Brook with a vision of how things should end. A finale with all three lives intact. Brook decided it was time to up the stakes.

'I'm not here for your money, Mr Ashwell. I'm here to extract payment of a different kind. I'm The Reaper and my currency is life.'

*   *   *

DCI Hudson hurried back to the car with the two coffees as a heavy shower began to pelt him. Grant leaned over and opened the door for him and he sat down awkwardly with the cellophane-wrapped sandwiches under his armpit.

Grant took her chicken salad from him and peeled the lid from her Americano.

Hudson took a swig of his tea. 'Bloody weather. You get north of Watford and you're straight into the next ice age. You're not going to need those,' he said, nodding at her sunglasses.

Grant removed them with a smile. 'My eyes get tired at the moment.'

'I hope you haven't come back to work too soon, luv. You know what these viruses are like.'

'I'm fine, guv. But I'd feel better if we weren't going up to Derby,' said Grant, giving her protest another airing.

'I thought you liked the idea.'

'Until I realised that Brook should be coming down to our turf. That's how we pressure him.'

'With what? Look, darlin', he isn't back at work until tomorrow morning. I know you think this is a courtesy too far but, trust me, it's best we make the effort.'

'You think we'll catch him off balance?'

'It's worth a try. If he thinks he's got away clean he won't be expecting questions, never mind a visit – it gives him less time to think.'

'I don't know. On his home ground he might be more at ease. And we'll be outsiders.'

'Home ground,' smiled Hudson. 'No such thing. Damen Brook is the outsider wherever he is.' Hudson took another mouthful of tea and swilled it round his mouth.

'You sound like you know him.'

Hudson cocked his head. 'I do sort of, though mainly by reputation – I only met him twice.'

'What's he like?'

'Brook doesn't make friends easily, or go out of his way to earn the respect of colleagues. He was a DS to one of my mates when I was up in the Smoke. You remember I told you about DI Charlie Rowlands? A legend and a fantastic copper. When he died, Brook was at the funeral. He gave a reading. We shook hands. No more.'

'So he won't remember you, guv?'

'I doubt it.'

'What did Rowlands think of Brook?'

'Charlie was in charge of the first Reaper inquiry in North London in 1990. Harlesden, it was.'

'Sammy Elphick, Mrs Elphick and their son.'

Hudson smiled at her. 'I see how you spent your evening. No wonder you're tired.'

Grant shrugged. 'We need to be ready.'

Hudson nodded. 'Well, Sammy was small time, a petty criminal like the other victims. They found him and his wife tied up with their throats cut. But before they died they watched their son die – he was only ten but The Reaper strung the boy up from the ceiling and cut two of his fingers off and the parents cried while they watched. Then there's the blood message on the wall.'

'SALVATION!' nodded Grant. 'Religious nutter?'

'Seems like.'

'So what went wrong with Brook?'

'Brook was Charlie's DS but Charlie told me Brook ran the entire thing. He said he was the most brilliant detective he'd ever worked with and he'd worked with a few. But the problem Brook had was getting on with ordinary coppers, coppers who weren't as good as him. He came across as arrogant and condescending, and they despised him for it. Still do. And when The Reaper came along . . . well. It was his first failure.'

'What happened?'

'You've read the files.'

'He had a breakdown after Brixton in '91. It doesn't say why.'

'From what I can gather, Brook started to take it home with him, started brooding about the stuff he'd seen. His marriage started to suffer.'

'Not unusual.'

'No. But there was another case . . .'

'Not The Reaper?'

'I can't remember it very well, luv. It was after the Elphick killings had died down. There was another murder, not related. Some runaway schoolgirl called Laura something – Laura Maples. That was it. She'd been raped and murdered in some grubby squat. Brook found the body but not before the rats had been at her.'

'And that tipped him over the edge?'

'Who knows? By the time the second family were killed in Brixton . . .' Hudson looked across at Grant.

'Floyd Wrigley, common-law wife and daughter,' she answered hesitantly. 'Throats cut. "SAVED" written on the wall.'

Hudson nodded. 'By then Brook was starting to veer off the rails according to Charlie. Soon after he had some kind of breakdown and a couple of years later he put in for a transfer to wind things down and get some peace. In 1993 The Reaper killed in Leeds but Brook got nowhere near that. Roddy Telfer, a small-time drug dealer, had his head blown off and his girlfriend was strangled.'

'Different.'

'Very. There's still a thought that it may have been a copycat because of the MO.'

'Sounds completely wrong for The Reaper.'

'It was, but the perp wrote "SAVED" on the wall after the killings. So . . .'

'And then nothing for over fifteen years until two years ago in Derby.'

'No. And nobody knows why. But it was all there in Derby. The parents, Mr and Mrs Wallis, and their young daughter had been drugged. The Reaper had delivered some food. It was doctored with scopolamine and morphine . . .'

'Twilight Sleep.'

'Right. He delivered the food and came back when they were out cold and cut their throats. The parents had cried so it looks like he made them watch the girl bleed out. It's a signature. "SAVED" was on the wall again and some art poster. And there was some classical music playing while they died. Another signature.'

'What's that all about?'

Hudson shook his head. 'No idea. Something to let us know The Reaper's a cut above your average killer, I guess.'

Grant nodded. 'Well, he's been in the wind for twenty years so I suppose he is. Just Brook's luck to be in Derby for The Reaper's comeback. Or is it?'

Hudson drained his tea and managed a half-note chuckle. 'You think The Reaper struck there to send Brook a message? Could be. But here's the measure of the man. The Reaper kills the Wallis family. Brook's back on the case. A week or two later he gets himself suspended – why, we don't know – but his career's over for all money. Then a few weeks later he solves the Laura Maples case, after nearly twenty years. He confronts some rich old geezer on his deathbed – Svensson or Sigurdsson or something – gets him to confess to the rape and murder of the schoolgirl. On *videotape*, mind you. Then the guy poisons Brook and cuts his own wrists. But Brook survived and that catch saved his career.'

'SAVED.' Grant looked down at the dregs of her drink and nodded. 'Convenient.' She looked up at Hudson, her eyes suddenly shining.

'What's wrong, luv?'

Grant ignored him and reached into the back seat for a file. 'I know why he got suspended, guv.' She handed a sheet of A4 to Hudson and indicated a date at the bottom of the page.

'Fuck me. Good spot, Laura. Brook assaulted Harvey-Ellis six days after the Wallis murders. He went AWOL in the middle of one of the biggest investigations of his career because he found out about his daughter and her stepfather.'

'And he came down to Brighton to sort it out.'

*

The man sipped on his glass of Californian Zinfandel and extracted a notepad from his rucksack. Caleb Ashwell had slipped back into unconsciousness, his head slumped on his chest, his double chin fanning out like a goitre.

Billy Ashwell shifted on his knees and eyed Brook. 'What you gonna do, Mr Brook? Pop ain't so good. He needs a doctor.'

Brook picked up the cup of coffee and put it on the floor next to Billy.

'Drink it.'

Billy shook his head. 'Ain't supposed to drink coffee. It keeps me awake nights.'

Brook smiled. 'That won't be an issue, Billy. Drink it!' he said softly, brandishing the gun and hoping the boy wouldn't spot his lack of ease with the weapon. Again Billy shook his head. 'Why? What's in it?'

'Don't know. Pop makes it.'

Brook nodded. 'Will it kill you?'

'Nope. Knock you out though.'

'Then drink it or I'll shoot your father, then I'll shoot you.'

Billy hesitated then withdrew a hand from his pocket and flicked the lid from the cup. 'It's cold,' he said, before realising it would make no difference to Brook. He took a wary sip and scrunched his face.

'More,' said Brook. Billy stared back sulkily then took a huge pull on the cup, almost draining it.

'Okay,' said Brook. 'That's enough. Put the lid back on.' Billy did as he was told. A few moments later his head began to roll and he couldn't sit upright. Brook was able to take the cup from the burly young teenager without a whiff of resistance.

He retreated to a chair to watch and was pleased to be able to put down his gun. He began to write down all of Billy's symptoms. At the top of the page he wrote 'Sleep', because that's what Caleb had called it, followed by 'Twilight' and a question mark. After a few moments of writing he closed the notepad. Billy's eyes were now just slits, he behaved with all the somnolence of a junkie.

'Stand up.' Billy lifted his head and tried to stand but his limbs wouldn't obey. Brook smiled. 'Perfect.'

A groan came from Caleb Ashwell, still slumped on the rocking chair. He shook his head and tried to right himself on the chair, but failed. Brook poured him some wine into a plastic cup. Ashwell drank, licked his lips, then opened his eyes.

'Sorry I don't have a proper glass.'

Ashwell blinked then fixed Brook in his sights. 'You lousy bushwhacking son of a bitch. Get these cuffs off me, you fucker, or I'll kill you.'

Brook smiled back but remained perfectly still. 'I see you're not a wine drinker, sir. Can I get you a beer instead?'

'A beer? Fuck you. I said, get these cuffs off, dammit, 'fore I take a baseball bat to your ass.'

'Do you think abusing and threatening me is the right way to secure your release?'

'I don't give a cold shit in hell what you think, you Limey fucker.' He tried again to right himself. He noticed Billy on the floor beside him. 'What you done to my boy?' Then he saw the cup. 'You son of a bitch. You fed that coffee to my boy?'

71

'Sleep you called it. Would that be from Twilight Sleep?' Ashwell didn't reply. 'Twilight Sleep, caused by a mixture of scopolamine and morphine. In small doses it can create a zombie-like compliance – in larger doses, death. I'm impressed. Where would you get that sort of knowledge? And, more importantly, where do you get your scopolamine?' Still Ashwell remained mute. 'Maybe you know it better as hyoscine.' Brook took a sip of wine. 'Let me assure you, sir, that unhesitating and well-mannered cooperation is the only way you and your son have a chance at seeing the dawn.'

Ashwell continued his sulk, but the barriers in his mind had crumbled. 'Used to be a fly boy down South America. Had my own charter service. When I went to Colombia I found out about scop. They use it a lot down there for robbing folk. Rape too. It comes from Borrachero trees. Brung some saplings back with me to grow.'

'Where?'

'Oh, around,' Ashwell said with a grin. 'You want some, I'm sure we can come to an understanding.'

Brook took another sip of wine. 'So when you got back from South America you set yourself up in a lonely gas station miles from anywhere and started using it on people.'

'Not people, Mr Brook. Tourists like you.'

Brook smiled at the distinction. 'They get a spiked coffee and young Billy follows them in the tow truck until the drug takes effect.'

'S'right. When the drug kicks in, they pull over for a sleep. Then he robs them. And that's the operation, right there.'

'That's it?'

'Sure. When they wake up they don't know what's happened to them – scop causes amnesia, see. They just go on their way. No harm, no foul. Eventually they work out they been robbed. But what the hell? They're insured, ain't they?'

Brook smiled. 'Surely when they wake up and realise they've been robbed, there must be some evidence they've been here.'

'What evidence? We don't got no till receipt. We say it's broke and if they want one, we just write a chit. And we only take the ones who pay cash.' Brook smiled suddenly, his black eyes disappearing under a concertina of skin. 'You knew, didn't you? That's why you put your credit card back.'

'One of the reasons.'

'How in the hell you know what we was going to do? 'Bout the coffee an' all?'

'Let's just say I had a feeling.'

'Bullshit. Are you police?'

Brook fixed Ashwell with a wintry eye. 'You're going to wish I was.'

'Why? What you going to do? Nuth'n. You've had your fun. Now take our money and get on out.'

'You'd make a great salesman, Mr Ashwell.'

Brook pulled off his black gloves. He had a pair of latex gloves underneath. Then he stood, zipping his boiler suit up to his neck. 'I'm sorry I've got no great art to remind you,' he said. A cutthroat razor gleamed suddenly in his hand.

Ashwell saw it and began to talk a little faster, grinding his wrists against the handcuffs. 'Remind me of what?'

'Of how wonderful the human race can be if it aspires to greatness instead of evil. Ideally, you should die beneath a beautiful painting, with wondrous music as your companion to oblivion. Alas . . .'

'You're gonna kill us over a few dollars? You're gonna kill my boy?'

'You killed Billy years ago. I'm just here to make it official.'

'I ain't killed no one.'

'Really? Tell me, did you kill your wife before you murdered the humanity in Billy or after?'

'My wife?' screamed Ashwell.

'No matter. The chronology is hardly an issue now.'

'You son of a bitch . . .'

'So what happens to the children in your *operation?*' asked Brook, to forestall another rant. 'I hope it's quick and painless.'

'Children?'

'You know, the children who don't drink coffee – the children on holiday with their parents who could identify Billy. And the other people in the vehicle who can remember what happened to them – the people who can remember being robbed, the people who can remember the car crashing, the people who can remember Billy turning up to help, the people who can remember being towed back here, who know where you've parked their car, with all the other cars in the clearing out back.'

Ashwell smiled his green and yellow smile and thought for a second. Then he seemed to come to a decision. 'Oh, those people.' He seemed to drift off for a moment, remembering secret pleasures. 'Well, that's why I choose tourists like you, Mr Brook, on holiday, hundreds of miles from home. It could be months before some of *those* people are missed. And even when they are reported missing . . .'

'Of course. They're travelling. They could be anywhere,' nodded Brook, his mouth beginning to harden.

'Exactly. And if the crash ain't killed 'em, we bring 'em back here and have some fun. We party with the wives in front of their menfolk. They don't like that.' He chuckled at the memory. 'Then we kill the men in front of their families.

They sure do make a hollering. We kill the little 'uns straight off usually but if the kids are old enough, we keep 'em a while and show 'em a good time. I get to bust the girls then give 'em to Billy when I get bored. If we get a real squirrelly little bitch, I invite my brother Jake over for a blind date.' Ashwell sniggered. 'They're old enough to bleed, they're old enough to butcher. That's what Jake says.'

Brook walked over to Ashwell's chair. 'I hope Jake's already dead because I've got a lot on at the moment.'

'Ain't no call to take on so, Mr Brook. We kept the sweet stuff for you. Got plenty of money left. Lot more than two hundred dollars. You can have it all. And don't forget we got you on camera, Mister Brook.'

Brook circled slowly round behind him.

'I bought some gas and left,' said Brook. 'No harm, no foul.' He moved directly behind Ashwell so that the cuffed man had to strain to keep him in view.

'We got your licence plate too.'

'Same answer,' whispered Brook in Ashwell's ear.

Ashwell's head was yanked back so his Adam's apple strained at the skin of his throat. Brook placed the blade of the razor onto the submerged blue of the carotid artery.

'We got a mic in that camera, Mr Brook,' squeaked Ashwell. 'They'll know your name.'

'Oh, I doubt that.' However, Brook appeared to hesitate as he processed this new information. Ashwell waited, hope seizing him. 'See, that's the other reason I didn't give you my credit card. My name's not Brook,' said the man. He began to hum the Requiem . . . then sliced cleanly into Ashwell's flabby neck.

Chapter Five

Damen Brook opened his eyes but remained motionless in his sleeping bag. The trees near the tent were creaking under the wind's assault and an owl hooted off in the distance, but the noise that had woken him had not been one of nature's sound effects. He looked at his watch – two in the morning. Maybe a car at the bottom of the field had woken him – but at this hour and in the depths of the Peak District? It seemed unlikely. He felt around for his water bottle and took a short drink.

He closed his eyes but reopened them at once. Someone or something was definitely moving around outside his tent. He lifted his head from the makeshift pillow and followed the source of the noise. Beyond the mound of his feet, framed by the moonlight, Brook could see a shadow on the other side of the canvas. The paper-and-comb noise of a zip unfastening sent Brook scrabbling for his torch. Flicking it on he trained it on the tent's flap, but this didn't halt the unfastening – it merely hastened it.

Fully alert now, Brook sat up and cast around for a weapon. He reached for his walking boots but the mention of his name turned his muscles to solid ice.

'Who is it?'

'Damen. Damen. It's me.' Brook didn't recognise the little-girl voice. 'Laura.'

Brook's heart, already working hard, went into overdrive. Sweat dotted his forehead. 'Laura?'

The flap opened and a pretty young girl popped her head through the gap.

She smiled at him and proceeded to crawl into the tent on all fours. 'Laura Maples. You must remember,' she grinned. Her skin was pale and she wore nothing but the briefest silk night slip, which did little to conceal her small breasts as she climbed onto his sleeping bag. 'I've come to thank you for Floyd,' she smiled and proceeded to unfasten his sleeping bag.

'What?'

'You must remember Floyd,' she said. Her smile vanished and she massaged her neck briefly, then showed her fingers to Brook. They were covered in blood. 'I do.' She moved towards him, recovering her smile, and climbed on top of him.

Brook shone the torch onto her unblemished peach-fuzz face. He felt a hand pulling at his sleeping bag. 'Stop.' He grabbed her hand – it was icy cold.

'Please, Damen. Just once for love.' She pushed his arms down and kissed him with her frosty lips. Brook could feel her soft flesh trembling in her too thin slip and tried to pull away, but she pressed closer to him for warmth, her tongue beginning to search for his.

A stench so foul Brook thought he might retch made him push the girl away and he swung the torch back to her face. The blackened skull and orbs of her eye sockets glared back at him and he shrank back to the wall of his tent, almost collapsing the frame. The broken beer bottle protruding from her neck glistened in the artificial light, grimy panties still dangling from its neck – testimony to her killer's final incriminating act.

'You're not real,' shouted Brook. He darted the torch this way and that, searching for her corpse. She had gone. Brook heaved a sigh. A second later he felt the movement at his feet and knew at once what it was. He scrambled to pull the sleeping bag off his legs but the seething, roiling mass of rats struggling for air at the bottom of his fetid bed gouged and scraped their way to freedom over his quivering torso.

77

Brook sat bolt upright and took several huge gasps of air. When his heart returned to near normal, he poked a bleary head out into the sharp, cold air of the morning. Although only wearing underpants and T-shirt, he spilled out onto the sopping grass and raised his six-foot frame to its full height, welcoming the fingers of dawn massaging their faint warmth into his face.

He closed his eyes and rubbed the fatigue from them. It had been years since he'd dreamed of Laura Maples, dreams he thought he'd left behind forever. Her killer, Floyd Wrigley, was in the ground – Brook had seen to that – and his nightmares had been buried with him. Or so he had thought. Two nights in a row. He heaved a final huge sigh. Something was wrong.

He looked at his watch and scrabbled back inside the tent, emerging with a box of matches inside a plastic bag. The first two matches he removed failed to ignite, but the third obliged, and Brook slid it under the kettle of his one-ring camping stove and made some tea.

Brook returned to the tent, dressed quickly, then packed his sleeping bag, camera and other meagre possessions into the side of his rucksack.

He then set to work taking down his quick-erect tent. He worked rhythmically, occasionally looking around as he folded, but there was no landowner or farmer to complain this early in the morning.

Brook packed his stove, kettle and mug and struck out down the path that would eventually spit him out into the small hamlet of Milldale, on the River Dove in Derbyshire's Peak District. Forty minutes later he was standing on Milldale's ancient footbridge, admiring a nearby heron and feeling the warmth of the low sun spread its balm.

He clambered up the steps to the municipal toilets. After an icy wash, Brook gazed at his bleary face in the cracked mirror. He then set off up the path next to the river that would eventually take him to his home in the village of Hartington. He walked steadily, ignoring the hunger gnawing at his tight belly and feeling quiet pleasure at the newfound strength in his legs and shoulders. Two weeks of wild camping, walking fifteen miles a day and eschewing alcohol and cigarettes had left Brook feeling as fit as he had in years. But the dream of Laura Maples gnawed at him. What did it mean?

Brook power-walked the last mile into Hartington and up the small hill to his front door, stopping only briefly to get a pint of milk and a loaf of bread at the corner shop. As he was extracting his keys from a side pocket, his eye wandered to the small, lavender-scented front garden of Rose Cottage next door. He noticed that the 'To Let' sign, which had been there for many a month, had now been taken down and laid flat along the side wall of the cottage. At the same time, he noticed that several upstairs windows had been opened to air the place out.

He unlocked his front door and stepped into the porch, kicking the large pile of unopened mail to one side. As soon as he entered the inner door he heard the urgent ping of the answer phone alerting him to messages. Two weeks away, two messages. He pressed the play button.

'Hello, sir. Hope you've had a good holiday wherever you've been.' It was DS John Noble. 'I thought I'd give you the rundown on The Reaper book. It came out on Tuesday and got a fair amount of attention. Brian Burton was interviewed on *East Midlands Today* apparently – I didn't see it. Surprise, surprise, he has a go at you in it, about the way the investigation went, you know the routine, and the BBC rang up to find out if you or the Chief Super wanted to be on with him. The Chief's said no. As he doesn't know you all that well, he's fretting that you might get sucked into saying the wrong thing. Don't worry, I told him you don't talk to anyone if you can help it, least of all journalists . . .'

Brook smiled at this and muttered, 'No comment!'

'Anyway . . .' The message cut off at this point but was picked up again in the next one. 'It's me again. Just to say I've taped the interview for you if you can face it. I've also left a text on your new mobile just in case you actually manage to take it with you, remember how to turn it on and have learned how to access your messages. Unlikely, I know. See you tomorrow. Oh, BTW,' Brook rolled his eyes, 'Jason Wallis was released a couple of days ago. Thought you might want to know.'

Brook's expression hardened. 'So you're out at last, you murdering little coward.' He made some tea and took a sip while glancing through the side window at the memorial to his slaughtered cat. He reflected on the night two years ago when he'd risked everything and played The Reaper, holding Jason hostage, confronting him with his crimes and threatening to cut his throat unless he turned himself in for the murder of Annie Sewell, an old woman in a sheltered home.

He looked back to the cat-shaped stone. He'd underestimated Wallis. A week later Jason and his crew had come after Brook, wrecking his down-at-heel flat and killing his cat.

Brook smiled suddenly. 'The Reaper's dead, Jason. Did I forget to tell you? For all you know he could be waiting round the next corner or passing you in the street. It could be anyone. It could be me. Sweet dreams.'

Brook finished his tea and deleted the messages. He took out his brand new mobile phone and turned it on, confirming there was a text from Noble, but didn't bother to read it. He wasn't comfortable texting but had no desire to endure the how-was-your-holiday conventions of a phone conversation so he painstakingly tapped out: 'Jason Wallis. Did anyone inform the Ottomans?', making sure he took the time to add the capital letters and question mark.

A few minutes later Noble replied – 'who' – without punctuation or a capital letter.

Brook was disheartened on two fronts. 'A pity we don't remember the victims as we remember the criminals,' he muttered and switched off the phone.

Then he booted up his computer and went to take a shower.

* * *

Special Agent Mike Drexler drained his espresso then turned his attention to the orange juice. He took a long slow sip and grinned at his companion.

'Yummy. I never imagined things could taste like this and I could feel this good on top.'

Special Agent Edie McQuarry flashed him a sarcastic smile and exhaled tobacco smoke over him. 'A month away from the weed and you turn into some kind of goddamn evangelist. It's sickening.'

'I got news for you, Ed. I haven't had alcohol for three weeks either.'

'Well, give the man a prize. While the rest of humanity is out getting drunk and laid, you'll be able to stay home nights and brush up on your macramé.'

'What's that?'

'I've no idea but my sister says she does it on her coffee mornings.'

'Sounds kinky.'

'Well, if you ever get a hankering to wear a poncho I'll hook you up.' McQuarry eyed her partner before taking another long pull on her cigarette and twisted her mouth to exhale the smoke away from the other tables. 'Sorry. I shouldn't have mentioned sisters.'

Drexler looked up. 'Ed, it's been ten years now. I'm over it.'

'Glad to hear it. So how'd it go last week?'

'How'd what go?'

McQuarry raised an eyebrow. 'It's October, Mike. And I'm your partner.'

Drexler smiled bleakly into the distance. 'How do these things usually go? You place the flowers, wipe the dirt off the headstone, say a few words. "Hey, sis, let me tell you about my year."' He smiled at his partner. 'Gotta keep busy standing over the dead.'

'You visit your mother?'

Drexler's smile was a mask behind which words were carefully selected. 'What's the point? She doesn't know who I am. I barely know myself. Since Kerry died . . .' He shrugged. What else was there to say?

Opposite McQuarry, a large woman sitting next to her even larger husband and two grossly overweight boys, caught her eye to purse her lips in disapproval, before opening them to fork in a mouthful of syrupy pancakes.

Drexler followed McQuarry's gaze to their table. 'If anyone complains I'm going to have to arrest you.'

'We're outside, goddamn it, Mike. What more do they want?'

'It's a public place. There are laws.' Drexler tried to keep a straight face but couldn't maintain it.

'My first smoke of the day ruined.' McQuarry stubbed out her cigarette, then briefly examined her left hand.

'How is it?' asked Drexler.

She grinned at him, then flexed her hand more vigorously, trying not to wince at the discomfort from the scar tissue. 'Good as new, Mike.'

Drexler nodded. A tension rose within him and McQuarry knew what was coming. 'Listen, Ed . . .'

'If you're gonna start that crap again, Mike, we're gonna have a problem. You're my partner. You saved my life. I got cut 'cos I got careless, and if it hadn't been for you I could've been filleted by that piece of shit. End of story.'

Drexler managed a smile. 'Okay. You won't hear me mention it again. But I never got to say thanks, you know, for still wanting to saddle up with me and backing me in front of the Board. I owe you.'

'You don't owe me shit, Mike, it was a good shoot. Just how many more times aren't you ever gonna mention it?'

Drexler returned her grin. 'Coupla hundred.'

McQuarry drained her coffee and they both stood in

unison. Drexler counted out a few dollars and dropped them on the table. She eyed the morbidly obese family as they passed their table. 'You know, I don't complain about lardasses encouraging me to weigh my heart down with fat,' she said, a little more loudly than was necessary, as she stalked away from the restaurant.

They walked down Placerville Main Street through the morning sunshine, back to their dark blue Chevy. They'd been partners in the FBI for nearly three years and were comfortable in each other's company. Drexler was thirty-three, slender and tall with curly brown hair, a handsome face and a lopsided smile.

McQuarry was thirty-eight and two years away from being a fifteen-year veteran. She looked younger, or so Drexler always told her, and despite his occasional teasing she saw no reason to disbelieve him. Her hair was also brown, but darker and shinier, and she tied it in a pony-tail when on duty. She was a foot shorter than Drexler and full-figured, though she tended to think she was over-weight and had been 'careful' with her diet for most of her adult life.

'Nice place, this,' said Drexler.

'You're kidding, right?'

'No. I can see myself living in a place like this in a few years. It's safe, got great fishing . . .'

'Safe,' sneered McQuarry. 'Sacramento's not safe enough for you? It's the most boring city in the world.'

'You'll never get over 'Frisco, will you, Ed?'

'No, I never will – the most beautiful place in the world. And they got a ballpark. And another thing – the most dangerous activity in San Fran is being a tourist who says 'Frisco. It's San Fran or SF – never 'Frisco. Got that?'

'Go easy on me, officer, I'm just a country boy who don't know no better.'

McQuarry threw the keys at him. 'Amen to that. Now let's move it, Mike. We got another hour on the road.'

*

Grant grabbed her small suitcase from the boot before Hudson could attempt to carry it for her. They walked from the residents' car park to the reception area of the Midland Hotel and checked in. They found their adjacent rooms and Hudson paused at his door.

'What do you fancy for dinner? French? Italian? Spanish?'

Grant tried not to laugh. Her superior had many qualities, but subtlety wasn't one of them. She'd ridden this merry-go-round so many times since they'd first started working together and it always stopped at the same place. Hudson wanted a curry. He always wanted a curry, but he insisted on going through the motions of asking his sergeant for her preference before deciding.

Grant was tired and decided to shortcut the process. 'You know what, guv? I quite fancy a curry.'

Hudson's eyebrows rose, as if entertaining the proposal for the first time. 'Curry? Good call. I think I can manage that.'

Grant tossed her case into her room and locked her door.

'Going out?'

'We've been in the car a long time, guv. I think I'll stretch my legs.'

'Scope out a curry house while you're at it.'

Grant left the hotel and walked into Derby railway station next door. She looked around to get her bearings, saw the newsagents tucked in a corner and went to buy a local paper. She also bought a cheap baseball cap with 'Derby Pride' as its slogan. She fixed it on her head, briefly amused at her new cap. She'd never had clothing that endorsed one of the seven deadly sins before.

She set off along a nondescript road, on one side of which sat a row of brick terraced houses, identical even down to the colour of the paintwork on doors and windows. On the other ran a metal fence separating the pavement from the station car park.

Enjoying the cooler air, she walked on past a dilapidated railway building, which sported a 'For Sale' sign, no doubt trying to tempt developers to see the potential for apartments. She reached a set of traffic lights and stopped to look around. There wasn't much to see. Across the road was a smart redbrick building developed pre-credit crunch. It had a shiny new entry phone system and several buttons next to the main door. Beyond that there was a flyover which ferried traffic in and out of Derby. As Grant stood in the gathering gloom, she was oblivious to the telescopic lens pointed at her, too distant to hear the frantic whirring of the camera recording her image.

*

Drexler pulled the Chevy across the highway onto the dusty forecourt of the gas station. There wasn't a lot of room to park with all the flashing Highway Patrol cars, an ambulance and the other support vehicles squeezed into the available space. There were always more people than you'd expect to see at a crime scene. It didn't help that the space between the gas pumps had been taped off by the CSIs to prevent the corruption of potential tyre, finger and footprints.

Drexler brought the car to a halt tight up against a patrol car and he and McQuarry both stepped into the unseasonal heat. A short and heavyset middle-aged man in brown uniform and a wide-brimmed hat walked out of the mêlée to greet them. He had a brown moustache flecked with grey and chewed mightily on a piece of gum. He stood resting both hands on his gunbelt as he watched the agents approach.

'This is Special Agent Mike Drexler; I'm Special Agent Edie McQuarry.'

'Sheriff Andy Dupree, Markleeville PD. Thanks for coming so quick.'

'No problem, Sheriff,' nodded McQuarry.

They shook hands briefly. 'Welcome to the Ghost Road.'

'The Ghost Road?' said Drexler.

'This is the Ghost Road?' McQuarry looked around at the highway with new eyes. ''89, of course.'

'S'right, ma'am. Some people think it's haunted, some people think there's creatures in the forest. Latest I heard, aliens are to blame.'

'To blame for what?' asked Drexler.

'Unexplained crashes. Vehicles disappearing. This is like the Bermuda Triangle for cars, Mike,' explained McQuarry.

'Started twenty years ago this year. I was just a green-horn trooper back in '75. We lost a family between Yosemite and Tahoe. The Campbells. Five of 'em. Mom and Pop, two teenage boys and a ten-year-old girl. Left Yosemite on a bright breezy morning one Easter and were never seen again. They got reported missing two weeks later . . .'

'Two weeks?'

'They was on holiday, Agent Drexler. No one to report them overdue. Except the manager at the condo, but why would he phone it in? Happens all the time. He gets to keep the deposit and re-let the apartment.'

'Right.'

'Far as we know, other families disappeared on this road too. Last one was just a couple of months ago. Family name of Bailey set out from San Diego in a VW camper. They . . .'

'What do you mean, *far as we know*?' Drexler was unable to keep a trace of censure out of his voice.

Dupree took a pause and shot Drexler a lingering look, then allowed himself a thin mocking smile. 'Well, when we can be bothered to take a break from hunkering down on the Krispy Kremes, and there's not a Klan meetin' or a rodeo on the tube, we sometimes squeeze in some police work.'

'Excuse my partner, Sheriff,' said McQuarry. 'He flunked the diplomacy training.'

'He's excused, Ma'am.'

'What the Sheriff means, Mike, is there could be other families who've disappeared.'

Dupree nodded. 'S'right. My kinda vacation. Load the wife and kids into a Winnebago and set off for the horizon. Who knows how many others do the same? We don't get notified in Markleeville if a car full of people from Alabama goes missing unless there's a paper trail that puts 'em here. Don't mean they didn't drive up 89 with a pocketful of cash. Know if it was me, I'd be paying cash for my gas. Out in the backwoods that can still be the only currency.'

Drexler nodded. 'I see.'

'And is that why you've called us in, Sheriff?'

'Not exactly, Ma'am. But I think we can rustle up a connection.' Dupree turned and led them towards the gas station.

Drexler noted he had a slight limp. 'So what *have* you got for us, Sheriff?'

'Two bodies so far. Caleb Ashwell, owner of the gas station. The other one's in here. Customer found him round six a.m. We figure this one was killed second, as he's got blood spray from the first on him.'

They walked into the low building where two CSIs were going through their various procedures. A harsh strip-light illuminated the dark office, but nothing else. McQuarry decided not to ask where the specialist crime scene lighting was. They probably didn't have any and there was no sense drawing attention to it and causing further offence. She pulled her latex gloves from her pocket and put them on. Drexler did the same.

A well-built young man, seventeen, eighteen at most, hung from a steel rafter in the low ceiling.

'Ashwell's son Billy,' said Dupree. McQuarry gazed up at him. His face was pale and his lips slightly parted and discoloured. Nearby a chair had been knocked over on its side and discarded plastic packaging lay on the floor. Otherwise there was order.

McQuarry clicked on a small Dictaphone. 'White male, Caucasian, mid-to-late teens. Lips and tongue cyanosed. Probable cause – asphyxia.'

Drexler stood near the plastic packaging. 'This is for a tow rope, Ed.' He looked behind the counter. Several more ropes in their untouched packaging sat on the shelf. 'Taken from the store here. The hanging was improvised. Suicide?' he asked Dupree.

'Homicide,' said Dupree. Both agents were slightly taken aback by his confidence. Hangings were rarely clear cut, the majority being suicides as it was not the easiest way to kill and would usually require multiple assailants, particularly to subdue a strong young man.

'Who found him?'

'Old Ben Gardner called in for gas round six this morning. Says he saw the boy hanging when he got to the door. He'd had to pump his own gas, which was unusual – the boy usually ran out to serve you before your engine was off. Ben said he was clearly dead. Well, he was in 'Nam so I guess he'd know. He rang it in straightaway – didn't touch anything, didn't even walk through the door.'

McQuarry nodded and clicked off the Dictaphone. Until the body was cut down they wouldn't be able to say more. She looked over at Dupree who nodded in response and led them out of the back door of the station onto a dirt track which took them to a small, functional wooden cabin.

Both agents were beginning to sweat now as the midday

sun began to parch the bare track and they were relieved to dip under the cooler canopy of the trees.

It took them a few minutes to adjust their eyes to the murk of the cabin. They could see the shadowy form of Caleb Ashwell, tensed and twisted from his death throes. They could see the sinewy debris of his throat and the dark pool of drying blood on his grubby vest. They could see the handcuffs behind his back and an opened wine bottle on the table. It took a while to make out the words daubed in blood on the wall, though, as the darkening stain was nearly lost in the gloom.

'"CLEARING UP THE GROUND",' read McQuarry. 'Interesting.'

'That's what we figured until . . .' began Dupree.

'What we are destroying is nothing but houses of cards and we are clearing up the ground of language on which they stood.' Dupree and McQuarry turned to Drexler who smiled apologetically. 'Sorry. Philosophy major. It's Wittgenstein.'

'Cute,' said McQuarry. 'Doesn't change what looks like a classic murder–suicide to me. Boy kills father. Boy feels guilty and kills himself.' She turned to Dupree. 'But this message makes you think it was a double murder?'

'No, Ma'am. Something else.'

*

Brook rubbed his eyes and took another scant mouthful of his baked potato. He washed it down with a slurp of cold tea and returned his gaze to the computer screen. He reread the FBI report and then clicked on a link to take him to the Los Angeles PD Homicide Report on the death of the Marquez family.

He read carefully: although the father and eldest son's petty criminal background fitted the profile, several factors marked this down as something other than a Reaper killing. The time-line was fine. The Marquez family had died in 1995, at the same time the original Reaper Victor Sorenson had lived in LA, but the use of both a shotgun and several different knives on the two parents and four children pointed away from The Reaper. In addition, the two girls, one fifteen the other twelve, had both been raped at the scene, a violation to which The Reaper had never stooped. Sorenson killed his prey quickly. He didn't want them to suffer; he just wanted them to experience beauty before they died – a piece of art, a beautiful aria, a glass of expensive wine. Then they could cease to exist, happy in the knowledge that they were leaving behind lives that weren't worth the living, knowing the world was a better place without them.

Brook looked at his watch. It was past eleven. Three hours spent scouring the unsolved murder files of various US law enforcement agencies had left Brook feeling in need of another shower. America sickened him and he resolved never to go. What was it Sorenson had said just hours before he died? Something about a nation that called itself the Home of the Brave presiding over such appalling murder statistics? No wonder Sorenson felt The Reaper's 'work' would be lost in America and had returned to England to strike in Derby. Brook had been searching for months to find cases that fitted The Reaper's MO and wading through so much stuff had left him numb.

He logged out of the FBI site and clicked onto his Hotmail account for something to do. He cleared the usual junk and was left with nothing. Not surprising. Apart from some of the US agencies he'd emailed asking for information about families murdered in their homes, nobody even knew he had an email address.

Brook stood, stretching his legs, and went outside to his back garden, sucking in the sweet night air. He shook his head. Why was he still looking? Sorenson was dead. The Reaper was gone. What was he hoping to achieve? To unmask Sorenson to the world? Why? So he wouldn't have to carry the knowledge alone? There had to be something else driving him. Guilt? The dreams?

A black cat dropped down from a neighbour's wall and headed

straight for Brook's legs, purring in anticipation of the pleasure to come. 'Hello, Basil, you little monkey. I haven't seen you for a while.' The cat fell onto Brook's foot and writhed around his ankle until Brook leaned down to scratch its head and neck. After a couple of minutes, Brook extricated himself from its clutches and went back into the house. He re-emerged with a saucer of tinned tuna for the cat and a measure of malt whisky for himself and sat down on the bench, dividing his gaze between the feeding cat and the cotton-wool stars.

He was tired now, torn between the comfort and novelty of his own bed and the urge to go for a stroll, to feast on the chill air. In the end he did neither and satisfied himself with a bare-footed amble around the lawn, enjoying the freshly nourished Basil's acrobatic skills as he chased the nocturnal insects that had dared to enter his territory.

Finally Brook drained his glass, and returned to the cottage. Unusually, there was an email alert on his computer. He clicked on his inbox and was greeted by a message with the tagline 'REAPER' and the subject 'CONGRATULATIONS'.

Brook hesitated for a moment, then clicked on the message.

Damen,

My dear friend, how could I have underestimated you? Well done. Disposing of your daughter's abuser was a noble act and one which I should have known you'd attend to in the fullness of time. I hope he suffered the way you suffered.

And now, my friend, it's time for you to really take flight and show the world what you can do. I know you've been waiting, biding your time, planning, but now it's time to fear The Reaper once more.

Remember how good it felt to avenge Laura Maples? There's a lot more work to be done. They're out

there, Damen, the dregs of humanity, waiting for you
to show them how life should be lived. Make them
see beauty. Make them appreciate the wonder.
   Good luck, though I know you won't need it.
   Your friend Victor.

Brook stared at the screen unblinking for several minutes, then drained his glass and went to fetch a refill. He stared at his monitor some more. This was a hoax. Sorenson was dead. And who knew his email address apart from a few FBI agencies? He reread the message before logging out of Hotmail and typing 'Tony Harvey-Ellis' into a search engine. He was rewarded with several hits, all local Brighton papers, reporting his drowning. He read all of them without expression, then his eyes fell onto the phone. He cast around for his address book, looked up a number that any normal father would've known by heart, and dialled.

Terri picked up on the first ring. 'Hello?'

Brook hesitated. He opened his mouth to speak but no words came out.

'Hello? Who is this? This isn't very funny.' Her tears were on the way when she slammed the phone down a few seconds later.

Brook replaced his receiver more gently, ashamed. His own daughter. He couldn't even speak to his own daughter. But what could he say? *I hope the man you loved, your mother's husband, the rapist who took your virginity, is burning in hell.* It needed a little work.

He took a deep breath. Two years. His ex-wife and only daughter were strangers. A misery he'd suppressed longer than he cared to think surfaced in him until he looked back at the reports of Harvey-Ellis's death. Maybe things could change. Now Amy would have to face the truth about Tony; maybe after a suitable time, when the dust had settled, there could be contact, some kind of reconciliation. Maybe.

He glanced back at the phone. Terri had sounded different.

Brook realised now how much he missed her. The only good thing he'd ever done with his life was her. They hadn't spoken in two years. Not even a phone call. Not since that day on the pier when she'd confessed to her affair with her stepfather – just fifteen years old – standing before him in her school uniform, laying claim to womanhood.

Brook sat down with another drink of whisky to gaze at the email purporting to be from the late Victor Sorenson. Everything about it was right, the laconic, gently probing style, the over-familiar yet stiff formality of the language.

But Sorenson was dead . . .

A banging on the door made Brook's heart lurch and, after clicking the message onto his toolbar, he padded to the porch. For the first time since his move to the crime-free peace of Hartington, Brook hesitated before opening the door.

'Mr Brook. I saw the light was on so I thought I'd take a chance.'

'Tom.'

Tom Hutcheson hesitated on the step, waiting for an enquiry. When Brook remained mute he pressed on. 'Aye, it's the cottage, Mr Brook. I thought I'd let you know . . . Are you all right?'

Realising that his manner was causing concern, Brook stirred himself to remember the social conventions. 'Tom. Sorry. I'm tired. I've been away. Do you want to come in?'

'No, that's all right. I thought I'd pop round about next door. I saw you were up and thought you'd like to know that it's let for the next six months.'

'Oh, okay. I saw the sign was down.'

'And no need to worry. No kids this time.' Brook allowed himself a thin smile. 'Some writer or researcher, or some such thing. I forget. He flew in from Boston this morning. Picked him up at the airport.'

'That was good of you.'

'Was it, buggery. He's paying through the nose in advance till next May.'

'That's great news, Tom.'

'Aye. And he seems like an okay bloke. About your age.' Brook merely nodded, taking nothing in. When Tom saw he was drifting out of the conversation, he paid his respects and left.

Brook returned to his whisky bottle for a refill and took a pack of unopened cigarettes from the desk drawer. He cracked open the cellophane and lit up his first cigarette in six weeks or more, grimacing at the harshness of the smoke.

*

An hour later, Brook was still on his garden bench with a blanket, sucking in the country air. He'd stared at the email until his vision had blurred, but eventually had to give it up to let his overheating brain cool.

He shivered and looked at his watch. Gone one in the morning. Work tomorrow. Today. It was cold now, in spite of the blanket he'd brought out to swaddle him, and even though he knew he wouldn't sleep, it was time to go to bed. He took a last pull on his cigarette, drained his glass and left the bench. As he prepared to go indoors, a noise made him spin round.

A darkened figure emerged from the gloom of next door's garden and stepped towards the dividing wall between their properties.

'Can't sleep either?' the figure queried in a mild American accent.

Brook hesitated for a moment then turned fully towards his new neighbour. 'Same as yourself.'

'But I've got an excuse,' he chuckled. 'Don't tell me you're jetlagged as well?'

Brook smiled on a reflex, though his new neighbour would be unable to see it. 'No. I've been on holiday and I'm reluctant to let it end. Work tomorrow.'

The man nodded. 'Holiday,' he repeated in a low voice, as though the word was a complete mystery to him. 'Must be nice. Go anywhere special?'

'Just around the Peak District. Camping,' Brook added, as though further explanation were needed.

'Sounds good. This is a beautiful area.'

'You've been before . . . ?'

'Mike. Mike Drexler. No, never. Only what I've read and seen from the car on the way from the airport.'

Brook waited, wanting to be away. He had already exhausted his quota of small talk. He realised the reason for the pause and stepped forward into the moonlight. 'Damen Brook. Nice to meet you.' Drexler also stepped forward. He seemed to be around the same age as Brook, perhaps a little older, with thinning brown hair, greying at the temples and sideburns. Brook's garden was below the level of next door's, so a handshake was problematic, and so they both settled for an upraised arm.

'Damen,' Drexler nodded. 'Good to meet you. Interesting name. Perhaps we have a German ancestry in common?'

'I'm from Barnsley.' Brook smiled under cover of night.

Drexler hesitated, 'I'm not that familiar with the homeland, Damen. Is that in Bavaria?'

'It's in Yorkshire, Mike. The nearest any of my ancestors came to Germany was a holiday in the Norfolk Broads.'

Drexler chuckled finally. 'I see. And what about that cute black cat I saw earlier?'

'That would be Basil and the guaranteed path into his affections is cooked chicken.' Again Drexler chuckled. Brook had reached politeness overload and wondered how to withdraw.

Fortunately Drexler seemed to have reached the end of his own small talk. 'Well, thanks for chatting, Damen. I'd better let you hit the sack. See you later.'

'Good night. And welcome to Derbyshire.'

A few minutes later Brook was in his bedroom. As he opened his bedroom window, he noticed the orange glow of a cigarette in next door's back garden.

Chapter Six

The next day, Brook drove to the Drayfin Estate. He bolted up the path to the house of John and Denise Ottoman. The middle-aged couple had been interviewed two years previously in connection with the Reaper murders at the Wallis family home.

On that occasion, Brook and Noble had remarked on their ordered existence, everything in house and garden spick and span. Now Brook looked around at how much things had changed. Their manicured front lawn was full of weeds and animal faeces. Their fence and front gate were rotted and the windows of the house sported curls of peeling paint that testified to neglect.

Brook knocked on the door, wondering if they'd moved. Eventually there was movement and the front door opened just a crack. He saw a haggard face and long straggly grey locks.

'Mrs Ottoman. Inspector Brook. Do you remember me?' The woman didn't reply but lowered her eyes in pained recognition. 'I've called as a courtesy to let you know, if you didn't already, that Jason Wallis has been released.' No reply, just a baleful red-rimmed eye lifted towards his own briefly. Brook could discern the formation of a tear, so brought matters to a close. 'There's absolutely nothing to worry about and no reason to suppose that he'd be any threat to you or your husband, but don't hesitate to contact—'

The door closed and Brook heard the figure shuffling back into her tomb.

* * *

Brook walked through the main door of the modern St Mary's Wharf police headquarters, his mind churning from the contents of 'The Reaper' email from the night before.

As Brook walked through the reception area, Duty Sergeant Hendrickson lifted a brand new copy of *In Search of The Reaper* in front of his nose. Pretending to read intently, he grinned maliciously as Brook passed. His grin faded only slightly when Brook barely gave him a glance. Hendrickson turned to one of the PCs and nodded.

'He knows about it all right. Fucking nailed him, the useless toffee-nosed twat.'

'Sarge?' inquired the unsuspecting constable.

'DI Brook!' urged Hendrickson. 'Fucking nailed him to a tree. This book,' he continued, nodding at it to underscore his point. 'Don't tell me you don't know about it . . .'

*

Dupree, Drexler and McQuarry stood huddled around the monitor in the back office of the gas station. The picture was nearly black and at first Drexler and McQuarry thought the monitor wasn't working. Then they realised they were looking at the customer service area of the gas station. They couldn't make out any detail because the building was cloaked in darkness. A second later the screen was flooded with light as the fluorescent strip sputtered into life. A slight figure, dressed head to toe in black overalls and black ski mask, carried a chair into shot and placed it down. The figure left the screen briefly, returned with a brightly coloured nylon rope, threw it over a beam and left the shot again, evidently to secure the other end, because they could see the rope moving.

A few seconds later, the figure returned, leading the boy to the chair.

'He's nearly a foot taller. Why doesn't he resist?' asked McQuarry.

'Drugs.' The two agents nodded in unison.

'We figure. Though we ain't found any on the premises,' said Dupree.

They watched the rest of the show like automatons until the moment the figure in black kicked the chair away from the helpless Billy. Drexler stood up from the monitor as Billy fell. 'I've seen enough. He's just a kid, for God's sake.'

'Give it a minute, Special Agent.' Dupree put the tape on fast forward. When the tape returned to normal speed, the body was dangling lifelessly in space. The figure in black returned to the middle of the shot and, in a gesture that chilled the two FBI agents to the bone, turned his covered face towards the camera and affected a slight but noticeable bow. Then he walked off camera.

*

DS Noble was sitting at Brook's desk, reading his copy of Burton's book, when Brook walked into his office. He closed it sheepishly and stood up as Brook entered.

'Sir. Welcome back. You look well. Good holiday?'

'Fine. Don't get up, John.' Noble sat back down. 'Well?'

'Sir?' replied Noble.

Brook gazed at Noble, calm but unrelenting, waiting for Noble to crack. In the end Brook took pity on him. 'Is it any good, John?'

Noble smiled into the break of tension. 'Oh, this? Total crap. Burton doesn't have a clue. He can't even write that well.'

'You don't have to put him down just for me, John. But thanks.'

'I'm not. It's sh . . . rubbish and nobody in this station will believe a word of it.'

'No, John. Everybody in this station and probably this city, apart from me and hopefully you, will believe every word of it. By the way, my chair suits you, John. So does my office.'

Noble pushed the chair back and swivelled violently round, stopping to give Brook a sly grin. 'Maybe. But if they keep eking out the budget the way they are, we'll both retire as DCs.'

'Patience, John. These things move in cycles. Any news?'

'Nothing that can't wait – Greatorix is still on the sick.'

'Anorexia?'

Noble laughed. 'You really shouldn't, sir. His weight problem is glandular.'

'I should have paid more attention in biology lessons, John. I had no idea the mouth was a gland.' Noble shook his head in mock censure. 'Any messages?'

'Only the DPP. They're putting back the Andrews trial. And Charlton wants you as soon as you get in.'

'Really?'

'I think he wants to check you're on side about the Burton book. Don't worry. I told him you wouldn't piss on Burton if he were on fire.'

Brook looked at Noble with a thin smile, dismayed by Noble's imagery but amused that Brook's inability to get on with virtually anybody might be news to the Chief Superintendent. 'Thanks. I hope you made it clear that wasn't a direct quote.'

'I'm not sure,' mocked Noble. 'By the way, there were a couple of new faces in his office this morning. Rumour is they're re-inforcements to fill in for Greatorix. And one of them is a bit of a looker.'

Brook repeated 'A looker!', lingering over the phrase with distaste. He knew he was being teased and though he actively encouraged such mocking, he still felt obliged to reproach Noble for damage done to the English language. 'Well, we can't say we don't need some new blood in CID. I just hope he doesn't want me to play nursemaid like I had to with you.' He turned to march out of the office, ignoring Noble's offended expression, then turned back. 'Mark the worst pages for me, John. I'll need to take a look.'

'You sure?'

'Well, unless he says something *really* mean. I don't want to start wetting the bed again.'

Noble laughed. 'Sorry. Did I tell you? Jason Wallis got out of White Oaks yesterday. Good behaviour.'

Brook nodded. 'So they do learn new skills there. Did anyone inform the Ottomans?'

Noble returned a blank look. Brook smiled sadly. 'Denise Ottoman.' No response. 'The teacher Jason sexually assaulted during a lesson.'

'Right – they already know. Someone said the husband was interviewed about it on the telly. Want me to send someone round for tea and sympathy?'

'No need. I took care of it.'

*

'Sheriff, it looks like you've got a real interesting case here. Real interesting,' nodded McQuarry. 'The Tahoe Satellite Office told the Sacramento Field Office this was a Federal case, but all you got is two dead locals. Now I know it's the Ghost Road but I've got to say it's a stretch. We'll try and help you the best way we can. Our resources are available to any PD that wants to use them. But the only way we can take this from local state police is if it involves terrorism, or we know for sure the perpetrator or victims have crossed a state line . . .'

Sheriff Dupree smiled at Drexler. 'What was it you said, son? Clearing up the ground. Follow me.'

*

Brook knocked on the door and entered.

'Morning, sir,' said Brook.

Chief Superintendent Mark Charlton declined to stand up behind his desk. He rarely did when Brook entered, the contrast between their heights causing a shift in the balance of their relationship with which Charlton wasn't comfortable.

'Morning.' Charlton's grey eyes bored into Brook in that well-practised show of openness that the lecturer on his senior management courses had tried to instil in him. 'I trust you had a restful holiday, Inspector?' offered the Chief Super with so little attempt at inquiry that Brook made no effort to answer, distracted as he was by Charlton's guests who had both made the effort to stand. A man, a couple of inches shorter than Brook with a craggy, experienced face, and a woman in her late twenties/early thirties, with hazel eyes and a pretty, well-proportioned face, turned to acknowledge him. The man held out a hand which Brook, after a brief hesitation, gripped and shook quickly.

'Hello, Joshua. How are you?'

'I'm fine, Damen.' Hudson smiled back at Brook and turned to give Grant a private look.

'I didn't realise you knew each other?' said Charlton.

'I saw you at Charlie Rowlands's funeral,' Hudson continued, as though Charlton didn't exist, 'though we didn't get much of a chance to talk.'

'I remember.'

'A sad day.'

'A sad day,' answered Brook, turning to DS Grant.

'This is my DS, Laura Grant.'

Grant, already reseated, nodded curtly at Brook, her head bowed as if trying to avoid his searching stare.

Brook sensed the antipathy in her but had grown so accustomed to the reaction from others, that it barely registered. 'Laura – beautiful name.'

Grant blushed, with an unexpected tremor of pleasure that teetered on the brink of annoyance. 'Thank you.'

'Please sit,' said Charlton. Brook noticed the extra chairs and made for one. Clearly this meeting had been planned. 'Now DCI Hudson and DS Grant have come all this way to see you, Inspector

Brook and, as I have a liaison committee to chair, feel free to use my office.'

'Thank you, Chief Superintendent,' said Hudson, already turning his sights on Brook.

Brook held his gaze, staring back without emotion or apparent curiosity. Brook knew why they'd come.

'Inspector Brook. I will need to speak to you about this Brian Burton book this afternoon. I'll be back in the office at three p.m.,' continued the Chief Super. 'In the meantime I'll leave you to it.' Charlton was now forced to stand. To his discomfort, everyone else stood too and he became flustered, keen to flee this land of the giants. As soon as he could manoeuvre himself to the door, he scuttled out.

'Shall we sit down, Inspector?' suggested Hudson.

Brook fell back onto the padded chair and crossed his legs. 'Call me Damen.'

'Damen.'

'Thanks for agreeing to talk to us.'

'I haven't agreed to talk to you.'

Hudson and Grant looked sharply at Brook. Hudson broke into a quick smile. '*Would* you agree to talk to us, Damen? Strictly informal at this stage.'

'No problem. What's going on in Bromley that you need to come all this way to see me?' asked Brook, without a semblance of interest. 'We've had telephones here in Derby for months.'

Hudson couldn't suppress a chuckle, but Grant smiled coldly. 'I transferred out of Bromley eight years ago, Damen. I moved to Brighton for a quieter life. Fat chance, eh?' Hudson and Grant locked eyes on him for a reaction, but Brook was completely impassive. There was silence for a moment before Hudson spoke again. 'Your ex-wife and daughter live there. Aren't you worried that something may have happened to them?'

'You wouldn't have driven two hundred miles just to break it to me,' said Brook softly.

'I suppose not.'

'In fact, we saw them recently. They're in good health,' added Grant. 'Emotionally they're not too good.'

'Really,' said Brook.

'You see, your ex-wife's husband, Tony Harvey-Ellis, is dead. He drowned in the Channel.'

Grant and Hudson were mildly shocked to see Brook's thin smile.

'What a pity. Drowned, you say?'

'Yes.'

'However, it wasn't an accident.'

Brook's smile faded. 'He was murdered?'

'It looks that way,' nodded Hudson.

'Drownings are almost always suicides when they're not accidents, Inspector,' added Grant. She glared intently at Brook.

Brook smiled and nodded, pleased that they'd tried to wrong-foot him. 'You clearly didn't know him, Laura. Someone as smug and self-absorbed as Harvey-Ellis could never kill himself.'

'You still haven't asked about your ex-wife and daughter,' observed Hudson.

'You don't think Amy and Terri were responsible, I hope?'

'We're keeping an open mind.'

'Well close it. They couldn't have been involved. They wouldn't have the strength to drown a man – especially someone as powerful as Harvey-Ellis. He was a rugby player at one time.'

'Maybe not to hold someone like Harvey-Ellis under the water,' agreed Hudson. 'But a smack on the head with a baseball bat wouldn't be beyond either of them.' Brook said nothing. 'You don't seem to dispute your ex-wife and daughter might have had motive.' Brook shrugged. 'Can I assume then that you know about the affair between Harvey-Ellis and your daughter?'

Brook narrowed his eyes and sank further into the chair. Grant noticed his hands clenching into fists. 'You wouldn't be here if you weren't certain I knew what was happening, would you?'

'Honestly, no,' said Hudson. 'Out of interest, how did you find out about the affair? Did your ex-wife confide in you?'

Brook looked away. 'I'm a trained detective. I found out. Leave it at that.'

'You seem uncomfortable discussing this, Inspector,' said Grant.

'How would you feel?' Brook glared at Grant. 'Virtual strangers asking questions, about my daughter and her . . .'

'Affair.'

'Can we not refer to this as an affair? Affairs are for adults. Terri was fifteen. Harvey-Ellis is a predator. Was.'

There was a long silence while Hudson and Grant let Brook simmer. 'Strong feelings feed strong motives,' added Grant eventually.

'Which makes me the prime suspect.'

'Is that a confession, Damen?'

'No.'

'Any normal father . . .' blurted Grant, then stopped, annoyed with herself. Hudson had been very specific about avoiding any hint of an accusation. She apologised to her boss with a look.

'Are you a normal father, Damen?' asked Hudson, deciding he had no choice now but to run with it.

'Normal enough to threaten him,' agreed Brook. 'I assaulted him as well. I suspect you know that.'

'Nearly two years ago. Is that why you got suspended?'

'No. No-one knew about the assault. I was suspended for dropping off the grid at the height of the Wallis Inquiry.'

'To come to Brighton to confront Tony Harvey-Ellis?'

'Yes.'

'But that didn't stop the . . . relationship with your daughter.' Brook's eyes bored into Hudson. 'No.'

'So why didn't you do something?'

Brook smiled sadly. 'You're the second person to have asked me that.'

'Who was the first?'

'Someone I used to know in London.'

'And what was your answer? After all, you could've exposed him, made his life very difficult. You might have had a crack at putting him away, Damen.'

'I know. It's just . . . things got away from me. Later I realised how much they both loved him and hated me. There didn't seem much point after that. It's academic now.'

'Before we ask the next question I want to remind you that we're just having an informal talk,' said Hudson. 'But in view of your distinguished career, neither I nor DS Grant would feel happy if you felt you needed representation and didn't ask for it.' Hudson waited.

Brook nodded. 'Ask your question.'

'Where were you last weekend, Inspector Brook?' asked Grant. 'We'll settle for Saturday night and Sunday morning for now.'

Brook tossed his head back to concentrate on the ceiling. 'I'm not sure but I think I was either near Matlock or Tissington. It's in the Peak District. I was on two weeks' leave. I didn't take a calendar with me and quite often I didn't know what day it was.'

'You were on your own?' asked Grant, now taking notes.

'Always.'

'Did anyone you know see you?'

'I don't know anyone.'

'Well, would anyone you *don't* know remember you?' asked Grant.

'Unlikely. I was camping wild. The whole idea is to keep away from civilisation.'

'Isn't that illegal?' asked Grant.

'Sometimes,' nodded Brook.

'So you have no alibi,' concluded Hudson.

'If I thought I needed one, Joshua, I would have slapped a policeman in the face with my passport and stuck my birth certificate in his mouth.'

Both Hudson and Grant made sure to give Brook an appreciative chuckle, but Hudson knew that such flattery was unlikely to make him more forthcoming.

'Is there anything else?'

Hudson ground his teeth. After a few seconds he said, 'Funny, you're not asking for many details about the murder. I find that odd for a police officer. You've asked no questions about how a fit, forty-three-year-old male was forcibly drowned.'

Brook looked at Hudson and Grant in turn. 'I don't care about Tony Harvey-Ellis or how he died. I'm just pleased he's dead after the way he preyed on my daughter and betrayed my ex-wife.'

'You think of their welfare no matter how much they hate you.'

'I guess Terri doesn't hate me,' said Brook. 'But she loves her mum more. Amy probably hates me because I destroyed her first marriage and tried to do the same to her second. The fact that I was right to do so on both occasions is a detail as far as she's concerned.'

'And, if it were necessary, would you consent to giving us a DNA sample? In case we need to rule you out of our inquiries.'

Brook pursed his lips in a show of concentration, looking back at Grant. 'No. I don't think I would.'

'Really? Why not?' ventured Hudson.

Brook smiled back at him, unblinking. Grant and Hudson had just about given up on an answer when Brook said, 'I don't want to.'

'Officers are encouraged to volunteer dibs and dabs for the database,' said Grant. 'It's compulsory for new recruits.'

'Good for them,' replied Brook. 'Let me know when it becomes compulsory for me.'

Hudson decided he was going to have to play his one remaining card. 'Have you ever heard of Twilight Sleep, Damen?'

Brook's eyes widened and his mouth parted slightly. 'What?'

*

'Now I don't know too much about Vitmanstein,' said Sheriff Dupree, holding back a stray branch so the agents

could pass unhindered, 'but this here ground is a clearing, wouldn't you say?'

'No doubt,' nodded Drexler as he and McQuarry emerged from the undergrowth and approached the line of motor homes sitting alongside the twenty-foot rock wall that made up one side of a natural basin. 'This is a clearing.' He mopped his brow. The air in this bowl was oppressive, the breeze apparently unable to penetrate the dense foliage surrounding the amphitheatre on three sides.

The vehicles had been carefully parked against the wall of rock and were in various states of decay, the oldest on the far left, all the way to the newest on the right. Some were physically intact and others had clearly been in some kind of collision, whether it was just a dent or, in the case of the newest vehicle – a yellow VW camper with California plates – a hefty crash.

'The yellow camper you see there belonged to the Bailey family,' said Dupree. 'The last family to disappear.'

'Colorado, California, Nevada, Utah, Arizona.' McQuarry muttered, as she examined the motor homes' plates. 'Guess we're on board, Mike.' She approached the VW camper and tried the door handle. It opened and Drexler and Dupree saw her reach inside briefly. She straightened up again holding a rag doll with yellow string for hair, then turned to her partner, a sombre look on her face. She looked at the ground, surveying the well-dug soil. 'Not a lot of vegetation growing in the ground, is there?'

Drexler followed her eyes down, looking at his own feet. 'Jesus,' he breathed when the penny dropped.

'You think . . . ?' Dupree took a few seconds' pause as he and the two agents began to step backwards, away from the vehicles to the edge of the clearing, as though walking on hot coals.

Chapter Seven

Grant stirred the remains of her starter and pushed it away. A waiter made to remove it so she pulled it back towards her. When Hudson returned from the toilet and sat back down, she took a sip of her sparkling water.

'Have a lager, darlin'. We're on exes, remember. Make the most of it.'

'I'm not an MP, guv. Water's fine.'

Hudson shrugged and ordered another Kingfisher. 'At least give the case a break.'

Laura Grant smiled like a patient mother with an errant child. 'He's still our guy, guv, I'm telling you. He didn't turn a hair when you said it was murder – all that hooey about "what brings you up from Bromley". He knew from minute one why we were here and where we were from – which means he knew Harvey-Ellis was dead when he walked in.'

Hudson nibbled on his roti bread, nodding at Grant's starter. She shrugged her assent and Hudson attacked her mushroom puri.

'Sure he knew. But it doesn't mean anything. There's the internet. Maybe Terri or Mrs H phoned him . . .'

'He said he hadn't spoken to them for a long time.'

'He may have lied. But it's not enough.'

'He's got no alibi.'

'That doesn't put him in Brighton, Laura. We'd need a lot

more to put pressure on a detective inspector. Assuming we wanted to . . .'

'*Assuming we wanted to?* Why wouldn't we?'

'You heard him, luv. Harvey-Ellis was a sex offender – a paedo, strictly speaking. Good riddance, most people would say. We say it every day about the scum we're forced to deal with.'

Grant sighed. 'I suppose. It's just he was so damned cocky about it. It's not normal.'

Hudson raised an eyebrow. 'So you didn't like him. Or don't you like the fact that you did like him?'

Grant looked up from picking poppadom crumbs off the linen tablecloth. Her pretty face became surly for a moment, then eased. 'I can't deny Brook's got . . . charisma.' Hudson smiled. 'But do I find him attractive? Er, not likely. He's almost as old as you, guv.'

Hudson's smile thinned. 'Thanks a bundle.' He looked around at the décor of the smart Indian restaurant just down the road from the Midland Hotel. 'Nice curry house, this. Good find, Laura. The food's great.' Hudson folded the final forkload of mushroom into his mouth and sat back with a sigh.

'You know, there is one thing in his favour,' said Grant.

Hudson nodded, trying to clear his mouth to speak. 'Yeah. Twilight Sleep. That really threw him.'

'It *appeared* to throw him, guv. He could still have been faking it.'

'But why would he? Someone using The Reaper's MO – it's a big deal to Brook.'

'Maybe he was just surprised that we got onto it so quickly.'

'You're not going to let this go, are you, luv?'

Grant paused, tipping the rest of her bottle of sparkling water into her glass. 'You know guv, as a woman I probably shouldn't say this, but I know about rape, I've worked cases, I've seen . . .' a moment of remembrance darkened her countenance for a second '. . . I've seen the victims and what it does

109

to them. And, honestly, I don't give a shit about the *affair* with Terri. Fifteen or not, Harvey-Ellis did not coerce that girl into bed. Okay, he may have seduced a silly little girl whose self-importance got the better of her judgement, but he didn't hold her down and she wasn't drugged. I'll admit he deserved a tug for it but as far as I'm concerned, he didn't deserve to die. And if people think they can play God and take other people's lives because *they* think it's justified, then they're going to have to answer to me.'

Hudson stared at Grant, who merely glared at the tablecloth tight-lipped. After a few moments of silence, Hudson took a long pull on his Kingfisher and nodded at her.

'Fair enough.'

*

Drexler waited while McQuarry finished speaking with the satellite office in South Lake Tahoe. By the end of the conversation, Drexler knew that a small army of forensic pathologists armed with the latest equipment would be mobilising. In a few hours the entire site would be alive with people wielding state-of-the-art technology and expertise, working under protective marquees looking for bodies of the victims of the newly dubbed 'Ghost Road Killer'.

When found the bodies would be processed and tested, photographed and analysed, before going to the portable mortuary. And, assuming the latest victims had more than mere skeletons to tell the story of their deaths, there would be a further battery of tests as well.

When she'd finished speaking on Dupree's car radio, McQuarry rejoined Drexler and they followed the sheriff back to the station building. An empty ambulance now stood outside, the crew inside waiting with a gurney for the body of Billy Ashwell. As they entered, two Crime

Scene Investigators were standing ready to take Billy's weight as another prepared to cut him down. As the two CSIs wrapped their arms around the boy's lifeless trunk, something fell to the floor from the dead boy's pocket.

'What's that?' asked Drexler.

'Looks like some kind of flower to me,' answered Dupree.

'It's a red rose petal,' said McQuarry, stooping to examine it.

The CSI released Billy's legs and more deep red petals fell to the ground. One of the CSIs followed the trail back to Billy's trouser pocket, which had been forced open by the attempt to get him down. He pulled at the fabric so the sheriff and the agents could see that the pocket was full of the same dark red petals.

'Zuzu's petals,' said McQuarry to nobody in particular.

Drexler and Dupree turned to her. 'Zu who?'

'Zuzu. The little girl in *It's A Wonderful Life!*' she said looking back at them. 'The film. James Stewart? Rose petals in his pocket?' They didn't seem to understand her. The sheriff arched a puzzled eyebrow. She shrugged her apology. 'Sorry. Drive-in major.'

*

Brook was late setting off for home after his shift, having made a conscious effort to clear his backlog of paperwork. It was partly that things seemed to be pretty quiet at the moment, the colder weather being credited with a decline in drink-fuelled violence, and partly a result of his meeting with Chief Superintendent Charlton.

Charlton had been as unsubtle as he could manage without openly saying what he wanted.

'How old are you, Damen?'

Brook had sat blankly in his chair, flicking a discreet eye towards the copy of Brian Burton's book on Charlton's desk. He didn't like the Chief Super using his first name. It wasn't that he cared about Charlton's overfamiliarity, more that he resented its use as a tactic to soften him up for some ulterior motive that Brook was fairly certain he could guess. To make his point, Brook waited longer than was polite to respond, knowing that Charlton almost certainly knew the answer.

'Forty-seven, isn't it? Forty-eight just before Christmas. You know, I envy you, Damen.'

Brook eyed his superior coolly, trying to mask the contempt rising in him. 'You wouldn't if you knew the pain I've suffered, sir.'

Charlton was taken aback. 'Oh?'

'My parents tried their best to keep things special but it's an expensive time of year. Uncles, aunts and grandparents always gave me one present for Christmas, which had to double up for my birthday as well. All told, I calculate I'm down about seventy presents from my childhood.'

Charlton briefly looked at Brook as though he were completely insane, then pressed ahead with his own agenda. 'No, I mean that coming up to fifty, your thoughts must be turning towards retirement, getting out of all this . . . stress.'

'Must they?'

'Not that you're not a valued officer. But I know it's a young man's game, eh? Let them get on with it while you go off and enjoy yourself.'

'Enjoy myself.' Brook lingered over the words and Charlton began to realise that he'd been a bit too obvious.

'But that's not why I wanted to see you . . .' And he'd rapidly changed lanes to talk about the Brian Burton book and how much Brook was prepared to say on the record.

So, subliminal or not, Brook had left the meeting feeling a need to clear his desk, and had spent several hours doing just that. Whether it was the need to show he was still a competent detective, or a subconscious acceptance that he was ready to call it a day was more difficult to fathom.

* * *

Mike Drexler and Edie McQuarry sat at the table of the windowless room at Markleeville PD sifting through various papers. Some were faded faxes of car rental receipts; some were black and white images of driving permits. The most disturbing were the happy family portraits of the doomed families, grinning timelessly into the camera, shiny with hope and purpose, now immortalised as victims of The Ghost Road Killer – or killers. When the documentary makers moved in, these would be the pictures set beside the pictures of skeletons, like the rag doll found in the VW. And when the story became public property it might even weaken OJ's stranglehold on the front pages for a day.

'Okay, we got the Campbells from Brigham City, Utah, the Hernandez family from Prescott, Arizona,' said Drexler, slamming down a missing persons folder for every family. 'The Biscotti family from Las Vegas, Nevada, the Reeves family from Denver, Colorado and the latest victims, the Bailey family from San Diego, California. Five families matched to five different vehicles so far. That's in chronological order.'

'And the Baileys were the last family to go missing.'

'Right.'

'How long exactly?' asked McQuarry, shaking out a cigarette and lighting up with a precautionary glance over her shoulder.

'They were reported missing two months ago, but obviously may have been abducted before that. Or after. They were last seen on July fifteenth when their holiday started.' Drexler looked over at his partner. 'Ed, *outside* a restaurant may be a grey area, but now you're definitely breaking California state law.'

'You think state police give a hoot about a law forced through by a few rich anorexics in LA with too much money and time on their hands?'

'Probably not.'

'Then stow it and tell me about the Baileys.'

'Yes, ma'am. The Baileys. Four of them. Two daughters. Nicole and Sally. Fifteen and thirteen years of age,' said Drexler, lingering over the last snippet without really knowing why. 'Wife Tania Bailey, forty-one and her husband George, forty-seven. They were from England originally but were living full time in the States at the time of their disappearance. The husband is a chemical engineer and had been working in San Diego for two years. They were on vacation . . .'

'Wait a minute,' said McQuarry holding up a hand and closing her eyes. 'Did you say George?' Drexler nodded. 'George Bailey?'

'That's what I said. Problem?'

She laughed. 'George Bailey. Shit. Someone's messing with us, Mike.' Drexler showed no sign of understanding her. '*It's a Wonderful Life*, that film I was talking about. The character James Stewart played was called George Bailey. He finds rose petals in his pocket that his daughter Zuzu has given him . . .'

'You can't be serious.'

'I'm telling you, this is more than a coincidence. Someone's sending us a message with these rose petals.'

'What message?'

She took a pull on her Marlboro Light and thought about it. 'I think whoever killed Caleb and Billy Ashwell wants us to know that they were killed because of what they did to George Bailey and his family. George Bailey is the key to this. Where did you say he worked?'

*

Stepping out of his car in Hartington sometime after seven, Brook realised with a sinking feeling that his new neighbour was clearly the outdoors type. Framed against the dark sky, he could see the glow of a fire in Rose Cottage's small back garden and knew that he would have to stay indoors unless he wanted to endure an evening of tedious chitchat. With winter fast approaching, Brook had wanted to maximise use of his garden while he still could, and this impediment was a nuisance.

When he reached his door, however, he found the situation far worse than that. A note stuck out of his letterbox.

Damen
Having a house-warming BBQ tonight. Come and have
something to eat and drink.
Mike

Brook hovered over the note for a minute before screwing it into a ball and binning it. At least when the tenants had kids they didn't have time to bother him. He went into the house and neglected to turn on any lights, without quite realising why. Eventually he flicked on a small lamp next to his computer and immediately began to feel self-conscious. He kicked off his leather shoes and squeezed his feet into a pair of deck shoes before padding back into the kitchen and opening the refrigerator. It was empty except for a carton of milk, a baked potato skin, an opened can of beans and a bottle of champagne left over from his last night with Wendy Jones the year before.

After a moment's contemplation he closed the fridge door, but not before plucking the champagne from its cradle. He strolled next door, remembering to take a full pack of cigarettes with him. Despite his infrequent attendance at social functions in the last fifteen years, Brook remembered sufficient misery when plentiful alcohol and tobacco was not at hand.

As he knocked on the front door, Drexler came to greet him from the side path.

'Damen! Good to see you. How are you doing?'

'I'm fine. How are you?'

'I'm good,' nodded Drexler, unaware of the tic of annoyance his grammar caused Brook. 'Champagne. Thank you. That's thoughtful,' he added.

Brook managed a smile as he followed Drexler round to the back. 'The least I could do. Settling in okay?'

'Pretty good.' Brook looked around the garden of his new neighbour, half an eyebrow raised. 'Yeah, it's just us, Damen. Tom's been and gone.'

'Great,' Brook muttered under his breath.

'And Basil, of course.' Brook spied the black cat gnawing away at some blackened meat on the tiny lawn. He looked up briefly to be sure Brook wasn't about to steal his food, then returned to his meal. 'Please sit. Wine or beer, or would you like champagne?' smiled Drexler.

Brook was aware now that his host was slurring slightly. 'Not champagne, beer or red wine if you've got it,' he said cracking open his fresh pack of smokes.

'As you're still in the job, how about both?' asked Drexler, with a grin. Brook shrugged his assent and Drexler disappeared into the tiny kitchen of Rose Cottage, re-emerging moments later with a cold bottled lager and a large glass of red wine. He trotted back into the kitchen and returned with a plate of raw burgers. He slapped two of them onto the grill of the barbecue then put his feet up on a spare chair and tapped his bottle against Brook's. 'Cheers.'

'Cheers.' Brook braced himself for a conversation and went over his mental checklist, but Drexler satisfied himself with staring into the hot coals, punctuated with the occasional bout of burger flipping and organising the salad. When the burgers were nearly done, Drexler dropped a square of processed cheese onto one of them, and when that wilted he began to assemble Brook's massive double cheeseburger.

When his plate was plonked down, Brook tucked in with more

gusto than he thought possible. Since leaving the city, Brook's meagre diet had consisted of baked potatoes, beans on toast and the occasional takeaway. The unexpected pleasure of flame-grilled meat left him purring.

When it was finished, Brook licked the ketchup, mayonnaise and grease from his fingers, wiped his hands with a serviette and sat back with a sigh.

'Mike. That was the best burger I've ever had. Thanks.'

'My pleasure. Another?'

'That was plenty for me.'

Drexler nodded and took a pull on his beer, then turned back to stare at the dying coals. When the coals began to lose their heat, Drexler pulled out a small pot-bellied garden stove and lit the newspaper protruding from beneath a pile of dry sticks. It sparked into life instantly and they both got to work examining the spitting flames and taking the occasional chug on their drinks.

'So you're a writer,' ventured Brook.

Drexler bent his head towards Brook and smiled without parting his lips, then scrunched up his nose in an expression of scepticism. 'Not really.'

'I thought Tom said you were.'

'I'm getting there. It's a second career of sorts. It pays the rent.'

'What was your first career?'

'Same as you, Damen – law enforcement.'

Brook looked up sharply. He waited for a moment but Drexler didn't expand, either on his own career or how he knew Brook was a policeman. He was on the verge of asking him when he realised that Tom must have told him on the drive from the airport. Of course. Ask about the new neighbours. It was the most normal thing in the world to do, assuming you weren't as dislocated from the norm as Brook.

'Whereabouts?'

'California. Sacramento. It's the state capital, just north of San Francisco.'

'I've heard of it. But you flew in from Boston.'

'That's right. I moved to the East Coast in '01 after my book became a hit.'

Brook nodded. 'What was it about, your book?'

Drexler looked away. Brook had nearly given up on an answer when Drexler said, 'A case I worked for the FBI.'

'You were in the FBI?'

'That I was, Damen. A long time.' Drexler stared into the flames intently, before adding under his breath, 'Or maybe it just felt like a long time.'

Brook took another pull on his beer and wondered whether to further pick at what looked like an open wound. 'I've got to take my hat off to you, Mike. I mean, you deal with things in the States that we just don't see over here.'

'Plus the bad guys have guns.'

Brook smiled, now more forgiving about the quirks of sharing a language with another country. 'Plus the bad guys have guns,' he echoed. Interested now, Brook racked his brains for a way to probe further but then decided against it. He had a sudden flash of sitting with Sorenson in his study all those years ago, plied with drink, a fire nibbling at his toes, being similarly dissected.

'What's the book called?' he finally asked.

'*The Ghost Road Killers*.'

'And should I not ask you what it's about?'

Drexler turned to Brook with a bitter smile. Suddenly he chuckled. 'In case I'm scarred by it, you mean. In case I wake up every night screaming, sheets damp, brain on fire.' He chuckled again. 'No. You can ask me. I dare say you get people tiptoeing round you when it's not necessary. You being The Reaper Man and all.' Brook raised an eyebrow as Drexler laughed. 'Sorry. You mustn't blame old Tom. You know how it goes. It's our job to pull this stuff out of people, and we do it even when they don't want us to. Tom was a pushover once he'd let it slip.

Besides, you're even famous in the States – in police circles, at least.'

Brook shrugged. 'That's good to know,' he added stonily.

'I'm sorry, Damen. I shouldn't have mentioned it. It's been a while since I had to live and breathe the life, night and day. It always stays with you, but I guess you forget how personal it gets. And I gather some hack writer's done a hatchet job on one of your investigations. Must be tough.'

'I'll live.'

'Glad to hear it. Don't let the bastards grind you down,' Drexler added, offering his bottle to Brook for a sympathetic clink.

'The problem is, the last Reaper killing was only two years ago so it sits a little heavier.'

'I hear you, man. And I know it kinda grates when you ain't caught the guy.'

Brook gave Drexler a piercing glance but drained his beer to cover it. Drexler immediately picked up the empty and grabbed a couple of replacements from the fridge.

Brook wondered about the wisdom of drinking too much, especially in front of a stranger, and what's more, a writer. It struck him suddenly that maybe their meeting was not an accident. Maybe the subject of Drexler's next book was to be The Reaper. After all, Brian Burton seemed to be making a good living out of it, laying open Brook's faults for the entire world to see. Maybe Drexler was jumping onto the bandwagon. Maybe moving into the same village as 'The Reaper Detective' was a shrewd career move.

'So what are you writing this time?' Brook asked, trying to seem no more than politely interested.

'Actually, Damen, it's a kind of sequel.'

Brook was puzzled. 'A sequel? I thought you said your book was about a real case.'

'It is.' Drexler smiled enigmatically at Brook.

'But you've fictionalised it?'

119

'No.' Drexler continued to smile at his guest, his eyes suddenly boring into him. 'See, we didn't catch the guy either.'

'Oh? And is that what the sequel's about?'

'Not really. It's complicated.'

'So maybe I should just buy the book. Save you having to re-live it,' said Brook apologetically. 'There's always one case that won't go away, isn't there?'

'Like The Reaper?'

Brook laughed. 'Well, that's one that won't go away but The Reaper's crimes aren't what haunt me.' Brook looked into the fire, remembering the decomposing corpse of Laura Maples, the rats who consumed her and the face of Sorenson, her avenging angel. After a pause, Brook said, 'You know what's funny, Mike?'

'Yeah. Nothing's funny.'

Brook nodded his surprise. 'That's right. Nothing.'

They both chuckled and Brook was surprised to feel an unexpected surge of kinship with his new neighbour. For the next half hour they sat in silence, drinking their drinks, smoking their cigarettes and looking at the stars.

*

Drexler mopped his brow and glanced over at McQuarry, who was at the edge of the clearing sucking on a well-earned cigarette. The heat was stifling in the bowl, despite the disappearance of the sun two hours previously, and the dozens of people labouring away under the fierce glare of the arc lights were visibly wilting.

Sheriff Dupree was speaking to the lead forensic technician and pulled a blue handkerchief across his podgy red face to soak up as much sweat as possible. The Crime Scene Investigator he spoke with held a small brush in his gloved hand, the bristles of which were covered in dust, removed from newly uncovered skeletal bones. His face

was covered by a mask and his whole body by a protective suit. Only his eyes and the bridge of his nose were visible, but still the beads of perspiration stood out like ball bearings. Mosquitoes and flies hovered in the hope of a meal.

Standing below ground level, the CSI levered himself out of the trench with the aid of a hand from Dupree. He waved a hand towards the rock wall of the clearing, which had now been cleared of all the decomposing vehicles. Instead a network of trenches and body-sized holes covered the ground, and more were being marked out with tape by at least a dozen similarly attired men.

Drexler looked over at McQuarry. She caught his eye briefly before turning away to pull another cigarette from her rapidly dwindling pack and lighting it with an urgent inhalation of blue smoke. She'd been there when they'd found the vaguely recognisable bodies of three of the Bailey family in a pair of graves – the father George, fully clothed on his back at the bottom of the pit with a large bullet hole in the front of his skull, mother Tania, lying naked and on top of him, also with the telltale star-shaped hole, this time in the back of her head. One of the girls – possibly the younger daughter Sally, to judge from her frail physique – was in a separate shallow grave next to them, also naked, also shot through the back of the head. Her corpse seemed fresher than her parents'; she'd been kept alive for days or even weeks after her parents had been executed and that, in addition to her state of undress, had clearly flagged up the nature of her ordeal. Of the other daughter, Nicole, there was as yet no sign.

McQuarry, a battle-hardened veteran, betrayed no visible reaction but as they stood together over the tiny girl's grave while the CSI brushed the dirt from the exit wound in her eye socket, Drexler could almost hear the tension in her body as her knuckles clenched inside her protective gloves. He could see this one troubled her and McQuarry had barely spoken since the girl had been disinterred with all the respect and solemnity required.

She did say one thing that struck Drexler. At one point McQuarry had taken his arm and guided him towards the little girl's corpse, still being carefully disentangled from the earth. She pointed at the girl and turned to him. 'Take a long look, Mike. Remember that face.' Then she'd stalked away to devour another cigarette, her back to the excavations.

'How many?' asked Drexler when Dupree was close enough to hear over the whine of the generator.

Dupree held the clutch of missing persons reports up to his face to check, as though he hadn't already done the math. 'Sixteen bodies so far. From the MP reports we're looking for at least another nine, including a three-year-old child and two . . . babies. Six and eight months old.' Dupree couldn't hold Drexler's eye. Drexler knew then that the sheriff was a father and lowered his own head in vicarious commiseration. 'How's your partner bearing up, Mike?'

'She's fine, Andy. Ed's the thinker. Just giving her some room to work the angles.'

Dupree allowed him a watery smile. ''Course. Good idea.'

'Any preliminary forensics?'

'We've recovered several guns that belonged to Caleb Ashwell from the cabin so we'll see what Ballistics have to say when we dig out the bullets. But as for trace . . .' he shrugged '. . . in this heat, decomposition is a lot quicker. Some of these vics are over twenty years in the soil. The Bailey family will probably give us the best chance. They're freshest.' The two law enforcement officers exchanged a grim smile. ''Specially the girl.'

'Poor kid,' nodded Drexler. 'It's not hard to imagine . . .'

'Isn't it?' Dupree looked up at him sharply. 'Then for her sake, try harder. Let's give her that peace at least.'

Drexler lowered his head. 'Any sign of the older sister – Nicole?'

'Not yet. She may yet be in here but it's mighty crowded. We've found some human remains out in the forest so it seems they didn't always bury them.'

'That figures. I'd be dumping them someplace else, Andy. It'd be safer to leave the bodies in a shallow grave in the wilderness. The animals would soon cover your tracks for you. Nobody would ever find them whole.'

'Then why keep any of the bodies so close to the house?'

Drexler fixed him with a knowing eye. 'You sure you want me to answer that?'

Dupree looked around and shook his head. 'Right. Keeps the jackoff closer to home. God in heaven. Maybe it's time to put in my papers and buy a boat.'

'You'll get past it.'

'Maybe. But Markleeville's my home and it won't ever be the same. Gonna be a pervert's playground when this shit breaks. God knows how many ghouls and murder tourists we're gonna get around here, getting off on this.'

'Always someone knitting at an execution, Andy.'

The sheriff blew out his cheeks. 'Know what, Mike? If I'm reading this right, when we find whoever took out the Ashwells, we should strike them some kinda medal. Better yet, whyn't you and Ed just go on home and forget about this case and we'll let the people who done this to Caleb and Billy just live out their days in peace. God knows they've earned it.'

'Billy was just a kid, Andy. We can't be sure he was involved. He may have been coerced.'

'Coerced my ass.' With that the Sheriff spat heavily on the ground and walked back down the track and out of the clearing.

123

Chapter Eight

'We got three more female bodies from the clearing,' said Dupree, putting the phone down and finishing a note on his pad. 'That makes nineteen.' Dupree hesitated over the next piece of information. 'Two adult females, one naked . . . and one little girl. They're exhuming as we speak.'

He cleared his throat and looked up at Drexler and McQuarry sitting across the office. 'Where were we? Right, Caleb Ashwell and his wife Mandy-Sue bought the gas station in 1974, twenty-one years ago. The year after that the Campbell family go missing somewhere in the state while on vacation. Their vehicle was the oldest in the clearing. It's not a stretch to assume they stopped for gas and that Caleb, maybe with his wife's help, maybe not, overwhelmed the family and drove their vehicle into the clearing. The bodies are buried nearby, though there's no way of telling how long after they were attacked. Our best stab at motive so far is robbery, but I don't need to spell out other possible motives . . .'

'Wait a minute. There were five members of the Campbell family, including two teenage boys,' said Drexler. 'Are you telling me they roll up for gas and one man, and maybe one woman, somehow overpowered these people right there on the highway?'

'If they were armed and had the element of surprise . . .'

124

'Even so, Andy, it's far from a slamdunk. Another car could happen along, the family might fight back. A lot can go wrong. Yet Ashwell's been doing this for over twenty years, without any comeback. Seems awful risky.'

Dupree stroked his chin. 'See what you mean.'

'You're forgetting the state of some of the vehicles,' said McQuarry. 'They wouldn't need guns if their victims had just been in a car crash.'

'So you think Caleb and his wife just wandered up and down 89 in a tow truck looking for car wrecks?' asked Drexler.

'Wait, what if Caleb caused the crashes? We're pretty sure Billy Ashwell was drugged.' Dupree put on a pair of half-moon glasses and picked up some papers. 'He drank coffee before he died. If they served coffee to customers with the same kind of drugs Billy had? A few miles down the road the victims would either pull over or crash.'

'It's a theory. But surely there could be other cars around that maybe get to the crash site first.'

'So they drive on by,' said Dupree. 'Or maybe they stop and help like regular citizens. But there are plenty of crashes on 89. It's a tricky drive, 'specially at night. But if nobody's around they hook up the car and tow it back to the station. If the adults are drugged the kids will be easy . . .'

'And maybe they only pick out targets at night and only ones paying cash so there's no paper trail,' added Drexler.

McQuarry nodded. 'Sounds reasonable so far. Only one fly in the ointment for me. Why would a woman conspire to let her husband commit rape?'

'It's not unknown, Ed. Maybe she was glad it was them and not her.'

'Or maybe Caleb's wife didn't know about the rapes. Far as I can remember, she would only have been around for the first one. Maybe the Campbells were just killed and robbed. We have a gap of several years to the next one – the Hernandez family from Arizona,' continued Dupree. 'Mrs Ashwell left Caleb before that. She gave birth to a son, then upped and left six months later, leaving Billy behind with Caleb. Maybe she got cold feet after the Campbell killings and couldn't live with it. She leaves and a few months later Caleb picks up where he left off. 1978, the year the Hernandez family go missing. Only this time he wants more than just their car and their money.'

'Where'd Mrs Ashwell go?'

'Nobody knows, Ed. She ain't been heard from since.'

'Then how do we know she left at all?'

Dupree and Drexler looked up at her. 'You think maybe Caleb killed her too.'

'What mother would leave her baby with a monster like that? These three new bodies. How many you say were naked?'

Dupree looked at his notepad. 'One. An adult female.'

'So one adult female wasn't?'

'That's right. Material indicates she was wearing a dress.'

'So how many clothed adult female bodies do we have in total?'

'Just that one.'

McQuarry raised an eyebrow. 'And why wasn't she naked?'

Drexler snapped his fingers. 'Because Caleb didn't rape her. She was his wife.'

Dupree checked his notes. 'She was found in a grave on her own. Son of a bitch. You might be right.'

'Guess we'll find out soon enough.' McQuarry pulled out a cigarette in anticipation of a break.

'Poor Billy,' added Drexler. 'Without a mother, he didn't stand a chance.'

'You think Caleb trained him up to be just like him?' asked McQuarry.

'Monsters like that . . .' Drexler shook his head. His eye met his partner's, but he couldn't maintain contact. He shrugged. 'That's what they do.'

'Well, forgetting ancient history for a while,' said Dupree. 'What do we suppose happened to Caleb and Billy last week? This weren't no family fighting back. These folks were executed.'

'It's all about the rose petals, Andy,' said McQuarry. 'George Bailey's family are the key. They get killed but this time somebody either knew about it or worked it out.'

'How?'

'You got me. But whoever this is wanted us to know. The way he looked up at the camera after hanging Billy. This guy knew about the camera. This guy had been to the gas station before.'

'So?'

'Think about it, Mike. Without that single piece of film, we log this as a murder-suicide and just concentrate on the Ghost Road killings. We tag the Ashwells as serial killers who do their stuff until one night Billy can't stand it any more and goes over the edge. He kills his dad, writes about what's in the clearing in blood as a sort of confession, then hangs himself out of remorse. But this guy wants us to know. He makes damn sure we know. First the camera, then the petals.'

*

Brook woke in the early hours. He padded downstairs to make tea. He was on late turn today but instead of scouring the internet for old Reaper cases, he decided to read his newly acquired signed copy of Drexler's book.

The Ghost Road Killers is a faithful account of the activities of Caleb Ashwell and his son Billy who faced justice of sorts in 1995. Their murders ended a reign of terror in Northern California and shone a light on the disappearance of several families whose misfortune it was to cross their path. It may never be known just how many men, women and children the Ashwells terrorised and murdered on the California 89 highway because some of the victims have never been found, and because the mysterious murder of the Texas-born father and son robbed the investigation of its two key witnesses.

Brook took a sip of tea. Odd. The Ghost Road Killers were identified in the book's first paragraph yet Drexler had claimed they hadn't solved the case. Perhaps he just meant the full facts were never uncovered.

He read for a couple more hours until the sun was up then walked round to the corner shop. He walked back to the cottage through the faint morning light, sucking in the soft chilly air and shaking the slight fug from his head. He'd drank more than he'd intended the night before but had to admit he'd enjoyed himself more than he'd expected.

After some tea, Brook returned to the book. It was well written and easy to read, but the subject matter was hard going. Women and children were abused, tortured and in most cases raped. Caleb Ashwell was a monster and his son Billy was being moulded from the same clay. The trigger for the killing spree seemed to be the infidelity of Mrs Ashwell, soon after the birth of her son. Claiming she'd walked out on him, Caleb raised Billy by himself while the body of his wife lay undisturbed in the farthest corner of a clearing near the family cabin. This had also been the hiding place for all the cars belonging to, or hired by, the families hijacked by the Ashwells while travelling on Highway 89.

All the male victims were killed almost immediately. For the female victims, standing in for the late Mrs Ashwell no doubt, the nightmare had just begun.

Brook was disturbed by the slamming of a door and stood up to see Drexler walking out to his car. He nipped to the front door.

'Morning.'

'Good morning, Damen.'

'Thanks again for last night. I had a good time.'

'No problem.'

'You're away early?'

'Work, I'm afraid. I'm not the best sleeper and books don't write themselves. Am I right in thinking Ashbourne's easy to find?'

'Very easy. Turn right at the bottom of the hill. Up to the A515, turn right again and keep going until you hit it.'

'Thanks.'

'Do you need a map?'

'I'll be fine.'

'I'm enjoying your book.'

Drexler turned from the car and fixed Brook in his sights. 'Enjoying?'

'You know what I mean. It's very well written.'

Drexler gave an imperceptible nod and just stood there waiting, as though Brook had more to say. Then he turned back to the car and got in behind the wheel. 'Any questions?' he said enigmatically.

When Brook shook his head, Drexler started the car and drove away.

*

Dupree, Drexler and McQuarry stood by the glass partition trying not to stare too hard at the decomposing cadaver of little Sally Bailey on the stainless steel gurney. Her corpse had the tagged summation of a lifetime tied round her big

toe. Name. Sex. Date of Birth. Date and Cause of Death. Case number. No intangibles, no memories, no laughter, no pain, no Little League, no prom nights, no nights of love. No future. Her mother, in a more advanced state of decomposition, was on the adjacent trolley.

Drexler stole a glance at the other two. Dupree the father had been locked in the deepest recesses and only Dupree the law officer had turned up. McQuarry too had eyes like flint. The medical examiner bent over the microphone for the last time then tossed the last of his instruments into a steel bowl for a steam clean. He picked up a small bowl with the remains of the bullet and held it up to the glass.

'Same bullet as the others, seems like, Andy,' he said, so the microphone could just about pick it up. He nodded at an assistant, who began bagging and labelling the various organs.

The examiner, whose nametag said John Taybor, walked through a small door at the end of the room. He held out his hand, which each shook in turn after an initial hesitation to check his latex gloves had been removed.

'Andy. Special Agents.' He nodded.

'Well, John?'

'We're getting there, Andy. Gradually. We'll have the little girl's internals tomorrow. Promise. But I can give you one thing now. She was no longer a virgin and had been subjected to repeated sexual assault. The mother had engaged in sexual activity before she died too.'

'We figured as much.'

'As for Caleb and Billy, I'll have the official report typed up for you tonight but you know the summary. Before his throat was cut Caleb was struck with a heavy instrument. Front of the skull too. There was no violence against the boy before he was hung because he was drugged. The coffee he had drunk contained the toxin hyoscine, sometimes called scopolamine. There are also traces of morphine which is interesting. A combination of the two, carefully applied can cause cerebral sedation.'

'He was anaesthetised,' said McQuarry.

'Effectively,' nodded Taybor. 'The subject would have been completely unable to think or act. Even speech would have been almost impossible. Physically they might have basic motor functions, but the subject would be very easy to control. I'm told a variation of this stuff is used as a date rape drug so you get the idea. The interesting thing is I found traces of the same drug combination in George and Tania Bailey's systems.'

'That's not a surprise, John.'

'I can't tell you about the girl yet.'

'If we're right, John, the drugs would be confined to the coffee drinkers. What about the other families? We're thinking they were also drugged. At least the adults.'

'I'm afraid our equipment isn't sophisticated enough for samples that age. We've sent them off to Quantico for further analysis.'

*

Laura Grant looked at her watch, then round at the entrance to the breakfast room. Nearly ten o'clock. She'd finished her scrambled eggs some time ago and now the staff were clearing the tables. This wasn't like her boss. He was old school. People of his generation never passed up a free meal. Whenever she and Hudson were away on work, he always made a point of eating a gargantuan breakfast. 'If the taxpayer is footing the bill for this, we owe it to them to get VFM,' he always said. Why men of a certain age associated lining their arteries with saturated fat and Value For Money was a complete mystery.

She drained her Earl Grey tea and marched to Hudson's room, banging on the door.

'Guv. You've missed breakfast,' she said loudly. No answer. She banged again. 'Guv!' Still no answer. 'It's checkout in two hours. Are you okay?' She rattled the handle and the door opened.

Grant pushed into the room. It was in darkness. The smell hit her first, then the faint noise from the bed. She walked over to the motionless form sprawled across the high mattress.

'Guv,' she said softly, reaching an arm out to rouse him.

*

Jason woke as usual, panting and clutching his throat. After an urgent inspection for gaping wounds his breathing began to slow and he slid his damp frame from under the moistened sheets. It was a cold morning and the sweat on Jason's brow and chest was transformed into salty goose bumps within seconds. He pulled aside the heavy green curtain and peeked out at the winter morning. The sky was clear and blue and the ground covered in a light frost.

Jason checked his mobile. He had a text from Stinger.

My place 7 2nite got news be their

Wassup he texted back. A moment later the text was answered. Jason read it. Then he read it again. A puzzled smile creased his pale visage and he threw himself back on his bed. He took a deep breath and nodded.

'I'm ready,' he muttered, staring saucer-eyed at the ceiling.

*

Laura Grant walked quickly past the railway station back towards the Midland. The sun still shone and although it was lowering it still felt unseasonably warm.

She trotted up to the first-floor landing and opened the door to Hudson's room.

The room was still in darkness. 'Guv?'

This time the figure on the bed croaked out an answer. 'That you, Laura?'

'No, it's Britney Spears.'

132

Hudson managed a chuckle before moaning long and low. 'Oh, don't make me laugh, darlin'. My stomach can't cope.'

'How are you feeling?'

'Like death would be a blessed release.'

'But you managed to get some sleep?'

'Between projectile vomits and having the shits, yeah.'

'Good.'

'You know, I think there's a competition going on to see which of my orifices can expel the most stuff. I could sell tickets.'

'As long as we don't see it in the Olympics. Here,' she said, drawing out a paper cup from a brown paper bag.

'What's that?'

'Chicken soup.'

'No, I couldn't, honestly.'

'You've got to eat something, guv. It's good for you.'

'Not yet. Not after that bloody curry. Just the smell . . .'

'Maybe some Lucozade?'

'I'll try. Leave it by the bed. Everything sorted?'

Grant nodded. 'We've got the rooms until tomorrow. And I rang Maddy's office to tell him we needed an extra day to follow something up.'

Hudson nodded minutely. 'Fingers crossed I'll be okay by then.'

'You'll be fine – this isn't like you.'

'I know. What will you do with yourself?'

'I don't know. Read a book. See a film. Maybe have an Indian.'

'That's not funny.'

'But we're on exes, guv. We've got to fill our boots.'

Hudson sighed heavily. 'Turn the lamp off on your way out.'

*

Sheriff Dupree stared at the frozen monitor then sat back so that McQuarry and Drexler could see the image of the shaven-headed man handing over money to Caleb Ashwell. 'This is the last one. This is the only customer we

133

can't put a name to and the only one who left with a cup of coffee. Every other customer that day is a local I can vouch for, or paid by other means. Not this man. He paid cash.'

'He fits. It's 6.30 – just before Ashwell closed up for the night.'

'And he was driving a motor home – a Dodge Ram 250.'

'How do we know that?' asked McQuarry.

'Ashwell had some problem with thefts a while back,' said Dupree. 'That's why they put a camera in. They also started logging all vehicle plates with a time.'

'Did the DMV give us a name?'

'No, because the vehicle was sold recently by a party in LA. The paperwork hasn't caught up yet, but they're tracing it.'

'This guy looks the right height and build to be our hangman,' nodded Drexler at the monitor.

'It gets better. Watch this!' said Dupree. He pressed the play button and the man began to move away from Ashwell. But before he turned to leave, he raised his dark eyes up to the camera and gave an imperceptible smile. Then he left, clutching a paper bag and his large Styrofoam cup of coffee.

'What was in the bag? Rewind it,' said McQuarry.

'No need, I already seen. He bought one of these.' Sheriff Dupree placed a sturdy penknife on the table. 'Ain't a fella in the county who don't own one.' Dupree smiled at them but only McQuarry understood why.

'Am I missing something?' asked Drexler.

Dupree picked up his penknife and pulled out the corkscrew attachment before placing the knife back on the table. 'This is California. And in California we grow grapes.'

Drexler smiled. 'Of course, the bottle of wine. We need to find this guy.'

'And we need to ask him something. If he got a cup of coffee, how come he didn't crash like the others?'

'Only one answer, Andy,' said McQuarry. 'He didn't drink it because he knew.'

*

Jason pulled in smoke and passed the spliff on to Grets, who pounced on it and went through the same ritual, looking round in the hope of seeing fear and disapproval from Drayfin residents peering out from their homes. But the light was fading fast and most curtains were drawn against the encroachment of the outside world. Finally exhaling, Grets pulled the bottle of Diamond White to his mouth and took another huge draw.

'Gear, innit?' he said.

'Sick,' drawled Banger, who took his turn on the dwindling joint. 'Betcha din't get no blow up at the fag farm, blood.'

'Not this kinda blow,' laughed Grets, coughing up smoke as the others screamed their approval and jostled each other to try and make a dent on the vat of hormones and cheap booze sluicing around their bloodstreams.

'Get your hands off, you gay.'

'Whatever, minger.'

'You say you dun't fancy me, pussy boy?'

'Blatantly no way, man. If I *was* into rusty bullet, I'd give your spotty ass the swerve, you punk ass bitch.'

Reassured that gayness had been uniformly rejected, they all relaxed and continued tucking into Bargain Booze's finest apple beverage as they ambled along the misshapen pavements of the estate, scraping their trainers to mark their passing as they went.

'I'm starving, man. Let's go chippy.'

'No need, bredrin,' said Stinger, checking his mobile. 'My mum and Uncle Ryan are having a barby remember – to big up Jason's release. If you're okay about passing your folks' old place?'

'It's just a building,' replied Jason, resurrecting his toughest expression. 'And if it's like you say . . .'

'Swear down, Jace. I told you. We teafed a brand new barby last week and fuck me, if we don't go and win a load of meat and booze and stuff. They were bringing it all round tonight.' He flicked through his texts until he found the right one. 'Yeah, we're on. 'Bout an hour.'

Jason looked at Stinger for a minute, unable to speak. Maybe it was the Diamond White, but for a second he was incapable of understanding why he had a lump in his throat. 'And you definitely won it right?'

'S'right.'

'In a competition?'

'Like I said.'

Jason stood frozen in time for a second, eyes like nuggets of coal. 'They just rung you up out of the blue?'

'S'up, Jace?' asked Grets.

Jason failed to answer. A moment later a strange grimace deformed his face and he nodded at some private revelation. 'Nuttin. I'm ready.' He grinned suddenly. 'I . . . I love you, man,' he said, adding a loudly blown kiss.

'I thought you were mi mate, you fucking queer,' laughed Stinger, and the rest of the Drayfin Dogs joined in, punctuating their shambolic walk with more mock brawls and bellowed insults.

Jason's grin was a little more forced than the rest. Looking around as they jostled their way to Stinger's house, he wasn't skimming the floor looking for stones to throw at lampposts and parked cars. He was looking for The Reaper. The Reaper was near.

Yeah, I'm ready.

Grets came to a halt and laid an arm across the others. 'Who's that?' he said, peering into the gathering gloom and pointing at a figure walking towards them. A young Asian boy stopped and stared at the four of them.

Banger stepped forward, pulling a Stanley knife from his pocket. 'These fucking terrorists think they can walk about in our block. We're having 'im,' he screamed, darting towards the figure, who'd already turned to sprint away. Banger, Grets and Stinger hurtled after him, Jason bringing up the rear.

*

Brook glared at the computer screen then lowered his eyes. At that moment, DS Noble walked into the office so Brook quickly minimised the internet window.

'Bit late for you, John?' Their shift had finished an hour ago.

'I'm meeting some mates in town for a drink,' he said.

'The pub? At this hour?'

Noble smiled pityingly. 'We're off to Restoration.' Brook gazed back at him, none the wiser. 'It's a new bar in town. Nobody under the age of thirty-five goes to pubs any more, unless they're married.'

Brook found it difficult to digest this cultural insight. 'If you say so.'

Noble made to leave then turned back. 'If you've nowhere to go, sir, you're welcome to join us.'

Brook looked up. He was almost touched. 'Thanks, John, but I've been going nowhere for years and I know the way.'

'Sure?' Noble persevered, against his better judgement. Brook fixed him with a pointed stare. 'Understood.' He turned to mask his relief.

'You're a computer boffin, John.'

Noble turned back from the door. 'I wouldn't say that.'

'How easy is it to trace an email?' asked Brook, ignoring Noble's modesty.

'Not too difficult if you're an expert, which I'm not, and providing you're not tracing another expert who doesn't want to be found.'

'I see.'

137

'The first thing is to identify the server. If you've got it up, I can have a look and . . .'

'Don't worry, John. It's not important,' smiled Brook. 'How are you getting on with Brian Burton's book?' he added to close the subject.

'Put it this way. I don't need sleeping pills. Night.'

'Goodnight.' Brook clicked on the toolbar to reopen the inbox of his Hotmail account. The second email from The Reaper had already been opened and read. But Brook stared at the subject line again. *Tonight.* He stood and went to look out across the low horizon, lighting up again as he gazed out through the darkness at the twinkling lights of Derby. With a deep sigh he looked at his watch and returned to his desk to log out.

*

Drexler pulled the car across the highway and into the drive of an unseen house. He and McQuarry stepped from the car and peered through an imposing pair of iron gates, following the course of the drive as it wound its way towards the lake. They couldn't see the house but the icy waters of Lake Tahoe were visible, lapping calmly against the shore in the pale sunshine – a waterfront property in one of the most expensive real estate zones in the US. It didn't seem feasible that a resident here would have any connection to the late Caleb Ashwell and his son Billy.

McQuarry checked her notes. '879 Cascade Road. This is it, Mike.'

Drexler rattled the gates, but McQuarry took the trouble to find the intercom on the wall and pushed the button. There was a crackle.

'Yes?'

'Federal agents, sir. May we speak with you?'

No answer but the gates swung open noiselessly.

The two words that struck fear and often loathing into everyone who crossed their path had barely registered. Not a moment's hesitation. Normally, even the most right-eous couldn't help but take a second to review their ancient and recent past for forgotten transgressions. Reasons to be fearful, McQuarry and Drexler called it. But not today.

'Somebody's got a very clear conscience,' observed Drexler. The agents jumped back into the Chevy and drove slowly up to the house, taking in the splendour of the surroundings – large grounds shaded by mature white fir, lodgepole pine and aspen trees interspersed with bark-covered flowerbeds. As the trees thinned they saw the huge cabin-style house facing the shore, built with natural wood and local stone. The house stood on a bank, maybe ten metres above the water level and about twenty metres back from the lake. A wooden pier, bleached by the seasons, stretched its arm into the heart of the lake, though no boat was moored.

'Feel intimidated?' smiled Drexler.

'I'm quaking in my boots, Mike.'

They parked near a three-car garage at the side of the house, though there was only one car in residence – a small red Toyota.

'No sign of a Dodge Ram 250,' said Drexler.

'Care to give me odds it's been *stolen*, Mike?'

He smiled. 'No sale.'

A slightly built middle-aged man seemed to appear out of nowhere and strolled across the lawn to greet them. Drexler and McQuarry exchanged a private smile of recog-nition. But instead of the full head of wiry red hair from his passport photograph, the man's shaved head was as it was on Caleb Ashwell's CCTV monitor.

'Detectives, what can I do for you?' he said in an approx-imation of an English accent. He smiled at them, though his shrewd black eyes didn't seem to be in sympathy with his mouth.

'FBI, sir. This is Special Agent Drexler and I'm Special Agent McQuarry.'

'Special agents, how thrilling,' he said with an effort to be impressed. 'Just like in the movies.'

Drexler flipped open his notepad. 'And you are Mr Victor Sorenson?'

The man grinned, perhaps distracted for a moment by an echo from the past. '*Professor* Sorenson in fact.'

*

It was well past midnight but the fire still blazed in the old oil drum in Stinger's overgrown backyard. The air was cold and a fog was forming, but the heat radiating towards the four figures slumped on two decrepit sofas served to incubate the occupants. Stinger's younger brother had gone to his room to play computer games, shortly after Stinger's mum and her boyfriend Ryan had staggered off to bed. Stinger, Banger and Grets were close to coma and stared unblinking at the hypnotic flames.

Jason would have liked to turn off the boom box but that wasn't a runner – Stinger was on a major wreck and Jason knew from experience that he'd not let up until every drop of booze was drunk and every ounce of dope smoked.

'Turn it up, blood. This track kicks ass,' slurred Stinger, head lolling back on the bigger of the two sofas.

'Turn it up yourself, bitch.' Banger leered at the others, waiting for them to acknowledge the comic genius in their midst.

'It's pretty loud already,' observed Jason, regretting his comment at once.

'So? The fuck are the neighbours gonna say?' said Stinger, stumbling to the boom box nestled on the bonnet of his dad's demolition derby car. It was rotting on bricks in the backyard until someone on the estate took a chance and bought new wheels

140

for their own vehicle. 'The last time Osama came round to complain, Ryan gave him a right slappin', innit?' Stinger turned up the gangsta rap a couple of notches and slumped back down as they all started nodding to the beat.

'Bet he weren't happy though,' observed Banger before dissolving into hysterics – he was on a roll.

'And granny next door never puts her head outside after dark no more,' added Stinger. He threw another fencepost onto the fire. Sparks flew off into the night sky.

'Not unless she wants croaking like that other old bitch,' nodded Grets. They all laughed but there was a tension in their throats, and each felt the need to run his drunken eye over the others to make sure it hadn't been noticed. The moment passed and they were able to reposition their masks of invulnerability. But there was disquiet in their demeanour as each reflected on the night Jason's family had been slaughtered just a few doors away, the night the four of them had murdered an old woman for money and drugs but awoke to find their thunder stolen by The Reaper, Annie Sewell's death a mere footnote. Narked at first, each had since come to realise that the sensational events at the Wallis home had kept the Sewell murder out of the lime-light and left them free to continue numbing their lives.

Jason stared into the flames and remembered that night with something approaching shame. The face he could never forget – the old woman begging for her life, or at least a little dignity. That night she kept neither.

Thank Christ nobody knew. Not true. That leng, DI Brook knew. He'd come round his aunt's, got him loaded on cheap whisky. Brook had warned him, tried to make him 'fess up and name names. Had he imagined it? But he hadn't imagined being tied up. Being threatened. One thing Brook said, Jason would never forget. The Reaper was still out there, waiting for his chance – unfinished business. Trouble was, he didn't seem keen to finish it. Well, maybe tonight was the night and Jason was ready. Ready to make payment. Ready for an end to misery and fear. Ready to stop being a victim and start being a player. Ready for fame and a place in history.

Banger took a long draught of cider and offered the dregs of a two-litre bottle to Jason. He held a hand up to refuse, so Banger drained the rest, and threw it into the oil drum.

'It's late. I should peg it,' said Jason, trying to sound casual.

'Chill your beans, man. It's early. Don't be dread. This party's for you. You can crash here. I asked my mum.'

'Cheers, Sting. It's been sick. But I got stuff to do tomorrow.'

'So what? I got college. Ain't going though. It's boring.'

'Me neither,' piped up Grets.

'Yeah, but I promised my aunt.'

'So? Anyway, you'll never get a white cab this time o' night.'

'I was gonna walk.'

'Oh my days. It's bloody miles to Borrowash. And you'll be crossing enemy blocks.'

'Yeah, well. When you've done time, walking outside at night, when you're locked in . . . well, it's something you think about.'

'Thought you said it was easy time,' accused Grets.

'Look, I'm bladdered . . .' began Jason.

'The fuck you are,' spat Stinger. 'You've hardly had a drop. And you passed the spliff after one draw. We used to have to taser your ass to get it off you. Innit, Bang?'

'No doubt.'

'He might not be used to it,' explained Grets.

'That's no excuse.'

Jason eyed Stinger. 'Can't yer take a joke, bredrin?' he said eventually, finding his party face again. 'Pass me that bottle. Let's get this party started, fam,' he said, downing a litre of rust-coloured liquid in one go.

'That's the Jace we know. Don't neck it all, bitch.'

Chapter Nine

Brook looked at his watch. One am. He was early. Good. Another hour and he would know. The chill wintry air had turned to fog and clung to the potholed roads and bald grass verges of the Drayfin Estate. The noise of his car cut through the still air with a deliberation born out of Brook's desire to move quietly through the streets, as though not being noticed meant that he was somewhere else. He didn't want to be here, that's for sure, revisiting his past, a past that he thought he'd conquered once and for all. But The Reaper was calling him. Even in death, Sorenson would never let go. Brook should've known.

He turned slowly onto the road he'd been on so many times in his dreams, eased past number 233, not looking at the Wallis house, just knowing it was there. It had a presence even now.

Parking around the corner, he stepped from the car and gingerly closed the driver's door, leaving it unlocked – a rare deliberate act on the Drayfin. He walked back through the gathering fog to the scene of The Reaper's last atrocity – a path that perhaps The Reaper himself had once taken – and ran his eye over the former home of the Wallis family, as it materialised out of the gloom like a ghost ship.

The house was boarded up and, unusually for the Drayfin, had stayed that way. No need for the council to brick up the doors and windows. Nobody came near the place – no kids, no tramps and certainly no neighbours. The house was a lure only for passing ghouls, unlikely tourists who craved a glimpse at infamy, assuming they could find the place in this sprawling, redbrick jungle. Even then such visits were made only in daylight.

Brook stood before the house and turned again to see if his presence was being monitored. It appeared not. All neighbouring houses were dark, all streetlights inert and broken. Even the faint light of the moon had taken the evening off. Brook felt himself in the grip of a black hole, being drawn towards the Wallis house, unable to pull away, his orbit decaying, his body and mind hurtling towards the stench of evil that still lurked there.

As he stepped over the splayed front gate, Brook pulled his dark coat tightly round him and yanked up his collar. He approached the front entrance slowly and, as he moved, he heard something that the deep recesses of his memory had warned him to expect: music. Brook stopped to listen, glaring at the house to search for an opening. The years began to melt away, and Brook remembered standing at the front door of Sorenson's London home, minutes before their first meeting, listening to the aria from La Wally leaking out of the window in his study above.

Then he realised that the music was not coming from the Wallis house. Nor was it a song for The Reaper. The pulse of this music came from elsewhere. Brook looked around, sensing the direction – a neighbouring home, maybe even a garden. Some kind of rap music. The music of violence and confrontation, guaranteed to irritate and cow anyone over thirty, especially at this time of night and in this place. Even this late the self-centred who blighted the urban landscape saw fit to inflict themselves on long-suffering neighbours. *Mind yer own business. It's a free country. We can play our music loud as we like. What yer gonna do about it?*

Brook returned his eyes to the Wallis house. He moved to the door he'd last opened on the night of the murders. It was now a piece of chipboard. It had been wedged open, recently by the look of it. The gap was too slight for Brook to get through, so he forced the board further open and ducked through the enlarged gap. In the same instant, he snapped on a small torch to check the floor for scurrying rodents.

The hall was just as he remembered. No carpet now but the wallpaper was the same grimy flock. The door into the murder room was gone, taken away by forensics to eke out possible evidence from the bloody smears on the handle. There'd been no prints and no clues on the door, on anything. The carpets had eventually yielded a footprint and a shoe size, but neither Brook nor Inspector Greatorix, who'd taken over the inquiry after Brook's suspension, had ever found a suspect or even a pair of shoes to seek a match.

Brook stepped into the room in which Mr and Mrs Wallis and their daughter Kylie had been killed. No, not killed, slaughtered like animals for the table, almost as ritual. Their throats cut from ear to ear, their life blood everywhere except their veins.

The armchairs on which the Wallis parents had died were gone, so too the once-white rug on which Kylie and her unborn child had been butchered. Even the wallpaper sporting the bloody daub 'SAVED' had been torn away. The room was completely bare. Brook stepped further in, wincing at the explosion of sound that his shoes created on the uncovered floorboards.

His veins turned to ice at the sight of the bottle of wine sitting on the fireplace, exactly as it had the night the Wallis family had faced The Reaper. Next to it were two wine glasses. Both were grime- and dust-free. He was expected. He forced himself to step nearer. The bottle was uncorked and full. He stared at the label. It was a Nuits St Georges, the same as it had been two years ago. Brook picked up a glass with his gloved hand and sniffed it. Clean. This time The Reaper hadn't had a celebratory drink after doing his work. His work. The Reaper was dead. And what work was there for The Reaper in an empty house?

'Sorenson's dead,' Brook muttered softly, clenching his fists.

A creaking noise from above made Brook drop the glass.

It shattered at his feet. He abandoned all pretence at stealth and hurtled out of the room, bounding up the stairs three at a time and tearing into the bedroom above the living room, flashing the torch wildly to be sure he wasn't about to be attacked. But the torch was unnecessary. There was already light. A candle in a holder burned in the corner and had been alight for some time, judging by the knot of melted wax around the stem. Brook gazed into the centre of the room at a small mattress; next to it sat a small camping stove and a few unopened tins.

Brook nodded sadly and stepped closer. How many years since he'd been in Laura Maples's bleak squat in London? Twenty? And now here in Derby, in reproduction, it was just as he remembered it. But instead of her blackened, bloated, rat-infested corpse before him, Brook saw only the framed picture of the girl, resting on the mattress.

'Laura,' he said before he could stop himself. He kneeled to look at the likeness of the bright-eyed schoolgirl, staring back at him. It was the same photograph he'd used in her murder investigation in the early nineties. The one plastered over the *London Evening Standard* and printed onto flyers in a futile effort to find her, then her killer. It wasn't the face ravaged by hungry rats, the face that tormented Brook in his sleep.

Well, the dreams had ceased for a while because, where Brook had failed, Victor Sorenson had found Laura's killer and had executed his family for the offence, offering her killer up to Brook as a gift. A gift. To show Brook that The Reaper's work, the destruction of entire families, was righteous and just.

'Who's doing this?' he muttered to himself. He said it again, only louder, lifting his head to project to a nearby listener. His voice bounced around the bare room without receiving an answer. 'Sorenson's dead!' he shouted this time.

He picked up the picture frame and examined it more closely. The picture was a photocopy. The necklace with its silver hearts still winked at him, but Brook was able to draw comfort from the artifice. He pulled the picture from the frame and slid it into his pocket, then listened to the house exhale around him. The pulse of the rap music throbbed faintly outside. He looked at his watch again. Ten past one. Fifty minutes to wait for The Reaper. He wasn't coming, Brook knew that. Sorenson was dead – he'd seen it with his own eyes. But someone was pretending to be Sorenson, someone was tugging at Brook's memories of the Maples case, and he was determined to put a stop to it. He bent down to blow out the candle and sat behind the door to wait in the dark.

*

The man felt the heat from the blaze in the oil drum. He looked at the teenage boys slumped on the old sofas, all four bodies contorted and unmoving. Empty cans, paper plates and glass bottles were strewn at their feet, cigarette ends littered the ground. He turned to the old car on bricks, the portable CD player on the roof, its display drawing his eye.

The man listened to the music. It was soft and beautiful, guaranteed to soothe. He wanted to close his eyes and let his mind drift, but he knew he had to stay focused. He returned to the sofas and crouched down to examine his dark shoes and black trousers by the light from the fire. They were flecked with the stains of drying blood. He stood slowly and prepared to leave.

He glanced at the blood-smeared scalpel on the ground and picked it up as carefully as he could manage with his gloved hand. He placed it on the arm of the sofa next to Jason Wallis, watching where he placed his feet to avoid brushing through more blood.

As he prepared to move away, he noticed something in the boy's hand. He hesitated, then slid the mobile phone from Jason's blood-spattered grasp before moving the boy's hand to rest over the scalpel, pleased with this sudden inspiration. He squinted at the phone in the poor light. It wasn't a model he was familiar

147

with and it looked complicated. He thumbed at a number but his hands were clumsy in the thick black gloves so he peeled one off and dialled again.

At first the man said nothing when the voice at the other end of the line answered. He hadn't thought what he might say. He glanced around at the four bodies, clothes saturated with blood, massive wounds deforming the throats which had once carried oxygen to now inert lungs – all except the Wallis boy, whose injuries weren't immediately visible.

When prompted again on the phone, he answered briefly through the material of his balaclava, then threw the mobile onto Jason's lap, deciding he had stayed longer than he should. He started to walk away but as he did so he heard a groan behind him. The man froze and turned slowly around. Jason Wallis was stirring.

The boy opened his drunken, drug-addled eyes and gawked at the man, without really taking in what he was seeing. He tried to speak but couldn't. For a second the man fancied he saw the boy smile. He opened his mouth to try again.

'I'm ready,' breathed Jason and attempted to lift himself. Instead he slumped back onto the sofa, his eyes closing as he returned to the depths, oblivious to the spouts of darkening blood from his friends dotting his face and hair and soaking into his clothes.

*

Brook woke with a start. He looked at his watch. Two o'clock. It was time. He stood to stretch his aching legs as quietly as he could, listening for any sound from downstairs. He remembered the rap music and wondered why it was no longer pulsing, so he walked over to the window. The large piece of board covering the window had a couple of improvised catches holding it in place. He loosened the bent nails to allow the board to fall into his arms and put it down before leaning out of the glass-free window to look out over the quadrangle of high fences at the back of the block of houses.

He heard the music clearly now but it had changed; it was soft and melodic. He searched his memory banks and peered into the night. There was a bonfire in an old oil drum, two or three doors away. Brook could see the glow of the dying embers crackling and fizzing in the soft breeze. To his surprise he could also see a car and what looked like a couple of old sofas positioned around the improvised brazier. He fancied he could see the heads of several people on the sofas, their feet stretched out towards the heat.

He could even see the display of a CD player as it played, could see the lights through the fog, rising and falling with each note. He listened for a second to the soft tinkling of the piano. 'Clair de Lune', of course. Debussy. Something beautiful. Something . . .

Brook stiffened. His face set he turned and walked purposefully down the stairs and out of the house.

*

Sorenson led the two agents towards the cabin, his hands gripped resolutely behind his back. On nearing the house, he gestured towards a covered patio which had a large glass-topped table supported by a heavy wrought-iron base in the shape of a quartet of nymphs. On the thick glass sat a chrome-plated coffee pot and three cups and saucers.

As they approached, Drexler could hear music, opera in fact, and narrowed his eyes to try and place it. He knew it, he was sure. His mother had been a major Pavarotti fan before her illness and that was the voice that he recognised. At the table, Sorenson gestured at a pair of wicker chairs towards which the agents moved.

A book lay open on the table and Drexler took the

long way round to his chair to get a glance at the title. It was a slim paperback volume of *The Myth of Sisyphus* by Albert Camus. Drexler smiled faintly. Their host was a philosopher.

Sorenson saw him looking but said nothing. Without asking, he poured coffee into the two empty cups and pushed them towards the two agents before freshening up his own cup. 'Please help yourself to milk or sugar. I'm sorry I don't have any cream. I know how you Americans jump at any opportunity to increase your weight.' Sorenson beamed at the two agents to dissipate the insult.

McQuarry emitted a mirthless laugh. 'Don't worry, sir. I'm sure we can locate a box of Krispy Kremes when we're done.'

Sorenson smiled at her response.

The music was clearer now and Drexler saw it was coming from an open pair of French windows behind them. He remembered it now. He'd heard it in a movie, *The Untouchables*. Robert de Niro was Al Capone, sobbing his brutal heart out at a performance of *Pagliacci*. The climax of the piece, when the clown has to face up to his wife's infidelities.

'This is nice,' he said. '*Vesti la giubba*, isn't it?'

'Yes, it is. How gratifying. A man of culture. So hard to find away from the East Coast.' Drexler looked over to his partner as she narrowed her eyes at Sorenson. McQuarry was a straightforward person who spoke her mind, yet believed in good manners and only attempted humour with people she knew. Sorenson's blend of intellectual vanity and restrained taunting would not be familiar to her.

But most of the Brits Drexler knew from college interacted in a very similar way to Sorenson – constantly on the offensive, probing for a weakness to deride. Though it was not the norm for a Californian, Drexler had sought out their company and had learned to appreciate their mocking.

Sorenson turned to fix Drexler with his coal-black eyes. 'Please sit.' Drexler obeyed on reflex, suddenly unsure whether he should have mentioned the opera. He'd given Sorenson a free piece of information about himself and received nothing in return. Their usual working method was to let the suspect do the running and underplay their own hand.

'Were you expecting us, Professor?' asked McQuarry.

'Expecting you?' inquired Sorenson angelically.

'The coffee cups all laid out, sir,' explained McQuarry, not taking her gaze from him.

Sorenson beamed mechanically. 'I'm always prepared for guests, Agent McQuarry. Now what can I do for you? Have you found my car?'

'Car?' The agents exchanged a knowing glance.

'Yes, my beloved Dodge Ram 250. Stolen in South Lake Tahoe. Outside Safeway of all places.'

'The FBI don't make house calls over stolen vehicles, sir,' put in Drexler.

Sorenson chuckled, with a tinge of feigned guilt. 'Of course not. Stupid of me. Then why are you here?' he asked, wide-eyed.

'We were hoping you could provide some information about an employee of yours. George Bailey.' Drexler dropped in the question effortlessly and waited for the reaction.

For a few seconds, Sorenson said nothing but merely looked from one to the other. The music came to an end but another piece started up immediately. Drexler didn't know it.

'Fauré's Requiem,' said Sorenson, waving a hand at the

French window. 'Imagine listening to this as you die. How would that be?'

'A good way to enter the next world,' replied Drexler, before he'd given himself time to think.

Sorenson's eyebrow raised and his mocking smile intensified. 'The next world?' Drexler's smile turned to stone and he berated himself again – another free piece of information. 'I wouldn't have thought someone familiar with the works of Albert Camus would have believed in the next world.' Sorenson's smile disappeared. 'After all, death is not an event in life: we do not live to experience death.'

Drexler nodded, the anticipation rising in him. Sorenson may have seen him looking at his book, but the phrase he'd just quoted was Wittgenstein, not Camus. He racked his brains to finish the passage. 'Eternal life belongs to those who live in the present.'

'A good philosophy, Special Agent.' Sorenson stared into Drexler's eyes. His dead-eyed grin was unnerving.

Drexler looked over at McQuarry, but she seemed not to have registered her partner's excitement.

Drexler tried to figure it. The way he'd floundered, everything he'd said to Sorenson since they'd arrived, even the faint glance of recognition at Sorenson's reading material had been logged, had handed their host an advantage. But despite all that, and under no pressure, Sorenson had made a coded confession to Drexler, had revealed knowledge of Wittgenstein that told Drexler he was the killer they sought. Not a confession for a judge and jury maybe but, sure as eggs is eggs, Sorenson had killed Caleb and Billy Ashwell.

Drexler narrowed his eyes. But why give it up so easily? As an opponent, Sorenson was holding a good hand. Opponent. Is that what he was? Yes, like this was a game. If the notion weren't so absurd he could have sworn that hidden away behind the mask of civility, Victor Sorenson was like a child with a new toy, unable to hide his glee. Drexler was desperate to glance over at McQuarry to see if she'd read him the same way, but was unable to unlock his gaze from Sorenson's lifeless, black eyes.

'Drexler? Drexler?' said Sorenson, suddenly taut with concentration. 'Why do I know that name?' Drexler stiffened and looked over at his partner. Sorenson must have read about the Board of Inquiry's report in the papers. Drexler sipped at his coffee and tried to regain some equilibrium. It was cold.

'We're here to talk about George Bailey, sir,' insisted McQuarry, tapping a diversionary finger on the glass table.

Their host smiled but this time it was a sad expression, suffused with unexpected tenderness. 'George. You've found him, then?'

McQuarry sat up straight. 'Found him?'

'He's missing, is he not?'

Drexler smiled at the overemphasis of the present tense. Their host was trying a little too hard to avoid a timeless trap, one that they hadn't even set. It was odd. Whichever way the conversation turned, Sorenson was trying his best to encourage suspicion with his manner. Usually suspects tried to feign sincerity and deflect further inquiry and although they frequently failed, at least they tried.

'You know he is, sir. You reported it. Would you care to remind us of the circumstances?'

Sorenson nodded. 'George was on holiday – vacation, sorry – for a month. He'd been out here in California for a couple of years, helping to set up the American end of the business. Sorenson Pharmaceuticals. One of my best people and also a friend. It was a big wrench for them to come out here, what with two young daughters. But they

153

loved it, once they'd settled. He didn't get much of a break the first two years so he wanted to make up for it. The family had always wanted to see what your astonishing country has to offer, particularly California, so they packed their gear into a Volkswagen camper van and set off . . . Yosemite, Death Valley, Big Sur, the Mojave. For the final week they were supposed to be coming here to my house as my guests. I was in LA on business and as I say, George was a good friend . . .'

'Was?' said McQuarry.

Sorenson took a sip of his inky black coffee. 'He's dead, isn't he?'

'What makes you say that?'

'Please don't patronise me. You're not from the local Tahoe office. You've come all the way from Sacramento to pay me a visit and there can only be one reason.' McQuarry and Drexler stayed silent to confirm Sorenson's speculation. 'So it's true. Tell me.'

'We've found the body of George Bailey, his wife and one of his daughters.'

Sorenson nodded. 'I see. How were they killed?'

'Shot in the head,' said Drexler.

'Mother and daughter were raped,' added McQuarry to Drexler's surprise. The details seemed unnecessary but perhaps she had reason, perhaps she was searching for a careless response, an unguarded word. 'And the little girl was tortured.'

Sorenson hung his head. 'Poor Tania. Poor . . .' he stopped abruptly and looked up at McQuarry with a raised eyebrow.

'We believe the girl's body is his youngest – Sally.'

He looked away and shook his head. 'Poor little thing.'

'Being from England their dental records are problematic and we wondered if you'd know about next of kin. For the purpose of identification, you understand,' added McQuarry.

Sorenson closed his black eyes in tribute, an unscheduled moment of near silence. But the music played on.

'Sir?' Now McQuarry and Drexler were able to look at each other and manage a quick acknowledgement. McQuarry had arrived at the same page as Drexler. They'd found their killer, a vigilante who'd chanced upon the very spot in the middle of remote Northern California where a personal friend and employee had been slaughtered alongside his young family.

'I believe there's a grandmother in Derbyshire. England,' he added finally.

'What about brothers and sisters, aunts and uncles?' asked McQuarry.

Again Sorenson seemed lost in thought. 'George was an only child,' he answered at length.

'Unlike in the movie.' McQuarry threw the observation away, expecting nothing.

But instead Sorenson smiled at her. 'Exactly.' The sadness returned. 'If you need a provisional identification, I'd be glad. I mean, if it would help speed things up.'

McQuarry had already removed a photograph from her attaché case and placed it in front of Sorenson. 'Sally was killed well after her mother. She should be easier to recognise.'

Sorenson looked at the photograph of the tiny body without picking it up. Drexler and McQuarry watched him closely, but his stony expression didn't waver; he merely stared at the image of the frail corpse for what seemed like an age. No wincing, no averting of eyes, no exclamations of shock or outrage. Nothing. Eventually, aware of his audience, he relented.

'Yes, that's Sally Bailey. George Bailey's younger daughter,' he added in a formal tone, as though familiar with the routine.

Drexler and McQuarry said nothing in reply and waited for the inevitable questions, but they didn't arrive. Instead Sorenson continued to stare at the picture. Drexler raised an eyebrow at his partner.

'You don't seem too interested in who did this, Professor,' said McQuarry evenly. 'I find myself wondering why.'

Sorenson looked up at her. 'Death is the only detail. The rest is window dressing. She's beyond hurting now.'

'In a better place?' offered Drexler, with a hint of a sneer as payback.

Sorenson smiled bleakly and Drexler wished he'd said nothing.

'Where were you last Thursday evening, Professor?'

'Returning from a trip.' Sorenson didn't even blink or try to pretend to remember his movements.

'Where?'

'I drove down to Yosemite for a few days.'

'Looking for George Bailey?'

'Not exactly,' smiled Sorenson. 'Though I suppose, taking a similar route to the one George would've taken to Tahoe, I was more than a little interested in the terrain.'

'And what route was that?'

'You don't expect me to remember tedious road names, do you?'

'What about California 89?' asked McQuarry.

Sorenson's face brightened in childlike recognition. 'Actually, I do remember being on 89. The Ghost Road they call it.'

'Make any stops?'

'Certainly. At my age I need the toilet more often than I'd prefer.'

156

'And gas?'

'Of course.'

'On 89?'

'Absolutely.'

'What time would that have been, sir?'

This time Sorenson did make a bit more of an effort to play the game and stroked his chin, looking into the distance. 'Let me see. It's a bit hazy. I was tired.'

'So it was late.'

Sorenson pointed a bony talon at Drexler. 'Yes, you're right. I stopped just as it was getting dark. Some rundown fleapit on 89.'

'And what did you buy?'

'Just petrol. Gas.'

McQuarry pulled another picture from her small case and placed it in front of Sorenson. It was in black and white but he was clearly recognisable. He was looking at the camera and carrying a cup of coffee in one hand and a bag in the other.

'That's me,' said Sorenson with a chuckle. 'So the camera did work. He said it did though I didn't believe him. You should've seen the place.'

'We have,' said Drexler.

'You remember what else you bought now?' asked McQuarry.

'That's right, I bought a knife. It had a can opener attach-ment. I lost mine at the camp . . .'

'It also had a corkscrew.'

Sorenson grinned at Drexler. 'I believe it did.'

'And the coffee?'

'Oh, I didn't buy that. Mr Ashwell was kind enough to let me have it for free.'

'You remember his name now?'

Sorenson smiled his assent.

'Where did you buy the roses?' asked Drexler.

'Roses? I didn't buy roses.'

'The forecourt camera clearly shows red roses in your car,' said McQuarry.

Sorenson smiled warmly but his eyes were cold. 'Forecourt camera? I don't think so. But show me a picture. It might jog my memory.'

Sorenson was sure of his ground.

'And how was the coffee?' asked Drexler.

Sorenson turned to him and grinned. 'Surprisingly good.'

'Do you still have the cup in your trash, sir?'

'I'm afraid not. I left it in the Dodge so you'd need to ask the thief about its whereabouts. Tell me. Why all these questions about where I stopped on the road? Why don't you speak to Mr Ashwell and his son?'

McQuarry allowed herself a soundless half-laugh this time. She wanted to punch him playfully on the arm and say, *Cut it out, willya? We know you killed 'em. You know you killed 'em and you know we know you killed 'em* but she settled for, 'Mr Ashwell and his son are dead.'

Sorenson didn't bat an eyelid. 'Indeed?'

Twenty minutes later, as the Chevy snaked its way back to the highway, Drexler ran his eye over the beautiful grounds again to confirm what he already knew. Victor Sorenson was a wealthy and successful man. He had a lot to lose. The game had begun.

Chapter Ten

Brook jumped into the BMW, fumbling for the ignition key. Finally he jammed it into the ignition and started the car. He froze for a few seconds, gazing off into the murk, seeing only his past. He slapped the lacquered wood of his steering wheel with the flat of his palm and turned off the engine.

'Two years in the ground and still no peace.'

He took a huge breath and stepped out of the car. As though in a trance, he walked back along the road through the billows of mist. Instead of making his way to the Wallis house again, Brook stopped a few doors away, getting his bearings. He looked at the house on his right. Windows were closed but there was faint light coming from inside. He set off for the path at the side of the house, which might once have supported a garage but which was now a scrubby weed-infested driveway, along which two lines of paving slabs had been dropped rather than laid, to enable access to a car.

Brook approached the corner of the house and peered around it. He saw the smouldering glow of the brazier against the blackness. The music was clearer now, beautiful and gentle. He could see dark shapes ahead, barely outlined by the dying radiance of the coals. He took another huge breath and stepped towards the abyss.

*

Brook didn't know how long he stood in that yard before brain function returned. Later, in the peace of his office, he would calculate it at two or three minutes. Looking back, he would try to remember what he'd been thinking as he stared at a scene that wouldn't have been out of place in an abattoir.

In the aftermath, he could only liken the experience to some kind of seizure or maybe the deepest stupor of a heroin rush, inducing a paralysis so deep that he was powerless to move or prevent the flow of images from his past. The Reaper had returned and Brook stood in the gallery of the dead admiring the brush-work but feeling the detachment of the critic. The Reaper was outside looking in at humanity and Brook stood with him.

What brought him back was not a noise or a stray light, but a sensation in his nervous system so real, that he felt as though someone was rubbing a snowball up and down his bare spine. He wasn't alone. Brook could feel eyes burning into his back. He turned slowly, panning round a pixel at a time, until he faced a newer section of the yard's boundary, a single section of shiplap fencing that bridged the gap between two crumbling walls. The top of the fence was smeared and stained with what looked like blood and Brook took a step towards it. As he did so, another noise behind him made him turn again. For a moment he listened, but except for the music there was nothing. Brook gazed back at the shiplap panel but the sensation had passed, and some kind of thought process had returned.

He walked back to the front of the house, fishing in his pocket for his new mobile phone. A second later an arm folded around Brook's neck while another arm pulled his hand down by his side, forcing him to drop the phone onto the ground. Brook began to struggle and instinctively put his free hand up to protect his throat from a blade.

'Take it easy, mate. You're going nowhere, so relax,' said a voice into his ear.

'Don't struggle,' said another voice, 'and you won't get hurt.'

'We just need to know what you're doing here . . .' said the first voice.

160

'. . . and see some ID,' continued the second.

Brook held his body limp to signal acceptance of the terms and conditions and the arm around his throat spun him around to push him back against a wall.

'I'm DI Brook, CID.'

Suddenly the pressure on his torso evaporated and the voices lost their well-grooved tone and became tense and clipped. 'Sir! Sorry, sir. We had no idea.' Brook fumbled for his warrant card but a gloved hand touched his breast pocket. 'No need, sir. I recognise you now.'

'You could have asked for ID straightaway.'

'Sorry, sir. But we're responding to a 999 call.'

Brook was bending down to pick up his phone but looked up sharply. He hesitated for a second then said, 'I know. I heard the message from Dispatch and I wasn't too far away. Did you catch who called it in?'

'We're not sure exactly. Emergency services got a suspicious call from a mobile. Bit garbled but the caller left their mobile on so they located the signal and asked us to have a look.'

'Right,' nodded Brook.

'We'd have been here sooner but were on another call.'

'So sorry if we . . .'

'PC Duffy, isn't it?' asked Brook.

'That's right, sir. And PC Parker.'

'Well, we've no time to waste. Stay here and get back onto Dispatch. I've only been here a few minutes myself but we seem to have several bodies and one survivor . . .'

'Bodies?' repeated Duffy as though the word was unfamiliar to him.

'Bodies, Duffy. Murdered. It looks like The Reaper,' he added. It had the desired effect.

'The Reaper!' replied Duffy and Parker in unison.

'We're going to need ambulances. Also, very important, get onto Dispatch and get Forensics here urgently – as well as the duty police surgeon. Third – maybe you'd better write this down – we need to start the hunt now. I think the killer may still be close. We need patrol cars blocking all roads off the estate as soon as possible. We need to get the helicopter and the thermal-imaging cameras up in case he's hiding in someone's garden. Also Traffic. We need to keep an eye on all suspicious movement on the roads linking Drayfin to all major routes, especially the M1 southbound . . .'

'What about northbound?' asked Parker, scribbling furiously.

'Why not? And investigate any vehicle driving erratically or speeding away from Derby, particularly vans with anyone in over-alls or protective clothing. There won't be many this time of night.'

'Anything else, guv?' asked PC Duffy.

'Apart from not calling me guv, no. Wait . . . yes. Tell Dispatch to get DS Noble down here now.'

*

Noble arrived twenty minutes later and parked beside the flashing ambulance. For once, his customary poise, so studiously nurtured and encouraged by Brook, was under pressure. He approached Brook, who was standing alone at the front gate of the house pulling on a cigarette.

'Sir,' he said with admirable brevity. The two officers exchanged no more than a glance.

Brook was about to speak when two ambulance men wheeled out a body on a trolley. The detectives both turned to look at the face, disfigured by spatters of blood, an oxygen mask covering his mouth.

'That's Jason Wallis,' Noble shrieked in bewilderment. 'It can't be.' He turned to Brook who returned only an enigmatic smile. 'I don't fucking believe it,' he said, forgetting Brook's disapproval of swearing. 'Jason Wallis again?'

'Easy, John. How's the patient?' asked Brook.

162

The paramedic at the front of the trolley paused to address Brook. Despite years of experience, the man seemed shaken. 'He hasn't got a scratch on him – far as we can tell. He's well out of it, had a lot to drink. But none of the blood on him seems to be his.'

Brook looked at the bloodstained latex glove on the man's hand. 'Did you touch the scalpel?'

'I don't think so. We left it on the arm of the sofa, next to the mobile.'

'Good.'

The man paused and sought Brook's eye with an expression Brook had seen many times before. 'I've seen car wrecks . . .' He shook his head and continued toting the trolley to the back of the ambulance with his partner. Noble's eyes followed the flashing light down the street as the ambulance drove away, then turned to Brook. 'So it's The Reaper again.'

Brook decided not to challenge him. 'It looks like it.'

'And Wallis too. It doesn't make sense. Unless DI Greatorix was right. Maybe Jason did kill his own family and got a taste for it.'

'And managed to leave himself unconscious at the scene again? I don't think so, John.'

'Then what have we got?'

'We've got a sophisticated and ruthless executioner who seems to be staking out this estate like a great white shark. That's not Jason. But you're right in one sense. I think someone would like us to think it was Jason.'

'How do you know?'

'They left the murder weapon in his hand.'

Noble nodded, without showing much sign of understanding. 'How many? Bodies, I mean.'

Brook took a deep breath. 'Six.'

'Jesus.'

*　*　*

An hour later the house and garden was a hive of activity. The first of the arc lights had been hooked up to a portable generator and were illuminating the Scene of Crime Officers as they worked. One officer was directing the erection of two large marquees to shield the evidence from the elements, as well as from the enterprising journalists who would soon be mobilising to cover the story.

At Brook's prompting they also removed the piece of shiplap fencing in the backyard. As they took it away, Brook held his hand up to stop them. He peered intently at it and could clearly see the blood on the top panel where the killer – he refused to use the word Reaper – had brushed his bloodstained clothing as he made his escape.

'Okay, thanks.' Brook waved on the lead Scene of Crime Officer, who winked in acknowledgement.

The neighbour's house beyond could now be accessed. It was in darkness and though officers banged on the door to explain to the occupant what they were doing in the garden, there was no reply.

Brook returned to the front of the Ingham house. A small but vocal crowd was gathering at the edge of the hastily erected police tape, some drinking cans of beer, most just trying to stay warm, but all taking an interest. Mobile phones were glued to ears, grins were glued to faces as they basked in the glow of their newfound worth. They had news that friends and family would want to hear, news that people would listen to without interruption. This was their chance to make their mark, maybe even get on the telly. For years to come, the untalented would regale the barely conscious down the pub with stories of their involvement.

'Our Billy used to knock around with the Inghams!'

'Mrs Ingham used to do my hair!'

'You can see their garden from our roof.'

'Them fuckers nicked me hubcaps.'

'I reckon it was their Stephen done our house over that Christmas. Thieving little cunt.'

'The mum was a right slag. Good riddance to the fat cow and her brats!'

'I wonder who's having their telly? It's forty-two inch.'

'They've even got fucking helicopter out. Wave, we might be on the box tonight.'

*

Just after five in the morning, Brook stepped carefully along the roped path, even though the Scene of Crime Officers had already checked the ground. Behind him came Noble. As they rounded the side of the house, both men's eyes darted around greedily for the details recently illuminated by the large arc lights.

'That's a lot of claret,' remarked Noble, glancing at the three corpses on the sofas.

Brook nodded; his eye was a little more measured, as he'd already observed the scene, albeit by the glow of a spent fire. He glanced across the fences to the window of the Wallis house a few doors away, from where he'd stood looking down at the Ingham garden just three hours before. The protective board was missing, as he'd left it. He knew at some point he might have to direct Forensics to it, if he could come up with a justification that wouldn't incriminate him. For now, to Noble's mild bemusement, he'd merely stationed an officer at the front of the house. 'In case people decide it's a good place to sneak a look at what's going on,' was how he explained it to Noble.

'Where are the other three bodies?' asked Noble, his breath steaming in the cold.

'Upstairs bedroom. Two adults, one male, one female, and one male child, about ten years old,' replied Brook, turning his attention back to the scene before him.

Two sofas sat at right angles to one another, facing towards the heat of a fire, as they might in any living room. In this case

165

the near-dormant fire was a brazier made from a discarded oil drum in the bare backyard of the Ingham household. The closest sofa supported two bodies next to each other, stretched out, feet towards the fire. The second sofa held just one corpse, similarly positioned. The seat where Jason Wallis had been unconscious was now vacant and, as promised, the bloodied scalpel and mobile phone were on its arm, waiting to be photographed and bagged. On the ground were discarded plates, some with dirty cutlery, and some with remnants of the condemned boys' last meal. Burgers and hot dogs in half-chewed buns, stained by blood and ketchup. There were also a dozen or so discarded Special Brew and other assorted beer cans, some crushed and thrown at a bin some ten yards away, others upright, probably unfinished, by the side of the sofas. In addition Brook could see at least four empty two-litre bottles of Diamond White cider, the drink of choice for seekers of oblivion. Most of the revellers had not been disappointed.

Noble kneeled to examine one of several handrolled cigarette ends that littered the yard like confetti. 'Smells like zoot to me.'

Brook looked over. 'Got a hole in your tooth, John?'

Noble returned a bleak smile. 'Marijuana, sir. Street name, zoot. I'm down with the kids.'

Brook nodded and rolled his eyes towards the sofa supporting the single male corpse. The boy, a teenager, sat upright, though his head, baseball cap still in place, was twisted backwards over the back of the sofa, his gaping wound fully exposed. They'd both seen the twist of pink gristle of a severed windpipe before. The cleanness of the cut was consistent with The Reaper's MO – no hacking, no panicked slashing, clean, cold, efficient and almost matter-of-fact. A job to get done, then move on. Who's next?

'Good question,' muttered Brook.

'Sorry?'

'Nothing.'

Brook ran his eyes over the empty space next to the corpse. He had to peer round the still warm oil drum to get a view, but grunted when he saw what he was looking for. Or rather, what he was expecting to be absent. He motioned to Noble.

'Is that where Jason Wallis was sitting?' Noble asked.

'It was.'

'Which means Wallis can't be our killer,' said Noble. 'You were right.'

Brook nodded his approval. 'Good spot, John.' He switched his attention to the other sofa. Again both male victims were young, probably seventeen-year-olds if they were contemporaries of Wallis. Like the other boy, their heads were pulled back so their severed windpipes winked up at the heavens. All the young men wore similar clothing – baggy jeans exposing designer underwear, padded jackets or hoodies and grubby Nike training shoes. A peaked cap, espousing support for the New York Yankees, still clung to one boy's head, in spite of the muscle spasms he must have endured as his life had convulsed to a close.

Brook moved away towards the car that stood on bricks at the rear of the house. It was an old Toyota, battered and rusty and had flames daubed amateurishly on the side. The portable CD player sitting on the roof had been turned off. Brook was tempted to start the music again but resisted. It didn't stop the soundtrack from other Reaper crime scenes rolling around his head – Mozart's Requiem in Brixton and Mahler's Ninth from the Wallis murders two years before. His eye followed the extension cord through the back door to the now brightly lit kitchen.

'John.' Noble looked up at Brook, who nodded towards the internal wall through the kitchen window. 'SAVED' was written in large, bloody letters. All the letters oozed red tiny tears, as if of condolence, which had pooled on the grease-caked linoleum floor. Noble nodded back to Brook in recognition. The Reaper's unique sign-off.

For years Brook had puzzled over who was SAVED until his

final apocalyptic night with Sorenson. The worst petty criminals on the estate would have died tonight, The Reaper having seen fit to save honest neighbours from their malevolence. Summary and absolute justice as before – but it didn't make it any easier to look at.

One of the SOCOs working near Jason's sofa stood up and turned to Brook, holding two clear plastic evidence bags in front of him. One contained the bloody scalpel, the other a mobile phone, also stained with blood.

The officer pulled down his mask. 'Mobile's not been dusted but it looks like there's a print in the blood.'

'Sounds promising,' said Noble. 'Bit careless for The Reaper though.'

'It could be Jason's,' noted Brook.

'Or the ambulance man's.'

'No, I moved it off Jason's lap so they could take him to hospital. Can we get a list of the last calls and any texts?'

'Shouldn't be a problem,' said the officer. 'And if any pictures were taken.'

Brook and Noble nodded their thanks and moved further down the garden towards a shiny new barbecue, still sporting a couple of scorched burgers.

'This is a Weber, sir. Top of the range barby.' Brook recognised the distinctive brand from his evening with Mike Drexler. 'Looks new. Wonder where they nicked it,' smiled Noble, looking over at Brook, who seemed distracted suddenly. 'Something wrong?' Brook looked into his sergeant's eyes. To Noble he seemed to be wrestling with a different mystery a million miles removed from this blood-soaked scene. 'Are you okay, sir?'

'Maybe they didn't nick it. Maybe they won it in a competition, John.'

Noble's expression sobered as soon as the observation hit home. 'You think? The same MO. Cheeky sod.'

'Why change a winning formula? We'll need those burgers and

sausages bagged for analysis, John. They could have been . . . doctored.'

'Twilight Sleep again?'

'It worked last time.'

'What happened here?' asked Noble as they walked over to where the fence panel had been removed.

'Best guess? Emergency exit. The killer has finished his work and is about to leave. Maybe he hears my car or maybe even sees me coming up the path . . .'

'Pardon?'

Brook sighed, feeling suddenly very tired after his night's labours. He looked up at the washed-out dusty sky, dawn still some way off. 'It's been a long night, John.'

'You think you disturbed The Reaper?'

Brook hesitated, trying to find the right words. Ahead of him the path forked into two. One way required honesty and promised awkward questions, suspicion, maybe even removal from the investigation. The other was the path of deceit and would require a balancing act of exhausting proportions. He'd already taken a pace along it with his lie to PCs Duffy and Parker about his presence on the scene. 'I don't know for sure.'

'How long have you been here?'

He looked back at Noble. 'A lifetime, John.'

*

The house adjoining the Ingham backyard was still in complete darkness. Brook ran his torch around the neat little back garden.

'What are we looking for, sir?'

'Assuming our killer vaulted over the fence and landed in here covered in blood . . .'

'Panicking after you turned up.'

'. . . there might be bloody footprints on the path, maybe some fibres, maybe he left DNA on the front gate.' Brook was trying his best to ignore Noble's piercing glance.

'You realise what the Chief Super's going to say when he finds out? Never mind Brian Burton and the rest of the media. What were you doing here in the middle of the night?'

'It's complicated, John, and I'm tired.'

'That's not going to cut any ice with . . .'

'Odd.'

Noble stopped to look at Brook. 'What do you mean?'

'Look at the row of houses facing the crime scene.'

Noble scanned from side to side. Of the dozen houses backing onto the crime scene only the one opposite was in darkness. Every other household alerted to the calamity in their midst had numerous lights beaming, some of which outlined a human frame peering out to catch a glimpse of the horror. Only the house, past which the killer may have made his escape, was dark.

'Empty house maybe? Or whoever lives there could be away. Lucky.'

Brook arched an eyebrow at Noble. 'The Reaper? Luck? I don't think so. Get Duffy and Parker to knock on doors and find out who lives there and where they are. We need to get in there. And station someone out front for the foreseeable.'

*

Fifteen minutes later the two detectives climbed the now bare stairs to the Inghams' first-floor master bedroom and prepared to enter. They approached the door as a bright flash illuminated the dingy room to reveal a child's bare feet suspended in the air. Once Brook would have reeled from such a sight. Now he was detached enough to just wrap it into his calculations.

Twenty years had passed since Brook had gazed at the corpse of a boy hung from a ceiling in the flat of Sammy Elphick, a petty criminal who lived with his wife and son in a slum in North London. A family had died that day too. How many more would it take before The Reaper was satisfied?

Brook stepped just inside the door to survey the scene but

Noble, following right behind, let out an involuntary 'Jesus!' The various SOCOs looked up from their different activities then grinned at each other. They always relished the shock and awe of the unprepared.

'You're not going to blow chunks are you, detectives?' said one. Noble speared a contemptuous look his way.

'I reckon the Chief Super will be losing his bran flakes when he gets here,' said another and the low chuckle was taken up by the rest, but just as quickly died away.

'Just like the first one. Harlesden, wasn't it?' asked Noble quietly.

Brook nodded. Another camera flash made him realise how tired his eyes were. He tried to focus despite the fatigue. He looked up at the young boy swaying minutely at the end of a rope which reached up through a trapdoor-cum-skylight in the ceiling into the roof space. The same MO as Harlesden all those years ago when Sorenson had removed the Elphick boy's fingers, settlement for a V-sign the boy had flashed at him in the streets of Shepherd's Bush. Had that been this youngster's offence this time around? It seemed an extraordinary coincidence.

He couldn't look at the boy's face so busied himself with other details. The Derby County FC pyjama top had a small breast pocket with a slight blood-stained bulge; Brook knew the two removed fingers would be in there.

He checked the stumps on the boy's disfigured hand. The cuts were clean, surgical. Noble bent to examine the boy's feet. The soles were dirty and scuffed, except where several trickles of urine, expelled at point of death, had cleared small channels through the grime. A teat of liquid still clung to the right big toe.

Brook looked at the boy's ankles, visible under his pyjama bottoms. They were a bluish pink with the accumulating blood of post-mortem lividity.

Noble followed Brook's gaze. 'I thought lividity created a deeper purple than that,' he remarked.

'It does,' agreed Brook. 'After eight hours. It's nearly seven now.

He's only been dead about six hours at the most.' He leaned in towards the boy to examine more closely. As he did, the body swayed gently round and Brook was forced to see his face. 'Full circle.'

'Sir?'

'We've come full circle, John. This is a copy of the first Reaper murder in Harlesden.'

'A copy?'

'The hanging, the removal of the boy's fingers. See the spots of blood under the body.'

'I assume the fingers are in the pyjama pocket. And he would have been dead or dying before he was strung up, right? That's the same as Harlesden.'

'You've done your homework.'

Noble looked a little guilty. 'Brian Burton, I'm afraid.'

They moved past the boy to the centre of the room and were assaulted by other odours beside urine, smells Brook knew well. Emptied bowels and the sickly sweetness of ageing blood had temporary dominion over the stench of stale beer and tobacco, which hung in the air and leached from the peeling, yellowed wallpaper. But now the room also had a chemical edge as the forensic officers applied their sprays and gels.

Like the other Reaper crime scenes, the room was sparsely furnished. It was important that only death and its key details would take the eye. A large double bed and wardrobe had been pushed close to the far wall, and beyond that was an ancient oak wardrobe, the doors of which were no longer flush. The doors had no handles, only holes for fingers to prise them open. There was no other furniture except for the chair that The Reaper probably used to hoist the boy into the noose.

Brook berated himself with a small shake of the head. Sorenson was dead. The Reaper was dead. This bore the hallmarks of The Reaper's method but it wasn't the same. Something wasn't right. Something was different. Brook moved gingerly towards the bed for a better look, careful to avoid the officer kneeling nearby who was combing through the bare carpet. Two adult bodies were in the bed: on the far side the male, young and naked from the waist up; on the near side, the female in a silk slip, older and heavier. Both were still under the deepening red duvet, but neither was sitting up to face the boy. Brook narrowed his eyes to ponder this and made a mental note.

As ever, after the first Reaper killings in Harlesden, Brook searched for something tasteful, something wonderful, if only in reproduction, to give the dying a glimpse behind the curtain of humankind's lofty ambition. In Harlesden it had been a painting, 'Fleur de Lis', for the Wallis murders a poster of Van Gogh and the grandeur of Mahler, beautiful sights and sounds to usher the dying towards the pit with smiles on their faces.

Brook looked around at the bold and colourful posters that had been displayed to enliven grubby walls, but knew The Reaper hadn't brought any of these. Famous football players grinning for the camera adorned several walls, while other sporting posters suggested a passion for both Formula One and topless female motorbike racing.

'Well, Burton can write down the details but never having been at a Reaper crime scene, he wouldn't be able to tell you that this isn't original Reaper.'

'Why not?' asked Noble.

'It's not a carbon copy. It's not how . . .' Brook was about to put himself into the frame but managed to stop himself. 'It's not exactly how The Reaper would've done it.'

'You once said The Reaper liked to vary his MO from crime to crime. You know, to fool the profilers.'

Brook looked at Noble and smiled. 'That's it. Prove me wrong with my own words again. Derby CID will be in good hands when I finally head for the elephants' graveyard, John.'

Once Noble would have beamed with childlike joy, but now he merely looked away before muttering, 'Had a good teacher.'

A few seconds later he nodded at the walls. 'There's no poster, no art for them to enjoy while they die. That what you mean?'

'True. But assume the music's on loud enough to be heard in here. Maybe that was enough splendour to usher them across the Styx.'

As usual, Noble was able to breeze past Brook's baffling rhetoric. 'Okay. So what else is different?'

Brook smiled at Noble. 'You *have* been at a Reaper crime scene before. Why don't you tell me?'

Noble looked around the room with new eyes. He gave a half-smile to Brook, then called across to one of the SOCOs who was kneeling to dust a beer can next to the bed. 'Are the bodies in the bed exactly as they were found?'

*

When Brook and Noble returned to the ground floor, DS Morton was waiting for them. He held up a rubbish bin containing a selection of discarded blue and white plastic wrappers.

'Looks like our victims had a lot of meat in them, sir.' Morton nodded at the contents. 'Sausages, burgers, kebabs. Think we can rule out cholesterol?' he added with a grin, which froze under Brook's baleful stare.

'What does it say on the packet?'

'Moorcrofts,' chipped in Noble. 'It's a local butcher in Normanton.'

Brook nodded. 'Makes sense if the meat was a gift from the killer. Asda has CCTV.'

'Also local butchers might struggle to pinpoint when the meat was bought.'

'There's a good chance they'll remember someone buying barbecue food in winter. Get those packets bagged and get someone round there,' instructed Brook.

At that moment DC Cooper popped his head round the door. 'Chief Super's here, sir.'

'Thank God,' said Noble. 'I feel safer already.'

Brook and Noble left the kitchen. As they rounded the corner of the house, Noble muttered, 'What the hell are they doing here?' Brook followed his stare. DCI Hudson and DS Grant were donning protective clothing alongside Chief Superintendent Charlton. 'Sir, they've got no place . . .'

'Calm yourself, John. More pairs of eyes can't hurt. Morning, sir,' he shouted over the drone of the helicopter passing overhead.

'Inspector. Sergeant. What's good about it?' returned the Chief Super.

'Nothing if you're a member of the Ingham clan, sir.'

'Quite.' Charlton hesitated, realising Brook, and especially Noble, expected further words from him. 'I sent a car for DCI Hudson and DS Grant so they can have a gander and share their impressions with us – as they're in the vicinity. More hands make light work, eh?' he finished with a half laugh, unable to meet Brook's eyes.

'Morning, Joshua, Sergeant Grant,' smiled Brook. 'I thought you'd be back on the south coast by now.'

'Lucky we weren't,' muttered Grant, a little louder than she intended, and Brook narrowed his eyes to divine her meaning. It didn't take long.

'You don't look so good, Joshua,' observed Brook.

'No. I had a rough night. I didn't have time to have all the vaccinations before we came up north.' Noble took tight-lipped offence but Brook, not being a Derby native, just smiled. 'Is it true?' ventured Hudson. 'Is it another Reaper killing?'

Brook paused for a second. 'It has all the hallmarks.'

'Hope you don't mind us taking a look, Inspector?' added Grant, clearly hoping that he did.

'Not at all. The more the merrier.'

'They're here at my request,' put in Charlton as though Brook had somehow voiced an objection.

'It's a good idea, sir. A fresh perspective would be useful,' said Brook, glancing at Noble's pained expression.

With that, the party set off for the garden and Brook set about removing his latex gloves and coveralls. As he scrunched up his protective suit, he noticed Grant turn at the corner of the house and run her eye over Brook's clothing.

Brook caught her eye and nodded. She smiled mechanically and continued after the others. Hudson and Grant had come to Derby to nail Brook for the murder of Tony Harvey-Ellis. Now a new Reaper killing put him even more squarely in the spotlight as far as they were concerned. He shrugged. He had nothing to hide . . . at least nothing that wasn't already well hidden.

Chapter Eleven

Sheriff Andy Dupree poured himself a black coffee and plucked a sugar-coated doughnut from the box next to his wide-brimmed hat. His Marine-crop haircut was severe and both Drexler and McQuarry realised this was the first time they had seen him without the hat.

Dupree took a small bite of the pastry and washed it down with a sip of coffee so strong it left a black slick along his upper lip. 'What did he say when you told him about Ashwell?'

Drexler looked at McQuarry then at the table. 'He said, "Dear me".'

Dupree let out a laugh. 'Dear me? Mr Sorenson, you just survived a visit with the Ghost Road Killers. And all he said was "Dear me"? These fucking Limeys, I gotta tell you.' He shook his head and chuckled again. 'He say why he didn't come forward?'

'He claims he didn't know the Ashwells were dead.'

'With all the media and shit. How's he expect us to swallow that?'

'He doesn't have a TV, Andy.'

'Well, there's some weird shit right there.' Dupree shook his head. 'But he don't deny being there?'

'How could he?' said McQuarry.

'Or buying the knife and the coffee?'

177

'The coffee was free but no, he didn't deny anything about being there.'

'So he coughed to murdering Ashwell and son.'

McQuarry raised an eyebrow and helped herself to coffee. 'Damn, I forgot to ask him that.'

Dupree smiled. 'And you think this Sorenson knew they killed the Baileys?'

'We're sure of it,' said Drexler. 'Why else would a rich and powerful man bother taking out those two lowlifes? He's been flagging it up from the get go. He takes the rose petals to stuff into Billy's pocket to tell us why the Ashwells have died. He writes some Wittgenstein on the cabin wall when he's done, then starts quoting him at me almost before we'd said hello.'

'Why the fuck would he do that?' pondered Dupree. 'We coulda looked at him for a while then moved on. Now he draws a lot more heat.'

'Mike has a theory,' said McQuarry with a hint of scepticism. Dupree turned to Drexler.

'He wants the heat, Andy,' nodded Drexler. 'He wants the attention and for us to know he did it.'

'Why?'

'It's some kind of Bored Rich Guy game. He kills Ashwell and his boy and is challenging us to prove it.'

'More than that, Mike. He's challenging us to care,' said McQuarry.

'And do we?' asked Dupree. 'Don't give me that look, Ed. I'm serious! This Sorenson's done the world a favour, far as I can see. Let's give it a day then move on. Spend our time looking for some real bad guys.'

'You've got a point, Andy. But there's one thing I have to understand and it's the reason we have to pursue this,' said Drexler.

'What's that?'

'Caleb Ashwell's been bushwhacking folks on the Ghost Road for twenty years and not only did he not get caught, but no one actually knew that crimes were being committed.'

'So?'

'So how the hell did Sorenson know? How did he see what no one else has ever seen? How did he know to stop there? How did he know to pay cash? And how did he know not to drink the coffee?'

McQuarry and Dupree stared at the table. A few minutes of head-shaking later, they looked up at Drexler, who was waiting for his moment.

'Okay, Mike.' nodded Dupree. 'Why don't you tell us?'

'There's only one explanation, as far as I can see. This isn't his first murder.' Dupree and McQuarry considered the statement but neither could raise a counter. 'Victor Sorenson is made of ice. He was looking for the Ghost Road Killer and because he knew Bailey's route, he knew vaguely where to look. He's a hunter. And a hunter knows how others hunt. That's how he knew and that's why we have to stop him.'

*

'It's bang out of order, sir,' seethed Noble.

'So you've said.'

'You're taking this very well.'

'How should I be taking it, John?'

'You should be sticking up for your division, sir,' said Noble icily. 'What about our reputation? I suppose you . . .' He stopped in mid-sentence.

Brook stared at him, taken aback by this sudden glimpse of old grudges he thought had withered. 'But I'm not from this division, am I? I'm an outsider who was imposed on it. That's why I don't care about its reputation. That what you wanted to get off your chest, John?'

Noble looked away, tight-lipped; Brook heard him mutter, 'Not exactly . . . maybe.'

Brook sighed and looked around. 'We shouldn't be arguing in front of the troops.' He walked Noble a little way from the house, although privacy of any kind was impossible. 'John, look at it from Charlton's point of view. Greatorix is on the sick list. And I'm in the doghouse because of Brian Burton's book. I'm tainted, John. Past and present. There's a long and well-documented history of my failure to catch The Reaper, on top of which . . .'

'On top of which?'

'On top of which . . . they're here. And they're already investigating a possible Reaper killing in Brighton,' he added quietly.

'What?' exclaimed Noble. 'What killing?'

'Tony Harvey-Ellis.'

'Who's he?'

Brook nodded towards the Ingham house. 'I'll tell you later.'

Chief Superintendent Charlton had emerged from around the side of the house. His face was ashen and he appeared to be having a little difficulty walking, to judge from the attention he was giving to where he stepped. Brook fancied he was blind to everything apart from what he'd just witnessed. Behind him followed Hudson and Grant. The latter detached herself and headed over to the gap in the fence. She gazed across at the darkened house opposite before approaching a uniformed officer. Brook watched her, trying not to be obvious about it. The uniformed officer pointed towards PCs Duffy and Parker who were kicking their heels next to a Scientific Support van. Grant marched over like any good detective would. Talk to the first officers on the scene. Basic police work. It wouldn't be long now.

Brook flicked his eyes back to Charlton who, together with Hudson, was approaching. Brook realised he had never seen the Chief Super out of uniform before. Minus his protective suit, he was soberly dressed and wore a large camel coat from which he now extracted a pair of brown leather gloves. He pulled them on, without breaking his sightless, unblinking stare.

On reaching Brook and Noble, Charlton finally managed to find his voice. 'My God.' He shook his head and squinted up at Brook suddenly. Brook gazed down into his confused eyes and fancied he detected a morsel of sympathy in there. Sympathy for the victims no doubt, but also some realisation of what it must be like for CID, at the sharp end, to have to deal with such sights.

'We need a win on this one, people,' Charlton said. 'We've got to catch whoever did this. And not just for the stats. Who could do such a thing?'

'How long have you got?' nodded Hudson grimly. 'Honestly, that was nothing, Chief Superintendent. One of the neatest crime scenes I've ever seen.'

'Is it The Reaper?' asked Charlton, fixing Brook with a look.

'It's a creditable copy,' replied Brook, keeping a peripheral eye on Grant, who was still talking to Duffy and Parker.

Charlton nodded. 'You can tell me how you know that later. What's being done now?'

'We've forty or so uniformed officers searching all the neighbouring gardens. I've got my CID team going door to door for witnesses, asking about the history of the Inghams, feuds, disputes, known enemies. The Forensics people are obviously doing their thing. We've got a scalpel as murder weapon and a mobile phone, which may have prints on it. We assume it was the one used to call emergency services last night so we'll be getting the tape for that this morning. We've got a brand new barbecue, which may provide a link to previous Reaper investigations. It may have been delivered to the Inghams as a prize. That's a Reaper signature to gain access.'

'What else?'

'The bodies will be going to the mortuary within the hour and Dr Habib has got his team prepared . . .'

'What about the survivor, Inspector Brook? This Jason Wallis.

He's now survived two Reaper attacks, shouldn't we be looking at him as our killer?'

Brook looked doubtful. 'Sir, I wish it was that simple . . .' Brook broke off as DS Grant rejoined the group. At first her face had carried an expression of confusion, but this had given way to satisfaction as she approached. She locked her gaze onto Brook, a thin smile curling her lip.

'It's not possible, Chief Superintendent,' explained Hudson, taking up the reins. 'The surviving boy must have been seated throughout the attack. That's why the back of his seat is clear of bloodstains. It would have been covered in the arterial spray of the boy next to him if he'd been moving around, cutting throats.'

'I see,' nodded Charlton. 'Then why was he here? And why did he survive? Again.'

'Those, sir, are two very good questions,' agreed Brook.

Grant continued to stare at Brook, an odd grin deforming her features. 'Maybe he's some kind of mascot,' she offered, making little effort to remove her gaze from Brook.

Charlton turned to her with a painful expression on his face. 'Is that meant to be funny?'

'No, sir,' she replied. 'Far from it.'

'Someone trying to scare him, you mean?' put in Noble.

'Or impress him. *Look at what I can do to your friends, any time I like.*' She shrugged. 'Just a thought, but we have a living witness and it seems unlikely to be an oversight,' she added.

Brook was the only one to notice her use of the word 'we'.

'Chief Inspector, is there anything you'd be doing that DI Brook's not doing?' asked Charlton. Noble took an audible breath and looked at Brook but he was staring at DS Grant and didn't seem to be paying much attention.

'Presumably you're hunting up any possible CCTV around the area?' Hudson inquired of Brook. 'And Traffic film should be examined in case our doer isn't local. Vans are good. Harder to see into.'

'Both in hand,' answered Noble for him.

'Have you got ANPR cameras here yet?' asked Hudson.

'Not yet,' said the Chief Super. 'Maybe next year . . .'

'Pity. But you can still check with the motorway boys who will have them,' interrupted Hudson. 'Not only can they automatically recognise number plates, but any potential criminal's car will have a marker on them.'

'Marker?' asked Noble.

'If an ANPR camera sees a stolen car that's in the system, the computer will throw out an alert within seconds. They're state of the art, Sergeant,' observed Charlton, happier now to be on home ground.

'He's probably long gone by now,' threw in Grant. 'Or he could be in our midst,' she added, continuing to burn her eyes into Brook.

'The helicopter cameras couldn't find anyone,' said Noble, missing the insinuation.

'And I don't have to ask if your search will include bins, grates and unlocked sheds, do I, Damen?' asked Hudson.

'Looking for what?' asked Charlton. 'We've got the weapon.'

'Well, we're assuming he has transport, but if he doesn't he's going to need a change of clothes if he wants to get far without being noticed,' replied Hudson. 'Which might mean dumping what he has on.'

'Excellent!' nodded Charlton. 'Excellent thought.'

'We're all over that, sir,' countered Noble. 'Standard procedure.'

'One other thing, Inspector Brook – why have you put a man on that house over there?' asked Grant, pointing at the officer examining his nails in front of the dilapidated Wallis house.

'That's where Jason Wallis's family were butchered two years ago, Sergeant,' said Noble.

'I'm surprised Wallis could come within half a mile of the place,' she observed. 'That doesn't answer my question though.'

Brook smiled suddenly and Grant was taken aback momentarily.

'She's very good, Joshua,' he said to Hudson. 'Glad to see you're not being allowed to soft pedal before you retire.'

'She keeps me on my toes,' answered Hudson.

Brook smiled again. 'I see she does.' She knew. She'd spoken to Duffy and Parker, assuming they were first on the scene. But they weren't. And a detective of Grant's ability wouldn't accept the lie about Brook picking up the call on his radio as easily as Duffy and Parker had. And the fact that Brook didn't have an in-car radio would soon nail that lie. 'It's part of our crime scene, Laura. The Reaper – sorry, the killer – was there last night before he came here.'

'How do you know that?' she said back at him.

'Because so was I.'

*

A half hour later Charlton, Brook, Noble, Hudson and Grant had gathered in a small conference room back at St Mary's Wharf for a meeting to get everyone singing from the same hymn sheet before the initial inquiry briefing at four p.m. and the media briefing after that.

Charlton ordered coffees before kicking off. 'This is very difficult for me, having no background in CID, but I'm determined to get a positive result, and we must start out with that in mind. I'm very aware that nearly two years ago my predecessor lost her job on account of mistakes made on the Wallis Inquiry, mistakes that she didn't necessarily make herself, but for which she had to bear responsibility.'

Brook was impressed that Charlton didn't look over at him at that point.

'We have to get the direction of this investigation right, from the start,' Charlton continued. 'I fully intend to be involved in all aspects of decision making and personnel, like it or not. Now, some might think that's just me covering my back, and they wouldn't be totally wrong, but my aim is to structure this inquiry for maximum efficiency. Comments, anyone?

'No? Okay. The first thing we need to decide is who directs the investigation.' Charlton looked around to see if either Brook or Noble were prepared to take offence, but as neither seemed to be reacting, he pressed on. 'I know, Damen, that you're nominally the Senior Investigating Officer on this inquiry but I don't think I need to tell you what problems that throws up. Firstly, the publicity surrounding this journalist's book . . .'

'Sir. May I say something?' asked Noble.

'John!' warned Brook. 'You don't know the full . . .'

'No, I think it needs to be said, sir.' Chief Superintendent Charlton invited Noble's contribution with a wave of his hand. 'I was on the Wallis Inquiry with both DI Brook and DI Greatorix and I've read Brian Burton's book. As far as I'm concerned there was nothing more that DI Brook could've done to hunt down The Reaper. Most of Brian Burton's book is complete nonsense. It's full of unsubstantiated rumours and half-truths that have been twisted to fit Burton's own prejudices . . .'

'The content's irrelevant, John,' put in Brook. 'It still puts the inquiry and my involvement under more of a spotlight than normal. It muddies the waters in which we have to swim.'

'Which puts the investigation at an immediate disadvantage,' added Hudson.

'What about the advantage of having an SIO who's uniquely qualified to catch The Reaper, sir?' said Noble.

'Not helped so far, has it?' observed Laura Grant with a humourless smile.

'Take it easy, Laura,' said Hudson. 'We're all friends here.'

At that moment, Charlton's secretary brought in the tray of coffees to shortcut potential bad feeling. After she'd left, Charlton removed a contemplative forefinger from in front of his mouth. 'Sergeant, I won't be basing any judgement I make on the contents of that book. But, as DI Brook has pointed out, its existence will impact on the amount of scrutiny we come under.'

'We're talking about The Reaper here, sir. How much more scrutiny can we attract?' asked Noble.

'A good point, Sergeant, but Burton's book is not the only impediment here,' added Charlton. He looked over at Hudson, who nodded and turned to Noble.

'I don't know if you've been brought up to speed by your DI, Sergeant, but let me do that now. The reason DS Grant and myself came to Derby is to question DI Brook about a murder that took place in Brighton ten days ago.'

'While Inspector Brook was on leave,' chipped in Grant.

'The victim was the husband of DI Brook's ex-wife. Tony Harvey-Ellis was his name. I'm not comfortable going into detail about why DI Brook and Mr Harvey-Ellis might be, shall we say, enemies – for want of a better word – but suffice to say that two years ago, at the height of the Wallis Inquiry, DI Brook turned up in Brighton and assaulted Mr Harvey-Ellis.'

Noble turned to Brook. 'Is that true?' Brook looked squarely back at Noble and gave an imperceptible nod. 'And now he's dead and you're a suspect?'

'So it seems, John,' conceded Brook.

'A strong suspect,' added Grant.

'It's purely circumstantial at this juncture,' noted Charlton.

'But added to last night's events . . .' continued Grant.

'Last night's events?' exclaimed Noble. 'You can't possibly think Inspector Brook . . .'

'That's enough, John,' said Brook. 'We're all grown-ups here. I can see why I'm a suspect. As for last night, that's an unfortunate circumstance . . .'

'Unfortunate for the Inghams,' noted Grant.

'. . . an unfortunate circumstance which I can explain.'

'We're listening,' smiled Grant.

Brook paused to choose his words with care. 'I was first on

186

the scene but I arrived too late. I was in the Wallis house before I realised what was happening. I got to the Ingham house a few minutes before PC Duffy and PC Parker. I surveyed the situation and secured the scene. When Duffy and Parker arrived, we called for back-up.'

'But you were there first, Inspector, and we've only your word for how long you were there.'

'That's true, Sergeant. But I have no motive to kill the victims. And it won't be hard to prove that I didn't make that emergency call, which puts someone else at the scene before me. Also, you were alert enough to check my clothing this morning when you arrived at the crime scene. I would have been covered in blood if I'd killed the Inghams.'

'Let's not get ahead of ourselves, Damen,' interjected DCI Hudson.

'You were at the crime scene alone,' insisted Grant. 'You could have changed, dumped the evidence before the responding officers arrived.'

'Let me know when you find the clothes.'

'That's just it. With you as SIO we never will.'

'That's enough, you two,' soothed Charlton. 'DCI Hudson's right. We're losing sight of the main objective.'

'Sorry, sir,' said Grant. 'But if we're going to entertain the notion that DI Brook should be involved in this inquiry, let alone run it, then I think we've a right to know what the hell he was doing at the Wallis house at that time of night.'

Charlton thought for a moment then nodded, looked over at DCI Hudson, who shrugged his agreement, and turned to look at Brook.

Brook put his hand inside his jacket and pulled out a folded piece of paper. 'I received this email yesterday.' He unfolded it and slid it across the table towards the Chief Superintendent. Charlton read the brief document aloud, then passed the paper round the table for examination.

Damen,
I'll be at the Wallis house at two o'clock tomorrow
morning. It's vital I see you. Come alone. I hope you
remember how to get there?
Victor

'Who's Victor?' asked Hudson.

'Victor Sorenson is . . . was a suspect in The Reaper inquiry in both London killings in the 1990s.'

'Was?'

'He died two years ago.'

*

Charlton, Hudson and Grant watched Brook and Noble leave the office. As soon as the door closed, Charlton arranged to have Brook's office computer taken away, to have the hard drive examined.

'You don't really believe this email guff, do you, guv?' Grant said to Hudson. 'It's easily faked.'

'Give me some credit, Laura. It's about as convincing as the evidence that Brook's The Reaper.'

'What does that mean, Chief Inspector?' asked Charlton.

'This email is a pretty terrible alibi and Brook must know that,' Hudson replied.

'So?'

'So, we're looking for a killer who's been active for nearly twenty years and Brook must know his methods better than anyone.' Charlton was still confused. 'In all those years, a viable Reaper suspect has never been identified. The Reaper's killed two families in London, one in Leeds, two now in Derby. Five crime scenes. And what did Forensics find at the first four crime scenes?'

'What?' asked Charlton.

'Nothing,' said Grant. 'No fingerprints, no DNA, no witnesses, no CCTV, no fibres. Nothing.'

'Add to that the fact that The Reaper has no clear motive,' added Hudson. 'Even a copper as good as Brook can't beat those odds.'

'I see,' said Charlton, clearly not seeing.

'And now we're supposed to believe that Damen Brook, the man who has hunted The Reaper for all these years, is actually The Reaper. If so, he wouldn't be caught at the crime scene with only a poxy email as an alibi,' said Hudson, pulling out a cigarette and lighting it before Charlton could object. 'If someone as smart as Brook was The Reaper, he would've been better organised than that, believe me.'

'Okay,' nodded Charlton doubtfully.

'And that's not the only strange thing. Suddenly there's more evidence at the Ingham house than we can shake a stick at. I spoke to one of the SOCOs. The killer used a mobile phone to alert the emergency services to the murders. Not only have we got a useable print on it, but we're going to have the killer's voice on tape.'

'That's good, isn't it?' said Charlton. 'It'll tell us about Brook one way or the other.'

'Yes. But it also tells us that either The Reaper has got very sloppy or we're dealing with a copycat, like Brook says. Whatever you think of him, Brook is a brilliant detective. Believe me, nothing we have will point to him for this – nothing.'

Hudson took a large pull on his cigarette and exhaled towards the window, suddenly aware of Charlton's aversion to the smoke.

'What about this Sorenson that Brook talked about?' asked Charlton.

'You're welcome to have a look, sir, but if there was no evidence to prove Sorenson was The Reaper when he was alive, it'll be ten times harder if he is dead. And it almost certainly won't help you with the Ingham investigation.'

'Unless we can trace that email, guv.'

'Don't hold your breath, luv.'

'And can you think why someone would want to copy The Reaper?' asked Charlton.

'Good question,' said Hudson; Charlton tried to hide his pleasure. 'His methods provide a workable blueprint for anybody wanting to be a serial killer,' answered Hudson. 'After all, he's never been caught.'

'But it doesn't fit the profiles,' added Grant.

'Profiles?' said Charlton.

'Serial killers fall into two categories,' explained Hudson.

'By definition, the compulsive killer can't stop himself,' said Grant. 'He repeats because he has a compulsion, one which eventually trips him up, because he has to kill even if it means taking risks.'

'And there's often a sexual angle, which generally leads to DNA,' put in Hudson.

'Then there's The Reaper. A killer like that is more organised and gets his kicks from power, not sex. He enjoys the fear of the public and the inability of the police to find him. These killers use their crimes as a secret well of omnipotence, to dip into when their self-esteem needs it.' Grant looked at her two superiors with a frown. 'However . . .'

'Problem?' asked Charlton.

'Vanity,' said Hudson.

'Right. This type of serial killer wouldn't usually copy another killer's MO. His ego needs to know he's an original, a one-off. If caught, he can revel in that knowledge, show off his superiority.'

'Then again, Laura, leaving a print is not evidence of great organisation.'

'We still don't know it's the killer's, guv.'

'Well,' said Charlton with an air of finality. 'This is all very interesting but gets me no closer to solving my dilemma. Even if Brook scrubs up clean over last night, can I afford to keep him as SIO?'

Hudson smiled at Charlton. 'Can I make one further suggestion, sir?'

*

DI Brook and DS Noble hurried down the stairs two at a time and arrived at the entrance to the lab. The place seemed deserted so Noble rapped on a frosted glass door and entered. A portly, completely bald, middle-aged man chewing on a slice of pizza turned towards the door. He wore a white coat flecked with crumbs and sported an ID badge with a picture of a thin long-haired stranger, taken many years before, and the name 'Donald Crump'.

'Hello, John, Inspector Brook,' Crump said, not looking at the senior officer. 'What do you want? Haven't you given us enough to do?'

'Where's Benny?' asked Noble. 'We need a quick scrape and tape. Clothes, fingernails, hair – the lot. Urgent.'

'He's next door sorting out the photos and sketches. Then he's off to the mortuary to record the autopsies.'

'You'll have to do it then, Don,' said Noble.

'I've already got six sets of bloodstained clothing on their way over,' Crump complained. Noble grinned and raised his eyebrows. 'So it looks like I've got a bit of time to do a rush job,' he added through gritted teeth. 'I'll get my gear. Where is it?'

'Right here, Don.'

Crump turned around to see Inspector Brook removing his clothes.

*

It was afternoon by the time Brook got home. Noble had returned to the Drayfin Estate to coordinate activity around the murder scene so that the Chief Super could go into the press briefing fully informed. Meanwhile, the key pieces of evidence to emerge were being walked through by individual detectives. DS Morton was the exhibits officer and was following the bloodied mobile

191

phone through its various examinations, the lifting of the finger-prints being the most important. DS Gadd was walking through the scalpel, also to be tested for prints and DNA, and DS Grant was collating the information on the 999 call.

When he pulled up, Brook was relieved to see his new neighbour's hire car was absent and he could pass unseen between his car and his front door. He was tired from his labours but Brook hadn't come home to rest. Although unable to bring his skills to bear on the current case until formally cleared by Donald Crump's various tests, his experience of The Reaper was a unique resource and Charlton was expecting him to deliver his opinions at the initial briefing.

However, much to his relief, Brook was to be allowed nowhere near the media. Charlton, at Josh Hudson's instigation Brook suspected, would handle the public face of the inquiry and be its titular head, with the occasional support of one of the senior officers if needed. Both DCI Hudson and Brook, assuming he was cleared, would lead a joint taskforce investigation into the deaths at the Ingham house.

Brook had to admit he was impressed by this sleight of hand. Instead of throwing him off the investigation and creating a media storm, Hudson had ensured that Brook was kept close to the inquiry while at the same time seeing to it that his power to influence events would be severely restricted. Although nominally in charge, Brook knew he would be under intense scrutiny; his every move would need to be approved by Hudson and Charlton, both of whom would be mindful of any attempt to sabotage the hunt for The Reaper. As far as Hudson and Grant were concerned, regardless of forensic tests on his clothes, Brook would remain a suspect, and what better place to keep an eye on him than right under their noses?

After a quick shower and shave, Brook settled down with a cup of tea to gather his thoughts. He fired up the computer and clicked on his Hotmail account to double-check he'd already deleted the first email from the fake Reaper, the message congratulating

Brook on the murder of Tony Harvey-Ellis. He had, and he'd already emptied the deleted folder. Brook was confident he hadn't opened the first email in his office so unless they took his home computer as well as his work laptop, it was unlikely the document would ever see the light of day again.

*

An hour later, Brook, suitably attired, went out to his car. He hesitated a moment, then flung the bag of protective clothing in the back seat and marched quickly round to the back garden of Drexler's cottage. The Weber barbecue was still there – the same brand as the one at the Ingham house, whatever that was worth. He examined it briefly without knowing what he was looking for. On an impulse Brook knocked on the back door, though he knew Drexler was out. He turned the handle and was surprised to feel the door open.

'Hello. Mike?'

Brook stepped into the small kitchen and looked around. He poked his head through the door into the tiny living room and noticed Drexler's passport on the arm of a chair. Looking around furtively, Brook gathered it up and something fell onto the floor as he did so. Brook picked it up. It was a train ticket. He stared at it for longer than was really necessary, then flipped open the passport. When he found the page he wanted, he examined the immigration stamp closely. Putting the train ticket back inside the booklet, he placed it back on the arm of the chair. He left quickly, stepping smartly back to his BMW in case Drexler drove up and saw him.

*

The taxi pulled up outside the Midland Hotel and Grant and Hudson stepped out, walking quickly to the reception desk. They leaned against it pensively and waited to be noticed.

'I only brought a holdall,' said Grant.

'Me too,' answered Hudson, trying to get some attention from the hotel staff.

'I mean, I'll have to get some more clothes from somewhere,' she insisted.

'Funny. I've got enough for two weeks.' Hudson grinned back at her.

She rolled her eyes. 'See, guv, I tend not to wear clothes until they rot on my body.'

'Interesting idea.'

'It's a girl thing.'

'Well, let's make sure they haven't given our rooms away first, and then I think I'm finally ready for a bite to eat.'

A few minutes later the pair sat in the Midland Hotel lounge, both feeling the effects of a disturbed night – two in Hudson's case. Grant poured two coffees from a coffee pot and handed one to Hudson who took a hearty draught around a mouthful of ham sandwich.

Finally Grant broke the silence. 'Guv. You were pretty sure about Brook.'

'What do you mean?'

'Telling Charlton he's not The Reaper.'

Hudson rubbed the six o'clock shadow on his chin. 'It's all wrong, luv. Five families killed in their own homes and sandwiched in between The Reaper supposedly kills a fit jogger in a public place. It makes no sense. The only connection we've got here to Brighton is the drug used in the Wallis killings, two years ago in Derby. Apart from that, nothing else The Reaper's ever done connects with Harvey-Ellis. Wrong MO, wrong victim. The Reaper didn't kill Harvey-Ellis.'

'Then why dangle his murder in front of Charlton?'

'It got us on the taskforce, didn't it? Let's face it, the Chief Super didn't need much pushing. This way he covers all bases. Besides we're getting bugger-all-where with the Harvey-Ellis

Inquiry and our chief suspect is here. This is where we need to be. This is where we find our killer.'

Laura Grant nodded. 'Brook.'

'It's possible. He has motive *and* opportunity for Harvey-Ellis. But there's no way Brook killed this or any other family. It's not him. Not without a good reason.'

'Maybe he *has* finally gone off the deep end and is starting to become what he's hunted all these years.'

'Bollocks. You've seen him. He's as cool as they come. And he wouldn't have been caught red-handed. No, there's something going on here . . . something interesting.'

'Like what?'

'I don't know yet but I'd like to find out. If we flip this thing over and assume Brook's telling the truth about that email, and that he didn't kill that family last night, it means that somebody took the trouble to lure him there and make it look like he did.'

'And you want to know who, guv.'

'I want to know why. And there's something else. I don't know anything about this Victor Sorenson being tagged as The Reaper, but he's the guy Brook nailed for killing that schoolgirl, Laura Maples and got him to confess. The one who tried to poison Brook – I remember the name now.'

Grant nodded. 'Interesting.'

Hudson yawned and looked at his watch. 'The briefing's at four. I think I'm going to have a shower and grab an hour's shut-eye.' He pulled a book from beneath his overcoat. 'Then I'm going to do a bit more background.' He flashed Grant the cover of Brian Burton's book.

'Where did you get that?'

'I borrowed it from the desk sergeant, Hendrickson. The one I spoke to on the phone. He had several copies, couldn't wait to give me one. I'll see you in here at three. What are you going to do?'

'Same as you – after I buy some underwear.'

195

Chapter Twelve

When Chief Superintendent Charlton entered the Incident Room with DCI Hudson and DI Brook, the hum of conversation stopped immediately. The room was filled with about twenty officers, some CID, some senior uniformed officers – Traffic, Community and others – whose input might initially be called upon in a potentially massive inquiry.

Charlton walked over to the table, hesitated for a second while he assessed whether he could ask everyone to sit, then, realising there wouldn't be enough chairs, he leaned against the table. Brook was next to him, standing several inches taller.

'Stand easy, everyone,' he said and most of the assembled throng either sat down on chairs or sagged onto nearby tables.

Brook looked around at the crowd. As well as Hudson and himself, there were several detective sergeants, including newly promoted Jane Gadd and Rob Morton, who'd both worked on the Wallis Inquiry two years before, in addition to Laura Grant and John Noble, who were chatting in one corner of the room. Another six detective constables had been added to the team, including DCs Bull and Cooper who had also been in Brook's previous team to catch The Reaper.

'We don't want this to take long because we've got a killer to apprehend,' continued Charlton. 'But I want to know that this inquiry has everyone on the same page,' he added. 'I can confirm that DCI Hudson and DI Brook are jointly heading up the taskforce to find this man; but this is a Derby inquiry and I will have ultimate responsibility.

'I will also take charge of the public face of the investigation as much as possible, and will deal with the media, allowing senior detectives to focus all their powers on bringing this madman to justice. Now, this is most important. My predecessor brought me up to speed on mistakes that were made on the Wallis Inquiry two years ago. One thing beyond her control was the leaking of information to the local media and this is something I will *not* tolerate. Anybody undermining this investigation with little whispers to the press, will find themselves back in uniform doing match-day duty at Ilkeston Town.' A general groan was followed by a few guilty titters. 'And I mean *anybody*!' He glared around the room. 'Anything to add to that, Inspector Brook?' Brook shook his head. 'Chief Inspector Hudson?'

Unlike Brook, Hudson had a few people skills and grinned at the assembled team. 'I'd like to thank everyone at this station for the warm welcome. I know it can't be easy to integrate new officers into a successful CID unit overnight, especially a hand-picked and talented team like yourselves. DI Brook and I know we can rely on your support to get a result.'

Brook darted his eyes around the assembled faces – all seemed to be buying into the middle-management drivel.

'I'll be leaning heavily on the expertise of all Derby officers,' continued Hudson. Brook was almost relieved to spot the expression of scepticism flash across Laura Grant's face. 'Because they have more direct experience of this killer and this MO. But remember, anything anybody wants to say to me or DI Brook about the direction of the inquiry, please don't hesitate to speak. My door is always open.'

'Where is your door?' asked a likely-lad DC. A peal of laughter broke out around the room. Only Charlton didn't join in.

Hudson smiled. 'It's a symbolic door at the moment, but we're sorting something out.' He glanced at Brook, who stood to address the briefing.

'DS Noble has been organising most of the information we've gathered so far, but we'll assemble again tomorrow morning to talk through further developments. John.'

It was DS Noble's turn to stand and face the throng. 'We'll have hard facts by tonight for full briefing tomorrow morning at eight a.m. sharp . . .' more groans followed '. . . yes, I know. You'll just have to set your alarms.'

'Enough of that,' bellowed Charlton, folding his arms.

The noise subsided quickly and Noble began again. 'Let's deal with what we know. As we speak there are six corpses lying in the mortuary.' He waved a hand at the crime scene photographs on the boards behind his head, as if it were necessary to prompt colleagues to examine them. As well as the crystal-clear SOCO pictures there were a couple of grainy mobile phone shots taken by PC Duffy using Brook's phone before the ambulances had arrived. They showed an unconscious Jason Wallis on the sofa, first with the bloodied scalpel under his hand and then with his phone on his lap.

Consulting a notebook, Noble continued. 'The crime scene is 229 Drayfin Park Road. Miss Chelsea Ingham, a thirty-two-year-old unemployed beauty consultant, was found in the main bedroom of the house. In the same bed was her current partner, twenty-three-year-old Ryan Harper, who we've identified from his fingerprints. He appears to be an unemployed labourer though he has a fairly long jacket of minor offences, the most serious of which was assault.' Brook and a few others were nodding in recognition at the name. 'Both of these victims had their throats cut. Also found dead in the bedroom was Miss Ingham's nine-year-old son by a previous partner. D'Wayne I think it is – that's the son, not the partner. The lad had been hung, although the pathologist is not certain that was the cause of death. He'd also had two fingers removed and placed in his pyjama pocket – a Reaper

signature from the first killings in Harlesden twenty years ago.'
All parents in the room lowered their heads. The rest stared
unblinking at the relevant photograph. 'The files on all the
previous killings are on the system so any spare minute needs to
be spent reading up on The Reaper's MO.'

'Anything on the ex-partner?' asked Hudson.

'In the clear, sir. He's a builder and working in Dubai,' answered
Noble. After a pause to shake out any further questions, he
pressed on. 'Also, in the backyard of 229, we have the bodies of
three seventeen-year-old males. Stephen Ingham, Miss Ingham's
elder son by another partner, and Benjamin Anderson. The third
body we believe is David Gretton. Those IDs are dependent on
formal identification by relatives. A fourth male, Jason Wallis, is
now in the Royal Derby, recovering from mild hypothermia.
Most of you know his history from the previous Reaper investigation nearly two years ago.

'The three deceased outside the house all had their throats
cut in identical fashion to the two adults in the bedroom. The
cuts were clean and professional, there were no signs of hesitation and the weapon used was a scalpel recovered at the scene
from Jason Wallis's hand. Provisional blood analysis would seem
to suggest that, apart from the little boy, all victims were killed
where they were found. Lividity would seem to confirm that.

'The three older boys were sitting on two old sofas in the yard
and had probably been consuming significant amounts of alcohol
and soft drugs.'

'What drugs?' broke in Charlton.

'Marijuana definitely, sir, but the post-mortems will give us a
clearer picture. Now at the moment we're assuming that whoever
attacked the Ingham home is still at large.' Grant glanced across
at Brook with a raised eyebrow. 'Jason Wallis did come under
brief suspicion for the killing of his family two years ago but
was subsequently cleared, and we're reasonably sure that once
again Wallis is not our killer. However, his presence at a second

Reaper killing is unusual to say the least. His *survival*, for the second time, is even more unusual, so we can't rule him out. We hope to interview him later today, provided he's regained consciousness. As Jason's the first living witness to survive a Reaper attack – if you discount the Wallis baby – we may have some significant details for tomorrow's briefing. The murder weapon, the scalpel, was covered in blood and presumably will have Jason's prints on it . . .'

'Sarge, am I missing something?' asked DC Cooper. 'Why can't Jason Wallis be our killer? Seems straightforward to me. Sole survivor. Weapon in hand.'

'It appears the weapon was placed under Jason's hand rather than in it.' Noble indicated the picture on the wall showing the scene before Jason was lifted onto the stretcher. 'Also, had Jason been the killer, he would have had to stand behind the victims, and the sofa where he was found unconscious would have been covered in blood spatter even if he had sat back down. It's not.' Noble looked round for any follow-up.

'Our best guess on time of death is between 1.00a.m. and 1.53a.m. this morning. You'll find out why 1.53 in a minute; obviously that's provisional and as the three older boys were out in the cold it'll be more difficult to pin down in their cases. We've already got door to door underway and we're coordinating any relevant CCTV around the area. Hopefully we can discover how the killer arrived at the Ingham house, but for now nothing is ruled in or out until we have something solid to get our teeth into.

'Until we get a heads up on definite leads from Forensics and the post-mortems we have to get stuck into the legwork. If the killer's local, fine, but if not it means looking at ways in and out of Drayfin *and* Derby, so we look at bus and rail passengers and cab firms, we check with Traffic and trawl through the cameras. We search the entire estate top to bottom.

'Van hire firms need checking as The Reaper hired locally two years ago. Also any hotels or B&Bs with male guests staying last night or the night before who have checked out. Get lists and addresses and any credit card details and cross-reference those with descriptions from previous investigations on file. But remember, assume nothing.'

'Why are we so sure it's a male?' asked DS Gadd. 'The Wallis victims two years ago were poisoned before they were cut open. That's a woman's MO.'

Brook spoke now, pausing briefly to find a way to give nothing away. 'That's true but the MO's not exclusive to women. Older, weaker men use it as well. Like Crippen.' 'Like Victor Sorenson' remained unsaid. 'And all descriptions from previous Reaper killings point to a lightly-built, middle-aged male. Possibly older.'

'Also we've something concrete on that shortly,' added Noble. Again he paused for any follow-up before continuing. 'We also look at the victims – we look into their history, see if there's anything in there that might have caused someone to do this to them. Two years ago we were sure the Wallis family were targeted because of their petty criminal background, specifically Jason Wallis's sexual assault on a Mrs Ottoman, a teacher at his school. The antisocial behaviour and petty criminal background of the victims would fit with previous Reaper murders.'

'Didn't the Ottoman woman have a nervous breakdown and attempt suicide?' said Laura Grant.

'I think she did,' said Noble. 'And that made her husband John Ottoman briefly a suspect in the Wallis Inquiry . . .'

'Then why suggest the offence was petty?' she asked.

'I didn't say it was,' answered Noble.

'You said . . .'

'How did this Wallis escape The Reaper last time?' asked Hudson, changing the subject. 'The files aren't clear.' He glanced over at Grant who read the signal and decided to leave the rest of her sentence unsaid.

'That's because we were never certain,' jumped in Brook, seeing Noble hesitate. 'At first we thought he was lucky and arrived

201

home after the murder of his family. We assumed he'd staggered home drunk and ate some of the drugged pizza delivered by The Reaper. He was unconscious at the scene and didn't even know his family were dead until the next day. It was only later we had to face the fact that The Reaper was probably at the scene the same time as Jason, but left him alive for some reason.'

'What reason?' demanded Grant, her eyes boring into Brook.

'Like I said, we were never sure . . .'

'I mean, why kill the daughter and not the Wallis boy? Sounds like a vicious little thug,' she added.

Brook shrugged, unable to meet her eyes.

'We asked the same question,' replied Noble. 'We're open to suggestions.'

Charlton spoke up while looking at his watch. 'I don't think we should get too bogged down in the past no matter how much it informs the present. Anything else, Sergeant Noble?'

'Just to remember that maybe there's a domestic lurking in here somewhere. The Ingham boys had two different fathers, one's out of the country but maybe there's an ex-boyfriend in the works. Even a neighbour pushed over the edge. Who knows? You'll get your assignments from DC Bull in a minute.'

'Thank you, John,' said Brook, pausing for a second to look around at the throng, some of whom were fingering coveted cigarettes in pockets. He could see in all of them that sliver of suppressed excitement that such a high-profile investigation generated; he wished he could share it. 'There is some good news before we get back out there. DS Grant.'

Grant stood up and nodded at all the strange faces. 'Yes, we think we have the killer's voice on tape.' There was an immediate murmur from the assembled officers. 'If it's him this would be a big leg-up. This 999 call was recorded this morning at 1.53 a.m.'

Brook looked at the floor. Around that time he'd been just yards from the killing ground. The killer had probably finished his work long before but the questions still nagged at him. Why lure him there? To make him think The Reaper was still out there? Or to try and frame him for the Ingham murders? He shook his head as minutely as he could. Surely this wasn't another attempt at recruitment? Get him to take up The Reaper's mantle? Is that why Jason was left alive again? Another gift for Brook. Like Floyd Wrigley all those years ago in Brixton.

Grant, with a little prompting from Jane Gadd, pressed the appropriate button on the machine.

'Emergency. Which service do you require?' The voice of the operator boomed out and Grant adjusted the volume. There was a pause, filled by an indistinct noise which might have been breathing, might have been the wind. Then Brook heard it, soft at first but still quite clear in the background. If he hadn't already known what it was, it might have taken him longer to identify. Clair de Lune. The soft melody tinkling away gently, distant but audible. Then the operator tried again. 'Emergency. Which service do you require? Hello. Are you able to answer?'

A few seconds later Brook heard the sound of a breath being exhaled into the phone, then a man's voice, 'They're all dead!' followed by a buffeting sound. Then nothing but the faint sound of the music with occasional interruptions by the operator trying to elicit further responses.

Grant waited a moment before switching off the machine. 'Now it's hard to distinguish from just four words, and whoever that was may have tried to disguise his voice, but you'll agree that's still clearly a male voice. And in the background is the music that was playing at the scene when DI Brook and the patrol car arrived to investigate.' Grant shot a glance his way;

'How did they know where to go?' asked Jane Gadd.

'The call was unbroken,' answered Grant. 'It was Jason's phone, found on his lap, covered in blood and a print, which is still being processed. I don't know Wallis but it's not the voice of a teenager as far as I'm concerned.'

Brook shook his head. 'It's not Wallis,' Noble agreed.

'What about the music?' asked DC Cooper.

'It's called Clair de Lune by Debussy,' said Grant. 'You may have heard it in the *Ocean's Eleven* film.' There was an outbreak of nodding from the cinema-goers in the room. 'Two years ago in the Wallis house it was Gustav Mahler playing, isn't that right, DI Brook?'

'As far as I can remember,' he answered, without looking at her.

'Any impressions about the voice, anyone?' inquired Hudson.

'Sounds local to me,' added Rob Morton. 'The way he said "They're all", like it was one word instead of two.' Brook looked over at him with a thin smile.

'Must be local if he's working the same street as two years ago,' someone said.

'Great. All we need now is a name and address,' grinned Hudson to induce a round of chuckles. 'There's a university here, isn't there? Maybe they've got a language guy,' he added quickly, suddenly aware that some might think he was having a dig.

'Linguistics,' said Grant, smiling – Hudson knew the correct word, she was sure.

'That's the one. Put that on your list, Rob.' Hudson nodded at DS Morton before looking over at Brook.

Brook stood up from the table. 'Before we get onto our assignments I want to give you some idea what we're up against.' He paused. He knew the words but he had to weigh them carefully. 'Two years ago this Christmas, and just a few doors away on the same street, the Wallis family was executed. I've chosen that word deliberately because these crimes aren't personal and, if this is The Reaper, he has no contact with his victims until he goes to take their lives. The only clues left behind two years ago, and in London twenty years ago, were what The Reaper wanted us to see. We got no weapon, no prints, no fibres or hairs or anything that might have been used to make a case against a suspect, even if we'd been able to identify one.'

Grant looked up at him with a half-smile on her face.

'This time it's different. The killer has left us with a lot of evidence to go at. For that and other reasons that we'll go into tomorrow, we're working on the theory that this may be a copycat. Certainly there was no suggestion of a Derby man being involved in any of The Reaper killings, including the Wallis case two years ago. That is a piece of information to be given to no one outside this room.' Brook paused to look round the room to ensure his message had been understood. 'And with the evidence we're compiling there's a much better chance of catching last night's killer. However, if it *is* a copycat, there's a much higher probability of him striking again soon so we need to be on our mettle. Even more so than usual,' he added as an afterthought to stroke a few egos. Brook wasn't a natural people person, but bitter experience had taught him that most people needed encouragement.

'All your assignments are absolutely crucial to the investigation as a whole so please don't think that if you're being asked to trace the origin of the barbecue from the scene, you're just following up a minor lead. Nothing we ask you to do is unimportant and the smallest detail could be critical.'

Brook turned to Charlton.

'And let me say again so there's no confusion,' said Charlton. 'Anybody who thinks it's okay to talk about details of this investigation to anybody, even if it's about the colour of the elastic bands in the Incident Room, will find themselves in serious trouble. Now let's move with a purpose, people.'

*

Brook stood back slightly from Hudson and Grant as they spoke to the hospital reception and fished the vibrating phone out of his pocket. He located and pressed the answer button, gluing it to his ear.

'John. What?'

'Good news. Ish.'

'Go on,' he said, ignoring Noble's linguistic mangling.

'The thumbprint on the mobile phone is not yours and it's not Jason's either.'

'So it could be the killer's.'

'Looks that way. However, there are no matches on the system. Whoever did this has a clean record.'

'It's something to go on.' Brook was silent for a moment. 'John. Any chance you could check the print against IAFIS?'

'IAFIS?'

'That's the US fingerprint database.'

'You're well informed.'

'There's a civil section for government employees, FBI, people like that. You might need some kind of permission.'

'Care to tell me why?'

'It's complicated.'

'I see. It's keep me out of the loop time again, is it?'

'It's only a hunch. But forget I asked, John.'

'Okay, okay, I'll see what I can do. Is Hudson with you?'

'Why?'

'We've got the results from your tests and I want him to hear them from me. Pass him the phone please, sir.'

Brook waved the phone at Hudson. 'For you, Joshua.'

Hudson took the phone. After listening intently for a few seconds, he nodded. 'Very good, John. Never doubted it.'

*

The police constable babysitting Jason Wallis stood behind the doctor. He made a drink signal to Brook who inclined his head and the fresh-faced young PC turned and headed down the corridor.

Brook peered at the curtain, behind which lay Jason Wallis, and wondered how the youngster would react to seeing him again. The morning after Jason's family had been butchered, Brook had been greeted by a face of hate as Wallis, unaware of events, had paraded his contempt for the police and all authority. By the end of that interview, the fifteen-year-old Jason had been jolted back to his childhood with questions about the murder of his parents and younger sister. A few well-chosen photographs had sealed the deal. Jason's lip had wobbled and he'd wept for the first time in years – for his family, yes, but primarily for himself. *What's going to happen to me?* What would his reaction be now?

'We've sent a blood test off to your Forensics people but physically he seems fine, if a little out of it,' said the doctor, addressing Hudson. 'If you ask me he's probably just had too much to drink and maybe a few too many puffs of marijuana. These substances always lower body temperature which explains the mild hypothermia. We'll keep him in overnight to be sure, but the main problem is likely to be shock.'

'What about stomach contents?' asked Brook.

'We did pump his stomach in case of toxins but it was virtu-ally empty,' replied the doctor, checking his chart.

Brook's eyes narrowed. 'Empty? He went to a barbecue. You're saying he didn't eat any meat?'

'Some breakfast cereal, that's all. Your people can tell you what kind,' he added with a shrug.

'Thanks, Doctor.' Hudson turned towards the screen as the doctor strode out of the ward. 'Well, if he saw anything of what went on last night he could be in shock for a while.'

Brook smiled. 'Don't underestimate the power of self-absorption, Joshua.' Neither Hudson nor Grant understood his meaning.

A middle-aged woman with short grey hair and sober apparel emerged from behind the screen. 'Hello, officers. I'm Maureen Welch. The social worker,' she added in lowered tones, looking around as though hoping no one else would hear.

'How is he?' asked Grant.

'See for yourself.' She stood aside and ushered them to Jason's bedside.

Jason Wallis had grown since Brook had last seen him, doped up and helpless in his aunt's house in nearby Borrowash. That wild and stormy night Brook had donned The Reaper's mantle and confronted young Wallis, offered him a way out from under the knife. But Jason Wallis had called his bluff.

Maybe he should have arrested Jason for Annie Sewell's murder when he had the chance. But it wasn't his case and, after much soul-searching, he'd decided that fear of The Reaper's return would be a more effective deterrent to Jason and his gang of teenage killers, robbing them of the peace of mind they might achieve in a locked cell. For all Jason knew The Reaper could return at any time to finish his work in Derby. Funny thing: The Reaper had returned but Jason was still breathing.

Brook looked him full in the face. His hair was a little longer than before and his face less spotty and perhaps a touch thinner. What was more striking, however, was Jason's demeanour. Where once he was snarling and scornful, now he seemed quiet, reflective. Instead of looking up to greet his visitors with suspicion and loathing, Jason remained motionless, merely glancing up. His eyes flicked momentarily towards Hudson and Grant but when he spotted Brook, they lingered for a few seconds longer.

Brook prepared himself for accusations, for finger-pointing. But if Jason remembered that night, he showed no sign. He was sitting up in bed, his eyes open, but seemed hardly aware of his surroundings. His eyes looked glazed as he resumed his thousand-yard stare, not even flinching when Grant waved her hand in front of his face. Brook wondered if he'd been given some kind of sedative.

'The doctor didn't tell us he'd been doped up,' grumbled Hudson.

'Oh, he hasn't,' offered Maureen Welch. 'They've given him nothing. That's how he is.' She moved to sit in a visitor's chair at the side of the bed.

'Jason. I'm Detective Chief Inspector Hudson. This is Detective Sergeant Grant and this is . . .'

'I'm ready.' Jason spoke softly but his voice seemed to echo around the room like a clap of thunder. For a moment the three officers looked at each other blankly.

'That's what he keeps saying,' chipped in Maureen Welch. '"I'm ready." That's what he says.'

Then Jason did the last thing Brook had expected. His face was suddenly transformed by a friendly grin. 'Hello, Inspector Brook.'

Hudson and Grant were puzzled. Brook was surprised but managed not to show it in front of his new colleagues. He'd expected hate. He'd expected fear or babbled accusations, but not this.

'I'd like to talk to you about what happened last night . . .' continued Hudson but broke off when Jason showed no sign of having heard.

Eventually he stopped grinning at Brook and turned to Hudson. 'Last night?'

'You were at your friend Stephen Ingham's house. Having a barbecue and a few drinks in the backyard, remember? Somebody killed your friend Stephen. Somebody killed your other friends too.' No reaction. 'Ben Anderson and David Gretton. Did you see who it was? Can you remember anything?'

'Did somebody use your phone, Jason?' asked Grant, holding a pencil superfluously above a virgin page of notepad. 'Was it The Reaper?'

At this Jason blinked.

'That's right, Jason,' coaxed Hudson. 'The Reaper! Did you see him? Do you know who it was?'

Finally Jason looked down at the bed, nodding. 'I saw him.'

Hudson and Grant exchanged a glance. 'Did you recognise him?' breathed Grant eagerly.

Jason's grin returned and he looked up at Brook and nodded his head gently. 'I recognised him.'

Grant sneaked a glance at Brook for signs of worry but he seemed equally eager for the reply.

'Who was it?' prompted Hudson, trying to fight the rising tide of excitement. After twenty years he was going to find The Reaper. A day on the case and one of the world's most sought-after killers was about to be unmasked.

'It was The Reaper.'

Hudson and Grant crowded closer in on young Wallis. 'How do you know?'

Now Jason fixed Brook with his grin once more. 'We've met before.'

'Can you describe him?' said Hudson.

'Bit smaller than Inspector Brook . . . chubbier. Not like you at all,' he said to Brook, with a suggestion of a tease.

To Hudson and Grant's consternation, Brook smiled back at Jason. Jason was telling him something. Telling him he remembered. Jason remembered their last meeting, but could only drop hints. Jason was as vulnerable as Brook to exposure. He was a killer, after all. If Jason was going to accuse Brook of being The Reaper he would've done it already.

'But who was it?' asked Hudson.

Jason shook his head. 'He wore a mask as usual. A woolly thing . . .'

'Balaclava? Ski mask?'

'S'right. It covered his face.'

'So you can't identify him,' said Grant. No reply.

Jason looked down at his sheets. 'I told you. He wore a mask.' He hung his head in shame briefly, remembering the tears and the terror of the chase. 'They're all dead.'

'I'm afraid so, Jason.'

Jason looked up. 'No. He said they were. The Reaper. That's what he said. I heard him. "They're all dead", he said.'

'Do you know why he didn't kill you?' asked Hudson. 'After all, he couldn't be sure you wouldn't identify him.'

Jason's grin returned and he looked from one to the other. 'He can't.'

'Can't what?' echoed Grant.

'Can't kill me. We're squared away, see.' Jason chuckled now.

'Squared away?'

'The Reaper and me. He can't kill me now.'

'You don't seem worried,' continued Grant.

Brook watched a more familiar expression, recalled from their first encounter, infect Jason's teenage face. 'Told you, you thick bitch. He blatantly can't touch me. You think I'm gonna walk into a trap if . . .' He stopped abruptly and returned his eyes to the bedsheets.

'Trap?' said Brook sharply.

'Never mind,' replied Jason with a cryptic smile and a dissembling touch of his nose with his finger.

Brook cracked a bitter smile and nodded. 'You didn't eat anything, Jason. Is that because you knew? You knew The Reaper was coming to the Ingham house, didn't you?'

Jason became hesitant, evasive. 'Leave me alone.'

'How did you know, Jason?' asked Hudson, trying to inject a little aggression into his voice.

'The brand new barbecue,' said Brook to Jason. 'The Inghams won it, didn't they? In a competition.'

'No. Sting said they nicked it last week.'

'Where from?'

'Dunno.'

'Then how did you know last night was a trap?'

'Stinger texted me. They won stuff – a load of burgers and sausages and shit. Booze too,' replied Jason after a pause. 'They was having a party with it.'

'And you knew, didn't you, Jason? You made the connection.' Brook stood back from the bed, now a little more animated. 'Just like the pizzas your mum and dad won two years ago. It was a gift from The Reaper to get access. And you knew he was coming but you said nothing.'

Jason's grin returned. 'I told you. He can't touch me.'

'But what about your friends?' asked Hudson. 'Why didn't you warn them? Why didn't you tell the police?'

He snorted. 'Tell the leng? Tell them what? I don't know nothin'. Anyway, it's not like they didn't deserve it.'

'What do you mean?'

Jason turned to Brook with a taunt in his eye. 'What they done. They told me. Stinger, Grets, Banger. They 'fessed up. Two years ago. They said they done some old woman over. Croaked her.'

Brook's jaw tightened.

'Old woman?' asked Grant. 'What are you talking about?'

'They strangled her in her flat. They told me about it. Same night as mi mum and dad and our Kylie.'

Hudson turned to Brook and shook his head. 'Do you know what he's talking about?' Brook was either unable or unwilling to speak.

'He knows,' Jason nodded at Brook. 'Ask him. Annie something. Same night, weren't it, Inspector?'

Brook nodded imperceptibly, finally able to comprehend what he was hearing. So there it was. The pay-off. Six lives lost to clear the slate for Jason. Three murderers, Jason's friends, were dead, unable to drag their accomplice down with them, with Brook, hands tied, unable to put the record straight. Neat. And Brook had thought him stupid.

'Annie Sewell,' he finally said.

'That's her,' nodded Jason cockily.

'Well, this is unexpected,' said Hudson, shaking out a cigarette. Then, remembering he was in a hospital, he slid it quickly behind his ear. 'And it looks like we've found a reason for The Reaper's visit . . .'

'You don't even know her name. You should at least know that.' Brook looked at the floor, unable to meet the triumph in Jason's eyes. 'Stephen's mum died too,' added Brook, trying to pick at a vestige of conscience.

'She weren't no MILF – a right sket, she were,' replied Jason.

'What about her young boy?' Brook spoke wearily, aware of the futility of his question and his search for a dormant indignation.

'Okay, Damen, it's not our job to judge . . .'

'Yeah an' he weren't no saint neither,' added Jason with a shrug. 'Worst o' the lot.'

'Nine years old,' said Brook.

'Still had an ASBO, din' he?' Jason sneered back.

Brook rose from his chair. 'He was hung by the neck.'

Hudson stood in front of him, assuming imminent violence. 'Okay, Inspector. Go and get some air. That's an order. We'll take it from here.'

Brook blinked at Hudson, Grant hovering behind him, aware that his body language was causing concern. He smiled faintly, mimicking Jason's faraway stare.

'Sure.'

*

Outside in the corridor, Grant allowed Brook to walk ahead of her and walked in front of Hudson to slow him down. She engaged her boss with a raised eyebrow.

'Well, guv, one day on the case and we're already in credit,' she said softly.

Hudson shrugged and stepped after Brook. 'We're not here to solve bungled burglaries, Laura.' He caught up to Brook. 'Well, Damen. What's the story on this Annie Sewell?'

'You heard Jason. He was pretty clear.'

'So she was killed the same night as the Wallis family?'

'That's right. But she got lost in The Reaper maelstrom.'

Hudson nodded. 'I can see how she might. Could those lads have killed her?'

Brook came to a halt and looked into Hudson's eyes. 'It wasn't my case. But yes, those lads could've done it.'

213

'Well, that's some measure of justice then,' said Hudson. 'That's a comfort.'

Brook smiled bleakly. 'Right. Three cheers for The Reaper.'

*

'What are we looking for, Mike?'

'You got me, Ed. Maybe I'll know when I see it.' Drexler shone the flashlight around the cabin, consciously avoiding the bloody writing on the wall. Wandering around at night at a deserted crime scene that had offered up over twenty corpses was good reason not to crank up the atmosphere any further.

'It's late,' said McQuarry, resolutely confining her own flashlight to watching her step.

'There must be something to connect, Ed. Assuming the Dodge is at the bottom of a lake, or burned out on some forest track, we can't tie the Ashwells to Sorenson. So we have to tie Sorenson to this cabin. If we can put him here then . . .'

'Then what?'

'. . . we can sweat him.'

'Thought you said he was made of ice,' retorted McQuarry. 'Look, Mike, Latent have been all over this place. They got Sorenson's prints from the garage but no matches in here, none on the wine bottle, nothing. He would've worn gloves. He's not stupid. We got no saliva in the wine, hell, he didn't even leave a glass. There are no footprints we can find, no fibres and no hairs.'

'He doesn't have hair.' Drexler shone his flashlight under the worn sofa then stood upright. He moved into the hall and opened the door to the third bedroom. The smell hit them like a wall of sewage, rancid and sour, and they puckered under its assault.

Drexler ran his fingers over the bolt on the door. 'This feels like it's been forced.'

McQuarry peered at it. 'Maybe Sorenson ransacked the place.'

'Looking for what?'

Drexler shook his head and swept the light around the windowless cell. The thin blanket and dank mattress were at Quantico and had delivered up their grisly secrets. The DNA of the Bailey girls was abundant in this room but nowhere else in the cabin – this had been their prison. Blood, hair, saliva, tears, urine and even traces of excrement were all found on the mattress. Two related females had spent time in this room, the mother, Tania, was not one of them – she'd been raped and then murdered in the clearing, probably in front of her family, according to the profiler. Young Sally had joined her parents a month or so later. They still hadn't found Nicole's grave. They probably never would.

The Ashwells had spent time here too. Their body fluids were all over the bedding, chiefly semen and saliva. Young Billy had evidently been fully initiated into the family pastime. It didn't paint a pretty picture but at least the fact leavened the agents' horror at the memory of Billy's feet scrabbling for solid ground as he dangled from the noose in the garage.

But there was something more. According to Forensics it wasn't just Caleb and Billy who'd been in the room: there were three different sets of DNA, all from the same family. A third male had been present, though less frequently it would seem, and Caleb and Billy's only next-of-kin was Caleb's brother, Jacob Ashwell. It seemed reasonable to assume he was the other participant and a bulletin was issued on him.

Inquiries had found Jacob's last known address in Las

Vegas but he'd since fled. And the fact that he hadn't come forward despite the media attention was telling. The gas station – while no gold mine – was a merchantable piece of real estate and Jacob Ashwell was the sole heir now that the corpse of Caleb's wife Mandy-Sue had been positively identified from her dental records.

Finally Drexler closed the door on the chamber of horrors and continued his tour. He unfolded the Forensics report from his back pocket and read it for the hundredth time. He went into the bathroom and opened the rickety bathroom cabinet with its cracked mirror.

'What are you looking for, Mike?'

'The drugs.'

McQuarry sighed. 'The CSIs went over this place twenty-four/seven for three days, Mike. If they didn't find the drugs then they're not here.'

Drexler looked at the sheet again. 'Billy Ashwell had coffee before he died, laced with hyoscine and traces of morphine. The combination depresses the central nervous system and causes paralysis and amnesia. George and Tania Bailey both received a similar cocktail of drugs before they died.'

'I read the report, Mike. But there's nothing here.'

Drexler sighed. 'Know what I'm thinking? Maybe Sorenson took it . . . for future projects.'

'Good luck getting a search warrant. It's past nine, Mike. I'd like to have some dinner and maybe a drink before I go back and collapse in my welcoming motel room.'

Drexler rubbed a hand over his face, then smiled. 'Sorry, Ed, you're right. Let's get out of here. Dinner's on me.'

'Damn right.'

They closed and locked the cabin door and walked back towards the darkened garage on the highway, Drexler swinging his flashlight and McQuarry greedily lighting a cigarette.

The noise of the forest was deafening and, but for their one pyramid of torchlight, the darkness total.

'It sure is lonely out here, Ed. I can't imagine anyone wanting . . .' Drexler halted in his tracks and swung his flashlight at the scrub on the side of the dirt track. He retraced his steps and got down on his haunches to examine something on the ground.

'What is it, Mike?'

'This hole. It looks freshly dug.' Drexler swung his flashlight over the hole. It was about a foot deep and six inches in diameter. He fingered the soil inside it. 'What do you suppose was buried in there?'

Drexler stepped back and swung his flashlight from side to side. There was a line, an avenue almost, of half a dozen small saplings planted equidistant from each other. The end tree was now missing. He approached the sapling nearest to the hole. The deep green leaves were large and oily, and horn-shaped creamy white flowers drooped towards the ground.

'Unusual. Don't think I've ever seen a tree like this. Know what genus that is?'

'Gee, Mike, is it a Californian Redwood?'

Drexler laughed. 'Sorry, Ed. I'm used to you knowing everything.'

'I know my stomach is grumbling.'

'I wonder what happened to this end tree.'

'There's been heavy traffic on the site, Mike. Maybe one of the ambulances or tow trucks knocked it over.'

He nodded. 'I'm sure you're right.'

*

It was cold, dark and beginning to rain by the time Brook, Hudson and Grant arrived back at the Ingham house. For that reason the crime scene was not as besieged as it might have been. There were still a few gawping locals hanging around the taped-off area, and media organisations were still represented, but the weather and the lateness of the hour had thinned out the crowd.

As Brook pulled the car into the nearest parking space, a few lights and cameras swung in its direction. A few friendly cries hoping to elicit an interview could be heard above the drone of the generators.

'Inspector. What progress are you making, if any?'

Brook turned to see Brian Burton grinning at him. 'No comment at this time.'

'Should I ask the Senior Investigating Officer?' Burton added with a leer. If Burton had been expecting a reaction from Brook, he was disappointed. 'Had a chance to read my book yet, Inspector?'

'I don't read fiction, Brian,' Brook replied coolly and the throng of Burton's colleagues bellowed with laughter. Brook walked calmly past the clutch of journalists and ducked under the tape, following Hudson and Grant to the crime scene. Cameras flashed behind him and Brook was halted in his tracks. Mike Drexler stood at the back of the crowd. He'd only caught a glimpse as the camera flash died, but he was sure it was him. He was standing some way off behind a knot of onlookers and seemed to be smiling in Brook's direction.

Brook stood and waited for the next camera flash. When it came a few seconds later there was no sign of Drexler.

The sound of booing erupting from a small huddle of people beyond the tape distracted Brook's attention. He turned to the group of no more than four people gathered in the dark, at least one of which was an elderly woman.

Hudson and Grant halted and came back towards him. 'What is it?' asked Grant.

'I'm not sure,' said Brook. 'Are they booing *us*?'

Grant narrowed her eyes against the slanting rain. 'I think they are.'

Seeing the three detectives now paying attention to them, the small group of people became more voluble. One shouted, 'Let The Reaper alone. If you can't keep the streets safe, let someone else do it for yer.'

Another shouted, 'Good riddance to the scum. Long live The Reaper.'

And yet another chanted, 'Scum in fear. The Reaper's near. Scum in fear. The Reaper's near.' The chant was taken up by the others.

'Fuck me!' said Hudson, throwing a cigarette into his mouth and continuing towards the house. 'That's a first. Three cheers for The Reaper? You weren't wrong, Damen.' Brook merely grunted.

Once inside the relative comfort of the police marquee, the detectives were joined by Noble.

'I take it you heard the Neighbourhood Watch out there?' asked Noble.

'Hell, yes,' answered Hudson. 'Bizarre.'

'Maybe you wouldn't find it so bizarre if you had to live next to the Inghams, guv,' observed Grant.

'She's right, sir. Door to door all round the estate, everyone we spoke to told us they lived in fear. Seems they were a constant nuisance and worse. The noise, the loud music at all hours, routine thefts, threats. They behaved like they owned the estate. Apparently the little kid was the worst. He was even put up for an ASBO. Nobody would raise their face to them, never mind a hand. And nobody went out without leaving lights and the TV on.'

'So good riddance to bad rubbish, eh?' nodded Hudson.

'It fits The Reaper's MO, guv. Target the troublemakers, the petty criminals,' added Grant. 'Maybe people are seeing the connection now.'

'Connection?' said Brook, fixing her with a look.

'The pattern. After five of these, people are starting to realise that if they're minding their own business and behaving themselves, they're safe. A few less villains on the street – who cares?'

Brook smiled. She caught on quickly. Under his breath he said, 'Nobody cares.'

Only Grant heard him above the background hum of the generators and she turned to him for the first time without hostility, giving him a bleak smile in return.

'Maybe we should piss off back to Brighton then, Laura. Let someone turn this road into a Reaper theme park,' Hudson observed, to his own amusement. 'Thought not. Bring us up to speed, John.'

'Yes, sir.'

'Call me guv, will you, John? Sir makes me sound like a fucking teacher.' Noble looked over at Brook, who affected disinterest. 'What about the bodies?'

'All gone and Dr Habib says he'll have something preliminary first thing in the morning. Forensics too.'

Hudson looked at his watch. 'Hopefully that'll give us something to chew on at briefing.'

'And you know the good news,' said Noble with a glance at Brook. 'We've got a clear thumbprint from the mobile phone. There are a few other smudged marks which are partials of Jason's. But the thumb isn't his. It doesn't match any print on the database. Criminal *or* internal!' he said, with more than sufficient emphasis. But, as if he were addressing first-day cadets, he felt compelled to add, 'DI Brook is in the clear. If there was any doubt.' Noble looked pointedly at Grant, who nodded.

'We never doubted it, did we, Laura?' said Hudson, encouraging his sergeant with a look.

'Not for a second, guv,' she answered in a monotone.

'And did we get anything useful from the street, Sergeant?'

Noble nodded. 'One lead – Mrs Patel, our nosy neighbour from two years ago, said she saw someone standing outside her house, watching the Ingham house. All the streetlights round here have been vandalised so she couldn't give us anything more than she thinks it was a man.'

'Doing what?' asked Brook.

'Like I said – just standing, watching.'

'Sounds promising. What time?'

'Around ten. She watched him for a few minutes and then he moved away.'

'That's a long time to hang around waiting for his opportunity,' said Hudson. 'Risky.'

'May not be our guy,' said Grant.

'If he moved off towards the Wallis house, it might still be him,' said Brook. 'But I agree. If he's using the Wallis house as cover, why stand in the road getting noticed? Anything else, John?'

'Just background. No other witnesses. Every curtain, every blind facing the Ingham house seems to be permanently drawn. Everybody on the Drayfin just wanted to block them out. Getting nosy invited trouble. And it was past one in the morning. Too late for most.'

'Did people hear the music?' said Brook.

'Everybody close by heard it but nobody looked at their clock. It was normal and people were used to tuning it out. One minute it was pounding out, the next morning it had stopped.'

'Pounding?' said Hudson.

'Some kind of rap music was on. Nobody heard the Chair de Lune.'

Brook smiled. 'The Moon Chair, John? No, they wouldn't have. The rap was for the neighbours. Debussy was only for the victims.'

'We found melted plastic in the oil drum. It's probably the CD the Ingham boy had on. My guess is that once they were out cold, The Reaper takes it off, tosses it in the fire and puts his own stuff on.'

'Did you find a case for it, John?'

'For the Debussy, no – could have been on the fire as well. But there's an empty case for a gangsta rapper on the kitchen table.'

221

'What about clothing? Anything dumped nearby?' asked Grant.

'Not that we've found. So far we've got some clear footprints round the barbecue but they match up with the victims' shoes.'

'What about the path and the gate?' said Brook, nodding at the darkened house that backed onto the Ingham house.

'If that's how he got away he left no sign and no one in the next street saw anything either,' replied Noble. 'They've taken the gate away for further tests.'

'No footprints or marks of any kind? With all that blood on him?'

Noble shrugged. 'Not that they can find. There's been some rain.'

'Maybe the killer left the Ingham house at the front?' offered Hudson.

'Then why the blood on the fence at the back?' persisted Brook. 'Did you find out who lives there?'

'Mrs Dorothy North. A pensioner. Lives alone.'

'Did she see or hear anything, anyone in her garden?' asked Grant.

'She's away. That's why the house has been dark through all this.'

'Any idea where?'

'No. Her next-door neighbour,' Noble indicated the house to the left, 'knows only that she's away for six weeks and left two weeks ago.'

'Okay, John. Get Cooper to re-canvass the entire block – both streets. Mrs North might have other friends in the street, so look for people nearer her own age. And check for any relatives. Find someone who knows where she went.'

'Is it important, Damen?' queried Hudson.

'Maybe not. But it's the house backing onto the Inghams and the woman who lives there is away. With The Reaper I tend to be suspicious of helpful coincidence.'

'I thought this was a copycat,' offered Grant, almost smiling.

Brook looked across at her. 'Either way.'

'Is this usual, Damen?' asked Hudson. 'As Reaper crime scenes go.'

'The Reaper always likes to mix it up. Assuming it is The Reaper,' he added with emphasis for Grant's sake.

'You still say it's a copycat?'

'Method can be copied Joshua. And yes, I shall say it's a copy.' *Sorenson's dead.* 'There are too many differences and too much evidence.' *And Sorenson's dead.*

'I mean the phone call for one. The Reaper would never do that.' *And did I mention Sorenson's dead?*

'We'll need to hear more on that in the morning. Okay, let's walk through again.'

For the next half hour the four detectives re-enacted the crime for their own benefit, arguing over a detail here and miming an action there.

Brook, who knew from experience how things had probably played out, watched Hudson and Grant go about their business. He had to admit he was impressed. They seemed well matched, each with differing talents that complemented the other's. They picked up on the significance of certain details and together sometimes came up with ideas that surprised or intrigued Brook. One such idea came to DS Grant as she had stood underneath the skylight in the bedroom ceiling. The rope that had hung the young boy was no longer in situ, having gone to the laboratories along with all the other evidence.

Brook noticed her as she stood gazing up into the roof space for several minutes, a finger twirling a few stray hairs.

'What?' he said.

Eventually she broke her reverie and looked at Brook. 'I'm not sure,' she said. 'But that rope seems desperately random,' she added with a smile that suddenly softened her features.

'How so?' asked Brook.

'Well, you say The Reaper's MO is to kill the child in front of the parents?'

'What of it?'

'But why a rope?' she said. 'He didn't need one to tie the parents up.'

'I don't follow, luv,' put in Hudson, walking over to them on the now bare floorboards.

'Why did he bring a rope?' It seemed a simple question, the significance of which had escaped Hudson and Noble.

Brook's brow, however, creased in thought. 'Why did he bring a rope?' he echoed, as though to hear the question again would help.

'What are you getting at?' asked Hudson.

'Well, you say he has a fairly fluid MO,' Grant reminded Brook, who nodded. 'In Harlesden the parents were tied up and the boy was strangled before being hung from a light fitting. He'd taken rope for the parents, so he already had it there for the kid. That sounds improvised to me. In Brixton a year later the daughter was tied up as well and had her throat cut. He may have taken rope for the parents but didn't need it because they were drugged.' She looked at Brook for confirmation.

'Heroin,' nodded Brook.

'Okay. There was no kid in the Leeds killings – not one that had been born anyway – and the Wallis girl was poisoned and her throat was cut.'

'You've done your homework,' said Brook, starting to see where this was going. 'And you're right. There was no rope at the Wallis house. The drugs did everything the rope could and more.'

'So?' asked Noble.

'So follow the pattern, John. Different MOs in each case.'

'To fool the profilers, you said,' replied Noble.

'Maybe,' agreed Grant. 'But look at how The Reaper's polished his act, how he's evolved. Harlesden and Brixton were twenty years ago, when he was younger and stronger.'

'He's making life easier for himself each time,' nodded Hudson.

'The physical effort required gets harder over the years, so he changes things.'

'But not this time, don't you see?' exclaimed Grant, warming to her subject. 'This time he's back to the rope, lots of physical effort, even brute strength is needed – which would seem to back up Inspector Brook's theory of a copycat.'

'So there's a younger healthier Reaper out there,' said Hudson. 'A disciple.'

Grant smiled and nodded at him. 'Exactly.'

'Seems to make sense,' agreed Noble.

Grant frowned suddenly. 'But even so, why not copycat the later killings? Even for a young guy, a rope isn't that easy to carry to the scene, especially if you don't know how much to bring. And another thing. How did he know he could get access to the roof space to tie it off? Unless . . .'

Brook looked excitedly at Grant. 'You think . . . ?'

'Definitely,' said Grant, catching the mood.

Hudson and Noble could only look at each other.

*

Brook led the way out of the Inghams' master bedroom, down the bare stairs and through the brightly lit backyard to the street. He marched towards the derelict Wallis house, Grant at his shoulder, Hudson and Noble trailing along in their wake.

The uniformed officer on duty outside the Wallis house stiffened and hastily hid the cigarette behind his back as the four detectives approached.

'Inspector,' he said.

'Constable . . .'

'Hopkin, sir.'

'Miserable duty, Constable,' said Brook without evident sympathy. 'Sorry you got lumbered. Why don't you finish your ciggy?'

PC Hopkin wasn't sure how to react. He'd only been in the

Force for a year and didn't know Brook very well, but what he'd heard had all been bad. 'Sir, I . . .'

Brook smiled. 'I mean it. Stand easy and enjoy your cigarette.' He made a play to look around at the deserted streets now that all the spectators and journalists had packed in for the night. 'Who's going to know?' With that, Brook and Grant eased past him and made for the front entrance of the Wallis house. The chipboard from the previous night had been removed by Forensics in the hope of finding some latent prints and Brook disappeared inside first, Grant following.

Hopkin's cigarette remained firmly behind his back until all four CID officers were safely inside the house.

*

Brook's eyes swept round the sparse but now well-lit room where he'd waited for The Reaper the previous night. But instead of the mock-up of the Maples girl's miserable squat, the room was now completely bare, apart from the crime scene lighting and a single wooden chair. The mattress had been removed for further examination by Forensics officers. The picture frame, candle, stove and unopened cans of food had gone to the laboratories too, as had the wine bottle and the glasses from downstairs.

'So there was a mattress here,' said Grant, waving a hand at the bare floorboards, 'and an empty picture frame on top.'

Brook nodded.

'But no picture in it. Why?' She looked expectantly at him.

Brook shook his head, remaining mute. Over the last few hours he was being forced to react to all sorts of information that had once belonged only to him. He wasn't about to open another seam into his past and produce the picture of the girl who had once haunted his dreams . . . not even for Laura Maples's namesake.

Hudson and Noble arrived at the top of the stairs and crowded into the derelict bedroom. 'Why all the excitement?' said Hudson.

Brook and Grant looked around. They both saw the stout wooden chair off in one corner and Grant picked it up to place in the middle of the room.

'The houses on this street are identical, Joshua,' said Brook, watching Grant climb onto the chair. 'That has to help with planning.'

Hudson and Noble turned to follow Brook's gaze and watch Grant lift her latex-gloved hand to the ceiling. She clenched it into a fist and gave the trapdoor a solid jab. At once the board fell on top of her, pushed down by the weight of something lying in the loft space above. She emitted a startled scream, lost her balance and tumbled off the chair, falling towards the floor. Fortunately Brook was well positioned and managed to catch her. He held his hands under her armpits and lowered her to the floor, their eyes locking briefly as her face passed his. Then they all turned to look into the roof space.

A rope tied to a rafter in identical fashion to the one used in the Ingham house had fallen into the bedroom. It swayed through the air gently and, at the business end of the rope, another young boy swung stiffly from side to side, his feet no more than five feet above the floor.

'Fuck me.' Hudson held out a hand to halt the motion of the body, as the noise of everyone's quickened breathing began to ease. He turned the form round and stared into the face with its sightless open eyes, abnormally red cheeks and happy grin. Hudson smiled back at the boy and tapped on his plastic mannequin's head with a knuckle.

'He did a dry run,' said Noble, now able to manage a relieved grin. Brook smiled back at him and Grant joined in. 'That's how he knew how much rope to bring.'

'The clever bastard,' nodded Hudson.

Chapter Thirteen

It was gone midnight when Brook pulled up outside the Midland Hotel to drop off the weary Hudson and Grant. It had been a long day – two days in Brook's case. They exchanged goodnights and Brook pulled away from the entrance and into the deserted streets. A moment later, he turned into a parking bay beside a line of former railway workers' terraced houses and turned off the engine. It was cold and a light rain was in the air again. Winter was on its way.

He stepped out of his car and shook out a cigarette from a near empty pack that had been donated by Hudson. He looked at his watch again. Less than twenty-four hours ago he'd set off to meet The Reaper not knowing what to expect, being sure only that Victor Sorenson wouldn't be on hand to greet him. So why on earth had he gone? He took a pull on his cigarette and faced up to the facts. How could he have stayed away? Whoever was doing this knew that he wouldn't be able to resist. Just as Sorenson would have known.

Brook pondered his options. Dr Habib had been prevailed upon to arrange a seven a.m. meeting to give up his findings on the Ingham killings and Brook debated the value of driving the forty-minute journey home. He'd have a couple of hours' more rest if he went straight back to his office and dozed at his desk rather than drive out to the Peaks.

He dropped the unpleasant cigarette down a sewer grate and

got back into his car. He was about to turn the engine on when in his driver's mirror he saw a figure emerge from the hotel on the other side of the street. He turned around to be sure. There was no mistake: it was Laura Grant. What's more, she was walking his way. Brook wondered what to do. He'd already bade his politest farewells to Hudson and Grant when he dropped them off and his already low reserve of social skills was severely depleted. Laura (he could call her that in his thoughts at least) seemed to have softened towards him as the evidence began to point away from Brook, but he knew she – and Hudson for that matter – would still be harbouring a kernel of suspicion about him, if only in relation to the death of Tony Harvey-Ellis.

He looked in the mirror again and reached for the ignition. But to turn on the engine would draw further attention, with Grant now only twenty yards away.

Feeling a fool, Brook resolved just to sit there and let her pass. If she spotted him, so be it.

A few seconds later, Grant drew level with Brook's car; out of his peripheral vision, Brook could see she had stopped. For a few seconds neither of them moved, then Grant crossed the road towards his car. There was now no doubt she had seen him. He turned to meet her advancing frame, tossed his head back in feigned surprise and lowered his window.

'Sergeant,' he said. 'Still awake?'

She reached his car door and, although not annoyed, she seemed a little puzzled. 'Are you stalking me, Inspector?' she asked with as mild a reproach as she could manage.

Brook grinned now and opened his door to get out. 'Actually no,' he said. 'Why, what are you up to?'

Grant looked at him, thinking. 'I'm about to arrest a kerb crawler.'

'Really? Need back-up?'

She laughed easily, the condensation from her amusement blowing between them. 'No. But what *are* you doing?'

'Honestly? Just thinking things through and wondering whether it's worth driving all the way home. You?'

She studied him for a moment then said, 'Don't laugh, will you? But I'm a bit of an insomniac, especially in the middle of a case. I often walk late at night by the sea. I love it. It clears my head.'

Brook smiled faintly, remembering his many battles with slumber. 'Why would I laugh? Must be common in the job.'

'It's a weakness,' she replied, betraying a hint of self-disgust.

'And you need to be strong.'

'In a man's world? Yes.' She smiled. 'So I handle it.'

'I'm sure you do,' he said. 'Mind if I walk with you?'

She looked at him and considered the question for a moment. 'Why not?'

Brook got out of the car and together they ambled off in the direction Grant had been taking, neither feeling the need to speak. After a few minutes Brook smiled. 'Four words,' he said. 'That was impressive.'

'Sorry?'

'"They're all dead." You said that was four words. In the briefing. You must have noticed everyone looking confused, mentally counting out the words. Most coppers would think it was three words. Some even two. Not you.'

She smiled but not at Brook. 'My dad was a real stickler for that sort of thing when I was at school.'

'Glad to hear it. But I must warn you to be careful about appearing too brainy if you don't want people to dislike you. In the job, I mean.'

'I know – it can cause resentment. I'm not very good at hiding things, I'm afraid.' She flashed a sideways grin at him. 'Like giving you a hard time. You may have spotted that.'

Brook laughed. 'I believe I did.'

'Sorry.'

'No need. That's nothing to the hard time I give myself.'

Grant looked up into his eyes. 'You too? Figures. I wish I could be more like Joshua – DCI Hudson.'

'Oh?'

'You know, relaxed about things. Treat it like any other job. Also he's very clever but he doesn't let it show.'

'He's got the common touch, has he?' smiled Brook.

'I thought you two knew each other?'

'Hardly at all. Mainly through a mutual colleague – Charlie Rowlands.'

'His old boss.' She nodded.

'And mine.'

They walked in a large circle through the darkened city centre of Derby for another twenty minutes, neither talking, simply walking and enjoying the freshness of the night air now that the rain had stopped and the sky had cleared. Brook felt comfortable in Grant's presence and she apparently felt the same.

They arrived back at the Midland's entrance. As Grant prepared to go inside, Brook said, 'If you love walking, Sergeant, you should come up into the Peaks. There's some wonderful scenery.'

She turned back to him and for a split second Brook thought he might have said the wrong thing, might have implied she come to his home and spend the night.

But a moment later she smiled.

'I'd like that.' She turned to go and Brook, already heading for his car, turned back at his name. 'Inspector Brook. Call me Laura.'

He smiled and continued on the way to his car. Laura. Beautiful name.

*

Forty minutes later, Brook pulled the BMW up to the door of his cottage and got out. Drexler's hire car was on the small drive next door and the house was in darkness. He held the car door open for a second then slammed it hard and locked up. He ran his eye over Rose Cottage to see if his lack of consideration had registered. It appeared not. Brook stepped softly onto the neighbouring drive and put his hand onto the bonnet of Drexler's car. It was still warm.

He resisted the urge to bang on Drexler's door and ask him why he'd been at the crime scene. Instead he crept back to his own house and poured a small whisky before heading upstairs. He fell asleep before he'd taken a sip.

*

Noble led the way to Pathology, Laura Grant beside him. Brook and Hudson brought up the rear, trudging in exhausted silence. They made their way to Dr Habib's office. It was seven o'clock, barely light, and after the last twenty-four hours, no one was much in the mood for small talk.

Habib was a short stocky man, in his early sixties and wore round pebble glasses. His unlined chubby face cracked into a soft smile when he saw Noble, though the sight of Brook chilled his cheery welcome somewhat. He hadn't fully forgiven Brook for giving him a hard time during the Wallis investigation.

However, he beamed at Laura Grant with undisguised pleasure. 'And who is this pretty lady you've brought for me to meet, Sergeant?' he said, grasping her hand and shaking it warmly. Grant, well used to the Jurassic outlook of men over a certain age, accepted his gushing with good grace.

'This is DS Grant, DCI Hudson.'

'Ah yes. You've taken over our CID, I hear,' said Habib, finally able to let go of Grant's hand to chortle conspiratorially.

'It's called liaison, Doctor,' insisted Hudson.

Habib grinned with pleasure. 'Indeed it is so. Let's hope you have more luck catching this killer than we had last time,' he added, completely oblivious to the implied insult to Brook and Noble. 'Bad business, bad business.'

'What have you got for us, Doc?' asked Noble.

'Well. It could almost be the Wallis family again it's so similar.

It is the same gentleman, is it not?' he asked with a brief sweep round all their faces, in case of correction.

'We're jumping to no conclusions,' said Grant. 'What you tell us will help determine that.'

'Yes, yes. I see. Well. Let's start with the three boys. Very straightforward really. All killed the same way. In each case the trachea was severed by a very sharp instrument – a scalpel, I gather. Makes sense. As with the Wallis case you're looking for a right-handed individual as the cuts sweep from near the left ear and finish at the right ear. You won't be surprised to hear the wounds were inflicted from behind – that's standard with this kind of slaying. What else? Yes, all three victims were seated and lividity confirms that they died where they were found. I imagine the blood dispersal will show the same.' Habib reached to consult a manila folder. 'Ah yes. Can't be as sure about the killer's height, but no reason to suggest it's any different from the Wallis murders. Below average certainly.'

'Remind us, Doctor,' said Hudson.

'Between 1.70 and 1.74 metres. Five seven or eight for the dinosaurs among us,' he added, with a cold glance at Brook.

'Were they drugged at all?' asked Brook.

'Not by the killer, I think. Plenty of other drugs though. Marijuana, amphetamines. And an enormous quantity of alcohol in the blood – to give you some idea, they were at least five times over the legal driving limit. But the boys, I assume, had self-administered, so perhaps he needed no drugs to control them.'

'So their food hadn't been doctored in any way?'

'Not the undigested meats they had in their stomachs.'

'What about the couple and the boy?'

'That's different. Or rather the same.'

'Same as what?' asked Noble.

'The Wallis family, John,' nodded Brook.

'That is so, Inspector. The Wallis family were poisoned with scopolamine and traces of morphine – our old friend Twilight

Sleep. Although I can find nothing in the males, it was injected into the woman and the child.' Habib turned to Grant and Hudson with an apologetic gesture. 'I'm sorry. You don't know about Twilight Sleep. Let me . . .'

'Actually we do know about it, Doctor,' smiled Grant. 'It was used in a murder in Brighton only recently.' She resisted a sideways peep at Brook.

'Indeed? How interesting. Then you'll know the history of the constituent drugs . . .'

'And that we're looking for a 150-year-old medical man, yeah, Doc,' smiled Hudson, throwing his joke into the mix again, but with less success than before.

'Did the woman's partner not get a dose?' asked Brook.

'No. Only the woman and the little boy – the man had taken a similar cocktail of drugs to the boys outside. The other two had only drunk a little alcohol . . .'

'Even the kid?'

'Oh yes. He would have been quite intoxicated, but he hadn't taken any of the other drugs, just the alcohol. Very strict some of these parents, you know.' He chuckled guiltily. 'There are differences though. The woman and the child received a much bigger dose than the Wallis family. Both would have died regardless of any other injuries; indeed the boy was near death before being hung. There's not enough trauma and bruising around the neck, which you'd expect from a hanging, what with all that struggling. Also there was no sign that his wrists or hands were bound. If the boy had been hanged anywhere near consciousness, the hands would have needed to be immobilised.'

'So the fingers were removed post-mortem,' added Grant.

'Indeed.'

'After he'd been hung?'

'From the angle of the cuts, probably. But you'll be able to determine that from the scene. Any spots of blood where he was hung would point to that.'

'Would a scalpel get through bone that easily?' asked Hudson. 'I mean, wouldn't the killer need some sort of saw?'

'In an adult, maybe. But the boy was only small. The bones in his fingers were young and thin. They wouldn't take much cutting with a precision instrument.'

'Right.'

'As for the adult male and the female in the bed, they were still alive when their windpipes were cut. They had very powerful blood dispersal. But the other difference is the male was killed with a backhand slash.'

'Why was that?'

'With his head against the wall, presumably the killer couldn't get behind him.' The doctor shrugged to signal the end of his contribution. 'Bad business.'

'Would the murderer have been able to revive them before killing them?' asked Noble.

'Not this time. I very much doubt it, Sergeant. Was there any indication that he tried?'

'None!' said Brook, with a glance at Noble.

'Is that significant, Damen?' asked Hudson.

'We think so.'

'Tell me on the way out. Better yet, tell us all at briefing.' Hudson looked at his watch. 'We'd better look lively. One last thing, Doctor – we're going to need a DNA profile from the three dead teenagers. They're suspects in another crime.' Noble raised an eyebrow at this, but Brook pacified him with a glance.

'Of course,' replied Habib.

They turned to leave but Brook hesitated at the door. He looked back at Habib who had already removed his glasses and was wiping them on a clean apron.

'Did you check whether the woman was pregnant, Doctor?'

Habib pursed his lips and replaced his glasses before blinking up at Brook. 'Yes. And no, she wasn't. That's why I didn't mention it,' he added tersely.

Chapter Fourteen

Due to the early hour the noise in the Incident Room was subdued and the yawning quotient high, the strong aroma of coffee testament to the preferred antidote.

The pale sun was just beginning to peep through the high windows, catching the belt of dust orbiting the room. Apart from the Chief Superintendent, only CID officers were present. This time Charlton stood at the back of the room as Brook, Hudson, Grant and Noble collated the information. More photographs were arranged around boards to one side, some of them the grainy snaps downloaded from the mobile phones of the victims.

When they were ready, Brook and Hudson faced the investigation team and silence fell. First Brook invited contributions from subordinates on various tangential aspects of the inquiry that had borne no fruit and Gadd, Morton and Cooper then skipped through the absence of leads from Traffic, Midland Mainline and the bus station. Trains and bus services were more or less nonexistent at the relevant time of night and they'd drawn the expected blank.

As for vehicles, vans were scarce in the early hours of the morning in question. Not one had been stopped or even spotted in the Derby area during the relevant time slot, and those few seen on the M1 had not joined at any of the local junctions, according to the traffic cameras. The same applied to other major access roads, the A52, the A38 and the A50. Van hire checks were ongoing, but without witnesses or a number plate, inquiries were problematic and potentially endless.

The corpses of the Ingham family had now been formally identified by a relative from Alvaston, as had the bodies of two of the boys killed in the yard, who had been named as Benjamin Anderson and David Gretton. Inquiries about family feuds were ongoing but not promising, and the fathers of both Ingham boys had alibis according to DC Jean Keys, who was acting as the Family Liaison Officer. Miss Ingham had had no assets of any importance and there were no financial incentives to murder either her or her boys. Her partner Ryan Harper had even less resources, having been living rent free with Miss Ingham and working casually as a labourer for cash-in-hand jobs on nearby building sites. He didn't even have a bank account.

DC Cooper worked through the inquiries made about single male guests in hotels and B&Bs but, again, there were few leads and those men who did match the descriptions they had for The Reaper either had alibis or had been in Derby on legitimate business.

Brook made his first contribution of the day. 'We may have to rethink on the lone gunman theory.'

Charlton raised an eyebrow. 'Oh? You're saying he had help?'

'He may have, sir. DS Grant spotted it. Laura.'

Grant stood, not noticing DCI Hudson's brief glance at Brook for using his sergeant's first name.

'We don't have the relevant pictures as the SOCOs are still going over the scene . . .'

'I thought they'd photographed everything already.'

'Not the Ingham house, sir, we're talking about the Wallis house a few doors away. The Reaper was there, presumably a few days before the Ingham killings.'

'How do you know?'

'Well, apart from the bottle of wine we found, which was identical to the one from the Wallis killings two years ago, we're now sure he was also in the bedroom. All the houses on the block are of identical design, something we realised last night could be significant. With identical houses, The Reaper could test the hanging in the corresponding bedroom of the Wallis house.'

'I don't follow.'

'He did a practice run using a beam in the Wallis loft and the same length of rope as at the crime scene. The same trapdoor was in the same position, giving the same drop. Even the knot was the same. We found a tailor's dummy just above the trapdoor in the roof space. That's how he knew he could bring rope *and* how much of it.'

'Plus, he might have stored the rope and other stuff in the Wallis loft indefinitely,' added Hudson. 'Helps his organisation. SOCO are going over it now.'

'Interesting,' nodded Charlton. 'But how does that lead you to conclude The Reaper had help?'

'It's not a definite conclusion, sir,' continued Grant. 'But if the assailant is five seven or five eight in height there's no way he could've climbed into the roof space without a leg-up from someone. DI Brook's six feet and even standing on a chair he couldn't pull himself up there.'

'What about a ladder?' asked Jane Gadd.

'There isn't one and he's unlikely to risk bringing and removing such a large piece of kit.'

'So we need to start from scratch on the hotels,' nodded Charlton, peering at DC Bull to be sure he made a note of it. 'I suppose it's too late for the vans.'

Brook nodded. 'Traffic were only looking for single occupancy but, regardless, the road blocks round the estate didn't stop any vehicles leaving at all, sir. Either the killers had already gone or left by other means.'

'Okay. What's next?'

'I played the tape to a linguistics expert at Derby University and although her conclusions come with all sorts of ifs and buts about how short the tape is, we are now starting to think seriously about this killer being a Derby man.' DC Cooper paused at this point to play the 999 call again. Everyone dutifully listened. 'She also says that the owner of this voice is a minimum of fifty years of age – apparently something to do with how speech patterns change from generation to generation.'

'Rob.' Brook nodded at DS Morton.

'The mobile phone belonging to Jason Wallis had some blood droplets from the victims in the yard. Obviously it also carries Jason's prints. However, there was one other print on and around the number 9 button. It was only a partial thumb but, as the phone was used to make the 999 call, we can safely assume it's the killer's. We have enough of a print to obtain a match but we've had no hits from the database, which is significant.'

'Why is that significant?' asked Charlton.

'Most serial killers are in the system for something, sir,' said Grant. 'Killing is generally the tip of the iceberg, the final step in their offending. What's odd is that we're up against someone who's been incredibly careful in the past, but who the other night took off a glove to call the emergency services on a mobile.'

Charlton nodded. 'Point taken. What about prints on the weapon?'

'Only a palm from Jason Wallis but we believe the scalpel had been placed under his hand by the killer, sir. The weapon is a Swann Morton PM60 scalpel,' said DS Jane Gadd, reading from notes. 'It has a heavy-duty stainless steel handle with a standard blade fitment, which includes bull-nose blades for added safety and protection against accidental sharps injuries.' This got an unintended laugh and Gadd couldn't help smiling as well. 'Used by morticians in post-mortems – very common in the NHS and virtually untraceable.'

'Think our suspect is some kind of health worker?' asked Charlton, again unafraid to show his ignorance to get answers to questions that occurred to him.

Brook shrugged. 'It hardly narrows the field but it's possible,' he said trying to keep the doubt from his voice. 'But then why leave the weapon behind to flag that up?'

'Good point.'

Brook looked at the floor briefly, then faced his audience. 'Okay. Sergeant Noble and I have been with DCI Hudson and Sergeant Grant for the last twenty-four hours. We've also spoken to Jason Wallis and, before we came here this morning, Dr Habib. We think we've pieced together a sequence of events. John.'

Noble walked over to the display boards behind him to point at an enlarged photograph. 'This is a Weber One Touch Gold barbecue. It was brand new and according to Jason Wallis it was stolen by the Inghams last week – from where we don't know and neither does he. We've got a call out to various local retailers, B&Q, Homebase and the like to find out. It's possibly stolen from other residents but no one in the canvass mentioned it, and the fact that it's new would seem to be against it.'

'Why does it matter where this barbecue came from?' asked Charlton.

'Maybe it doesn't,' answered Brook. 'But the Inghams acquired this barbecue the week before winning a large selection of meat supplied – we think – by The Reaper. With his MO it's unlikely to be a convenient coincidence. Go on, John.'

'The Ingham family used the barbecue to cook their last meal on the night of the murders. On the eve of the murders someone, we presume The Reaper or his accomplice, rang the Ingham house from an untraceable prepaid mobile phone. According to the Ingham's phone records that call took place at 6.32pm. We don't know the exact contents of the call, but we think it was to tell the Ingham family that they'd won a competition. It's the only call received on the Ingham landline in the two days preceding the killings. We know from text messages that Stephen Ingham texted Jason Wallis to tell him the same thing, and to ask him to come round for a barbecue the following night to celebrate his release.

'Jason Wallis confirmed to us last night that, according to Stephen, the family had won a hamper full of burgers, sausages and kebabs as well as a substantial quantity of beer and cider that was delivered after the call. How and when the delivery was made we've no idea, but obviously that's a question for door to door. Chances are, delivery was made after dark.

'As most of you know, two years ago the Wallis family were persuaded to believe they'd won a free meal of pizzas from a local takeaway. The pizzas had been doctored and so the Wallis family were left defenceless when The Reaper returned to slaughter them. Interestingly, none of the food or drink had been doctored this time but because all the victims had been drinking heavily, even the young lad, it wasn't really necessary. It looks like the food and drink was a tool to concentrate the Ingham family and friends in one location ready for the killing.

'A neighbour, Mrs Patel, claims to have seen a strange man loitering near her garden, which is across the street from the Ingham and Wallis houses. That was about ten o'clock so it may be nothing. Our best guess for The Reaper's arrival is around one o'clock in the morning. He—'

'How does he know the Inghams are going to have the barbecue the same night as he delivers the food?' interrupted Jane Gadd. 'I mean, it's not warm at the moment.'

There was a hush while people cast around for an answer.

'Maybe he didn't know,' said Grant. 'Maybe he was watching and waiting.'

'Where from?' asked Noble.

'There's the Wallis house,' she added.

There was an outbreak of impressed nodding from the CID officers. 'That is a very good thought, Sergeant,' said Charlton.

'Forensics hasn't come up with anything yet to suggest The Reaper spent any significant time in there, sir,' noted Noble.

'It doesn't mean it didn't happen,' said Brook. 'The Reaper of old would have left no trace.'

'Then given us his voice and a thumbprint?' noted Hudson.

Brook nodded. 'It's odd; I still can't explain it.'

'And if he was watching, it would explain why he didn't medicate four of the victims,' said Grant. 'He knew what condition they'd be in.'

Noble continued. 'So The Reaper arrives at the house to find his targets in the state he wants them. It's around one in the morning. There's a thick fog developing. Streetlighting is virtually nonexistent and he knows he's unlikely to meet anyone. Nobody sees him. Maybe he's got a car nearby, but nobody sees or hears that either. Possibly he's travelled the rest of the journey on foot – maybe even on a bicycle. At the moment we have no idea and door to door has produced nothing.

'He's got various pieces of equipment with him that tells us this is no random killer. Most importantly he has a scalpel, not the everyday weapon of choice. You won't be surprised to learn that not a single doctor or surgeon lives on the estate.' There was a ripple of laughter at this. 'Just a nurse and a few hospital workers.

'Okay. The four lads in the yard are unconscious when he enters the yard. We think he gets his Debussy CD from his bag or rucksack ready to play. The classical music is a Reaper signature. He has a length of rope which he puts to one side. He takes off the rap music and puts on his own CD, then takes out his scalpel and cuts the throats of Stephen Ingham and the Gretton and Anderson boys. In what order we're not sure yet, but we know they died before the couple and the lad because of the bloody smears in the house and transference onto the victims upstairs from gloves – latex probably. Also the boys would be the most able to defend themselves if they came round, so he has to get them out of the way.'

'But he leaves Wallis alive?' queried Charlton.

Noble shrugged. 'We can't explain it.' He paused, waiting for further interventions before continuing. 'After he kills the three teenagers he heads up to the main bedroom with the rope. Even though both the kid and the mother have been drinking, they would be unlikely to have drunk as much as the men so, probably as a precaution, the killer drugged them. But unlike two years ago he injected the victims directly into the neck, so obviously he has a syringe, maybe two.

'He covers Chelsea Ingham's mouth with his hand and injects her with a mixture of scopolamine and morphine, the same combination of drugs used to disable the Wallis family two years ago. It's a powerful and toxic narcotic that would have subdued her almost immediately.

'The dose is enough to kill her within half an hour if he wants to just leave her to die. Then he moves around the bed and cuts Ryan Harper's throat, this time with a backhand slash across the windpipe – he can't get behind him because the bed's up against the wall. While Harper's dying the killer goes into the boy's bedroom. He injects a lethal dose of the same cocktail of drugs into D'Wayne Ingham's neck and leaves him while he goes back to the main bedroom to set up the rope.

'He uses a chair, and/or possibly an accomplice, to help him climb into the loft space and tie the rope around a beam. The noose is already tied and the rope is just the right length because the killer has already tested his method in the derelict Wallis house.

'He goes back to the boy's bedroom and carries him through to the main bedroom and hoists him into the noose. According to Dr Habib, the boy was dead or on the point of death when he was strung up so The Reaper can do what he likes. He cuts off the boy's index and forefinger and puts them in a breast pocket, in a copy of the MO used in Harlesden, the first Reaper killing in 1990.'

'Why copy the MO in that killing?' asked Gadd. 'With the rope it makes it much harder. Why not copy the later murders? They were more polished.'

Brook looked up wearily. 'Harlesden was the first. I think that's why.'

Charlton's brow furrowed. 'I don't understand.'

Brook caught his eye. 'Whoever's doing this wants to tell us something.'

'What?' replied Charlton with a hint of exasperation in his voice.

'That The Reaper is starting again,' nodded Grant. 'That this could be the first of many.'

'Christ.' Charlton looked aghast.

Brook nodded at Noble.

'With the boy now in the noose, The Reaper replaces the chair against the wall then cuts Chelsea Ingham's throat, to pre-empt the drugs that would have killed her . . .'

'Why bother?' asked Morton.

'For effect,' answered Brook for Noble. 'It's what he does. The adults are more responsible. They deserve the humiliation and their corpses have to be defiled.'

'You seem very sure of that, Inspector,' Charlton said. 'But I suppose you've been carrying his profile around for twenty years, so we'll bow to your psychological insight.' Brook declined to thank him for the endorsement. 'What then?'

'Then he's back down to the kitchen. He uses Stephen Ingham's blood to write "SAVED" on the wall,' continued Noble. 'There are smudged marks around his neck to suggest someone dipping fingers into the wound. He places the scalpel under Jason's hand . . .'

'To frame him?' asked Jane Gadd.

'We can't think of any other reason, but it does seem a pretty lame attempt,' answered Brook. 'It took us about two minutes to clear Wallis.'

'But speaking to Wallis last night, we do now have a possible motive for the murders and an idea as to why Wallis was spared,' said Hudson. Brook pursed his lips and stared at the floor. 'Jason told us last night that the three teenage victims were responsible for the murder of an Annie Sewell two years ago, the night Jason's family were murdered. We're arranging for a DNA profile from the three lads and will look into it.'

'It doesn't explain why The Reaper didn't kill Jason as well,' said Noble. 'He's still a potential witness.'

'He's being kept alive,' said Laura Grant. Brook looked up at her. He gave her a half-smile of approval, which she noted with a glance.

'Why?' asked Charlton.

'I've no idea,' said Grant. 'But that's twice he's been saved despite being at The Reaper's mercy.'

'Is that what the blood message refers to?' said Charlton.

Brook considered the value of sharing information exclusive to him and decided it could do no harm. 'I don't think so, sir. "SAVED" refers to us, the community. The Reaper sees himself as a soldier of sorts. He's killing families like the Inghams to save *us* from *them*. And he seems to have found his audience. There isn't a resident on the estate who hasn't expressed pleasure, or at least relief, that the Inghams are dead.'

'Scum in fear, The Reaper's near,' chipped in Hudson. Charlton turned to stare at him. 'Not my words, Chief Superintendent, a group of residents who were at the scene. They were chanting it at us last night.'

'When they weren't booing us,' added Noble.

'I see,' said Charlton, tight-lipped. 'Well, if those residents want to share their feelings with the world that's their business but I don't want to hear of any member of this division repeating that little ditty or they'll answer to me. Understood?' The whole room nodded as one. 'Move on.'

'Finally,' resumed Brook, 'the killer finds Jason's mobile phone and breaks with all previous Reaper method by using it to call 999 – and he does it within earshot of Jason.'

'He does?' asked Noble.

'When we spoke to Jason he said he heard what was said. "They're all dead",' said Brook softly.

'Christ. It must have put the shits up him,' observed Morton. 'Sorry, sir,' he added in response to Charlton's glare.

Brook decided not to correct Morton. Jason's almost casual reaction and subsequent behaviour was something he hadn't yet been able to work out. A thought popped into Brook's head and his brow creased in sudden confusion. It was such an obvious anomaly, yet it hadn't occurred to him until now.

'Anything else, Sergeant?' asked Charlton.

'Only the exit route. Our killer doesn't leave the Ingham property by the front but climbs over the shiplap fence panel separating the Ingham house from the adjoining property. The house belonging to a Mrs North is unoccupied and there were no signs of forced entry so we assume the killer ran through to the adjoining street, Drayfin Park Avenue, to make his escape. He leaves blood transference from some of the victims on top of the fence and fibre from his clothing. We're hoping for his genetic material but nothing so far.'

'Why did he go out over the fence and leave us all this evidence?' asked Gadd. 'That's a young man's getaway.'

'Having called emergency services and left the line open he has to think the cavalry are on their way,' answered Noble, deciding not to mention Brook's arrival. He looked over at Grant, who seemed aware of the omission, and they both looked over at Brook. He seemed lost in thought.

'What other leads do we have?' asked Charlton, glancing at his watch.

'There are some indistinct bloody footmarks on the carpets and the kitchen lino, sir,' continued Noble.

'Footmarks not footprints,' said Charlton.

'Yes, sir. We're assuming the killer wore plastic overshoes. We might still get a shoe type and size but it will be more difficult. The boffins are working on it. Provisionally they believe the suspect wore some kind of sports shoes, size between 7 and 9.'

246

'If there are two of them, maybe it's both sizes,' observed Jane Gadd to another round of silent nodding.

'That it?' asked Charlton.

'No, sir. From the Wallis house, we have a bottle of wine, freshly opened but not drunk. As DS Grant mentioned it's the exact same vintage and source as the wine used two years ago. Nuits St Georges from Burgundy. In France,' Noble added for the benefit of the detective constables. 'No prints on the bottle or the glasses; also none on the empty picture frame, the mannequin, candle or anything in the Wallis house. They're still working though.'

'Anything on the food and drink from the Ingham house?' asked Charlton.

'We tracked down several of the alcohol batch numbers to a cash and carry in Leicester which supplies various off-licences and corner shops in Derby. The booze was bought in small quantities from at least five of these outlets over a period of time, making it impossible to trace purchases. Another pointer to a local killer. No luck at the butcher's, nobody remembers the purchase and no receipts match exactly so it's the same story as the alcohol.'

'Anything else, Sergeant?'

'Only that according to our sequence of events, Miss Ingham couldn't have watched her son die. Inspector Brook and I believe that to be significant.'

'Oh? Inspector Brook?' All heads turned to Brook.

Brook seemed lost in thought still. From somewhere the question materialised in his mind and he roused himself to answer. He spoke slowly, deliberately. 'Two years ago the Wallis parents had been drugged, but were revived to see their daughter murdered. They cried, knowing they were next. The same applied to Sammy Elphick and his wife in Harlesden, even though they'd been tied up. We found the salt track marks on their cheeks. It's a Reaper signature.

'In Brixton, Floyd Wrigley and his. . . . girlfriend were pumped full of heroin so they couldn't know what was happening to them or their daughter. They couldn't cry so the girl was killed without ceremony.' After a pause Brook added, 'The parents too. But usually The Reaper wants the parents to suffer for the misery they've caused, the dysfunctional example they've set their offspring. He wants them to know that they and their family will be wiped off the face of the earth. But as they die he gives them a gift, a sight or sound of something which represents the very best of what mankind has to offer – a great piece of art or a beautiful piece of music. Like Clair de Lune or Beethoven's Ninth or a Van Gogh print – something to tell them what they should have aspired to. But Miss Ingham and her partner were killed without being made to face either the son's death or the consequences of their actions in life. They didn't know they were about to die so there were no tears. That's why I believe it's a copycat.'

There was silence for a while as Brook's words sunk in, then Charlton and Hudson drew things to a close and the room became a hub of noise and activity as officers renewed their coffees or snuck out for cigarettes. Only Brook remained unmoving at the eye of the hurricane, staring into the distance. Noble had seen this before and broke away from briefing DC Bull to speak to him. Laura Grant was there a second before him.

'Inspector Brook?' she said, laying a hand on his shoulder.

Noble joined the intervention. 'Sir?' No reaction. Noble and Grant looked at each other, both unsure what to do.

Before they could ponder their next step, Brook spoke softly, to no one. 'They're all dead.'

'Sir?'

Brook looked up and saw the two sergeants in attendance. He smiled as though noticing them for the first time. '"They're all dead." That's what the voice said. Jason heard him. We heard him.'

'So?' prompted Noble.

Brook's smile faded and he shook his head. 'But they weren't, were they?'

Chapter Fifteen

Brook and Grant walked through the drizzle, eyes fixed to the floor to avoid the potholes and puddles. A splenetic pit bull marked their progress as they passed one house, yelping and straining at its chain. Brook checked Noble's text message, with Grant's amused assistance, and surveyed the small, redbrick semi. He had the correct address. Number 197 had a paved front yard and a simple wooden fence that was in a better state of repair than that of most of its neighbours. The barrenness of the yard was counterbalanced by the throng of multicoloured figurines on the sill of the front bay window – an area that could reflect the artistic expression of the household without fear of theft or vandalism. Brook could see several porcelain horses, dogs, ballerinas, cars and an amusing series featuring the same dishevelled leprechaun fishing, sleeping under a tree or leaning inebriated against a lamppost.

'I'll have five pounds on dogs playing snooker,' said Grant, mysteriously.

Brook had no idea what she was talking about but smiled anyway. He lifted the latch on the gate and walked towards the side door, which was slightly ajar. Steam drifted through the crack and the smell of boiled cabbage wafted across the divide to assault their nostrils. The door was opened further at their approach and a stout woman, well into her pensionable years, beckoned them in. She had a small wiry goatee and a full head of wild grey hair swept back in a purple scarf.

'Come in, sir. Come in, sir.'

'Mrs Petras? I'm DI Brook, this is DS Grant. We'd like to ask you a few questions about Mrs North.'

'Yes, yes, come in, sir, come in.'

Despite the lack of a personal invitation, Grant followed Brook into the tiny kitchen. She wasn't offended by her nonexistence; it happened a lot with the older generation. They always addressed Hudson when they were on a call in Sussex and would often not speak directly to Grant at all. Mrs Petras was not only old school but old country – Ukrainian in fact – and men came first.

'Hello, hello,' smiled Mrs Petras, offering her hand to Brook and shaking his hand briefly. 'Please go through to sitting room. I bring coffee.'

'There's no need . . .' began Grant but was interrupted by Brook.

'Thank you, Mrs Petras. We'd love a cup,' said Brook. He was keen to escape the kitchen which was stifling from the steam carrying the last of the cabbage's flavour. He turned to follow Mrs Petras's direction towards a small back room with a table and four padded chairs. In the main room at the front of the house sat a frail old man, who either couldn't or wouldn't acknowledge their presence. He sat in pyjamas and slippers and had a blanket wrapped around his legs, in spite of the electric fire glowing from the hearth. Gaze unbroken and chin on chest he was staring at a TV with pictures but no sound. Several people in a TV studio were pushing and shoving each other above the caption: 'My partner's mum is having my baby.'

'Hello, sir.' There was not a flicker of response to Brook's greeting.

Mrs Petras pushed past them and pulled the door of the front room closed. 'Please sit. No mind Jan. He not hear you. Just back from hospital.' She pulled her apron up to her eye and wiped away a speck of moisture, then gestured to them once more to sit. They went through to the tiny sitting room in which there was barely room to pull back the chairs, but Brook and Grant just about managed to slide their way onto a seat.

There was an ashtray in the middle of the table with several torn up cigarettes and unwrapped filters. Brook recalled his university days when his limited finances had meant he'd been forced to smoke rollups of old dog ends. He took out his own nearly full pack and looked up at the wall behind Grant. It was covered in a mixture of bright little trinkets and sepia photographs of stern-looking men and women. The largest picture was a print of several dogs sitting at a poker table, green visors on heads, playing cards. He indicated it to Grant with a flick of the head.

'You owe me five pounds,' he said softly.

She smiled. Something about the place made them feel they had to communicate in mime and whispers, and she was trying to communicate her reluctance to sit drinking coffee when Mrs Petras came in with a tray of cups filled with a tar-like black liquid.

Being the inferior, Grant was served first and she smiled her thanks. When Brook had received his cup he refused her offer of a pink cake from a plate of fancies, took out a cigarette and offered one to Mrs Petras. She accepted his offer eagerly and, after Brook had lit both their cigarettes, inhaled with a sigh of pleasure. The tiny room was instantly awash with smoke and Grant wafted her hand to fight for some unpolluted oxygen.

'You talk about Dottie,' said Mrs Petras, taking a gargantuan pull on her cigarette. 'She good woman. Keep me company, have tea when Jan . . .' She broke off to keep her emotions in check.

'She's gone away,' prompted Brook.

'Yes. Australie. I very pleased for her. She not seen her brudder sixty year. He in Sydney. She win competition . . .' She pulled urgently on the cigarette again.

Brook's eyes narrowed. 'Competition?'

'Yes. Someone come see. Say she win flight to Australie. All spends. Very nice. No pay a penny.'

Brook looked over at Grant. 'Do you know who came to see her?'

'No. People. She win competition and they look after house. Pay for taxi Manchester. All spends. She deserve. Very happy.'

'So these people. How many were there?'

'Not know. Not see. Maybe one, maybe two. Very happy.' She took a final pull on her cigarette then delicately stubbed it out in the ashtray for future consumption.

'But they took Mrs North's keys?' said Grant.

'Yes. They look after house. Part of prize. I do but for Jan. Need me here.'

Brook drained his coffee and prepared to leave.

'Do you have a spare set of keys to Dottie's house, Mrs Petras?' asked Grant.

'Yes. I get,' Mrs Petras answered, addressing Brook much to his amusement. 'Glad she away. Horrible things happen. Tank God horrible people die.' She looked around for somewhere to spit but thought better of it and instead made the sign of the cross. 'Must not say. All from God. Sorry.'

'Don't be,' said Brook. When she went to fetch the keys he added, 'Nobody else is.'

*

After phoning Noble to update him about Mrs North, Brook and Grant walked back towards the crime scene.

'So the house opposite the Inghams is empty for a reason,' said Grant.

'So much for luck and coincidence,' replied Brook. 'It's all been arranged well in advance.'

Grant nodded. 'I'm beginning to see why The Reaper's been at large for so long. The scope of this is breathtaking. Not to mention the resources behind it.'

Brook stood by the gatepost of Mrs North's house waiting for Forensics to arrive. He patted his coat pocket for his cigarettes.

'You left them at Mrs Petras's house, Inspector. I saw you drop them under the table.'

'Did I?'

'If you felt that sorry for her, why not just offer them some money?' inquired Grant.

'They're not kids standing outside an off-licence Laura,' he said. 'I didn't want her to lose her dignity.'

Laura Grant smiled and held her eyes on the back of Brook's head as he turned towards the Scientific Support van pulling up outside Mrs North's house. Noble approached them from the Ingham house, his mobile in his hand.

'It's legit, sir. Dorothy North did get on a plane to Sydney two weeks ago. The return flight is due back in a month. The ticket was bought in her name on a prepaid credit card assigned to a Mr Peter Hera – our old friend The Reaper using his anagram again.'

Brook smiled at Grant and explained. 'Two years ago The Reaper used that name to hire a van. He turned back to Noble. 'How much was the ticket?'

'Three grand.'

'Christ,' said Grant. 'What the hell are we dealing with here?'

Brook said nothing. If he didn't know that Sorenson was already dead . . .

'If she's in the way, wouldn't it have been easier to just bump her off?' shrugged Noble.

For some reason Brook took umbrage at this. 'An innocent old lady. The Reaper would never stoop to something like that.' Brook examined the house keys given him by Mrs Petras. 'This looks like the one.' He handed them to the lead Scene of Crime Officer. 'Quick as you can, Colin.' He missed the look of reproach from beneath Colin's protective mask.

*

'What are we looking at?' asked Brook, bending down to peer at the stain at the rear of Mrs North's house.

253

'Oil,' said Colin, through his mask. 'Two different spots. Here and here,' he said pointing. 'It's Three in One.'

Brook looked around the backyard. They were on a small pathway culminating at the kitchen drain. Beyond that, the yard was paved around a bordering flower bed with a few desultory plants trying to survive. There was no shed. 'From what?'

'Best guess – mountain bikes.'

Brook nodded. 'Two separate stains, maybe two bikes propped side by side. Perfect getaway. How do we know they're mountain bikes?'

Colin pointed at a colleague a few yards away preparing a bucket of plaster of Paris. 'We've got a tyre impression near that bush.'

Brook nodded and stood upright. 'How long before I can get in the house?'

'Half an hour.' Colin walked away.

'Okay. Good work, Colin,' Brook said after him, a second later. 'Thank your team for me.' A raised latex hand was the only acknowledgement. Brook turned to see Grant's smile. 'What?'

*

'Two bikes, two perps,' nodded Hudson, sipping his tea in Charlton's office. 'You were right, Laura. Nice catch.' Charlton, Brook and Noble nodded in agreement.

'So assuming Mrs North isn't The Reaper and is unlikely to own a mountain bike, let alone two, where are we?' asked Charlton, seated behind his desk. His eyes alighted on the four detectives one by one.

'We're in awe, sir. That's where,' said Grant finally.

'Why so?'

Brook took a deep breath. 'The scale of the planning that's gone into this is so meticulous that it almost makes me begin to doubt that we're dealing with a copycat. Leaving aside the elementary blunder of leaving us a fingerprint and the traces of his DNA from the fence panel, I'd say this was planned as thoroughly as any previous Reaper killing. If not more so.'

'Go on.'

'Two weeks before the Inghams die, the killer or killers spend a small fortune persuading Mrs North, an elderly widow, to move out of her house and go to Australia for six weeks. All expenses paid. Somehow they know she had a brother in Sydney that she hasn't seen in years. The house is to be looked after as part of the prize and they take a set of keys. It's perfect. They have time to prepare and quietly amass all they need in Mrs North's house, so they didn't need to risk storing things like the rope and the barbecue in the derelict Wallis house.'

'I thought the Inghams stole the barbecue?' interrupted Charlton.

'They did and they didn't,' said Grant.

'Explain.'

'It's so simple, sir, it makes me want to cry with admiration,' she continued. 'SOCO found the box and all the packaging for the Weber in Mrs North's house. So instead of wheeling it round to the Ingham house or risk being seen delivering it, they just let them have it.'

'I don't follow,' said Charlton.

'What's the best way to get something nicked on the Drayfin, sir?' asked Noble.

Charlton thought for a minute then shook his head. 'Tell me,' he said with a hint of shame in his voice.

'Carelessness. They just left it out in the backyard in plain sight – probably the week before the murder, I'd say,' said Brook. 'Mrs North's yard backs onto the Inghams' . . .' He shrugged as though the rest were too obvious for words.

'. . . and all they had to do was wait for one of the boys to see it, knowing they'd just help themselves,' concluded Grant.

'They probably even watched from an upstairs room to make sure,' said Noble.

'It's brilliant,' conceded Charlton.

'And when the Inghams won the meat from the phoney competition, the killers knew the Inghams would have something to cook it on . . .'

'And, as they're watching, they can see when they're going to cook it,' added Hudson.

Charlton nodded. 'Okay, I'm impressed.'

'It gets better,' said Grant. 'We found plastic wrappers for a tray of premium cider in Mrs North's house.'

'So . . .'

'We have a theory why no one saw any deliveries of food and drink,' said Brook. 'The killers have bought everything in advance, long before it was needed and transported it to Mrs North's house. The day before the murder, we know from Stephen's text to Jason that the Inghams had won a competition and were expecting a delivery, let's say sometime later that evening or the next day. Now The Reaper knows for sure someone's going to be at home waiting for their winnings. When it's darker, the killer or killers carry all the stuff from Mrs North's front room to the bottom of their yard. The Reaper knocks on their door. Or maybe even waits in the yard for someone to come outside, then calls over the fence. "Hey, are you expecting a delivery of meat and booze because it seems to have been delivered here by mistake?" Then they just hand it over.'

'It's beautiful,' agreed Hudson.

'Wouldn't they be suspicious of a neighbour handing over this stuff? Especially someone they don't know,' asked Charlton.

'Not enough to refuse them,' said Grant. 'They're on benefits after all. And the killer or killers could easily pass themselves off as relatives looking after Mrs North's house.'

'Don't forget people like the Inghams think all honest people are stupid,' observed Hudson. 'They wouldn't be suspicious of anyone. They'd probably have contempt for them. They certainly wouldn't be afraid.'

'So everything's in place,' nodded Charlton.

'Now all they have to do is watch and wait,' said Brook draining his coffee. 'The Inghams fire up the barbecue the next night and our killers start to prepare. They fill their syringes and prepare the rope. They're wearing some kind of protective clothing, gloves, overshoes, hairnets – assuming they have hair.'

'Like our own Scene of Crime clothing?' asked Charlton.

'Very likely,' agreed Brook. 'As a further precaution, key rooms in the house are covered with sheets to collect hair and fibres just in case. They touch nothing without gloves on and never put on a light.'

'Hang on. If the killers have access to Mrs North's house for two weeks, why don't they practise the hanging in *her* bedroom?' asked Noble.

'Mrs North's away and her next-door neighbour knows it,' replied Brook. 'Any noise could end up with the police being called. If anyone hears them in the Wallis house they'll think it's just kids.' Noble nodded. 'Now as soon as the barbecue is lit they spring into action and move down to the kitchen. They bring all the sheets down and carefully fold them into two backpacks or something they can carry with them and still cycle.'

'How do you know they put down sheets if they took them away?' asked Charlton.

'They left a new one behind in the kitchen, still in the plastic,' said Noble.

Charlton nodded. He wondered fleetingly whether to ask if they'd checked the wheelie bin outside but managed to stop himself. 'What then?'

'The bikes were kept in the living room – there's a small trace of oil on the carpet there. When all's quiet they wheel them outside, leave them out of sight from the road for a quick getaway. They wait for the boys to pass out. They lock the house and climb over the fence to the Ingham house. The rap music should

257

cover any noise. And maybe they put a sheet on top of the fence as an added precaution . . .'

'Then why have we got fibres and DNA from it?' asked Noble.

'I don't know. Maybe something went wrong and they had to hurry, but that's what I'd have done.' Brook remembered the few seconds after arriving at the crime scene. The feeling of being watched, coldly, scientifically, like a lab rat caught in a maze.

'One of them has already been to the Wallis house with the wine and glasses,' continued Grant. 'He just has to open the wine and go upstairs to light the candle and it's all ready for DI Brook.'

'And the point of that?' asked Charlton staring at Brook.

'Take your pick, sir. Maybe they were trying to spook me, maybe they were trying to frame *me* instead of Jason.'

'Then why not lure you to the Ingham house? And at the right time?' asked Hudson.

Brook shook his head and looked at the floor.

'Maybe they wanted you there when they were done,' said Grant. 'To humiliate you.'

Brook glanced up and held her gaze. 'Maybe.'

'So then what?' said Charlton.

'Then it's all on,' said Hudson.

'We think that both killers are present when the boys have their throats cut, just in case someone comes round. Maybe one is ready with a syringe while the other does the cutting. It makes life easier if they both go upstairs as well,' added Grant. 'Which would explain the different size footmarks in the house.'

'Once they've finished in the bedroom they go back down to the kitchen. One of them writes "SAVED" on the wall, dipping his latex fingers in Stephen Ingham's blood.' Brook stopped now, not sure how to go on. They all looked over at him. 'And this is where it gets a bit hazy. Maybe they get careless. Why, I don't know.'

'Panic?'

'It hardly seems possible but there it is. Anyway, the scalpel is placed under Jason's hand, maybe a last-minute idea to frame him, but how people this meticulous think that's ever going to stand up to examination beats me.

'Even more out of character they find Jason's mobile phone and, incredibly, one of them takes off a glove and rings 999, leaving us a print and his voice on tape.' Brook shook his head before continuing. 'They leave the phone on Jason's lap, not realising he's heard the phone call—'

'Jason didn't mention two killers when we spoke to him,' interjected Hudson.

'Maybe he didn't see both of them,' surmised Brook.

'The amount of drugs and alcohol in his system, I'm surprised he saw anything, guv,' added Grant.

'I suppose,' conceded Hudson. 'What then?'

'That's it. They vault back over the fence, depositing DNA and fibres on the top. They stuff their protective clothing into their rucksacks and ride away.'

'Where to?'

'No idea for now,' answered Brook. 'A van maybe. Parked a few miles away.'

'None were spotted by Traffic,' said Noble.

'Maybe they slept in it. Left the next morning,' said Hudson. 'But why don't they kill Jason? It still makes no sense.' Brook shook his head again.

'Maybe the sight of what they'd done started to affect them,' offered Noble.

'Both of them – after killing six people in cold blood?' queried Grant. Noble accepted this dismissal with a shrug.

'And were they so affected that after the 999 call they left the line open so we could run a trace and charge over there?' added Hudson.

'It's out of character,' nodded Noble.

'As is the killer's memory loss,' added Brook.

'What do you mean?' asked Charlton.

259

'"*They're all dead.*" That's what the killer said, sir,' explained Noble.

'What of it?'

Grant turned to him. 'Jason Wallis was alive.'

All heads except Brook's bowed for a few minutes to consider this anomaly. Finally Hudson broke the silence. 'I suppose Jason may not have been on the killer's hit list so they didn't count him.'

'That doesn't explain why they didn't kill him,' said Charlton. 'Surely these Reapers, whoever they are, have to consider that he's likely to be cut from the same cloth as the others.'

'And, more importantly, he's a living witness,' added Grant. 'Sorry, guv, but in their shoes what's one more body?'

*

Brook, Noble, Hudson and Grant walked with Charlton to the media room for the four o'clock briefing. Hudson and Charlton stepped inside to face the assembled media. Charlton had been fully briefed, more fully than he'd really wanted, because he now knew things he would have liked to share with the world in order to show his division, and perhaps himself, in a favourable light. But to his credit he would stick to the script.

His appeal for witnesses to any unusual events on the Drayfin Estate *up to two weeks before* the murders unleashed a volley of follow-up questions, which he batted away with all the skill of the political animal.

The investigation team was now seeking *two* individuals who had spent the two weeks previous to the murders bringing occasionally bulky items to Mrs North's house on Drayfin Park Avenue, the road adjacent to Drayfin Park Road, site of the Ingham crime scene. The mountain bikes and the brand new Weber barbecue were the most distinctive items that the public may have seen. And the perpetrators may have either cycled their bikes to this safe house or transported them on a car.

Brook, watching from the sidelines, felt sure that the bikes would have been ridden to Mrs North's house in the dead of night. The barbecue, however, would be more difficult and the appeal might just produce witnesses to its arrival.

*

A half hour later, Brook and Grant led a short debriefing for the dozen CID officers involved in the inquiry. Although the Forensics leads were strong, most of that evidence would only be of use once a suspect had been identified. Other leads hadn't panned out. They were no nearer identifying a shoe type or size from the blood-smeared footmarks left at the Ingham house, despite the use of an electrostatic mat.

Although he hadn't mentioned it to the other officers, Noble had taken Brook aside before the briefing to tell him that the email he'd received purporting to be from Victor Sorenson could not be traced. Brook had expected nothing less.

The bottle of wine had not been purchased locally and Brook believed it had to be from the same case as the one brought by Sorenson to Derby two years previously. The link with Sorenson worried him. If they were dealing with a copycat killer, why did so many things point back to Brook's original Reaper suspect? The wine, the financial resources, the meticulous planning. He thought back to the Wallis investigation when he'd wondered if Sorenson's cancer had made it necessary for him to bring an assistant to help carry out the murders. Could Sorenson now have handed the baton to a trainee Reaper? The idea was becoming more attractive by the day. Somebody younger, perhaps overseen by a more experienced individual with a background in law enforcement. Someone like Drexler.

The search for hotels and B&Bs that had housed two men on or around the night of the murder was not proving fruitful and Brook told Rob Morton to cross it off the list. Once the killers had made the call to the Inghams the day before the murder,

Brook was sure that he, or they, would have been holed up in Mrs North's house, waiting for the off. And there was no telling how long they'd been staying there. Perhaps several days.

All grates, dustbins, manhole covers and even three skips within a five-mile radius of the Ingham house had been searched and nothing of interest found. Every garden on the two-street block had been fingertip-searched and this had also produced nothing. Brook was able to produce a cast of the mountain bike tyre taken from Mrs North's garden and directed Uniform branch to concentrate on all likely, and then unlikely, cycle routes out of the estate. But given the design of the estate and its proximity to fields, there must have been a hundred different escape routes avoiding the roadblocks on major arteries.

The meat packaging had shown that the burgers, sausages and kebabs had been bought from a local butcher, Moorcrofts, in nearby Normanton, which didn't have CCTV or any credit or debit card details for a similar purchase. The clear inference was the meat products must have been bought with cash and in small batches, which made it much harder to pinpoint a time of purchase and pointed to a local killer who could stockpile the meat at home in a freezer.

Brook was about to bring things to a close when DS Gadd ran in carrying a laptop.

'Got something, sir.' She opened her laptop to show a series of indistinct images similar to those PC Duffy had taken with Brook's mobile phone camera at the crime scene.

'What are we looking at?'

'We've uploaded everything from the phones of the three deceased teenagers. These images were shot on Jason's phone the evening they died. About seven hours before. I've compiled them in chronological order.' She clicked her keyboard to start a slideshow.

Brook and the other officers watched intently as the pictures showed a young Asian boy on the ground, clearly in distress and surrounded by the Ingham boy, Gretton and Anderson, who were kicking and taunting him while adopting the poses glorified by American gang culture. The shots continued until Ingham bent over the victim and dragged something across his face. The final shots showed the three Drayfin boys laughing as the Asian boy covered his face with bloodstained hands.

Gadd froze the slide show and dropped a clear plastic bag onto the table. It contained a Stanley knife. 'This was recovered from Stephen Ingham's room, sir. There's human blood on the blade and none of it is a match for any blood found at the crime scene. It looks like he used it to cut this boy's face.'

'Happy slapping,' said Noble. 'What a shame three of them are dead.'

Grant nodded. 'It's a turf thing. Keep out of our territory or get marked. Gangs like to cut the cheek. There's more blood.'

'So we have another motive,' observed Brook. 'The waters are getting muddier. Good work, Jane. Take DC Cooper and check the hospitals. It shouldn't be too hard to track this lad down. Everyone not manning the phones hits the streets again.' Groans followed. 'I know. But you heard the Chief Super's briefing. We have more questions for Drayfin's good citizens. Just think of the overtime.'

*

Brook pulled his coat tightly around him. November was underway and at this time of night, with a moonless sky, the estate was dark and forbidding. Every door he and Grant had knocked on had opened only after a lifted curtain and a shout through the door.

'Mrs Patel? DI Brook.' Brook smiled reassuringly at the face squinting through the inch of open door. 'Do you remember me?'

'Ah, yes, Inspector.' Mrs Patel pulled the door open and stood before them in a magnificent gold and purple sari. 'From two years ago. Hello.' Her smile faded as she stole a glance at the

Wallis house over Brook's shoulder. 'How could I forget? Is it about that man loitering outside?'

'It is.'

'You'd better come in.'

'Thank you. This is DS Grant.' Brook and Grant stepped over the threshold into the spicy warmth of the brightly decorated hall. Mrs Patel stepped back and pulled a door closed to block out the sound of the family meal.

'You're eating,' noted Grant. 'We can come back.'

'Not at all. I eat afterwards anyway. Helping the police is more important.'

'Thank you. We just want to go over what you told my officer about the suspicious man outside your house. My officer said it was around ten o'clock . . .'

'No, it was exactly ten o'clock, Inspector. The news was just starting.'

'And what did the man do?' asked Grant.

'Like I told the other officer, he just stood there. He seemed to be staring across the road for some reason. I didn't know at the time—'

'Towards the Ingham house?'

'Yes. He seemed to be waiting for something. Or someone.'

'How long was he there?'

'About five minutes.'

'You're sure it was a man?' asked Grant.

'As sure as I can be. He looked quite big through the shoulders – like my Sanjay – but he wasn't tall.'

'And how was he dressed?'

'It was very dark, Inspector. He was dressed all in black or at least very dark clothing, with a balaclava.'

'And which way did he go when he left?'

'To the Ingham house.' Brook and Grant looked at each other. 'To the gate, I mean, what there is of it.' Her voice betrayed a sliver of disgust.

'But he didn't go in?'

'No. Just tried to peer into the yard . . . then he walked away.'

'He walked. You didn't see a car or a bicycle?' Grant prompted.

Mrs Patel shook her head. 'He walked.'

Brook nodded and signalled Grant to the door. 'Once again, thank you for your vigilance, Mrs Patel. One more thing.' He pulled a picture from his coat pocket. 'Do you know this young man?' He held up the clearest picture of the young Asian boy they had been able to come up with.

'Oh dear.' Mrs Patel put a bejewelled hand to her mouth. 'No, I'm afraid not. What are they doing to the poor boy?'

'The last bad thing they'll ever do to anyone, Mrs Patel,' said Grant.

Mrs Patel looked at her, a little startled, then she seemed to nod, satisfied. 'Good.'

When they were outside, Brook and Grant exchanged a look. 'Is there anyone on this estate upset about these murders?'

'Scum in fear, The Reaper's near,' Brook replied.

Chapter Sixteen

McQuarry eased her chair back and rubbed her neck. She closed her eyes for a second and began to drift off with her arms resting on the wheel. She roused herself and looked at the clock on the dash – five before ten – then glanced across the road at Sorenson's wrought-iron gates and beyond, down the drive towards the lake.

The main highway was dark and deserted now. In summer, lakeshore tourists would've have been moving around the resort to bars, restaurants and casinos, although most of the traffic would've been on the east side of South Lake Tahoe, across the state line. Tahoe was never empty; it was also a winter resort with skiing in several locations around the lake, including Heavenly in South Lake Tahoe itself. But if any time of year could be described as downtime for Tahoe it was this shoulder period between summer and full-blown winter.

On the California side things were a good deal quieter. Residents were wealthier, their houses grander, and the blending of the architecture with the landscape more thoughtful. But travel into South Lake Tahoe and cross into Nevada, across a road in town, Stateline Avenue, and the high-rise gaudiness of the gambling palaces reached up to the sky the second you hit the sidewalk on other side. South Lake Tahoe was the Jekyll and Hyde of American resorts.

McQuarry looked at the clock on the dash again. It was Drexler's shift. She leaned over to wake him but hesitated. Drexler had taken the day shift today while McQuarry had slept at the motel – they alternated each day and took the night shift together. He'd been pushing himself hard these last few weeks. The case had clearly gotten to him. The tenth anniversary of the death of his younger sister Kerry hadn't helped.

In 1985 Kerry had been found at the bottom of a ravine near their home in a burned-out car. Drexler's mother had collapsed at the news and had been in an institution ever since; she hadn't said a word to anyone from that day to this. A double whammy if ever there was one. McQuarry looked over at her partner. She couldn't imagine how a person might deal with that. She decided to let him sleep a little longer.

She opened her window to inhale the pine-scented air and began to shake out a cigarette. She paused over the pack, distracted by a light reflecting on the trees, and turned to see a car travelling from Sorenson's house towards the highway.

'Mike, we're up.'

Drexler let out a deep sigh and looked blearily out of the car. The gates across the highway opened noiselessly and a small black convertible emerged. A blond-haired woman was at the wheel but didn't even glance towards Drexler and McQuarry.

The car turned left towards the resort, sweeping its lights across the Chevy. Both Drexler and McQuarry instinctively ducked to avoid the headlights, though their car was easily recognisable as the one that had been parked in the same spot for much of the last two weeks. In that time they had seen Sorenson come and go maybe four times. He hardly ever left the place. People came to him though. His groceries were delivered and a nurse visited three times a week. Apart from that, they hadn't logged a single visitor to his house since they'd been staking it out. Sorenson was a virtual recluse.

'It's the nurse,' said Drexler, sitting up. 'She didn't even look over at us,' he added.

'I told her better not to acknowledge us at all.' On a solo shift a few days before, McQuarry had reported following the nurse and interviewing her when she stopped for gas. After certain assurances from the FBI agent, the nurse had revealed she was treating Sorenson for a minor lung complaint.

Drexler nodded. 'She okay with it?'

'She's fine, Mike. I told her it was a financial investigation and just to carry on treating him. She's in no danger but obviously she's not to mention our interest to Sorenson.'

Drexler lay back down on his reclined seat.

McQuarry was halfway down her cigarette when Sorenson's red Toyota drove through the gates towards the highway a few minutes later. This was the first time Sorenson had left his home at night in the two weeks they'd been watching him. McQuarry tossed her butt into the wet undergrowth and reached for the ignition. Sorenson turned left and, after a suitable interval, McQuarry turned the Chevy across the highway to follow.

She and Drexler were pleased to see that a slight crack in Sorenson's driver side taillight meant they could drop back without losing their prey. They tracked the Toyota towards South Lake Tahoe on the Emerald Bay Road, which was technically still the same State Highway 89 that ran past the Ashwell gas station forty miles away.

On they drove towards Tahoe Airport, passing Fallen

Leaf Road, which skirted the lake of the same name, not once nosing above thirty miles per hour.

'Think he's trying not to lose us, Ed?'

'Could be.'

Soon after the lonely road entered a more populated area, Sorenson turned east onto US 50, towards downtown Tahoe and the state line. A few minutes later, the high-rise hotels and buildings on the Nevada side of the line rose up like teeth in a shark's mouth and the garish lights adorning each casino left no one in any doubt as to where they should come to part company with their cash.

On they travelled into the night and back into the enveloping darkness, following US 50 along the lakeshore, past Elk Point and Zephyr Cove and towards Glenbrook where the road headed inland towards Carson City.

Some forty minutes later, Sorenson came to an intersection and turned north onto US 395. He pulled off the highway into a lot and parked in a bay outside an unremarkable, low building with a sign that said 'Golden Nugget Motel'.

McQuarry and Drexler pulled in just before the exit and watched their target step out of his vehicle. Sorenson seemed to examine his watch in the gloom. It had taken just over an hour to get here. He spent five minutes walking up and down the front of the motel, lingering for a moment outside the room farthest from reception. He appeared to write something in a notebook then walked back to the bright lights of the office. He disappeared for a moment then re-emerged, returned to his car and crossed the highway back towards Tahoe.

McQuarry pulled out to follow but as she drew level with the office, Drexler jumped out of the car.

'Back in a minute, Ed.'

* * *

Brook drew up outside his cottage before midnight. He parked with some difficulty as Drexler's recycling bin was out on the street for tomorrow's collection. His neighbour was home and, judging from the lights, clearly still up. Brook resisted the urge to call and trudged into his house. The whisky he'd poured for himself yesterday evening was the only thing in the fridge, save a half-pint of milk and an opened can of beans. He examined the beans but plopped the rusted tin in the bin and closed the door.

'First impressions, Damen,' he muttered to himself, his mantra since the Wallis investigation when his blossoming relationship with PC Wendy Jones had been threatened by his inability to see how out of control his life had become. For Brook, an empty fridge was the litmus test of a mind in turmoil, and he vowed to set matters right the next day.

And he was hungry. That was a good thing. At the height of his obsession with work, his stomach had never grumbled and Brook had needed reminders to take on food. He wagered that Josh Hudson's life never became so chaotic that he forgot to eat.

Brook sat down in his armchair and flicked on a small lamp. He pulled out the photocopy of Laura Maples's picture that he'd removed from the Wallis house and unfolded it. He looked into the clear eyes of the schoolgirl, now dead nearly twenty years, the thin necklace with the heart-shaped links winking up at him. He placed the picture reverentially in a drawer.

He took a sip of his chilled whisky and looked across at his neighbour's house, remembering the delicious burger of a few nights ago. He flicked the lamp back off and sat motionless in the dark, eyes closed, enjoying the momentary sensory deprivation. It didn't last. The sight of the Ingham boy was upon him before he could slam the sluice gates on the flood of gore – stretched out before him, head pulled back, throat twisted like a gargoyle. He saw the other boys as well, smelled them, reeking of blood and fresh, steaming urine and excrement.

Finally Brook saw Drexler's face in the dying flash of the camera at the crime scene. He opened his eyes, downed his whisky, left the house and walked down the side path of Rose Cottage.

*

'Hi there.' Drexler stole a glance at a folded handwritten sign on the desk – *T.J. Carlson, Night Manager*. 'Say, Mr Carlson, did I just see my old buddy Vic leave a second ago?'

The manager looked up evenly at Drexler, removing a well-chewed cigar butt from his mouth but showing no inclination to answer. He was an overweight figure with grey whiskered jowls and a mass of unkempt greying hair swept incongruously into a minute ponytail at the back of his neck. He scratched at a flabby bare arm. 'Do you need a room, fella? It's thirty dollars for the hour or forty-five for the night.' He returned his gaze to a small TV, showing a college football game.

'So that wasn't Vic?' Carlson returned his disinterested eyes back to Drexler and cocked his head. The penny dropped and Drexler fumbled in his trousers for a five-dollar bill and handed it over. 'See, he's my best man and he's cooking up something for my bachelor night and I'd as soon know what it was.'

'Took a card. Wanted to know what our quietest night of the week was.'

'What did you tell him?'

'Tuesday.'

'Anything else?'

'Yeah. He wanted to know if I'd be working Tuesdays because he wanted someone he could rely on. Someone with discretion.'

'That all?'

271

The manager gave Drexler a cryptic smile. Drexler fished in his pocket for another five-dollar bill.

'He gave me a twenty.'

'That's what I got, friend.'

Carlson shrugged and wrapped his podgy fingers around the money. 'I told your friend I'm on every Tuesday. He booked all the cabins for a week Tuesday.'

'All of them? He say what for?'

'Nope. And I didn't ask. I got . . .'

'Discretion. I get it.' Drexler turned to leave.

'For another fi' dollars I can tell you his name.'

Drexler turned. 'It wasn't Victor?' The manager returned his interest to the football. Drexler pulled out his diminishing roll of bills. 'All I got is three ones.'

The manager glared at him and muttered something which sounded like 'Cheap motherfucker', then gestured with his chubby hand. Drexler handed him the notes which he pocketed before answering.

'Reservation's under the name Hera. Peter Hera.'

*

The small pot-bellied stove was still giving out heat but the embers were dying. The kitchen door was open and Drexler was sitting at the tiny kitchen table, cigarette in hand, looking at a bunch of papers strewn across the surface. Brook watched him from the shadows, debating whether to turn on his heel.

Suddenly Drexler looked up and for a split second Brook imagined he saw fear there.

Brook stepped out of the dark. 'Mike. I saw you were up.'

Drexler found his Californian grin and stood, casting a sly glance around his tabletop as if to check the sensitivity of the documents, before coming outside. He closed the door behind him, extinguishing much of the light.

'Damen. Quite the stranger.' He gestured towards a chair in

the garden and brought out a pair of blankets, tossing one to Brook. He then busied himself feeding wood and newspaper into the small stove; the air was distinctly chilly now and both men were glad of the flames that began to catch.

'Work, I'm afraid.'

'I've been reading the papers. Six people. I won't ask you about the case. I'm guessing you need to get away from it.'

'You can ask me.'

Drexler studied him for a moment, but let the opportunity pass. 'So what can I do for you?'

Brook hesitated, a little embarrassed to be scrounging for food. 'I saw the light.'

'God be praised!' grinned Drexler, throwing his arms in the air.

Brook smiled politely. 'We have a lot to talk about.'

Drexler's smile disappeared. 'Yes.'

Brook decided to deflect him until he was ready. 'Your book for one thing.'

'I thought you'd have questions. Hungry?'

Brook nodded, as if to suggest the idea hadn't occurred to him. 'I could eat.'

Drexler returned to the kitchen and Brook fancied he was using the time to hide his papers. But it also allowed more time for Brook to finalise his side of the ensuing conversation. Drexler returned with a ham salad sandwich and two bottles of beer. They clinked bottles and Brook ate in silence as Drexler chugged on his bottle.

'That was good. Thanks.'

Drexler nodded, but his good humour had dissipated. He stared into the fire, waiting, but Brook wouldn't be hurried.

Finally Brook was ready. 'When did you arrive in England, Mike?'

Drexler stared into the fire. A moment later, he said, '*Never ask a question you don't know the answer to.* An interview technique my old FBI tutor taught me. I guess you had a similar mentor.' Brook waited, his eyes piercing Drexler. 'About a month ago.'

Brook nodded. 'Then why tell Tom you'd just flown in from Boston when he picked you up last week?'

'I flew to Manchester from Heathrow. I told Tom I live in Boston and he assumed the rest.'

'But you didn't bother to put Tom straight?'

'I didn't lie.'

'So telling me you had jetlag wasn't a lie?'

'Actually I think I asked you if you had jetlag.'

Again Brook was silent, assessing Drexler, who didn't appear to be flustered at all. In fact he seemed calm and untroubled.

'And Brighton?' Drexler's eyebrow shot up. 'There was a train ticket, which dropped out of your passport.'

Drexler nodded, sombre now. 'I can see I'm going to have to beef up security round here. I didn't have Hartington down as Sin City.'

Brook felt a pinprick of shame. 'I'm sorry. I called round and your door was open.'

'Was my passport open too?' The two men stared into each other's eyes, neither willing to be the first to drop his gaze. Drexler found his grin again. 'No harm no foul, Damen. I've got nothing to hide.'

'Lucky you. You haven't answered my question.'

Drexler's grin eased but a smile remained. 'I went to Brighton to look up an old friend.'

'This old friend wouldn't happen to be called Tony Harvey-Ellis, would he?'

'No. Who's that?'

Brook was studying him for signs of deceit, but Drexler was a tough read. 'Never mind.' He took a final swig from his bottle of beer. 'And why are you really in Derbyshire, Mike?'

'I told you. I'm writing a book.'

'I've read your book, Mike.'

'All of it?'

'No. I've been busy. But enough – enough to know the case was solved. It says as much on the sleeve, yet you say you're writing a sequel.'

'I am. But it's nothing to do with solving the case.'

'You'll have to explain that.'

Drexler took a long pull on his beer and stared into the fire. 'You're a cop. You must have seen it, Damen. The aftermath. The effort that goes into explaining – the press, the TV, the psychiatrists, the writers, even the fucking clairvoyants get a piece.' Drexler looked over at him. 'I got tired of books about the killers, Damen. It sickened me how much people wrote about the upbringing which caused them to kill, about the psychology behind the murders, about how we need to understand the killing to correct our society. About what they had for fucking breakfast.

'We've got to the stage where killers are so famous that we've got schoolkids taking weapons into school to kill their classmates. Sure, they do a little dance, make a videotape, upload something on to YouTube to say why they did it. *The music made me. I've been bullied. I can't get girls. My teacher gave me an F in English.*' Drexler laughed now. 'Stupid little fuckers! Like we don't know the real reason. Like we don't know they're just lazy and desperate. Desperate for fame. *No one notices me. Gimme a gun.* Success through hard work? *Fuck that. Gimme a gun.*

'I'm ashamed of that first book, Damen. It's about the killers. It's about turning pieces of shit into historical figures. So I'm correcting that. I'm writing a book about the victims, about the families destroyed by those butchers. I'm giving them back their lives. Not the way the news media do it. To me the victims aren't just names, dates and addresses, end of story. They're people who lived and loved and dreamed. And died before they were supposed to. That's why I'm in Derbyshire, Damen. I'm speaking for the dead.'

'In Derbyshire?'

'You haven't read that far, have you? The last victim was George

Bailey and his family. He was a chemical engineer, originally from Ashbourne, Derbyshire. He'd only been in the States for a couple of years. He was murdered. His wife was raped and murdered. His youngest daughter Sally was drugged, then tortured, then raped and then murdered. Shot in the head when her usefulness was at an end.' He took another drink of his beer. 'They weren't even buried in the same hole. Even in death they could never be a family again. I'm doing a book for them and the other victims, Damen. To correct the balance. You of all people should understand that.'

'Is that why you were on the Drayfin Estate the other night?'

Drexler smiled. 'So you did see me. Yes, I took an interest. I'm a writer. But don't worry. From what I hear these vics had it coming.'

Brook nodded but said nothing. His final question was left unasked. *Never ask a question you don't know the answer to.* It didn't feel like the right time. Besides, if Drexler had been the copycat Reaper or, worse, had been recruited by Sorenson, he was hardly likely to confess it. He looked at his watch and finished his beer. 'It's late.' He stood to leave but turned back to Drexler. 'I'm sorry about going through your stuff. The door was open . . .'

'Forget it. We're cops. It's what we do. Like I said, I've nothing to hide. Tell you what, put these empties in the recycling and we'll call it quits.'

'Fair enough.' They said their good nights and Brook set off for home. He paused at the recycling bin, flipped the lid up and dropped in his bottle with as much noise as he could manage. He returned to his kitchen with Drexler's bottle, peeled off an evidence bag from a stack in a drawer, and slid the bottle in.

Ten minutes later he was in bed with Drexler's book. His eyes were already starting to close and he soon dropped the book onto the floorboards, but not before turning to the index and the glossary to check out the three key phrases he'd used in countless internet searches – 'Victor Sorenson', 'Twilight Sleep' and 'scopolamine'. His search was in vain.

Chapter Seventeen

DCI Hudson drained his sweet tea and picked at a piece of bacon stuck in his teeth with a fingernail. It was a cold morning and the sun was slanting in low through the windows of the Midland's breakfast room. Even on a weekday, when the hotel was close to fully booked, the pair ate alone, so early were they up and about.

Hudson looked over at Grant, who was nursing her black coffee and yawning.

'You should eat something, luv.'

Grant opened her eyes and shielded them with a hand. 'It's the middle of the night, guv.'

'You should still eat something. Most important meal of the day, breakfast. Besides . . .'

Grant held up a hand. 'I know, guv, but I'm sick of hotel food, restaurants too. Exes or not. I miss the sea and I miss my flat. I wouldn't mind working a sixteen-hour day if I had something better than a trouser press to welcome me home.'

'You're missing a man in your life. Like Damen Brook, maybe.' Grant stared at him. Hudson laughed. 'Come on. Don't pretend you haven't softened towards him big time. *La-ura.*'

Grant refilled her coffee cup and took a sip. 'Okay, guv. He's not what I expected. There's something . . . sad and gentle about him. And he didn't kill the Inghams, I'm with you there.'

'And Harvey-Ellis?'

Grant considered for a couple of minutes. 'I'm less sure than

I was.' She decided against telling her boss about Brook's invitation to his cottage. Hudson was a true dinosaur and wouldn't view it as a chance to get closer, as she did. 'We'll see where the evidence takes us but you're right about something else, guv.'

'What's that?'

'Catching The Reaper is the bigger prize.'

*

Brook was also up early to see Noble before the morning briefing. He handed over an evidence bag.

'A beer bottle? Where's that from?' Brook didn't answer and Noble understood the look. 'What do you need?'

'You remember the US fingerprint database?'

'IAFIS?'

'Did you check the print on the phone against it?'

'Still going through channels.'

'Here's a shortcut. There's a set of prints on the bottle. Compare them with the print on the phone. There should be plenty for comparison and . . . er, there may also be some of mine.'

Noble eyed him, thin-lipped. 'Any other news? Besides you going out on the town with The Reaper?'

Brook emitted a one-note laugh but Noble wasn't to be placated. 'Even if they're not a match, I want all the details you can get about their owner. Cases he worked, partners he worked with, places . . .'

'Hang on. You already know whose prints they are?'

Brook sighed and looked around the briefing room. He led Noble out by the arm. 'Look, I know it's irregular but I have good reason.' Noble did not move, maintaining a deadpan face. 'He's a retired FBI agent from California. He's renting the cottage next to mine for the winter.' Still no reaction from Noble. 'Okay. Victor Sorenson lived in California when . . .'

'I remember him. Apparently he was the chief suspect in The Reaper Inquiry, wasn't he?'

Brook paused. He led Noble further from the briefing, which was now due to start. 'I deserve this, John. You've every right. I never told you about Sorenson because . . .'

'Because . . . ?' Noble lifted his eyebrows to turn the screw.

'Here's the thing. He moved to California after the Leeds killings in '93. Business reasons. I know he lived in Los Angeles and also had a house on the edge of Lake Tahoe. He told me he continued his work in America. His work – that's what he called it. I didn't see him again until the Wallis investigation when I went to London, to satisfy myself that he couldn't be The Reaper.'

'And did you? Satisfy yourself?'

Noble wasn't making this easy. Brook was unsure now how to continue. He settled for, 'He was very frail. He had terminal cancer.' Brook barely glanced at Noble, hoping he'd said enough.

'And so?'

'And so ever since the Wallis investigation I've been . . . *surfing the net*' – Noble couldn't resist a grin at Brook's awkwardness with the language – 'to find cases in the US that might have a connection with Sorenson. So far without luck.'

'You've Googled Twilight Sleep?'

'. . . and scopolamine and Victor Sorenson and "SAVED". I've tried everything, John. Nothing.'

'And now?'

'And now, I don't know. I start getting emails from a dead man. Then a retired FBI agent from California moves next door to me and another family is slaughtered – coincidence? I don't think so. He's also written a book, *The Ghost Road Killers*, about a serial killing he investigated near Lake Tahoe. Where Sorenson lived.'

'You should get a copy.'

'He gave me one. There's something else. I saw him in the crowd at the Ingham crime scene.'

Noble nodded finally. 'I'll get onto it straight after briefing.' They turned to go back into the Incident Room. 'I doubt you'll find Twilight Sleep mentioned in the US by the way.'

'Oh?'

'The phrase was coined by the British in the First World War in the battlefield trenches.'

'How do you know that?'

'I'm a professional detective,' said Noble, a grin forming. Brook pursed his lips in mock annoyance. 'And did you Google the American names for scopolamine?'

*

McQuarry caught up with the Toyota and they dutifully followed Sorenson back to his home. At twenty minutes past midnight Sorenson turned back into his driveway and activated the electric gate.

McQuarry looked at Drexler and shook her head. 'What the fuck? What a royal waste of time. I'm heading back, Mike.'

'You don't think we should do another hour?'

'I don't think we should do another minute.'

Drexler looked over at her. She seemed exhausted. 'Okay. Let's call it a night.'

They travelled in silence for ten minutes until Drexler broke it. 'What do you think about the Golden Nugget? Weird or what?'

McQuarry put a hand up to her face and rubbed her eyes.

'Mike, right now I don't give a fuck if he's planning to kill Clinton, I'm going back to our motel, having a swim and a couple of Jacks and grabbing some shuteye. I've had it and so have you.'

'I think he's setting it all up, Ed. He times the journey and books all the rooms at the motel, so he's unlikely to get disturbed. He scopes out the cabin farthest from the office . . .'

'So what, Mike? Who cares?' McQuarry snapped. A moment later she sighed. 'We can't keep doing this.'

'But if we . . .'

'No, Mike. Tomorrow I'm going to get up round ten o'clock and have some waffles then I'm going to pack my bags and drive up to Markleeville and shake Andy Dupree's hand. Then I'm heading home.'

'We're giving this up?'

'Hell yes, we're giving this up. We've been out here for nearly two months, Mike. The Ghost Road Killers are in the ground, the paperwork's done, we've been up Sorenson's ass for nearly a month and, even assuming he killed Caleb and Billy Ashwell, we got precisely buttkiss for evidence. We can't get a search warrant and we got no PC . . .'

'Who needs probable cause? You know he did it.'

McQuarry sighed. 'Know what, Mike? Even if I did know, I'm caring less and less . . .'

'Don't you care about Sorenson's arrogance, that he *wanted* us to know . . .?'

'No. Because, you know what, the reason he wanted us to know was so we could tie ourselves in knots, exactly like we're doing. As far as proof is concerned, Mike, he's squeaky clean. And if he's lining up another lowlife like Ashwell to put in the ground then I might just be chipping in for a medal with Andy. Now I'm the lead in this and I'm telling you, it's out of juice.'

Drexler nodded and was silent for several minutes as McQuarry drove back to the motel. 'Suit yourself. I've got some vacation time coming up.'

McQuarry looked across at him in disbelief. She was about to speak, then thought better of it.

*

The briefing was a short affair consisting primarily of a discussion about whether it was feasible to DNA-test every adult male in Derby. Genetic material had been obtained from the fence panel but, as with the partial print, it had produced no matches from the database. Everything else had been done.

The Forensics teams had been at breaking point with three separate houses to process. The Wallis house had produced exhibits but no leads. The rope, the old mannequin, the wine bottle and glasses carried no prints, DNA or saliva. The old mattress contained about a dozen samples of DNA, which was not surprising in a derelict house. All were too degraded for sampling, suggesting they'd been deposited a long time before the Ingham murders. Other artefacts from the Wallis house had also yielded nothing.

In the North house Forensic officers were still working, but the house had been kept scrupulously clean by the killers. The tyre track found in the backyard was from a very common twenty-six-inch tyre available at hundreds of outlets nationwide. Its size and width suggested a tyre for a standard-sized mountain bike. The set of keys used to gain entry to the house hadn't been found and searches of the surrounding area had produced nothing.

In the Ingham house only DNA material and fingerprints belonging to the victims had been collected. The footprints issue was no clearer: maybe sports shoes had been worn, maybe the prints showed two pairs of feet – one size 7 and one size 9. The fact that protective overshoes could have created prints of both sizes from one suspect further confused the issue.

The Family Liaison Officer, DC Keys, went through the background of both Ingham boys, Ben Anderson and David Gretton again. Although no angels, nothing they had ever done seemed sufficient cause to provoke such violence against them. However, the unsubstantiated allegations about the murder of Annie Sewell were still pending, as all Scientific Support services were critically overstretched.

As far as other relatives were concerned, most members of both families had given each other alibis, not surprisingly, given the time of day their sons/nephews had been killed. Nevertheless they had been printed and swabbed after assurance from Chief Superintendent Charlton that their samples would be destroyed after comparison and they were in the clear.

The final item for the briefing was the assault – the happy slapping – of the Asian boy. He still hadn't come forward and it was decided to release the photograph for the *Derby Telegraph* front page. A television appeal had been mooted by Charlton but, as the incident may have had nothing to do with the eventual murders, it was deemed excessive for the time being.

After the briefing, Hudson and Brook decided that senior detectives should meet to determine future actions, so they gathered in Hudson's borrowed office with the four detective sergeants. It was still early and Gadd, Morton, Grant, Noble and Hudson all grabbed a coffee before traipsing into Hudson's temporary office

'Okay, people. Leads are going nowhere and things are starting to peter out. Any suggestions?' asked Hudson. 'Damen, I assume you've reached this point in a Reaper inquiry before. What now?'

'We do the only thing we can do. Get back on the doorsteps. The good news is that learning about the time spent by the killers in preparation at the North house means we've got different questions and a different time frame to ask about. Even if the killers snuck in and out of there at night, someone may have seen them. We get onto the utilities, paper boys, postmen – anybody who might have had business there in the two weeks previous. See if they noticed anything. Also get back to the local taxi firms. Mrs North didn't walk to the airport. If that was part of the prize, one of our suspects may have arranged it in person.' Hudson motioned Morton to make a note while Brook continued.

'We show the pictures of the assault. Maybe someone knows the victim. We know when but someone else might know where it happened. And remember, the lad is not a suspect but a witness at this stage. We have to stress that – possibly why he hasn't come forward before now. Also, we talk to Jason again. He's seen one of these men. And, no matter his condition, we may get a better description.'

'Sounds like a plan,' added Hudson. 'There's still life in this then.'

'We're in better shape than the Wallis investigation. If we can identify a suspect at least we can prove it one way or the other.'

'Didn't you have any suspects at all apart from Victor Sorenson?' asked Grant.

'We worked on the theory that Jason's sexual assault of his teacher caught The Reaper's eye,' said Noble. 'So we interviewed her and her husband. But that was it.'

Brook nodded. 'It did cross our minds briefly that John Ottoman could have done it. He was Kylie Wallis's primary school teacher; he had motive and the necessary intelligence.'

'We should at least have another talk with them,' nodded Noble.

'Agreed,' said Hudson.

'I think John and I should do it,' said Brook. 'Familiar faces,' he said to Grant, who shrugged. 'We'll do it to tick it off, but they're not involved.'

'You're very sure.'

'Jason Wallis survived. His sister Kylie died. Ottoman would have had that the other way round.'

'It could be he panicked,' offered DS Gadd.

Brook rubbed his hand over his face. 'I don't think panic is in The Reaper's lexicon, Jane. We've got to understand. The Reaper slayings are not ordinary crimes. The MO is unique. Motiveless, cold-blooded, multiple executions are usually the stuff of organised crime. But even a gangland hit is carried out with some venom, because it has to send a message to others. And killing children rarely sends the right message. There's just no profile that fits what The Reaper does. Finding a suspect on that basis has proved impossible.'

'But you found Sorenson. He fitted the profile,' said Hudson.

'Yes and no. He found me and he virtually had to tell me he was The Reaper to keep me on the hook.'

'But you don't think he killed the Wallis family two years ago?' asked Noble.

Brook looked over at him. 'Sorenson was dying of cancer when Jason's family were killed. At the time, yes, I thought it was possible he might have stretched himself for one last hurrah . . . but you know what? Maybe he didn't. Maybe he just set it up or *maybe* he had help. Two Reapers. That tallies with our thinking on the Inghams. Two killers, not one. The only question now is . . .'

'Who stepped into Sorenson's shoes?' nodded Grant.

*

Mike Drexler pulled his Audi A6 out of the parking lot of the Lakeside Motel and drove west on US 50, feeling refreshed after his shower. He looked out over Tahoe as the wind ruffled the waters. No boats were out this morning; summer was long gone. Squally snow drove across the water, up the stony beach and swirled around the exposed highway. In two weeks the ski season would start and Drexler's motel would be fully occupied. For now he was the only resident and had the best apartment with a view of the deserted lake. It cost him sixty-nine dollars a night but what the hell, he was on vacation.

He smiled and looked in the driver's mirror. The bags under his eyes told their own tale. He'd been at the motel three nights already, but the bed had still not been slept in.

When Drexler reached the intersection he turned onto 89 but, instead of heading west for Sorenson's house, he turned south towards the airport. An hour later he reached the gas station and parked. He took out his new camera and wandered up the path at the back of the station to

take pictures of the saplings he'd noticed during his nocturnal search of the cabin.

He wasn't the only visitor. Any car that passed the station made a point of stopping. Sometimes the people wouldn't get out but just talk and point at the decaying slab of a building. Other times the occupants would get out for a few minutes to take pictures. They rarely moved too far from the car though, and never turned off their engines.

Half an hour later Drexler shook hands with Andy Dupree at the Police Department building in Markleeville.

'Good to see you, Mike,' said Dupree, holding onto Drexler's hand long enough to keep his attention. 'Vacation, you said? I sure hope this one's not under your skin, amigo.' Drexler just smiled in response. 'Like the lady said, it's squared away. Save your ulcers for the deserving.'

'The Ashwell deaths are unsolved, Andy.' Dupree shook his head, then gestured Drexler into the building. 'Any trace of Ashwell's brother yet?'

'Not a one. Guess he knows what's waiting if he puts his head above the trench.'

'Any other developments?'

'Nothing. 'Cept this one here.'

*

The wind had freshened by midmorning and officers were hunched against the spitting, driving rain. The streets around Drayfin weren't nearly as full of police vehicles as they had been on previous days, but this morning the pavements were well lined with officers asking the questions about the North house that had been generated by inquiries so far.

Brook and Grant were coordinating visits on Mrs North's side of the block while Hudson and Noble banged on doors on the Wallis/Ingham side. Noble and Hudson approached a house eight doors away from the Ingham house and Noble's knock was greeted by a pretty young Asian girl in an orange sari.

'Sorry to bother you, Miss . . .'

'Dhoni. And it's Mrs Dhoni as of two weeks ago,' she said with an air of something close to disbelief. 'Mrs Dhoni.'

'Congratulations,' said Hudson, smiling.

'You've come about the pictures, have you, officers?'

Hudson and Noble looked at each other. 'Er, yes,' nodded Noble with more confidence than he felt. 'The pictures.'

'Well, we knew you'd be along for them sooner or later, as soon as you found out about the wedding. I would have brought them in myself but I've had quite a job collecting them from everyone. Now they're digital, so would you like them on a memory stick or should I just email them somewhere?'

'Depends how many there are, Miss . . .'

'Mrs Dhoni,' she giggled. 'At least three hundred. Some are just family portraits but there are plenty of others that show the houses.'

'Houses?'

'Yes. The Ingham house and the Wallis house beyond. Where all those people were killed. Horrible people. I shouldn't speak ill of the dead, but to have a wedding reception and have to listen to the abuse from those . . . animals. But we have our duty to do. My grandparents would be livid if we didn't help. They came to this country to be full citizens and . . . well, you know.'

'Yes, we do know, Mrs Dhoni,' beamed Inspector Hudson, 'and a memory stick would be great if you can spare it.'

'I'll just go and get it.' She returned and handed it to Noble. She hesitated for a second. 'You know, I've got to say. Over the last two years, nine people have been murdered in houses that we can see from our back garden. But the funny thing is we've never felt safer than this last week. My husband and I have done our duty but, honestly,' she paused over the words, 'I hope you don't catch him.'

*   *   *

287

Brook stood in Mrs North's back bedroom looking out over the Ingham yard. The room was tiny, but still fussily furnished and the smell of damp was a background note that a pensioner with dwindling senses might not detect. The view over the killing ground was stunning, however, and details in several rooms of the Ingham household were easily visible.

Brook sat on the mattress, the sheets having been removed for fruitless tests, seeking a good viewing position. When he had settled on the best spot, he began to look around to see if anything had been missed. He was about to return to Grant in the kitchen when he spotted something on the floor, underneath the curtain. He kneeled down to pull the curtain aside then rubbed a finger over the carpet. There was a small indentation on the fabric, as though something had been placed there over a period of time. He pushed the bed back a few feet and stroked the carpet in wide sweeps with his hands. He found two other small indentations.

'Say cheese.'

He returned the bed to its proper position and trotted back down to the kitchen. 'I think they had some kind of tripod set up in the back bedroom.'

'What for?'

'Hard to tell. Binoculars maybe? Though my money would be on a camera. I think if I were The New Reaper I might want some souvenirs.' Brook looked at his watch. 'Must be nearly time.'

Grant nodded and stepped outside. Brook was about to follow when something began to nag at him. He looked around the kitchen, trying to draw it out, but failed and followed Grant to the front gate.

A few doors down, the postman was talking to a uniformed constable who pointed towards the two CID officers. The postman nodded and walked towards them, smiling. A few yards away, he put up a single digit and jogged down the path of a neighbouring house and out of sight.

'Cheeky sod,' said Grant. 'We should have asked him down to the station.'

Brook smiled at her. 'Patience, Laura. If he's got anything for us he'll remember it better on location.'

When he re-emerged, the postman jogged towards them, panting. He was about forty, thin with long bleached blond hair and an unnatural tan. He sported LOVE and HATE tattoos on each hand and wore frayed denim shorts, despite the winter bite. The ear studs augmented the impression of a self-appointed ladies' man. 'Sorry to keep you,' he said. 'Bad luck to retrace your steps.'

'How unlucky is it to get arrested for wasting police time?' asked Grant.

'I said I was sorry. I'm here, aren't I?' the postman countered.

'DS Grant's just pulling your leg, Mr . . .' said Brook.

'Blake, but just call me Tommy,' he grinned.

'Tommy. You know why we're here?'

'Those murders obviously.'

'Right.'

'Terrible. Those Ingham boys were right rogues, no two ways, but they were good kids deep down. And their mother . . .' A private grin invaded his features, in spite of his attempts to suppress it. 'Well, enough said.' Grant's stony gaze wiped the grin from Tommy's face. 'What do you want to know?'

'Simple,' said Brook. 'We want to know if you've seen anyone in and around Mrs North's house since she's been away. That's up to two weeks before the murders happened.'

'Mrs N's. No, I can't say I have. I mean, I knew she was going away, she told me. I like to keep a lookout for people, you know, sift out all the flyers and junk, so callers don't realise the house is empty. All part of the service, mind – though it don't hurt round Christmas,' he added with a wink. 'But Mrs N had some people looking after the place so the mail didn't pile up.'

'People?' repeated Grant. 'Did you see any of these people?'

'You know, not once.'

'Okay, thanks anyway.'

'She's back in a few weeks. She can tell you herself. Six people.' Blake shook his head. 'She's got a shock coming when she rolls up in that car.'

'Car? What car?'

'The car that picked her up. It weren't no taxi. I assumed it was a relative.'

'What time was this?'

'Well, early on that Saturday. I was on my way to work. It would've been before six in the morning.'

'How do you know it wasn't a cab?'

'I didn't see any licence or nothing. And if the driver ain't a . . .' Grant raised an eyebrow '. . . an Asian.' He shrugged. 'It just looked like a private car,' he finished, looking at the ground.

'What kind of car?'

'It was dark. I'm not Jeremy Clarkson, you know. More of a Harley man myself,' he sniffed, glancing at Grant to see if she was impressed.

'Think. What about colour?'

'Black, I think. Or dark blue.'

'And you couldn't have a guess at make and model?'

'A saloon. If I had to guess, I'd say foreign.'

'BMW?' asked Grant. Brook gave her a sidelong glance.

'Maybe. No. I don't know. Something powerful.'

'And the driver was white?'

'Oh, yeah. Not only that . . .'

*

Brook and Grant marched into Hudson's temporary office. He and Noble were having a lunchtime sandwich and staring intently at the monitor of a laptop. Before Brook or Grant could get a word in, Hudson grinned up at them. 'We've caught a break. We've got photographs of the North house the week before the killings. We may have one of our doers on film and you'll never guess . . .'

Brook's expression never wavered. 'Is it a woman by any chance?'

Hudson's grin faded but Noble managed a smile. 'We think so. How did you know?'

'Postman Pratt saw Mrs North getting picked up by a car,' said Grant. 'He said he thought the driver was a woman.'

'Any description?'

'He only got a glimpse. He got as far as petite, then he saw she was older than him and stopped looking.'

'He and Laura hit it right off,' said Brook.

Hudson smiled and turned the laptop round to them. Brook and Grant leaned into the monitor. The happy smiles of the wedding party took up most of the screen but there in the background was the North house. And, just as clearly, there was a figure in the back bedroom window, sitting on the bed in the exact same position Brook had been sitting earlier that morning. The face was a ghostly blur but it was possible to discern medium-length grey hair parted in the middle and a Caucasian face. The figure was turned towards the Ingham house, oblivious to the festivities taking place in the neighbouring garden.

'It's not very clear,' said Grant. 'I don't know how you conclude that's a woman. The hair maybe.'

'Can we get the boffins on to it? Get it cleaned up.'

'Just where we were going,' said Hudson. 'There's something else.' He clicked through several pictures and stopped at one, then turned the monitor back to Brook and Grant. Behind the brightly clothed revellers, sitting astride the shiplap fence, a young boy was clearly visible, mouth open to shout something and holding two fingers aloft to the photographer.

'D'Wayne Ingham in all his glory,' said Brook.

'And getting maximum use of his fingers while he still could,' observed Grant, inducing a round of bleak laughs.

'And this one.' The angle was slightly different but D'Wayne

Ingham was still on the fence, looking not at the party but down into the backyard of Mrs North's property. Hudson picked up a pencil and indicated a partially obscured round shape. 'Could that be the barbecue?' Brook nodded. 'And this was taken three hours later.' Several clicks stopped at an ensemble picture, which the photographer had obviously taken from a first-floor window. All the revellers stood in their vivid finery, waving happily to the camera. Hudson's pencil indicated what could only be the Weber barbecue, but this time it was sitting up against the back wall of the Ingham house.

Hudson leaned back on his chair, hands behind his head. 'So, a middle-aged woman. Do we know any middle-aged women connected to the inquiry, Damen?'

*

Brook and Noble headed for the car park. As they passed Brook's office, Noble nodded towards a manila folder on the desk.

'Michael Drexler, FBI. Sounds like an interesting guy.' Brook picked up the folder and looked up at Noble. Noble shook his head. 'No. The prints on the bottle don't match the print on Jason's phone.'

Brook nodded. 'Okay. Thanks, John.'

'Did you expect they would?'

'I don't know.' He smiled at Noble. 'But, honestly, I'm pleased they don't. And you're right. He is an interesting guy.' But, he had to admit, so was Sorenson.

*

'Nice to meet you, Jeff.' Drexler shook the young man's hand but stole a look at Sheriff Dupree, who returned it with an inscrutable shrug.

'It's okay, Special Agent,' said Jeff. 'I know I look young to be doing this.'

'You look like you should be surfing in Hawaii,' smiled

Drexler, examining his bleach-blond curls and designer stubble.

'My fee today will get me some of the way,' he laughed. 'My sister was born deaf so, although I'm only twenty-eight, I've been around this most of my life.'

'Okay,' nodded Drexler.

They turned into an office and Jeff continued. 'I've had a couple of runs through it and I've got to say there doesn't seem an awful lot there of interest. The guy buys ten dollars' worth of gas and that's pretty much it.'

'Then you get an easy paycheck, son,' said Dupree. 'You sure it was ten dollars?'

'No question,' replied Jeff.

'Mmmm.'

'Is that significant, Andy?' asked Drexler.

'You can't fill an empty tank with ten bucks' worth of gas, Mike. Know what I think? I think Mr Sorenson stopped at every station on the way to Tahoe.'

Drexler nodded. 'So it was no accident he happened to stop at Caleb's. Why?'

'Because he didn't know who killed George Bailey. He took a stab at what might have happened and went out there looking until he got the vibe.'

'The hunter hunting – could be. At least now we know he's not superhuman.'

'I already knew that, Mike.'

They sat down at a large monitor and Jeff took up a sheaf of notes. The CCTV footage of Sorenson entering the Ashwells' gas station flickered onto the screen. 'Okay, the guy called Caleb is welcoming him to Alpine County and telling him his name. Pretty friendly. The bald man says "Evening", and asks if he's on the road to Markleeville. Caleb says yes, you're on 89 and asks where he's headed. Then he tries to get the customer's name. Caleb calls him Mister and waits for the customer to fill in the blank. You can see the guy thinking about it. Then he replies and says he's headed for South Lake Tahoe.'

'What does he say his name is?'

'It's very short. I made a list of possibles.'

'His real name is Sorenson,' said Drexler. 'Victor Sorenson.'

Jeff shook his head. 'That's not what he said. It's one syllable.'

'And what do you think it is?'

Jeff stopped the film and reversed over it two or three times. 'See how abrupt he is. It begins with a B or P.'

'Any suggestions?'

'I think it's Brook.'

*

Brook looked around the garden of the Ottoman house, then back at Noble who hadn't been there for two years. Back then they'd admired the care and effort that had gone into the lawn, the path and even the condition of the gate which had once opened smoothly and without noise. But now, Noble and Brook were required to scrape the gate along the ground to gain access to the weed-encrusted, flagged path.

'It's hard to believe,' said Noble.

'That's what being a victim does to you, John.'

There were further signs of decay. The fence had several missing and rotted pickets, and the paint on doors and windows was peeling. At one time a punctilious and well-ordered couple, the Ottomans it seemed, had succumbed to the traumas of victimhood. Brook had seen it all too often. Denise Ottoman couldn't be the woman in Mrs North's house. He doubted she had the courage to leave her own.

He walked across to the garage, looking for either of the two cars he remembered they owned, but it was empty. He looked towards the house. All the curtains were drawn. Either the Ottomans were away or they wanted to give that impression.

Noble stood on the step and rapped on the door again, then shrugged at Brook, who signalled him away.

'Let's try the school.'

*

The headteacher of Drayfin Primary, Mrs Grace, seemed very tight-lipped about John Ottoman's absence. 'I don't know what more I can tell you, Inspector. John rang me on Monday morning to tell me, not ask, tell me he wouldn't be in and was taking a fortnight's leave. His wife . . .' She waved her hand in the air.

'Denise, yes, we know what happened.'

'Of course. But it was two years ago for goodness' sake. I suppose this latest . . . it's brought it all back, what with Jason Wallis being involved again.'

'It would,' nodded Brook.

'The little sod,' she whispered under her breath. Brook and Noble were both taken aback. 'I'm sorry, but we had the little angel here before he went off to spray his scent over the secondary school. There ought to be retrospective abortions for some chil-dren, Inspector. I shouldn't say that, I know. But no matter what you do, there's a minority that are irredeemable. And to think he'll soon be starting a family of his own. We had D'Wayne Ingham here too and, honestly, he made Jason look like Martin Luther King. He was due back in from suspension this week. You should see his tutor now D'Wayne's . . . you know, gone. She's walking on air.'

'So Mr Ottoman was here on the Friday and rang in on the Monday; you didn't speak to him face to face?'

'Oh, no, he telephoned. Didn't want to see my reaction, I expect. And I can tell you something else. I think he was already a long way away.'

'What do you mean?'

295

'Long distance. You can just tell, can't you? All the noises on the line. He couldn't ask me in person, could he?'

*

'What teacher would take a leave of absence and go away in term time?' asked Noble, manoeuvring the car out through the primary school gates and ignoring the five mile an hour speed limit.

'One who wants to get his wife away from Jason Wallis's picture in the paper, I guess. It can't be easy having to face what happened all over again. But you're right. It doesn't look good. The Inghams are killed in the early hours of Sunday morning . . .'

'. . . and the Ottomans are gone by the Monday. Maybe sooner. The headteacher was less than supportive.'

Brook glanced across. 'Know any management that are ever happy when you're ill? I had the same thing in the Met after my problems. The first thing Brass does when you go on long-term sick is mark the calendar when they can put you on half-pay. It's all about budgets.'

Noble was heading the car back to the Drayfin Estate when Brook received a call from Grant. It was a rare occurrence and Brook, under Noble's amused gaze, managed to locate the answer button without disconnecting.

'Hello?' Brook listened for a moment then rang off with a massive depression of the thumb.

'DS Grant. Head back to St Mary's.'

*

The man draped his arm around his son to comfort him, but the boy stared ahead, terrified. 'Ravi. You must tell the police.'

The boy's eyes began to fill again and he started to sob. Unable to close his mouth properly because of the large plaster over his cheek, the boy dribbled as he cried. His voice turned to a high-pitched wail, 'They said not to tell no one or else.' He turned and buried his head in his father's chest.

His father pulled him away and forced eye contact. 'Ravi, they're all dead.' Mr Singh's choice of words provoked a glance between Grant and Brook. 'They can't hurt you no more. Now tell the police.'

'Have another drink, Ravi,' soothed Grant, easing an opened can of Fanta towards the boy. 'The sugar will make you feel better. You can tell us everything. Your dad's right. They can't hurt you.'

The boy reached obediently for the soda and took a large swallow, before looking up at Brook and Grant through red-rimmed eyes. 'One of 'em's still about though. Him in the papers. Jason.'

'Tell us what he did and we'll make sure he's put away, Ravi,' said Brook.

'He din't do much. It were the other three. He kept lookout.'

'Tell us,' said Grant softly.

After a deep breath, Ravi said, 'I were off home and it were getting dark. I stayed out too long . . .'

'You know not to go across the Drayfin, Ravi, you've been chased before . . .' said his father.

'Please, Mr Singh. Let Ravi tell us.'

'Sorry.'

Grant nodded encouragement and Ravi continued. 'I came back across the Drayfin and they saw me. They chased me.'

'For the tape, Ravi, by "they" you mean Stephen Ingham, Benjamin Anderson, David Gretton, as well as Jason Wallis?'

Ravi nodded so Grant gestured with her arm. 'Yes,' he said at the prompt.

'And where did they catch up with you?' asked Brook.

'Near the field, before the bridge.' His lip started to wobble. 'They just started booting me, takin' it in turns, while the others took pictures, innit? Then that big one called Stinger . . .'

'Stephen Ingham.'

'Yeah. He told 'em to hold me down. The other two of 'em

did. Then he did this.' His eyes began to water as he gestured at his cheek and he put his hands to his face. 'I screamed . . .'

'Was Jason Wallis holding you down?'

'No, he were keeping lookout, like I said. I think he were embarrassed, he couldn't look at me . . .'

'Why was he embarrassed?' asked Brook.

''Cos he knew me. I used to go round with his sister at the primary.'

'His sister Kylie?'

'S'right.'

'Go on.'

'Well, then that bloke shouted for them to stop . . .'

'Bloke?' said Brook and Grant in unison.

'Yeah, that teacher.'

'What teacher?'

'I didn't recognise him at first, all dressed in black like that.'

'You knew him?' said Brook.

'Yeah, I used to go to primary like I said. He were a teacher there. I can't remember his name 'cos I never had him.'

'John Ottoman,' said Brook softly.

'That's it. Mr Ottoman. If it hadn't been for him . . .'

Chapter Eighteen

Jason Wallis woke early the next morning from a deep sleep. He sat up with a controlled sigh and yawned. He flicked on his mobile: just gone seven. He sprang out of bed and dressed in his new tracksuit and running shoes before tiptoeing downstairs. For the second night in a row, he had no need to shift his chest of drawers from behind his door.

He downed a glass of orange juice and pulled on a woollen hat, also new, before leaving the house. He broke into a slight jog as he headed down towards the bridges, taking the same route he had when fleeing The Reaper the day after his release. This was his second early morning and his lungs weren't quite as bad as yesterday, though he still required frequent stops. His head felt clear after three nights without booze and tobacco.

When he reached the towpath he actually broke into a sprint for about fifty yards, finally giving in to the stabbing pains and stopping to hack up the noxious sludge lining his throat and lungs. When his pulse returned to normal he set off again, this time managing a longer stint that took him all the way to the weir, near which he'd once cowered in terror from The Reaper.

Jason smiled. *The old me.* He set off again, following the same path to Elvaston Castle that he had on that fateful night of terror, the night he'd finally had to face his demons, the night he'd begged The Reaper for his life, sobbing like a girl. He eased to a halt at the very spot his bowels and bladder had opened, the place where the seed of the new man had been planted. He looked around in the pale dawn light enjoying the blood pumping through his heart. He was on holy ground. He'd been resurrected here, had seen the light or heard the voice; however you put it. *He* was alive, his friends and family were dead. He was a survivor. He must be doing something right.

No more dreams. No more weakness. The weak died. To be a victim was to live in fear of the death that sought you out. Cowards die many times. Jason Wallis was no coward. He'd faced The Reaper time and time again and still he was here. If The Reaper couldn't kill him, who could? He smiled and set off jogging back to Borrowash.

'I'm ready.'

*

Drexler began to doze. The heating in the car was cranked up to combat the chill of sub-zero temperatures and, despite being still light, he was in no shape to resist the sedative effect. His notebook slipped from his lap and his head dropped down onto his shoulder. Soon he was snoring.

He woke up some twenty minutes later feeling refreshed. Light snow had built up on his windshield and he moved the wiper switch to clear his vision. Sorenson's black eyes were burning into him.

Drexler stiffened, his feet kicking the fast-food cartons strewn across the floor of the car. He cursed himself for keeping his firearm in the trunk.

Sorenson grinned and his breath steamed as he mouthed something. He walked through the bank of slush to the driver's side window. Drexler opened his window no more than a crack.

'That *is* you, Special Agent. Are you lost?' He grinned confidently at Drexler, who didn't return his smile.

'Just pulled over for a nap, sir. I was on my way to our satellite office.'

Sorenson's grin remained. 'I was just walking around the grounds and I saw you.'

'Walking in this weather with a bad chest?'

Sorenson smiled coldly. 'My chest's fine. And, coming from England, this weather is normal. It's the heat that does for me.' Sorenson seemed to weigh his next utterance. 'Would you care to join me? I've got another fifteen minutes to walk then I'll be having a hot drink.'

Drexler nearly laughed. He was about to dismiss the invitation when he realised it was an opportunity he couldn't pass up. 'Sure, why not?'

Sorenson nodded, pleased, then jogged arthritically back to the wet highway to wait for Drexler to lock up his car.

After the two men passed through, the gates swung noiselessly together. Drexler looked round as they closed and Sorenson pulled a remote gleefully from his pocket. 'You Americans. Considering the privations you suffered creating this country, it amazes me that you can't open or close your own gates or garage doors. Dangerous to have things so easy, don't you think? This way.'

They set off away from the house, following the boundary wall. They walked in silence for five minutes, though not, it seemed to Drexler, as a result of any detectable awkwardness.

'How's your case faring?' Sorenson finally asked.

Drexler smiled. 'I'm not at liberty to talk about ongoing investigations.'

'Ongoing? So you still seek the killer of Caleb and Billy Ashwell? Why?'

'Why what?'

'Why do you seek the killer of two people who would

never have been allowed to see decent society ever again? Assuming they escaped the death penalty.'

Drexler didn't answer for a few moments. Finally he said, 'The man who calls at every gas station on a highway looking for his victims has to be a cold calculating killer. No matter what happened to the Baileys and those other poor families, the man who led Billy Ashwell to the end of a rope couldn't possibly have known he was involved in his father's crimes. But he was prepared to execute him anyway.'

Sorenson laughed then his tone became serious, almost accusing. 'But he *was* involved in the crimes.' Drexler raised an eyebrow. Sorenson smiled now. 'So I gather from the newspapers.'

They continued walking in silence for a few minutes before Sorenson said, 'Do you ever dream, Mike?'

Drexler looked across at him. 'Sometimes.'

'An American dream? A dream of betterment?'

'What's your point?'

'In Europe our dreams are different. Our governments don't promise us happiness. But the American Dream is about being so much better than you are – as though that would make you happy. A pity then this country cannot grasp greatness, Mike. It's there, right in front of you but always out of reach.'

'What are you talking about, Professor?'

'You. The FBI, the government, the ruling elite and all you represent.'

Drexler paused, trying to divine Sorenson's meaning, without success. 'Which is what?'

'The enforcement of laws that, for all their high-sounding rhetoric, keep the uneasy peace in one of the most vengeful nations on the planet. You know, this country imprisons children who accidentally shoot other children with guns legally kept in the home, by "responsible" adults. Those adults are protected by the same constitution that allows children to be exposed to violent films and games that glorify these weapons. When children become fixated by these guns and accidents inevitably happen, everyone throws up their hands in horror and astonishment.

'That's hilarious enough, but just to make it even funnier your nation maintains the pretence that it's the children's fault and locks them away for years, with hardened criminals. Only in America,' he added with a malicious grin.

'Is there a point to this lecture, sir?'

'Just that everyone in this nation would be happy to justify the execution of Billy Ashwell, including your partner. Everyone, it seems, except you.'

'With respect, you don't know what my partner thinks.'

'She's not accompanied you this last week, I notice. A parting of the ways?'

Drexler hesitated and turned to Sorenson. 'She's busy. I'm working this solo.' He was unhappy with his answer as soon as he said it. It made him sound like a lone wolf, a misfit going off the deep end.

'Using your vacation to persecute an innocent man?' Sorenson couldn't prevent a snigger.

'What makes you think I'm on vacation?'

'Just an impression.'

'My partner may disagree with me, but she understands why I have to do this. We have a bond.'

'Ah, yes. That would be the bond created at the residence of the late Reverend Hunseth.'

Drexler turned towards Sorenson's mocking smile, feeling his fists clench. The moment passed and Sorenson's nose remained unbroken. His thoughts swam around his head like a draining sink. Where did this old man get the confidence to goad somebody like him? It was unnerving. Sorenson played a dangerous game but played it with a confidence that made Drexler uneasy. Everything Sorenson had said felt like an assault, his words like the most invasive probe, against which he was powerless to defend himself and his country.

For an instant he imagined being under Sorenson's power and almost began to feel sorry for Caleb Ashwell. He imagined Sorenson opening his bottle of wine to drink a toast, grinning at his captives, telling them what he was going to do to them . . . and smiling as he did it.

After an age, Drexler's lungs began to slow and his mind began to reassemble. But once more he was to be wrong footed.

Sorenson looked down at the ground, apparently ashamed. 'Forgive me, Agent Drexler. I shouldn't have flung that at you. It was crude.'

'Who told you about Hunseth?'

'This is America. I'm rich. And everything and everybody is for sale,' said Sorenson. 'But I didn't need to pay for that information, Michael. May I call you Michael? Special Agent is so impersonal.'

'It's Mike.'

Sorenson nodded. 'Mike. As you better than most must know, your government's fantasy of a free society is maintained by a few clever gimmicks. Freedom of information is one. It's all in the records.'

Drexler nodded. 'But you have to know what you're looking for, Professor.'

'Call me Victor. Now come and have that hot drink, Mike. You look cold.'

*

Brook slouched against the patrol car, sucking on one of Hudson's cigarettes and watching a small crowd gather in the dusk. Brian Burton stood on the other side of the police tape, arguing with a uniformed constable about his right to trample all over potential evidence in the cause of free speech. Brook turned away from him and looked back towards the Ottomans' home. He shook his head as a SOCO gingerly carried away the bloodstained mountain bike from the house.

'Guess that's a clincher,' said Hudson, grinning widely. 'It takes all sorts, Damen. You of all people . . .'

Brook looked up at him with a bleak smile. 'I suppose.'

Laura Grant walked back towards them. 'The neighbour two doors down said they set off on Sunday morning before nine o'clock. She said she hadn't seen Denise out of the house for two years so it was a shock when she saw them loading up the car. And apparently they were having words.'

'Okay, luv. Do us a favour and scrounge a few CID coffees off one of the neighbours, will you? Try the one two doors down. She sounds accommodating. We won't be getting in until Forensics have strutted their stuff.'

Grant gave Hudson one of her looks then turned on her heel to pass the instruction to a PC.

'They didn't waste much time hitting the road,' said Hudson.

'What kind of car?' shouted Brook.

Grant turned round. 'What?'

'Ask the neighbour what kind of car they were driving, Laura.' Grant nodded and turned to leave. 'And . . . Laura!' She turned round expectantly at Brook's call. 'No sugar.'

She grinned at the two senior officers, mouthed a mute obscenity and walked away.

'I don't see them driving something black and powerful.'

'Cars can be hired, Damen.'

'They're just not up to it, Joshua. They're teachers, for God's sake. The nearest they come to homicide is slapping an unruly pupil on the spur of the moment.'

'They're educated, Damen. You said yourself they had the intelligence.'

'Really? Joshua, they didn't even wipe the blood off the bike.'

Hudson shrugged. 'Blind panic. You do what they did and try not to let it affect you.'

Brook looked up at him, but could discern no ulterior meaning. 'When I visited last week, Denise couldn't even open the door properly. You heard what the neighbour said. I doubt Denise ever leaves the house, especially at night.'

'Well she's left it now,' replied Hudson. 'Look, Damen. Stress does funny things to people. Then again, maybe she's not involved. Maybe it's just her husband looking for some payback . . .'

'And leaving Jason Wallis alive again?' Hudson shrugged at this. 'Then who's the woman watching in the bedroom?'

'All good questions, Damen. Want some good facts to go with them? The Ottomans have motive. John Ottoman is the right age, build and height. He's on the estate the night of the murders. He's wearing black clothing. A bloodstained mountain bike with the same tyre tread found at the scene is in his home. The next morning the Ottomans pack their bags and make a run for it. Want another fact? DS Noble has been listening to the 999 call and thinks it's Ottoman's voice.'

Brook was quiet for a moment, trying to get past the accumulated evidence. For a second he was prepared to accept it, then he thought of Sorenson. 'It's not them,' he muttered.

A Scene of Crime Officer walked down the path carrying several items in plastic bags. Cups, a telephone, a remote control – all items likely to carry fingerprints.

'Where's the other bike?' asked Brook.

The SOCO shook his head. 'Only one bike on the property.'

Brook looked at Hudson who shrugged again. 'They can explain it when we catch them.' Hudson grinned again and nodded towards the house. Brook turned to see an officer holding up a bloodstained black balaclava from the top of a bin bag.

* * *

Brook and Hudson waited with Charlton for the assembled journalists to be ready. Charlton and Hudson were in high spirits at the prospect of the press conference. They were determined to avoid triumphalism, but were finding it hard not to smile. This would be a huge feather in their caps once John and Denise Ottoman were in custody. Brook was less thrilled at the prospect. He could see Brian Burton in the second row preparing his questions; no doubt some would be fired in his direction. With the lights not yet on, Noble entered from the side door and passed a piece of paper to Charlton, who read it with satisfaction before passing it on to Hudson. Brook read it with a sinking heart. The thumbprint from Jason's mobile phone belonged to one of the Ottomans. As Jason had heard a male voice at the crime scene, it was fair to assume the print was John's. In addition, blood from the mountain bike had been matched to one of the victims – Stephen Ingham. DNA samples from various artefacts recovered from the Ottoman home were still being tested against the DNA taken from the fence panel.

'Excellent,' said Charlton, under his breath. 'Now we all know what we're going to say. The key thing is not to get ahead of ourselves, keep it simple and state clearly that our suspects are wanted only in connection with The Reaper killings in Derby. We make it clear that we have no evidence for the murders in London and Leeds until we interview . . .'

'Wait a minute. I didn't agree to that. We can't connect them to the Wallis murders as well . . .' began Brook.

'Why can't we?'

'There was no evidence; they were never suspects. And there are still loose ends in the Ingham deaths.'

'The Chief Inspector and I are agreed. As far as we're concerned, the Ottomans are connected to Jason Wallis and have tried twice to kill him in revenge attacks for the assault on his wife.'

'Then why is he still alive? Jason himself heard John Ottoman

307

talk to the emergency services. If he was there for Jason, why didn't he kill him first?'

Charlton noticed several journalists, including Brian Burton, start to take an interest in their conversation. 'Keep your voice down, Inspector. I don't need to tell you how criminal plans can go wrong . . .'

'And I don't need to tell you, sir, that both you and DCI Hudson were nowhere near the Wallis Inquiry. Trying to tie the Ottomans to that crime is not supported by any evidence . . .'

'But fortunately we have a surfeit of evidence from the Ingham murders which provides circumstantial . . . Where are you going? Inspector, sit back down,' Charlton hissed. But Brook was gone. Charlton turned around with a smile glued to his face, hoping nobody had noticed the disagreement. The lights came up and Charlton's smile disappeared.

*

Brook arrived back at his office to collect the folder on Mike Drexler. He slumped in his chair and stared out of the window at Derby's low horizon, across the flyover and on past the cathedral. The daylight was almost gone and people would be sitting in their homes watching Chief Superintendent Charlton and DCI Hudson giving their press conference. By the next morning John and Denise Ottoman would be on the front pages of every newspaper in the country and, in spite of the delicate policespeak employed by Charlton, presumed guilty by every editorial and reader. He wondered what such publicity would do to Denise Ottoman's fragile mental state.

He opened a window and sat down to read the file on Drexler. There were only three pages so it didn't take long. He tossed it onto his desk then lit a cigarette. His thoughts returned to the Ottomans and the media jackals preparing to tear their lives apart. How to save them?

Brook stubbed out his cigarette and dropped the filter out of the window, before closing it.

He stood to leave, picking up the Drexler folder. The Ottomans hadn't been convicted yet. There was still time.

*

Brook passed through the Incident Room on his way to the car park. Grant and Noble were talking over a coffee.

'You missed the press conference,' said Noble. 'We're just going out to celebrate. The rest of the team are already in the pub. If you care to join us.'

Brook paused. 'Two dangerous teachers have escaped and could be roaming the streets of Derby issuing detentions even as we speak. And you want to celebrate?'

Noble darted a smile at Grant. 'We're safe for now, sir. They're out of the country. They caught a ferry from Dover to France, Sunday lunchtime. We just heard.'

'So it's a plain old hide and seek now,' put in Grant.

'They got away. Then maybe a celebration *is* in order, John. Do we know what car they were in?'

'Volkswagen Polo.'

'Is that black and powerful, Laura?'

She smiled. 'No, it's green and small, but the car Tommy Blake saw might have been a legitimate taxi. We just haven't found it yet.'

'And has he been shown a picture of Denise Ottoman?'

Grant sighed. 'He has actually. No joy though. We also showed him the cleaned-up picture from the North bedroom to compare. It's not come out much clearer.' She handed him the printout, which Brook examined. 'Tell me, Inspector, do you always take a good result so badly?'

'There are no good results in our game, Laura.' He looked into her eyes. 'Joshua tells me you're driving back to Brighton tomorrow.'

Grant turned to Noble. 'Can I have a minute, John?'

309

Noble hesitated, then said to Grant, 'I'll meet you downstairs.'

When he'd left the room, Grant turned to Brook. 'Yes, sir, we're going home. We'll be back when the Ottomans are caught. But I thought I might take an extra day in Derby.'

'Oh?'

'I prefer to take the train. Besides,' she said, a smile playing around her lips, 'I've got a standing invitation to go walking in the Peaks.'

*

Drexler sank back in the sofa and accepted the hot chocolate from Sorenson's wrinkled hand. He took an immediate sip of the dark sweetness.

'It was a righteous shooting, Professor. Agent McQuarry supported me. The Board of Inquiry supported me. The Reverend was a secret drunk and an abusive bully.'

'How did you know that, Mike? Did he have a T-shirt to that effect?'

Drexler glared at him. 'I knew his type. He also had a knife. He'd already beaten his wife and threatened her with it. Drunks do that. When we got there we could see hesitation cuts on her neck. But I knew from experience he wasn't hesitating out of reluctance. He was putting the knife against his wife's neck again and again to let her feel its unforgiving steel, to amplify her terror.'

Sorenson drifted over to the hearth and turned on a gas tap. He lit the jet with a taper and flames began to crackle around the dry logs placed above. With a sharp breath, he turned to face Drexler, his black eyes boring through the smoke to his core.

When Sorenson said nothing, Drexler felt compelled, he didn't know why, to fill the silence. 'For a while she'd gotten away from him. She was wailing in the corner. Her face was all beat up and the man of God was three-quarters through a litre of vodka. Ed tried to talk him down, but she

310

must've got too close, I don't know. He went for her. Then it all turned to shit.'

'So it was your partner's fault.'

'No! It was my fault. The thing is . . . I should've been talking to Hunseth not Ed. The profile of a wife-beater is never wrong. A strong woman trying to reason with him, talk him down – that was always gonna rile him and we knew it. It's just that I . . . I guess I just froze. So when Hunseth lunged at her, she cut her hand pretty bad and damaged her tendons. She had to have rehab. She tried to get away but when he went for her again, I fired.'

Sorenson smiled and sat opposite Drexler. 'And after that, there wasn't enough rehab in the world to save the Reverend Hunseth.'

'No.'

'Not with four bullets in him.'

Drexler managed to hide his surprise. How did Sorenson know? How could he zero in on all his weak spots so unerringly? It was probably in the transcript but even so, only a professional would raise an eyebrow at that. 'What do you mean?'

'You're a very fine shot, Mike. Two in the heart and two in the head. The Reverend took some stopping. Is that why the Board took so long to clear you?'

Drexler's heart began to beat a little faster. 'I don't understand.'

'Did they ask you off the record, because it doesn't say in the file?'

'Ask me what?'

'At whom you fired the third and fourth bullets.'

'They were fired at Hunseth.'

'Physically, yes. I know that, Mike. Forget who you were firing at and just tell me one thing. Why fire the third and fourth bullets at all? If your first didn't stop him, the second

311

must have done. One in the heart, one in the head. But you fired two more.' Sorenson cocked his head to one side, to deliver his payload. 'Who else were you killing that night?'

Drexler smiled now. Of course. Never ask a question you don't know the answer to. The end was in sight. But then what? What purpose was this serving? What did he want from him? 'Don't stop, Professor. It's just getting interesting.'

Sorenson stood. He seemed satisfied with Drexler's reply. 'I'm glad you're not taking this personally, Mike. I think we can be friends.' Drexler raised an eyebrow at that. Sorenson caught it. 'In time.'

He moved over to a large walnut cabinet and opened a door. 'First some Beethoven . . . and a glass of malt whisky.' Sorenson pressed a button and music began to play – beautiful and lingering piano notes swaying dramatically against the worsening weather gathering on the lake. He poured two generous measures into heavy tumblers and handed one to his guest. Drexler prepared to refuse. He hadn't touched alcohol for nearly three months and hadn't missed it.

'Don't worry, Mike. It's not drugged.'

Drexler smiled and took the glass. This had to be part of the game. He accepted his whisky and sniffed at it without drinking. It didn't smell like ordinary whisky and he was tempted to take a sip but needed his wits about him if he were ever going to get a crack at his agenda. He felt the need to occupy himself and stood to stroll as nonchalantly as he could manage across to the large glass doors which were being pounded by wind and snow now driving across the water.

He turned to look around. Everything about the place was expensive and tasteful. The room was sparsely furnished as befitted the single man, indicated by all the information they held on Sorenson. The space was large and open and smelled of pine, though there was a slight chemical edge in the air that reminded him of hospitals.

A mezzanine balcony, serviced by a generous wooden staircase, ran along one wall and seemed to lead off to other enclosed rooms. The fire, framed in wood and stone, dominated another wall and arranged to face it were a polished oak coffee table and the two comfortable dark leather sofas on which Drexler and Sorenson had been sitting.

There was no TV but across an end wall stood a large walnut chest holding a few weighty books. There was a music centre that fed the speakers, which were placed discreetly under beams at the four corners of the room. The chest also housed the drinks cabinet from which Sorenson had produced the two glasses of whisky. The darkness was gathering and Sorenson switched on a pair of lamps.

'Cheers.' Sorenson raised his glass to drink and Drexler decided to follow suit with a minute sip which burned his tongue with its smoky fire.

Drexler returned to his seat, leaving the toast unanswered. 'What do you want, Professor?'

Sorenson seemed a little surprised. 'What do I want? I want to know who you are and I want you to know who I am. I'd like you to think of me as a friend.' Drexler pulled a face. 'Or at least as someone who can help you.'

'Help me? How?'

'Make you realise you're not alone in your pain, Mike.'

'Pain?'

'With me it was my twin brother – with you a drunken, abusive father. Families cause such pain. I don't know why.'

Drexler glared at Sorenson, determined not to react to the constant probing, though each pick at the wound made it harder. 'Makes you just want to wipe them out, doesn't it, Professor?'

313

Sorenson smiled faintly. 'Yes, it does. For instance your father, James Drexler, was also a religious zealot, Mike. A drunk too. And as you saw with the Reverend Hunseth, religion and alcohol can be a dangerous combination. Did he quote the scriptures at you as he beat you? Did he beat your mother and call her the devil's harlot? Did he call damnation on your sister after her suicide?'

Drexler dropped his glass and lunged towards Sorenson but froze a few yards away. The 9mm M9 automatic had appeared in Sorenson's hand as if from nowhere. 'Sorry, Mike.' He gestured the gasping Drexler back to the sofa and sat down on the other. 'Truly I am. I push too hard sometimes. But I had to be sure.'

'Fuck you. Kerry would never do that. It was a traffic accident,' panted Drexler, still breathing harshly.

'There were no skid marks, Mike. She wasn't wearing a seat belt. She drove herself into that ravine to end the torture of life with your father. Her love for you couldn't conquer the pain he caused, so she snuffed out her life and left you and your mother to pick up the pieces.' He paused to assess Drexler's willingness to lunge at him again before lowering the gun. 'Now that is information I did have to pay for. I'm very sorry. But I have to know why you're still coming at me so hard. It's the same reason you put four bullets into Reverend Hunseth, isn't it? Am I really the same as him?'

'An authority figure with power over life and death. And not afraid to use it. What do you think, Professor?'

'I think whoever killed Caleb and Billy is more like you than you know. An avenging angel, removing those who abuse their position, those who torment and kill the innocent to satisfy their basest urges. With your father and the departed Reverend, it was a twisted religious mania and a love of the bottle; with Caleb Ashwell, carnal pleasure and financial gain. Face it. You didn't have to kill Hunseth. You could've disabled him. The Board knew that but gave you the benefit of the doubt. But you get more than that from me and Hunseth's tortured family. You get their gratitude. You ended the tyranny of his life and saved those close to him.'

'Saved?'

'As surely as the killer you seek saved other families from the tyranny of Caleb Ashwell.'

'And Billy?'

Sorenson put down the gun and took a sip of his whisky, eyeing his guest. Drexler wondered briefly whether to make a grab for it but decided against it. 'Of course. Stupid of me. You see me as Caleb and yourself as Billy – as much a victim as George Bailey and his family. And do you know something? You're right, Mike. Billy was a victim. But it was too late for rehab. Billy could never be that child again. The clay had hardened.'

'Clay?'

'That's right. He was moulded by his father. You see, Billy didn't have your strength.'

'My strength?'

'Mike, when will you embrace what you've become? Those four bullets have bestowed a power on you that you weren't aware of before. You were moulded just as Billy was, but did you become Billy? Did you help your father beat your mother? Did you help drive your sister to despair? No. You conquered the urge to find safety under his cloak. And to do so kept you a victim. You chose the hard path. But not Billy. He took the hand that led him to oblivion. He would've become Caleb. No power on earth could've stopped that.' Sorenson got up with his glass and picked up the gun by the nozzle. 'Terrible things, guns.' He threw it to Drexler who caught it.

Drexler checked the magazine. It was full. He flicked the safety off and caressed the weapon in his palm and looked over at Sorenson who was at the drinks cabinet, his back turned.

'Another drink, Mike?'

Drexler contemplated for a few seconds, then put the safety back on. He put the gun in his pocket and picked up his spilled glass. He walked over to Sorenson and held out the glass which his host refilled. Then he drank the whisky down in one swallow and held his glass for a further refill.

'So what do you want, Professor?'

'What I said, Mike – understanding.'

'You want me to understand you?'

Sorenson smiled and shook his head. 'No, Mike. I want you to understand yourself. You've studied philosophy. Apply those skills. Make friends with your past. You're not Billy Ashwell. Billy raped and tortured people.'

'So you killed him.'

'Caleb Ashwell and his brother Jacob killed him. They killed him as surely as if they'd put the noose round his neck. Your father didn't drive your sister over that ravine. But he killed her just the same. And he tried to kill you. But you won that battle.'

'I didn't kill my father if that's what you're implying. He left us after Kerry died. Ashamed, he said. The ultimate sin before God, to take your own life. I haven't seen him since.'

'Yes, you have, Mike, remember. You put two extra bullets into him and saved your partner's life. You killed your father that night. In absentia, as it were. Tell me, Mike. How did you know I called at every gas station? They can't all have had security cameras.'

Drexler took a sip of his drink, brooding over the value

316

of that information. 'You could only get ten bucks' worth of fuel in your tank. I figure if you drove up 89 looking for George Bailey's killers you're going to need a reason to stop at every station. So you filled up each time.'

Sorenson seemed puzzled for a second. 'I'd say that was good police work, Mike – especially as there was no record of the sale. I'm amazed that Ashwell's camera was good enough to pick out the ten dollars.' He took a sip of whisky.

Drexler returned Sorenson's gaze. He said nothing. No more free information. No more showing Sorenson his hand. He wouldn't ask about Brook. He wouldn't ask Sorenson what was to happen at the Golden Nugget on Tuesday. He knew. The wait was over.

'Thanks for the drink. I have to go.'

'Stay a little longer. I have a proposition for you. How would you like to earn what you've always wanted?'

'What's that?'

'I think you know.'

Drexler stared at Sorenson for several minutes. 'And you know where he is.'

Sorenson smiled back and patted his pocket.

'Where?' asked Drexler.

Sorenson's smile remained while the black eyes did their work, poring over every detail of Drexler's countenance as if he was some kind of behavioural experiment. For a moment Drexler considered taking out the gun and ramming it into Sorenson's mouth to force him to reveal his father's address, but somehow he sensed that that would be a variable that Sorenson had already assessed and included in his calculations.

Drexler couldn't hold his eyes and stared off into the fire. 'What do I have to do?'

*   *   *

'Not joining your colleagues for a knees-up, Brook?'

Brook, preparing to get behind the wheel of the BMW, turned to see Brian Burton's yellow grin. 'Aren't you getting a bit old for all this, Brian? Up all hours, filing your copy when the rest of the world is enjoying life.'

'I could say the same about you. Why did you walk out of the press conference?'

'No comment.'

'Have you got a problem with the investigation?'

'No comment.'

'Or maybe you're having another breakdown.'

Brook swung onto his driver's seat and pulled at the door but Burton grabbed it. 'Get off or you'll get hurt.'

'My photographer would love to see that. He doesn't like me!' he shouted at a thin-lipped man hovering with a camera a few yards away. 'You don't like me, do you, Inspector?'

'I don't ever think about you. Now get away from my door.'

Burton held on. 'I've interviewed the Ottomans before. Or tried to. After the Wallis thing. Charlton and Hudson don't know them like we do, Inspector. If Mrs O trod on a spider she'd cry herself to sleep. And now we're meant to believe that the pair of them murdered six people. Nine if you include the Wallis family.'

'What do you want?'

'I want to know if you're happy with the result. That's all.' Brook held onto his driver's door but stopped pulling. 'Just a couple of words.'

Brook took his hand off the door and stared off into the darkness, resisting the temptation to deploy the two words that entered his head.

Burton seemed temporarily wrong-footed. He took his own hand from Brook's door and straightened up. Brook made no move to close it or start the car.

'Okay. You don't want to talk to me. But if I ask you if you think John and Denise Ottoman are innocent and you don't reply that's what I'll be putting in tomorrow's paper.' Brook looked up into Burton's red-rimmed eyes and held his gaze. After thirty seconds he raised an eyebrow and reached for the door handle. A smile spread across Burton's face.

*

Drexler pulled up his collar against the biting wind and trudged wearily along the tree-lined drive, his mind still in turmoil from the psychological battering he'd suffered at Sorenson's hands. Andy Dupree was right. He should have left it alone, walked away. Now Sorenson was in his head, had insinuated himself into his very DNA. Sorenson had read between the lines of the report and worked out what had happened.

But one thing Sorenson couldn't change. In shooting Hunseth, Drexler had killed his father; he didn't need to do it again. Not if it meant pawning his soul, his freedom, to Sorenson. The Ashwell case was over, Sorenson was untouchable. He knew that now. To continue would be to surrender his own will, to risk losing himself, to become Billy. Drexler made a decision. He'd get in his car and drive back to Sacramento that same night. He wouldn't kill again at Sorenson's behest.

He quickened his step, keen to be away. The lamplight was barely adequate and the moon cowered behind angry clouds, which made walking difficult. He stepped gingerly over sodden, slippery leaves and hopped over puddles. He gazed up at the bare branches of trees swaying in the wind. Their striptease done for the year, they tried to hide their blushes behind the modesty of the evergreens, but Drexler registered nothing.

Halfway back to his car he stopped cold. He peered at a patch of newly broken ground where the dusting of snow seemed lighter. He stepped a couple of metres off the tarmac for a better view. He wished he had his flashlight but had to manage with the pale yellow glow of the avenue's lighting. He stared at the freshly-planted sapling in the gloom and touched the deep-green leaves, which were large and oily. He ran his thumb over his finger and sniffed the sappy resin on his hand. Then he rustled the horn-shaped creamy white flowers with the back of his hand.

He stood and made his way back to the car, a grim smile spreading slowly across his face.

*

Brook got home forty-five minutes later and turned on his computer. After clicking onto Wikipedia, he typed in 'scopolamine' and read for ten minutes, jotting down several alternate names for the drug. Then he jogged up the stairs to fetch *The Ghost Road Killers*. He turned to the index to check for hyoscine and got a hit on his first attempt. He turned to the page and read with a quickening pulse:

> *Victims, predominantly the adults who were driving the vehicles, were found to have ingested quantities of hyoscine, combined with traces of morphine, which would render the recipient drowsy, malleable and prone to hallucinations. It is believed that the drug was introduced to victims in the coffee provided at the gas station.*
>
> *Inevitably drivers became somnolent and, if unable to pull to the side of the road, were liable to crash their vehicles. Several of the motor homes recovered from the gas station had been involved in a collision, though not usually with other vehicles and in only one case was damage more than minor. However, damage to the bodywork of their vehicles was the least of the worries for the unfortunate occupants . . .*

Brook looked at the faded picture of a happy and grinning Bailey family on the opposite page and nodded. The parents at the back, arms entwined, the girls at the front laughing at some remark from their father, oblivious to their destiny. Unfortunate indeed. He stared at the picture longer than he should, then turned back to the index for any mention of Victor Sorenson. It was fruitless but that was hardly surprising. There was no mention of Sorenson in Brian Burton's book either, nor any of the hundreds of Reaper newspaper stories over the last twenty years – not even in Brook's own police reports.

Victor Sorenson only ever existed between the lines. Like The Reaper, he was a ghost. Nothing proven, nothing recorded. For years Brook had thought himself the only living person who could connect Victor Sorenson to The Reaper – and only then because the professor had wanted him to know.

But now, despite Sorenson's death, The Reaper was back. And a former FBI agent had moved next door to write a book about a fifteen-year-old case in California. Brook was starting to read between the lines and Sorenson was there.

He threw the book aside and left the cottage. Drexler's car was in the drive but the house was in darkness. He checked his watch. It was nearly midnight. He walked down the side path and knocked. No reply. He tried the door but this time it was locked. He considered breaking in but thought better of it. As he turned to go, however, the outside light came on, the lock turned and the door opened.

Drexler stood before him, apparently unsurprised to see him. 'Damen.' He made no effort to invite Brook inside.

'Can we talk?'

'It's late.'

'We've found a suspect.'

Drexler's head cocked to one side. 'The Reaper? You'd better come in.'

Chapter Nineteen

McQuarry opened her eyes at the first ring. She craned towards the clock – three in the morning – then flopped back down with a groan. A few seconds later she flicked on a lamp and pulled the receiver to her ear.

'Ed. It's me.'

McQuarry rested her head on her spare hand. 'Who else? What's up?'

'We got him.'

'Who?'

'Sorenson.'

McQuarry opened her eyes and sat up. 'You've arrested him?'

'No. Nothing like that. Listen, you have to come back to Tahoe.'

McQuarry looked around for her cigarettes but couldn't see them. 'Why, Mike?'

'Because we can connect him to the cabin.'

'How?'

'You know that freshly dug hole near the cabin? The one we saw that night we searched the site.'

'Vaguely.'

'Well, there was a small tree in it. Same as the other ones in the row, remember?'

'A tree . . . Mike, I don't . . .'

'Ed, that tree was taken and replanted in Sorenson's grounds.'

'How do you know?'

'Because he invited me in for a drink and I saw it.'

'He invited . . .'

'Know what I think? That tree is some kind of natural source of those drugs Ashwell was using on tourists. Like deadly nightshade or something. That's why we couldn't find anything in the cabin. Ashwell must've told Sorenson before he died or maybe Sorenson worked it out – he's an industrial chemist, remember – so he takes one of the trees for his own use . . .'

'Mike. Slow down.' McQuarry got out of bed and walked to a small table. She picked up a pack of cigarettes and lighter and put one in her mouth. She opened the double doors to her apartment balcony and stepped out in her pants and 49ers sweatshirt to light her cigarette. The cold air woke her up with a jolt and she glanced off to the blinking lights of Sacramento below. 'That doesn't mean it's the same tree. You've no proof that he took it.'

'That's not all. I had a lip reader look at the film of Sorenson buying his gas at Ashwell's garage. Ed, he lied about his name. He told Caleb his name was Brook . . .'

'Brook?' McQuarry took a large pull on her cigarette and tried to gather her thoughts. 'So what?'

'So, I thought I'd check it out. I've got a friend in the Metropolitan Police, the London . . . branch or district or whatever they call it, where Sorenson has a house. You remember those murders four or five years back? In England.'

'Remind me.'

'The Reaper murders in London. Serial killer. He ghosted into family's homes and killed everyone, children included. It even made the papers here because there was talk of him being another Jack the Ripper.'

'The Reaper . . . I remember.'

'You remember he cut their throats? Like Caleb. One boy was hung though – the son of one of the victims. Yeah? Like Billy. And another thing, all the victims were petty criminals . . .'

'Unlike Caleb and Billy.'

'. . . and listen to this,' Drexler continued, missing the objection. 'One of the investigating officers was a Detective Sergeant Brook.'

McQuarry took another draw, her mind absorbing the information. 'It's a bit thin. Sounds like a common enough name.'

'There's more. Victor Sorenson was interviewed by this Brook in connection with the Reaper killings.'

'He was a suspect?'

'Well, according to my friend, no, but that's still a connection. And apparently Brook became so obsessed with this Reaper . . .'

'Sound familiar?'

'. . . that he had to take a leave of absence. Mental problems. His marriage failed . . .'

'Mike. Okay, okay, I get it.'

'One more thing, Ed. Remember the Golden Nugget Motel? Sorenson booked all the rooms for the day after tomorrow, under the name Peter Hera.'

'So?'

'Peter Hera is an anagram of The Reaper.'

McQuarry looked across at her bags, already packed. 'I'll be there tomorrow afternoon.'

*

'Should I open that bottle of champagne now, Damen?'

'Not tonight, Mike.'

Drexler nodded. 'No. The end of a case is never for celebrating.

It just frees you up for the next human train wreck. Who's the suspect?'

'A man called John Ottoman – a teacher. But he escaped to France. He'll be caught soon enough.'

'Did he do it?'

'There's a lot of evidence.'

'I'm sure you were very thorough.' Brook detected an undertone and narrowed his eyes to dredge up the inference. He was on the point of asking for a clarification but let it pass. He didn't want to be sidetracked tonight.

Drexler indicated an armchair for Brook, opposite his own and facing a small but robust coal fire. A small chintz lamp gave out light to see by, but not enough to dispel the gloom. On Drexler's chair sat a leaded glass, half-full of what looked like malt whisky. On the cushion was Brian Burton's upturned book. Brook sat down while Drexler brought him a tumbler and showed him a green bottle.

Brook nodded and stretched his feet towards the fire while Drexler poured the whisky and handed him the heavy glass. Brook examined the bottom of the glass but could see no sign of anything untoward. He sniffed its intense peaty bouquet and half-smiled at remembrance of things past. Brook took a small sip, recalling the taste from his meetings in Sorenson's London home. He looked up at Drexler who seemed at ease and Brook felt a tremor of anxiety. He was in the home of a man he would soon denounce as The Reaper but he feared that, like Sorenson, he was unlikely to be troubled by it.

'Are you enjoying Burton's book?'

'It's badly written. Though a fascinating subject,' said Drexler, closing it. 'But he doesn't have a good head for those little details that make all the difference. The details cops notice and lose sleep over, but people like Burton can't see.'

'Such as?'

'This kid, Jason something.'

'You don't even know his name.'

'I know he's still alive, against all the odds. He's survived The Reaper not once but twice. Anybody but a cop could put it down to an oversight and move on. But we know better, don't we? We know all too well why he was left alive.'

'Do we?'

'Sure we do – it's called division of labour. Why kill someone when you can get someone else to do it? And when that someone else has killed for you, well, then there are two of you to work the next Reaper killing – and after that three of you. And before long . . .'

'Before long there's a whole Reaper network to do the killing,' said Brook.

'*Many hands make light work* . . . a bit of a commie mantra but it fits. But here's the mystery, the thing this Burton will never think to address. Someone has failed to deliver on this kid. Twice.'

'Makes you wonder, doesn't it?' said Brook. 'About some people's commitment to the cause.'

Drexler grunted his amusement. 'It does. But go careful, my friend. Even an untalented flatfoot like Brian Burton spotted one thing.'

Brook raised his glass and fixed his eye on Drexler. 'Oh? What's that?'

'How many times you've failed to catch this guy.'

Brook took a sip of his drink. 'He doesn't rate me very highly,' he said with a thin smile.

Drexler nodded. 'Another of those details missed, Damen. That's why Burton's a fool. He actually thinks you're incompetent. But he doesn't know you at all. Personally, I think it must take a special type of genius to keep letting The Reaper slip through his fingers and still look like he's doing his job properly.'

Brook eyed his host for a moment, trying to organise his thoughts. The gloves had been peeled off and he would finally get some answers. Time to throw his first punch.

326

'Well, on this side of the pond, Mike, we have something called the rules of evidence. We're not allowed to execute suspects just because they have a knife in their hand.'

Drexler smiled back. 'I see you've been doing your own background reading. You're referring to the Reverend Hunseth. Seems like a long time ago.' He looked off into the fire, as Sorenson had all those years before. Then he looked back at Brook. 'I got some grey hairs over it, sure, but I'm fine with it now. Nobody missed him. Nobody mourned him – 'cept maybe the local liquor mart. But you're wrong, Damen. Even on my side of the pond they don't like unexplained shootings. Questions were asked. People were interviewed. But I was a federal agent and my partner was in danger. I was able to answer them and that was enough. See, back home, the good guys have guns too.' He laughed at a private joke. 'I suppose that makes *me* The Reaper, Damen.'

'You were for the Reverend.'

'Hunseth got what he deserved.'

'Did your father?' Brook was pleased to see the icy expression infect Drexler's face, his knuckles whitening for a few seconds.

Finally Drexler smiled and affected a slight nod, to acknowledge a blow well aimed. 'Always go too far, because that's where you'll find the truth.'

Brook nodded. 'Albert Camus.'

Drexler eyed him. 'You know Camus. Why am I not surprised?' He took a sip of whisky. 'So tell me, Damen. Is this teacher, Ottoman, getting what he deserves? Is he The Reaper's disciple?'

'He didn't do it, Mike.'

'You amaze me,' said Drexler in a monotone. He cocked his head and considered Brook as though anew. 'What happened? Were they getting too close? Was it too obvious to your superiors? Did you have to throw them a bone? The professor wouldn't be pleased. He's not keen on civilians getting hurt in the crossfire.'

'Sorenson's dead.'

Drexler nodded. 'That's the rumour.'

'That's a fact,' said Brook. 'I was there.'

Drexler took another sip of his drink. He walked over to a small stereo and switched it on. He checked the disc then pressed play. 'But he lives on through others, Damen. His will be done.' A deep sonorous note sounded from the speakers and a choir took up the opening verse.

'And what's that exactly?'

Drexler swivelled to face Brook. 'Cutting out the dead wood, Damen. So the tree can grow stronger.'

'Is that what you're doing here, Mike – strengthening the tree?'

'I'm writing a book, my friend, for the good guys who already died. That's why I'm here.' He reached into the drawer of a nearby chest. He pulled a gun from it and placed it on the arm of the chair then looked away, remembering, a sudden sadness invading his features. He closed his eyes, but Brook resisted the urge to make a lunge for the gun. 'Fauré's Requiem. Imagine heading for the next world with this rolling around in your head.'

Brook's eyes burned into Drexler's death mask. 'There isn't a next world.'

Drexler grinned, his eyes still closed. 'No, there isn't.'

'But I'd prefer the Debussy if I have a choice.'

Drexler opened his eyes. 'I don't have any.'

Brook nodded. 'No, of course.' He looked at the weapon and then at Drexler. 'If this is my reward for breach of contract,' Brook paused for effect, 'then I'm ready.'

'Ready?'

'But first I'll tell you what I told Sorenson. The Laura Maples case . . . I was young and in a bad place. I made a mistake. Floyd Wrigley was a mistake and one that I am never going to repeat. No matter what Jason Wallis has done to me I'm not going to kill him, nor am I going to join your little network. I'm not like Sorenson and I never was.' Drexler stared at him and Brook fancied he could detect uncertainty for the first time tonight.

His hesitancy pleased Brook, so he continued. 'So if it's all right with you, I'd like a last cigarette and then you can do what you've got to do.'

'Last request – just like in the movies.' Drexler looked down at his gun, then smiled. 'Don't get the wrong idea, Damen. I'm no tough guy. Just careful. I don't know how far off the reservation you've strayed. But one thing about Sorenson, you of all people should know, is that when the good guys get in the way, that's when you get out. Those are the rules. No civilians. No John Ottomans. No matter what the cost. You've served. I've served. We're the thin blue, my friend. We've got rights.'

Brook's eyes narrowed. Answers. Fat chance. All he was getting here were more questions. Why had Drexler killed Harvey-Ellis? And why was he still in Derbyshire? The Inghams were dead. His work was done. Was he hanging on for Brook to deliver on his contract with Sorenson? Or was he planning another atrocity?

'You can forget about me, Mike. I won't kill Jason Wallis.' Brook stared hard at Drexler who wouldn't look back. Instead he put his hands together, immersed in the music. 'When are you leaving?'

'Soon. A week.'

'You paid six months' rent in advance.'

Drexler smiled. 'I won't starve. My research is nearly done. I just need to speak to one last person and I'll be on my way.'

'And who's that?'

Drexler fixed him with a twisted smile. 'Don't you know?'

Brook rose to leave, declining to finish his drink. 'Thanks for all your hospitality, Mike.' Drexler accepted with a nod of the head. 'I won't bother you again. But don't contact me and don't send me any more emails. And, rules or no rules, if you come back to Derby . . .' Brook turned to be sure he locked onto Drexler's eyes '. . . I'll kill you.'

Drexler picked up the gun and followed Brook to the door,

pulling a cigarette from a pocket and throwing it into his mouth. Brook walked into the blackness without looking round. 'Goodbye, Damen.' Drexler aimed the gun at Brook's retreating back. He squeezed the trigger briefly then relaxed and let the gun fall to his side. He went back inside and lit his cigarette, removing the clip from the M9.

He sat down to finish his drink, examining the weapon. Sorenson's gun. It had never been fired in anger since the professor had given it to him. Maybe it never would be. Maybe Sorenson really was dead. Maybe he really was chasing ghosts.

*

When Brook woke the next day, it was to the sound of knocking on his door. He jumped out of bed and glanced at the clock. To his surprise it was ten past nine. He padded to the window over-looking the lane and saw a taxi in the road. A second later, Grant stepped back from the door and looked up. She was dressed for walking. She saw him at the window and waved.

Brook acknowledged her and pulled his trousers on, fastening them up as he skittered down the stairs to open the front door. On the way, he picked up the folder on Mike Drexler and put it in a desk drawer. For the first time since moving to Hartington, Brook had bolted his door and he slid it open as she turned away from the departing taxi.

'Laura? What are you doing here?'

'I'm here to go walking, remember?'

Shivering in his T-shirt, Brook looked at her. He hadn't thought she was serious, but he beckoned her in and returned to the semi-warmth of the kitchen to turn on the kettle.

'We said nine o'clock,' he threw over his shoulder in mock admonishment.

'Yeah, sorry to keep you waiting,' she smiled back. 'I had trouble finding a cab to come all this way.'

'I'll bet.'

'Brought you the local paper.'

Brook looked across at the headline: CHIEF SUSPECT INNO-CENT, SAYS REAPER DETECTIVE

He smiled faintly and continued to make tea. 'I suppose I'm back in the doghouse,' he muttered, handing Grant a mug.

'Not with us. Joshua doesn't care. But I haven't spoken to Charlton. There's more,' she said, turning to page three. 'We got a DNA match from Stephen Ingham and Benjamin Anderson to the two samples taken from Annie Sewell's sheltered accommodation the night she was murdered. Jason Wallis was telling the truth . . .'

'. . . but not the whole truth,' added Brook. Grant raised an eyebrow. 'Never mind.'

Brook read the first few paragraphs then took his tea upstairs to get fully dressed. After a quick glance across at his neighbour's house for signs of life, he returned to the kitchen to make a flask for his rucksack. 'I didn't have time to make sandwiches,' he said.

Grant grinned at him. 'I noticed. Didn't you think I'd come?'

'Honestly . . . no.'

'I couldn't sleep so I figured why not. I need a day to wash the case out of my brain.'

Brook smiled at her. 'A day?'

'All right. A month would be better, but it's a start. I know Josh would've been talking it through all day in the car . . .'

'About how and why I killed Harvey-Ellis?'

She smiled as they stepped out into the cold. 'Day off, remember.'

'We'll see.'

They struck out down the lane into Hartington, past the Devonshire Arms and the post office and were almost through the village when Brook led them onto a path beside a municipal toilet building. Through the gate and following the path across fields, they eventually came to a small copse and stepped through another gate. Within a few minutes they were walking next to the River Dove, following the heavy winter waters through the steep-sided valley. They met few other walkers and were content to walk in silence for the first hour.

At a small footbridge over a tributary, Brook swung off his rucksack and poured two cups of tea from his flask. 'I didn't bring sugar.'

'That's fine.'

They sat against a large rock, sipping their tea. It was ten minutes before Grant spoke again. 'You know, there's one thing I've begun to understand about the Reaper murders, Damen.'

'What?'

'That one of the reasons he chooses who his victims are going to be is to make us question whether we care about what he's done. And, whether we like it or not, because we realise that the dead aren't going to be missed, we don't do our job properly . . .'

'I hope—'

'No, I don't mean we don't do everything we're supposed to do to catch him. We're professionals after all. It's just that . . . it doesn't matter as much. When we see crowds cheering The Reaper outside the Ingham house, we're not disgusted – surprised maybe, even a little amused, but we're never going to go that extra mile as we would for a murdered toddler or a beaten pensioner. Do you know what I mean?'

Brook nodded. 'I think so.'

'I suppose what I'm trying to say is that I can see Harvey-Ellis died for a legitimate reason. It's hard to care that he's dead. Whoever killed him, if it's because of the way he behaved in life . . . then, I guess that doesn't mean his killer is necessarily a bad person.'

Brook smiled. 'Is this where I say "gee thanks" and you throw the cuffs on me?'

Grant smiled. 'It wasn't meant as a trap.' She looked at him. 'Besides, you didn't kill Harvey-Ellis, did you?'

Brook looked back at her, once again feeling a surge of

admiration for her abilities. Day off or not, he knew he'd have to be on his guard. 'When's your train?'

'Six o'clock tonight.'

Brook checked his watch. 'If we walk to Alstonefield we can have lunch at the George. Taxi back to my place and I'll run you into town for six.'

'Thanks.'

'Where's your luggage?'

'At the hotel.'

Brook packed the flask into his rucksack and they set off again. The sky had darkened and a light rain began to fleck their clothing. A half-hour later they approached a wooden footbridge across the river and Grant crossed as Brook removed his boot to shake out a stone. With his boot retied, Brook climbed over the bridge and followed Grant steadily up the steep path. She skipped up the gradient but Brook caught her at the top of the slope where they both sat panting. Brook made his three thousandth resolution to give up smoking for good.

Once rested, they followed the footpath past a YMCA and onto the road, into the pretty village of Alstonefield. The George sat on a small triangular green and, after kicking off their boots and ordering a couple of pints, they were soon sitting in front of a roaring log fire to contemplate the menu.

'So why did you do it?'

'Do what?'

'Brief that journalist. Not a great career move.'

'I've not had a great career, Laura.' He took a sip of his beer. 'I did it because they're innocent.'

'In the face of all the evidence.'

'Yes.'

'Is this just a feeling or something more concrete? I'd like to know. For the interview.'

'It's not them, Laura. They're . . .' Brook remembered his conversation with Drexler the previous night '. . . civilians.'

'Civilians.'

'Yes. The Reaper is fighting a war against ugliness and there's no room for civilians. They get in the way.'

'But Ottoman was at the scene. The DNA doesn't lie.'

'I can't help that, Laura. But when we get them back to Derby we'll ask him.'

'Think Charlton will want you on the interview, Damen?'

'He may not want me on the case. I have a bad habit of getting myself removed from investigations. That's why you need to know. So you can ask him.'

'What should I ask him?'

'Keep it simple. Ask him why he was there, why he got his prints on the scalpel and his DNA on the fence. Ask him why on earth he would kill everybody present except Jason, the one person he and his wife must hate above all others. Ask him why he made the call to the emergency services. Ask where the second mountain bike is.'

'We don't know for certain that there ever was a second bike.'

'Two killers. Two bikes. Ask him.'

Their sandwiches and chips arrived and they waited for the waitress to leave but the conversation had dried up and they ate in silence apart from the cracking and spitting of the logs. When the food was finished, Brook stretched out his legs and closed his eyes.

'So why didn't he kill Jason Wallis?' asked Grant finally.

'Wrong question, Laura. Ottoman didn't kill anyone.'

Grant smiled and shook her head. 'Why not?' Brook flicked a glance at her. 'Flip it over, Damen.'

'What do you mean?'

'Okay. Assume he's there by accident. Assume he didn't kill the Inghams. Assume what you like, but Ottoman was there. And the person he hates most in the world was there, helpless before him. He had the scalpel in his hand – we know he did. So even if he didn't kill the Inghams, it's all set up. Why not just do it? It's the right question. You were on the scene alone

334

at one point. If Wallis had hurt you in some way, could you have killed him?'

Brook opened his eyes and looked into the distance, remembering his dead cat, head smashed in by young Wallis two years ago. Then he remembered the sensation, the frisson of power as he picked up the scalpel in his gloved hand and moved it from under Jason's hand and held it against his throat. He took a sip of beer. It *was* the right question.

*

After lunch Brook and Grant took a taxi back to Hartington. They were both damp after their exercise and Brook insisted on Grant taking a shower. He gave her an old T-shirt and sweatshirt to wear so she had dry clothes for the journey. After making coffee he checked his answering machine. There were six messages. He listened to them all. Two were from Noble warning that Chief Superintendent Charlton was after Brook's blood. The other four were from Charlton, his tone clipped and increasingly angry at each renewed attempt to get through to Brook without success.

'Aren't you going to answer those?' asked Grant from the doorway, rubbing a towel through her hair.

Brook shrugged. 'Maybe tomorrow.'

He took his own shower and dressed in his bedroom. Again he looked briefly across at Rose Cottage but, although a light was burning somewhere in the back, he saw no sign of his neighbour.

When they set off for Derby it was already dark, but traffic into town was light and they reached the Midland Hotel forty minutes later. Grant disappeared into the hotel and re-emerged with her small case and Brook walked her on to the platform.

'Thanks for a lovely day, Damen,' she smiled. 'You don't need to see me onto the train.'

'I don't mind. It's only twenty minutes.'

She looked into his eyes and leaned forward to give him a

kiss on the cheek. 'Go. I'll see you in a few days.' Brook handed over her bag and turned to leave. 'And the next walk we do, we can go a lot further.'

Brook smiled at her. 'I look forward to it.'

*

'He's leaving it late.' McQuarry blew out smoke through the window and flicked the butt into the middle of the road. She looked for the spray of orange but the lashing sleet extinguished the smouldering cigarette before it hit the ground. She closed the window to block out the buffeting wind and horizontal rain howling around their car.

Drexler looked over at her, his hands superfluously gripping the steering wheel of the stationary vehicle. 'It's tonight, Ed. Tuesday.'

'There's only three hours left before Wednesday, Mike.'

'Trust me.' Drexler watched McQuarry put the pack in her pocket, resisting the urge to ask her for a cigarette. 'He's laid the ground too carefully. And how perfect is this weather for discouraging stray witnesses?'

'You shoulda let me call out the cavalry.'

'He won't move unless it's just us.'

'He said that?'

Drexler pursed his lips. 'I just know.'

McQuarry shrugged and took out her weapon. She checked the magazine before returning it to her belt, then lay back and closed her eyes.

Ten minutes later the glint of a headlight heading away from the lake alerted the agents to Sorenson's approach. They both slid down further in their seats. The gates opened smoothly and the red Toyota stopped at the highway. It took an age to turn onto the deserted road so the two agents lifted their heads to identify the problem.

Sorenson was sitting in the driver's seat, staring directly at Drexler and McQuarry's car. Despite the poor visibility, they could clearly see Sorenson smiling at them, his dead eyes creased in chilly amusement. A shiver ran down Drexler's back. Finally the Toyota turned left towards Tahoe and continued as sedately as it had the last time.

'How sure of himself is this guy?' smiled McQuarry over at Drexler. The smile faded when she saw the vacant expression on Drexler's face. He fired up the engine and, as though in a trance, manoeuvred the Audi onto the highway in pursuit.

They didn't speak again until they rolled up to the Golden Nugget Motel an hour later, coming to a halt in a darkened corner of the deserted parking lot. Sorenson's car had pulled up outside the reception office.

*

Brook walked out of the station and back to his car. As the Ingham case was largely on hold until the Ottomans could be run to ground, most of the officers involved were taking a couple of days to recharge while Forensics continued compiling the evidence against the couple. Hudson was back in Brighton now and Grant was on her way. He thought of Terri and resolved then and there to visit her as soon as the case was over. Really over.

He lit a cigarette. It was a strange feeling to be at the end of something that hadn't ended. But for Brook the case could never end, not until he knew, so he set off for Drayfin, pulling up outside the Ottomans' house about twenty minutes later.

He nodded to the constable at the gate and bounded up the steps to the house. Two SOCOs were still at work even at that hour and Brook exchanged a few strained pleasantries before wandering in and out of the rooms. He went to the master bedroom and pulled several pairs of shoes from the Ottomans' wardrobe and examined them. John Ottoman was a size ten and his wife Denise a size six. Close, but not the shoe sizes of the bloody footprints found in the Ingham house. That was one thing going for them at least.

He headed down to the pitch-black garden and pulled open the shed door, although it had already been searched for the second mountain bike. He shone a small torch on the floor, looking for signs of oil. He couldn't find any. He returned to his car and looked back at the house, which was of similar design to the Ingham and Wallis houses. A thought occurred to him and he jogged back up to the front door.

'I suppose the loft has been searched, hasn't it?' he inquired of the officer standing in the hall.

'You suppose right, sir,' he replied through his mask. 'Nothing. DCI Hudson even worked out they had an allotment, but there's nothing there either.'

Brook nodded, wondering if there was a slight dig somewhere in the last sentence. Hudson seemed to achieve that easy rapport with people, especially subordinates, that Brook found impossible to master, and it was plain, outsider or not, that Hudson was already popular with Derby officers. He trudged back to his car and drove in to the station, stopping to get a coffee on the way.

At the entrance Brook spied Sergeant Hendrickson at the duty desk. With Charlton on the warpath, Brook paused until the portly sergeant was distracted by something at the rear of the duty office then walked quickly and quietly to the stairs.

The Incident Room was empty when Brook arrived. He sat at a desk and remembered the implied promise of Laura's parting words. He took a sip of coffee and roused himself to look through the latest paperwork. It made for depressing reading. The DNA found on the fence panel in the Ingham yard had been positively matched to that from a hair found in a comb removed from the Ottomans' bathroom.

Brook shook his head. With the couple away from home, bloodstained bikes and clothing could have been planted in their house. DNA at the crime scene was another matter.

Brook located the 999 tape and played it several times. He was forced to admit it did sound like John Ottoman.

He reread the interview notes with the butcher from Normanton who'd provided the meat for the barbecue at the Ingham house. A few card purchases for similar amounts had been followed up but no suspects identified. Not surprising. Brook was sure that The Reaper would have used cash. There was a footnote about the plastic bags used for packaging some of the meat having been discontinued three months previously. He closed the report and lifted himself to leave.

He paused, then sat back down and reopened the report. Three months? No wonder the butcher hadn't noticed any new customers the week before the killings. Brook pulled out another cigarette but didn't light it. There was something about the Ottomans and Mrs North that seemed significant all of a sudden, but he couldn't bring it to mind. Then it came and, like a solved crossword clue, all the knowledge fell in a heap in his conscious mind. He leapt up and marched over to the exhibits officer's desk and rummaged through a drawer, extracting a set of keys before quickstepping back to his car, ignoring Hendrickson's parting sneer.

He roared through the centre of town. Ten minutes later he crossed the ring road and five minutes after that screeched to a halt outside the Ottoman house once more. He bolted back up the garden steps and into the kitchen, almost colliding with the SOCO who was finishing up.

A thought struck Brook. 'That allotment the Ottomans have. Did they have a shed?'

'Apparently,' replied the officer, pulling down his mask.

'Was there a freezer in it?'

'A freezer? No. Just gardening equipment and a kettle.' Brook smiled and turned towards the fridge freezer in the kitchen.

'So this is the only freezer they've got.'

'We're just about to lock up, sir, if . . .'

'One second . . . Bernard,' replied Brook, having another stab at being a people person.

'Martin,' replied the officer tersely. 'And like I said . . .'

But Brook had already yanked open the freezer and was slinging the contents onto the table. Tupperware containers with labels in a neat hand and the occasional ready meal were strewn across the kitchen table until it was emptied. 'Vegetable lasagne, mushroom risotto, pumpkin soup, vegetable curry, vegetable chilli, ratatouille . . .' Brook read. When he finished he nodded with satisfaction and started to refill the cabinet. There was no meat from the butcher's shop in Normanton. There was no meat at all – the Ottomans were vegetarians.

Brook was encouraged. It was only circumstantial and not enough to clear them, but this was a big red flag against the Ottomans buying and handling meat to set a trap for the Inghams. The Ottomans would be unlikely to countenance the idea of storing flesh in their freezer for three months and upwards while they prepared to murder the Inghams. Being local, and assuming they could even think in those terms, the couple would more than likely purchase meats no more than a day or two ahead of time.

*

'Was beginning to think you were a no-show, Mr Hera,' said Carlson, the night manager, dropping the key into Sorenson's spidery claw. 'Number 7 as requested – the bridal suite. Nice and secluded,' he added with a chuckle.

'And all the other cabins are empty?'

'Just like you asked,' he grinned.

Sorenson's black eyes burned into him and the coolness of his Siberian smile wiped the leer from Carlson's face. Carlson plucked a sopping cigar butt from his mouth and rubbed a chubby hand around his whiskers. 'Well.'

'Thank you,' said Sorenson softly. 'Do you have a rest-room I can use?'

'Right there,' said the man, nodding at a door in the corner of the office. Sorenson smiled his thanks and disappeared, counting out change in his hand.

Carlson loped over to the office door and, shielding his eyes from the neon above the entrance, squinted out at Sorenson's car. A yellow-toothed grin slowly deformed his features and he returned to his reception desk, scratching his belly through his too thin T-shirt.

When Sorenson returned so did Carlson's lascivious grin. 'You get ever'thin' you need in there, Mr Hera?'

This time Sorenson patted his breast pocket and returned his grin with a wink. 'All set.'

*

Mrs Petras opened her door on the second knock and wiped her hands with her apron.

'I'm sorry to call at this hour.'

'Inspector Brook,' she beamed. 'Come in. I make coffee.'

'I can't, Mrs Petras.' She looked crestfallen. 'Urgent police business.' Her face hardened. She understood duty. Brook offered her a cigarette which she accepted gratefully, taking a long pull when Brook lit it for her.

'Do you remember seeing this woman, Mrs Petras?' Brook brandished the photograph of Denise Ottoman.

Mrs Petras looked at it briefly. 'Only from papers. She never see Dottie. Not see her before papers.' Brook showed her a picture of John Ottoman for good measure but got the same result.

Brook paused, unsure of the right words. 'Does Mrs North eat ready meals?'

'No understand,' she said.

'Er, ready meals. Frozen food.'

'Frozed. Never.' She looked like she wanted to spit, so Brook smiled to disarm the unintended insult. 'We proper cook. Go three times a week Eagle Centre. On free bus. We buy fresh. Young girls cook Iceland. Not me, not Dottie.'

Brook rushed back to his car. As he expected: pensioners bought fresh and cheap produce and cooked proper food. Meat and two veg. His late parents had been the same. It wasn't just the desire to eat healthily that drove them to the corner shop or the greengrocer's. It was also the daily balm of human companionship that drew them out of the house.

Five minutes later Brook removed keys from his pocket and opened the side door of Mrs North's house. It opened directly into the kitchen in which Brook had previously stood, trying to turn a nagging feeling into a solid fact. Brook opened her fridge. It was empty and spotlessly clean.

This time Brook opened the small freezer compartment. It took some doing as it was frozen solid. When he finally did manage to prise open the flap, the tiny space contained what could have been a tray of ice cubes. There was no room for anything else. There could be no doubt. Nothing had been stored in that compartment for months, if not years.

Whoever had committed murder at the Ingham house had prepared long in advance, had bought meat long before it was needed and stored it, then defrosted it before offering it up to the Inghams. To do so they'd need access to a freezer. But where?

*

Drexler's eyes had not left the office door all the time that Sorenson had been inside the office. McQuarry had readied her night-vision field glasses and was scanning the surrounding area for any activity. There was none.

When Sorenson re-emerged he returned to the Toyota and drove it across the lot to the farthest darkest corner, parking outside the end cabin. When the vehicle's lights

went out, Drexler found it hard to see what Sorenson was doing and nudged McQuarry for a look through the field glasses, an instruction that she ignored. Eventually the driver's door opened and Sorenson stepped out of the vehicle, framed by the safety light, and opened the rear door.

'There's somebody else with him,' said McQuarry.

'There can't be. We'd have seen.' Drexler squinted across the ground. He saw a figure emerge from the rear of the car and close the door behind, extinguishing all light again. 'You're right. There are two of them.'

'There must have been someone hiding in the back seat,' said McQuarry.

'Could it be a hostage or another victim? Drugged maybe.'

'Can't see any signs of it, Mike.'

'Then maybe it's an accomplice.' Drexler thought for a second. 'Maybe there are two Reapers.'

McQuarry lowered the glasses and looked over at him. 'You might be right.'

There was silence apart from intermittent gusts of wind. The car park was empty. Even the highway was near deserted. 'What can you see?' asked Drexler, laying his hand on McQuarry's shoulder. The tension had pitched his voice a semitone higher.

'See for yourself,' she said, nodding towards the cabin.

At that moment the door opened and Drexler was able to see Sorenson illuminated against the bright room. The other person was already inside, carrying something in either hand. Maybe a small case. Drexler didn't get a look as Sorenson closed the door behind him.

'What do we do now?' asked Drexler, a wave of frustration washing over him. He looked across at McQuarry's arched eyebrow as she removed her binoculars.

'We wait.'

Drexler opened the door. 'I'm going in. He could be slaughtering someone as we speak . . .'

'Mike! We wait,' insisted McQuarry.

After a few seconds' hesitation, Drexler pulled the door closed.

*

As Brook switched on the computer back in the Incident Room, a sense of dread began to overtake him. Two years ago The Reaper had murdered the Wallis family. The preparations were thorough and Brook had concluded that Sorenson must have spent time in the area. But, try as they might, they'd never discovered where the killer might have stayed. They'd scoured the local hotels and B&Bs but found no trace.

Eventually Brook had concluded that Sorenson had probably stayed somewhere out of town. After Brook was suspended from the inquiry, the question hadn't been pursued and certainly had never been answered. But now the knot in Brook's stomach was telling him that Sorenson had property in Derby. Rented or otherwise, it would explain so much about the preparations for *both* Reaper killings in the city.

He started with estate agents, listing then emailing all those he could find on the internet. He asked about rentals and purchases pertaining to the name Sorenson. Then he noted down as many telephone numbers as he could find for follow-up in the morning.

But two years ago Sorenson had been using a false identity. He'd shown a driver's licence in the name of Peter Hera when hiring a van to deliver pizzas to the Wallis home. So Brook emailed the estate agents, again asking the same question but with the new name.

Brook had an idea. If a property had been purchased before the Wallis murders, the name might have found its way onto the voters' register. He searched for the electoral roll and fed the same two names into the search bar. Nothing. As usual, Sorenson wasn't making things easy for him.

He tried again, this time using Drexler's name. Still nothing. Disheartened, he turned the computer off. He got up to go but found Chief Superintendent Charlton blocking the doorway.

'Sergeant Hendrickson said you were here.'

'Yes, sir. I was just on my way to see you, sir.'

'I'll bet you were – despite being too busy to answer your phone.'

'Have you been ringing me, sir? It's been out of order for some time.'

Charlton eyed him with studied contempt. 'Modern policing is all about communication, Brook, but I can see I'm not getting through to you.'

Brook noted the absence of his title and tried not to smile. 'Sir?'

Charlton looked up at Brook, trying to inject some swagger into his voice. 'I suppose you've heard by now.' Brook raised an eyebrow. 'The Ottomans were arrested in France this evening. They'll be on a flight to East Midlands Airport tomorrow afternoon. I'd appreciate it if you didn't pass that titbit on to Brian Burton, no matter how many drinks he offers you.'

Brook stiffened. He could hold his hand up to mistakes, but corruption was a different matter and for a second he wondered whether to put Charlton on the floor. It passed swiftly but Charlton must have detected the change in Brook's demeanour because his manner became hesitant.

'Well. Suffice to say you're not going to be involved with the case any further. Take a week off. Don't come to the Incident Room again. Don't talk to other officers on the inquiry. Clear?'

Brook nodded, declining to speak. His placid response stirred Charlton's superiority complex once more and his lip curled. 'You know, I was warned about you, Brook. There's no future for your kind in the Force, certainly not in a division I'm running. Think on that.' He turned smartly on his heel.

'Where were the Ottomans arrested, sir?'

Charlton half turned. 'In Paris – they were spotted in an Irish pub by some ex-pats.' Brook couldn't suppress his amusement this time. 'Something funny?'

'An Irish pub,' Brook nodded. 'Right. If I was a hunted serial killer, that's where I'd go.'

*

Twenty minutes later, the door to the cabin opened. Drexler nudged McQuarry who sat up and opened her eyes. They watched intently. This time Drexler had the night-vision glasses. Sorenson emerged from the cabin alone. He still had on the overcoat and gloves he had been wearing when he'd arrived. There didn't seem to be any sign of blood. He looked around before flicking off the light and pulling the door closed. As far as the agents could discern, he did not say anything to whoever remained inside.

Sorenson returned to the Toyota and started the ignition. Drexler reached for the keys but found McQuarry's hand on his.

'Let's wait a while.'

Drexler looked at her, saw the sense in her suggestion and sank back onto his seat, breathing deeply.

'You gotta take it easy, Mike. It'll happen. You can't force these things.'

Sorenson drove to the reception office and pulled up. He stepped out and strolled into the building.

Chapter Twenty

Brook got home late again that night. For once he'd stopped at the Coach and Horses and just managed to catch last orders. He sat in the snug there, nursing a pint, thinking about the Ottomans. He remembered Laura Grant asking him why Ottoman had spared Jason. An even more difficult question, he thought to himself, was why had he, Brook, spared him? The little thug had killed his cat. Smashed its head to a pulp and left the little mite for Brook to find. And there he was in the Inghams' yard, helpless before him. Why hadn't he done it? He didn't know. The Reaper had slaughtered everyone else. There was no one to stop him.

The Reaper. Brook nodded. This was no copycat. Even from beyond the grave this carried Sorenson's mark. No copycat would have lured Brook to the scene and left young Wallis for him to finish.

*

Half an hour later he pulled up outside his cottage. To his relief Drexler's car was nowhere to be seen. Brook knew he wouldn't be able to sleep so he made a cup of tea and fell into a chair, pulling out a notepad. A couple of minutes later Brook heard a car and pulled the curtain aside.

Drexler extinguished the headlights, locked his car and walked to his side door, unhurried and without the briefest glance over at Brook's house.

Brook picked up his pen and tried to put himself in Sorenson's shoes. If the professor had wanted a safe house in Derby how would he go about it, given his almost limitless finance? Brook made a list:

1. *Purchase property in cash. Rented accommodation may involve landlord visits.*
2. *No mortgage arrangements so less ID needed.*
3. *All bills on direct debit to account with appropriately large balance.*
4. *Low maintenance. No garden, etc.*
5. *Probably a flat. Secure/secluded parking space required.*
6. *Good security required because of infrequent use. Possibly upmarket block with janitor, entry phone, etc.*
7. *Can't be on ground floor or lack of occupancy easily noticed. Some kind of high rise?*
8. *Close to railway station and/or M1.*

Brook crossed out M1. It was miles away. If it was too far from Derby, journeys to the Drayfin would become more hazardous. So instead he wrote:

Flat needs to be central and anonymous.

Brook sat back and examined his list. Then he wrote down some of the problems he might encounter if he owned such a property:

1. *Utilities need annual access to meters.*
2. *Council tax requires entry onto electoral roll.*
3. *Unforeseen, e.g. burst pipe.*

He fell asleep in the chair, still trying to think of number 4.

*   *   *

Brook woke at six the next morning, still in the same chair. Without changing his clothes, he made a flask of tea and put it in his backpack along with the notes he'd made the night before and the folder on Mike Drexler. He drove through the darkness to St Mary's Wharf and entered the deserted Incident Room before seven. Charlton wouldn't be around until mid-morning, not that Brook cared about disobeying orders. He poured tea and began to distil some of his notes in order to create a profile of likely properties to send to estate agents. After sending out the emails, he sat back to rub his eyes. It was still too early for any response to his inquiries from last night or this morning so he clicked on his Hotmail inbox to read the sole email waiting for him. It was from The Reaper.

Whether it was frustration with the case, or lack of sleep, or both, Brook felt a rare anger bubble up through him. When would this stop? What did they want from him? This constant prodding – was this his life now? What did he have to do to be left alone? Kill Jason Wallis? Would that stop it or did they want more murders, more victims?

Brook walked around the room to calm down. He returned to the computer and clicked on the email. It was blank but a file was attached. He clicked on the attachment and after a few seconds a film began to play. It was poor quality and badly lit, but Brook knew at once it was the yard at the Ingham house. There was no doubt. In the bedroom of Mrs North, one of the killers had set up a camcorder on a tripod and filmed the crime scene. The fire in the oil drum still blazed and provided sufficient light to pick out the faint outline of bodies on the two sofas. Brook watched mesmerised, his eyes gradually adjusting to the gloom either side of the fire. He stared at the side of the Ingham house by the drive, waiting for his own arrival. It never came.

Instead another figure appeared from the same spot, dressed head to toe in black, wearing some kind of mask of the same colour. He – it looked like a man – crept towards the warmth of the fire but seemed to be staring towards Mrs North's house. A moment later he turned and approached the bodies. A few feet away the figure seemed to recoil as though in horror. Hands went to head and he was rooted to the spot for several minutes. Eventually the figure moved away towards where Brook knew Jason had been sitting.

'Ottoman.'

The man bent down to the ground, as though to pick something up, and moved towards the boy. Brook could only guess what was happening as the shadows hid the man's actions, but a few seconds later he could see the figure remove a glove then put something to his ear. After a minute or so the man threw what Brook assumed was Jason's mobile, onto Wallis's lap. His movements became jerky and his limbs seemed to have trouble obeying their master. Knowledge was starting to bite and panic would follow. A second later the man sprinted towards the shiplap fence and vaulted onto the top, climbing clumsily over. The film ended.

Brook was initially pleased – this could clear John Ottoman. But then he began to feel uneasy. Perhaps his own appearance had been filmed but had been edited out for later release. He wondered what it would show. According to the time and date display, the man (Ottoman?) had entered the crime scene some fifteen minutes before Brook. It seemed about right. And the fire would have been much dimmer when Brook arrived, making it even harder to see the action. Brook shook his head. He couldn't worry about that. He clicked off the film and logged off.

One thing was certain. If Ottoman's account tallied with the actions of the man in the film, he could be in the clear.

*

Brook stayed in the Incident Room most of the morning, hoping not to be noticed. At intervals the room began to fill up with

CID who noted his presence but, unusually, said nothing. News of his disgrace was clearly on the grapevine.

Noble arrived at ten o'clock and smiled at Brook. 'Morning, sir. Back on the case?'

'Not exactly, John. Just here to see justice done. Pretend I'm not here.'

Noble nodded. 'Shouldn't be a problem – though you might be better in your office.'

'I haven't got my computer back. Where's Charlton?'

'Gone to the airport to pick up the Ottomans. DCI Hudson and DS Grant are driving straight there too.'

Brook nodded and resumed his work. When DS Gadd arrived to finish off some paperwork, Brook passed her some papers and began to brief her about phoning the estate agents. She looked over at Noble, who nodded, and she was able to listen more attentively before getting to work.

'What are you looking for?' asked Noble.

'I think Sorenson has a safe house in Derby.'

'Sorenson's dead.'

'But the house remains, John. And somebody used it to store the meat for the barbecue. And everything else probably.'

Noble didn't seem excited by this theory so Brook returned to his notes. After half an hour he began doodling to soothe his overheating brain. He wrote 'The Reaper' at the top of a page followed by 'Peter Hera', arranging the letters in a disordered circle as he might when trying to solve an anagram from a crossword.

Finally he yawned and flung the pencil down. He put his hands behind his head and closed his stinging eyes.

*

Charlton led the way with Hudson, followed by John Ottoman in handcuffs being guided by a uniformed constable. Mr Ottoman was very pale and seemed to be in shock. Denise Ottoman, her eyes red-rimmed from crying, and a female constable were behind him, and Grant brought up the rear. She smiled weakly at Brook as she passed. She looked very tired from the strain of travelling down to Brighton and having to turn straight round and come back at news of the arrests; Hudson didn't look much better.

Only Charlton seemed ebullient, a mood which faded quickly when he caught sight of Brook. To his credit, he said nothing in front of the throng of officers, instead busying himself directing the two prisoners to separate interview rooms. Then he turned back to Brook and glared at him for several seconds before marching off with Hudson, Grant and Noble. Brook leapt up to follow.

*

'Forgotten something, Mr Hera?' said Carlson.

'Not at all. I've had what I came for so I'm checking out.'

The night manager's grin returned. 'What about your lady friend?'

'She . . . will check out tomorrow. I don't know what time, but don't disturb her. And when she does wake, she may be a little groggy and confused as to how she got here. She's a little forgetful. I'd appreciate it if you were the same.' Sorenson grinned, as if to say 'we're all men of the world here'.

'Discretion.'

'Exactly. Now what do I owe you?' smiled Sorenson and began peeling twenties from a roll. He stopped at four hundred dollars after a nod from the manager. 'Nice to do business with you.' Sorenson pocketed his remaining notes and made for the exit.

'Same here, Mr Hera,' said Carlson, counting his bills. 'You come back and visit soon. Always welcome.'

*

'This had better be good,' said Charlton, sitting on his desk. Hudson, Grant and Noble all pretended to be absorbed in something requiring intense concentration.

352

'Something's come up, sir. Another message from The Reaper.' Suddenly all eyes were on Brook.

'Saying what?' said Charlton.

'It's better if I show you – with your permission.'

Fifteen minutes later, Brook turned off Charlton's computer and looked around the room.

'You think that's Ottoman?' asked Grant.

Brook nodded. 'It's not me.'

'According to that he came in by the front gate and didn't even go in the house.'

'And when he arrived the three boys were already dead,' nodded Hudson.

'He may have been in the house before that,' said Charlton. 'This could be a second visit.'

'So he left a murder scene with six bodies, then came back to phone it in. Doesn't make sense.'

Charlton accepted Brook's point with a few sage nods, momentarily forgetting his animosity towards him.

'So what are you thinking?' said Hudson.

'I'd say we treat Ottoman as a witness,' said Brook. 'For some reason he was on the estate and stumbled into the middle of the Ingham killings . . .'

'What reason?' asked Charlton.

'Best guess: Jason Wallis. Maybe he was keeping tabs on him after his release.'

'In a black ski mask?' said Noble.

'He'll have a chance to explain himself,' added Grant.

'Well, you're not interviewing him, Inspector Brook,' barked Charlton, resurrecting a little righteous indignation. 'Not after your stunt with Brian Burton. Whether you're right about Ottoman or not.'

'That's okay, sir. Joshua and Laura know the questions.' Brook smiled over at Grant, who acknowledged his confidence with a nod.

Momentarily appeased, Charlton returned his thoughts to the film. 'I don't get it. If Ottoman's not our man, it means the killer shot these images. Shouldn't he be getting away?'

'And why send us the film at all?' asked Hudson. 'If Ottoman goes down for this, the real killer's off the hook. This film means we're still looking.'

'It's not about that,' said Grant, looking over at Brook again. 'Ottoman's a civilian. The Reaper doesn't want the innocent coming to harm. This film gets him off.'

'But that's not why they were shooting a film,' said Brook. 'You see, they lured me there hoping to shoot something to blackmail me.'

'Blackmail? You?'

Brook sighed. 'The Reaper has killed everyone but Wallis. He, or they, left him there for me. They thought I'd kill Wallis if they set it up.'

The room erupted.

'You?'

'What?'

'Why?'

When it died down Brook picked his way round the words. 'Two years ago Wallis broke into my flat and killed my cat. The Reaper thinks I'll take my revenge. He lures me there with the promise of a meeting and leaves the weapon for me to cut Jason's throat. He sets up a camcorder in the North house and shoots the film we just saw. Up to that point, everything has run smoothly. The Ingham family are dead, so are two of Stephen's friends. Protective sheets and bloody garments have been packed into rucksacks. The mountain bikes are waiting in Mrs North's yard for a quick getaway. They're just waiting for me. But there's a rogue element they haven't factored in.'

'Ottoman,' said Grant.

'He arrives and finds the bodies. Remember the phone call. "They're all dead." Ottoman has found Jason's phone and does what any good citizen would do. He takes off his glove without thinking and leaves a print. Only he gets it wrong. He thinks they're all dead but Jason's alive – ironically the one person on earth he'd like to see dead.

'Ottoman had already seen the scalpel and in his fevered brain thought he could lay these killings off on Jason. Some kind of payback for everything his wife has suffered. He picked up the scalpel and put it under Jason's hand. After the phone call it all started to crash in on him. Maybe he hears a noise, maybe Jason starts moving, but he gets spooked and jumps over the fence leaving us his DNA. But he has one piece of luck. There are two bikes in the yard. He grabs one and rides home as fast as he can. The next morning Ottoman is haunted by what he's seen. He has to get away. He argues with his wife, who is terrified to leave the house, but in the end persuades her to come with him and off they go to Dover.'

'Very interesting,' said Charlton. 'But what about our killers?'

Brook shrugged. 'They do what's necessary. They've done this before, they don't panic, they improvise. One of them gets away on the remaining bike, the other . . . on foot, I hope.'

'Where do they go from there?' asked Hudson.

Brook looked up at Noble. 'I'm starting to think they may have a safe house in the city. A property The Reaper's had for a while, maybe from before the Wallis killings even.'

'It would explain a lot,' conceded Hudson after a pause.

'What do you mean, you hope one got away on foot?' asked Charlton.

'He means that with one bike gone, the second Reaper either got away on foot or . . .' Grant hesitated, looking over at Brook. He confirmed her analysis with a nod.

'Or what?' demanded Charlton.

'Or he may have had to sit tight in the North house and watch us at work,' answered Grant. Brook smiled at her.

'Then how did he get away?'

'Oh shit!' exclaimed Hudson, putting a hand to his forehead. Charlton looked at him, still none the wiser. 'How many dozens of people did we have working on the scene in protective suits and masks?'

Charlton's brain was working overtime and a second later his mouth fell open. 'You mean he may have walked out of Mrs North's house pretending to be Scene of Crime? Oh God. If the press ever find out . . .'

'Let's just hope we didn't give him a lift back into town,' added Brook, with a grimace.

*

Brook and Charlton were forced to sit side by side. They were in the anteroom behind the one-way mirror that showed only Hudson, Grant and Ottoman in reflection on the other side. So far John Ottoman had refused to speak.

'Mr Ottoman, we have a witness who saw someone of your height and build, wearing a ski mask identical to the one recovered from your home, loitering outside the Ingham house just a few hours before a multiple murder. Any comment?' Ottoman looked away from Hudson, tight-lipped.

'We also have a witness who puts you on the estate at the time of an assault earlier that evening – an assault involving Jason Wallis, which you broke up. We know you were on the Drayfin that night.'

Ottoman ignored Hudson and stared saucer-eyed into the mirror. Brook felt as though he were visible and shifted his position.

Finally Ottoman relented. 'I've told you. Let my wife go first. Then I'll talk to you.'

'We can't do that, sir. One of you was at the Ingham house at or near the time of the murders,' said Grant. 'We've matched DNA left on the fence with a hair found in your home. Unless you confirm it was you at the Ingham house, your wife stays here until Forensics gives us a definitive match.'

Ottoman looked at her impassively, knuckles white.

'We have a thumbprint on Jason Wallis's mobile phone and your voice on tape, not to mention blood from the victims on your clothing and a mountain bike found in your home. Do yourself some good here, Mr Ottoman. If you've got a reasonable explanation for all this, now's the time to tell us.'

Grant looked over at Hudson, then back at Ottoman. She stood up and wandered away, affecting disinterest. 'One thing I don't understand, John. Why murder these people but leave Jason Wallis alive? With your history,' she shrugged, 'it should have been easy to cut the dirty little bastard's throat. And let's face it, nobody would ever miss him. If anyone deserved killing, it was that little shit.' Grant looked over at the two-way mirror and Brook stared back.

Ottoman looked at the floor then shook his head. He'd reached the tipping point. 'Scare him. That's all I wanted. Not kill.'

'You just wanted to scare him but the other boys wouldn't let you so you killed them. That what happened?'

Ottoman squinted into Hudson's face. 'I didn't kill anyone.'

'Then who did? Tell us.' Hudson paused. 'Give us a full statement now and I promise your wife will go home tonight.'

Ottoman stared at the wall, processing the deal as best he could. 'She'd need a lift. She doesn't like being outside.' Hudson held his hands out in agreement. Ottoman sighed. 'I was there. I'd been following Jason for a while, since news of his release. I waited outside his aunt's house. You know – the one in Borrowash. He was scared, I knew. Like all bullies. The Reaper was still at large so . . .'

'So you put on the black garb and stalked him.'

'That's right. To frighten him. That's all I did. I didn't kill anyone. I couldn't. All I did was stalk Jason. I followed him in Borrowash and round the Drayfin. He was afraid of The Reaper. Terrified.' Ottoman cracked a bitter smile. 'That first night he saw me and ran. I chased him for miles, up by the river, round the back of

357

Elvaston. He hid. But near dawn I caught him. And you know what? He collapsed – a young lad like that. I thought he was having a heart attack.' Ottoman laughed, forgetting his guilt for a moment. He remembered a second later, restoring solemnity. 'I stood over him and he cried at my feet. He begged me not to kill him, said he was sorry about some cat, sorry about some old woman.' Ottoman shrugged. 'I thought he meant Denise at first, but now I'm not sure. Then he said he'd do anything. Anything. He even offered to help me kill the other members of his gang to make it right. Can you believe it? Then he shit his pants – I could smell it.' Ottoman nodded. 'Know what? I was pleased. It was what he deserved . . . to live in fear like my Denise.' His saucer eyes blinked and he looked round at Hudson. 'But I didn't kill anyone.'

In the anteroom, Brook was nodding. That's why Jason had gone to the barbecue. He'd known it was a trap but, thinking he'd made a pact with The Reaper to spare his life, had gone anyway.

'Tell us about the Inghams.'

Ottoman nodded and looked away. 'That night, after that poor Asian lad got beat up, I hung around at the front of the Ingham house waiting for Jason. To teach him a lesson, give him a proper scare. They were having a party, I could hear the music. Thud, thud, thud – very loud. Anyway, time wore on until it got really late. The music had stopped, or so I thought, and I began to think Wallis wasn't going to leave, so I crept closer to see what was happening. That's when I saw her.'

'Her?'

'A woman I think, climbing over the fence. I only saw her for a second.'

'Did she see you?'

'No.'

'Was it this woman?' asked Grant, slapping down a picture of the middle-aged woman from the North house.

'I can't tell. She had her head and face covered like me.'

'Then why think it was a woman?'

Ottoman stared into the distance and shook his head. 'I don't know. The way she moved, maybe.'

'You didn't see two people? A man with her.'

'No. Just the woman.'

Brook nodded. 'Her partner would've been manning the camera at this point,' he whispered to Charlton.

'What was she wearing?'

'Dark overalls and a balaclava or ski mask like me. She had blood all over her but it was going on the sheet . . .'

'Sheet?'

'There was a sheet thrown over the fence. She dropped over the other side and pulled it over. And then she was gone. I didn't know what was happening or what to think. I heard the music, only this time it was soft. Classical. Then I saw the Ingham lad.' He shook his head. 'Terrible. All that blood. I looked round for Jason and . . .'

'You saw the scalpel on the ground,' prompted Grant. Ottoman nodded. 'Why did you put it under his hand?'

'I don't know. I wasn't thinking straight. I saw the phone and I realised what I had to do. But I didn't know what to say.'

'You said "They're all dead." You thought Wallis was dead?'

'Why wouldn't I? There was blood everywhere. Even on my clothes by now. Then it hit me, what I was seeing, and I started to fall apart. When Jason came round I just froze.'

'Jason was conscious?'

'Briefly.'

'What happened?'

'Something strange.' Ottoman shook his head and his eyes narrowed in confusion. 'He looked at me. I think he might even have smiled. He said "I'm ready" then passed out again.'

'I'm ready?' Hudson nodded. 'What do you think he meant?'

'No idea.'

'Then what?'

'I got scared. I thought I heard someone coming so I left the same way the woman left – over the fence. When I got down I saw there were two bikes. I took one. The next day we . . .' Ottoman took a deep breath. 'What about my wife?'

'She'll be on her way home soon, Mr Ottoman,' said Hudson. 'Trust us.'

'Trust you. Like I trusted you to deal with Wallis after he assaulted my wife.' Ottoman hung his head.

'This is different, John. Six people are dead.'

Ottoman's head lifted like a hunted deer. 'Six? What do you mean?'

Hudson glanced at Grant. 'Three people died in an upstairs bedroom, Mrs Ingham and her boy among them. It was all over the news.'

'I didn't know. The last thing we wanted was to listen to the news or read a paper. Six? Oh God. I didn't kill them. You must believe me.'

Both Grant and Hudson stared at the mirror through to Brook and Charlton. Hudson nodded.

'We believe you.'

*

'It's fine, love. They believe us, I think. I just need to stay a bit longer.' Ottoman pressed his hands into the knots of tension in his wife's back then held her away and looked at her tear-streaked face. 'You go with this officer. He'll take you home. I'll see you soon.'

'Don't be long,' she whimpered.

*

Brook opened his eyes and lifted his head from the desk and yawned. He looked at his watch and had to rub his eyes to see properly. It was past midnight. He hadn't been this tired for two years and he was unlikely to get much rest any time soon. His hunch about Ottoman having come good, he was back on the team. Charlton had already held a press conference to 'de-emphasise' – his very word – the significance of the arrests and to insist the Ottomans were witnesses not suspects. Denise Ottoman had been taken home and her husband would probably be released tomorrow after another interview.

Brook stood and walked around for a few minutes to stretch his legs, having already decided not to go home. Being in the house next door to Mike Drexler made him edgy and he had resolved to keep away from Hartington as much as possible until he had gone.

He sat back down at the desk and shook his flask. There was a little tea left in it so he poured it out and took a swig. It was cold.

He looked around the room and his bleary eye fell on the photo array on the boards. The sky had cleared and a full moon had cast its light onto the ghostly image of the middle-aged woman sitting in Dottie North's bedroom – the picture that had erroneously led them to Denise Ottoman. Brook picked up his pencil and looked at the anagram again. This time he looked for a female name among the letters. After ten minutes he'd come up with only three – Pat, Rae and Petra.

One at a time, he mangled all the remaining letters into unlikely sounding surnames and one by one typed all the options into the search bar for the electoral roll on the computer. He expected nothing and wasn't disappointed when he found nothing. However, after a dozen or so attempts, Brook keyed in 'Petra Heer' and was surprised to be rewarded with an address – 1b Magnet House, Derby.

His pulse began to quicken. 1b suggested a flat and Magnet House suggested a larger building. He reached for an A–Z and looked up the address. Magnet House was just down the road from the railway station and the Midland Hotel. In fact he must have passed it on his nocturnal ramble with Laura Grant.

He hastily wrote a note: *Everything you can get on a Petra Heer if she exists. Birth certificate, nationality, passport, picture of any kind, etc. DIB.*

He dropped it on DS Gadd's desk, gathered up his car keys and hurried out of the door.

*

Sorenson drove away from the motel, crossing 395 back towards Tahoe. Drexler reached for the keys.

'I say we wait, Mike.'

'What? Why?'

'There's somebody still in that cabin and I'd kinda like to know who.' Drexler hesitated, poised to spark the ignition. 'And I'm guessing Sorenson's headed home. It's way past his bedtime.'

Drexler exhaled and sat back. 'Okay. We wait.'

McQuarry pulled out her cigarettes and lit up. She looked over at Drexler and on an impulse offered the pack. Drexler hesitated then plucked a cigarette and put it shamefacedly into his mouth. McQuarry lit it for him and he inhaled and exhaled like it was his first kiss.

'Taste good?' grinned McQuarry, opening her window. Drexler smiled back a little sheepishly. 'I've not seen you like this, Mike. Not since the shooting.' He looked over at her. 'You really want this one, don't you?'

'I guess.'

'Why?'

Drexler thought for a minute. 'The wreckage.'

'What wreckage?'

'The wreckage of families. My family. The Campbells. The Baileys. Even the Ashwells. I thought when I killed Hunseth I was done with it.' He took a large pull on the cigarette and scowled at the taste. When he exhaled he looked over at his partner. 'I killed him, you know, Ed.'

'I know, Mike. I was there.'

'I didn't have to . . .'

'You saved my life.'

362

'But I could have brought him down alive. Somehow Sorenson knew that. I don't know how.'

'You were cleared, Mike. It was a good shoot.'

'I was cleared by the Board, Ed. I haven't cleared myself. Sorenson's a smart man. He told me I shot my father when I killed Hunseth. He was right. I saw Hunseth as I'd seen my father so many times, staggering drunk, carrying that bat around looking for my mom, looking for me, spitting rage and the Bible between slugs of moonshine. And Sorenson knew that, like he just reached into my mind and pulled it all out.'

'How could he know?'

'He just does.'

McQuarry tossed her butt into the night. 'It's in the past. Let's leave it there. You had an off day.'

'We both did.'

McQuarry looked up at Drexler. 'What do you mean?'

Drexler looked back at her and shrugged. 'You got careless, Ed. You got too close. And you got cut. Hard to believe, you of all people . . .'

'Mike!'

Just then, the night manager came out of his office and walked down the row of cabins to the end room. He knocked on the door and waited. Nobody opened the door. A moment later the portly bedraggled man turned the handle and slipped inside.

*

Magnet House was no more than five minutes from St Mary's at that time of day. A quick trip round the inner ring road and Brook was soon pulling up next to it, the building looming up out of Pride Park, the now-deserted industrial zone to the east of Derby. It was a perfect location. As well as its proximity to the train network, the area was sparsely populated and foot traffic at night would usually be minimal, most of the bars and pubs being located half a mile to the west in the city centre.

Brook drove past the redbrick structure, unable to keep his eyes from it, and parked in the forecourt of the railway station, some four hundred yards further on. He rummaged in the boot for his small torch and a pair of protective gloves. He also extracted a bunch of keys, the size of a small hedgehog, liberated from a serial housebreaker many years before, and set off towards the building. He wondered briefly whether to call in at the Midland and wake Grant, but decided against it. She'd had a wretched twenty-four hours travelling the length of England and might not appreciate a visit at nearly one in the morning.

As he neared the darkened building he was disturbed by a noise behind him. Without breaking stride or turning, he continued walking until an unkempt hedge provided cover. He pressed himself into the body of the hedge and scrutinised the ground to his rear. It was a clear night and he was able to train his gaze on the doorways and few parked cars all the way back to the station, but he could discern no movement, not even an animal. He waited a little longer then continued on past the dilapidated buildings on his right, towards Magnet House.

He stood in the shadows of the entrance, looking up at the building. To one side there was a security gate barring admittance to the car park, which evidently snaked around the back of the block. Brook trotted over to it but couldn't see any vehicles. The parking bays were probably under the building. He turned back to the entrance stairwell. There was a solid door and a steel grill with four shiny new buzzers at the side of a microphone. The name tag of the top buzzer was 'PH'.

Brook stood back again. Four flats in what looked like two storeys, so two flats per floor. Assuming the top buttons were for the flats on the top floor, he pressed the bottom buzzer. Several minutes and several attempts later a female voice answered.

'Inspector Brook, Derby CID,' barked Brook. After a brief hesitation the buzzer sounded and Brook made his way into the entrance hall. An inside door was opened as far as a chain would allow and a young girl ran a sleepy eye over Brook's ID.

'Miss Jane Gadd?'

'Pardon?'

'Are you Miss Jane Gadd?'

The girl let out a huge sigh. 'No.'

'My mistake. I'll see myself out,' he smiled, apologetically.

'Thanks a fucking bundle,' she said and slammed her door.

Brook returned to the stairs and climbed to the next floor. The second door of two had 'PH' on its nameplate. He looked at the crack below the door but couldn't see a light. Then he rang the bell. No answer. No sound or movement that he could detect. No shadow falling over the peephole. After a few minutes he took out his bunch of keys and selected one, then another, then another. The fourth master key turned and Brook pushed back the door and stepped over the threshold, closing the door softly behind him.

*

Carlson stood inside the doorway, listening in the dark. There was music coming from somewhere near the bed. Classical stuff, playing softly. Quite nice if you liked that sort of shit. He was more of a Bluegrass man.

He was tempted to turn on the light but thought better of it. Roofies or not, the girl might be half-conscious and manage to store a memory of him. Instead he took off his clothes until he stood naked in the blackness, listening for the sound of his early Christmas present sleeping. His eyes had adjusted to the gloom now and he tossed his grimy clothing on a chair and sniffed under his fetid armpit. Not great but not bad enough to waste time showering. Not with a boner like this to drain.

He had his party hat in his hand and pulled it over his

fat penis with a twinge of regret. He usually preferred to ride bareback but he didn't want to leave behind his DNA in case the girl ever worked out she'd been screwed – which was highly likely with his massive tool. Bitch may not walk for a week, he chuckled.

He moved over to the bed, following the sound of shallow breathing and sat on the edge.

'I hope you got plenty of the sweet stuff left for Uncle Jake, honey,' he chuckled again. No reply. This bitch was out cold. He hesitated, assessing the risk. Fuck it. He had to see what he was drilling, made it sweeter. He leaned over and flicked on the bedside lamp and turned to the girl. He liked what he saw. Long hair, slim but with tits and young, soft skin. Her eyes were firmly closed and her firm young body was clad only in bra and panties. He climbed on the bed and prepared to remove her underclothes and mount her.

'Oh honey chile, Uncle Jake's gonna light you up like Christmas.' He grinned at her motionless face, but then his mouth slackened suddenly. He pulled the blanket and narrowed his eyes at her. 'Wait a minute. I know you.'

The girl's eyes opened and her right fist emerged from the bedding and plunged onto Jake's throat. He fell back, clutching his neck and a second later pulled the empty hypodermic from his flesh, gasping as he tried to steady himself. He glanced at the hypodermic long enough to see the plunger was fully depressed and the chamber empty. He flung it away.

He moved back towards the bed and the girl screamed but Jake staggered on the threadbare carpet and fell to his knees, sweat pouring out of him in an effort to reach her.

'You . . . fucking . . . little . . . whore . . . I'm . . .' He sagged onto his vast stomach, one arm propped on the bed. The girl had wrapped a sheet around her and cowered against the head of the bed, legs pulled up, watching him grind out every word.

The door flew open and the two agents barked 'FBI!' in unison. Drexler flicked on the main light and was through the door first.

'Get on the ground,' he shouted superfluously at Carlson, whose head was already sinking onto the floor. The two agents stared at the barrel of a man, rambling incoherently, unable to move.

'Off the bed,' shouted McQuarry to the girl. 'Face the wall.' The girl did as she was told, still clinging to the sheet to preserve her modesty.

McQuarry checked behind the door – 'Clear' – as Drexler headed for the bathroom. 'You okay, honey?' asked McQuarry to the girl, looking all around, both hands on her gun.

'Clear,' she heard her partner shout and he returned to the bedroom clipping his firearm back into his belt.

The girl nodded, her face set in a grimace of fear, her cheeks beginning to run with tears.

'The girl's clean,' said McQuarry, holstering her own gun.

Drexler removed a pair of cuffs from his belt and went across to Jake. He placed the cuffs on him and turned him over, throwing a towel over his shrivelling manhood. The man groaned and Drexler helped him over to the wall and sat him up with some difficulty.

'What happened here, honey?' said Drexler to the girl. 'Why did Sorenson bring you here? Why'd he leave you?'

The girl turned from the wall pulling the sheet tight. She was calmer now and looked back at McQuarry, who was busy rifling through Carlson's clothes. Drexler could see she was no more than sixteen, possibly younger. She raised her chin but lowered her eyes.

'Jesus Christ, Mike,' shouted McQuarry. She stood by the

chair where Jake had tossed his clothes. She examined a wallet in her hand. 'That's Caleb's brother. This son of a bitch is Jacob Ashwell.'

Drexler looked over at the man still groaning, blank eyes open and glassy. 'You sure?'

'There's a picture of him with Caleb in the wallet. And here's his driver's licence.' McQuarry handed him the dog-eared snap of the two brothers, both holding guns, in front of the line of wrecked motor homes in the bowl near the Ashwell garage.

*

Brook tried the light switch. Nothing. He switched on his torch and swung it around the room, pausing on the lone mountain bike. It was identical to John Ottoman's bike, though the saddle and frame sported no discernible blood stains. One of the killers had been able to use it to get back to the flat – presumably the one with the greater need to be visible the next morning. Brook nodded. He knew now who that was.

He moved towards the large curtain-free window, catching his foot on a box as he did so and causing a sharp clanging noise. Brook slipped his hand into the box and pulled out a bottle of Nuits St Georges. Same label, same year as the two bottles left at the Wallis house. He tried a couple more. They were the same.

He rose from his haunches and moved over to the window. The moon was beaming down, bestowing sufficient light to pick out the various items stored in the room. One was a box packed with two bottles of a colourless liquid. One bottle was half empty. A different box, full of hypodermic syringes still in their sealed hygienic packets, sat beside it. Brook shook the colourless liquid then unscrewed the lid and gave the contents a tentative sniff. It was odourless. He replaced the top. Brook was willing to wager that this concoction was some incarnation of the drug used on members of the Wallis and Ingham families.

He swept his torch around the walls. In one corner rested a tripod, though it wasn't supporting a camcorder at the moment. Three doors lid off the room he was in and all were slightly ajar. Brook stepped through the first one and tried the light again. Still nothing. Perhaps Sorenson's account had run out of funds, though that hardly seemed likely. He shone his torch over the kitchen appliances, coming to a halt at what seemed to be a large chest freezer. He stepped over to it and opened the lid. He smiled faintly; there were at least a dozen of the same blue and white striped bags found at the Ingham home, containing meats from the butcher's in Normanton. He closed the freezer. It was working normally, the green light winking on the display. Clearly there was power in the plug sockets. Perhaps the fuse for the overhead lighting had blown.

Brook looked through several kitchen units, searching for the fusebox without success. Instead he found a set of wine glasses identical to those from the Wallis house and a small box of Swann Morton PM60 scalpels. He took a deep breath. It was all here – all the evidence they needed.

He went into another room. This was less of a storage area than the main room and the kitchen, this was somebody's space. He couldn't see any personal items on display, but there was a bed and a small sofa, a desk with a laptop and a shelf full of books. Brook examined them as he had Sorenson's library two decades before. He smiled when he saw *The Collected Works of Albert Camus* – Drexler's philosopher of choice. There were also a couple of slim volumes of Wittgenstein who, Brook knew from Drexler's book, had been quoted in blood at the scene of the California killings.

He turned on the laptop and approached the small stereo, next to which was a stack of about twenty CDs – all classical. Brook ran his eye down them. Debussy, Wagner, Fauré, Beethoven, Mozart, Shostakovich. How many people would die before these discs were exhausted? He opened the Debussy case. It was empty.

Brook continued his sweep. His torch alighted on a large

canvas lamp on the far side of the bed and he padded round to switch it on. It worked so he flicked off his torch. Now he had light, he saw the copy of *The Ghost Road Killers* on the floor. He checked for an inscription but found none.

He moved to the window to look out over the flyover and beyond to the red 'Westfield' sign of the new shopping mall. His eye dropped to the laptop on the table beneath the window. The welcome page was waiting for a password. He typed in 'The Reaper', then 'Sorenson', then 'Peter Hera', then 'Petra Heer' in turn. No joy.

He turned back to the room. In one corner sat a pile of papers topped by a large colour photograph. Brook picked it up. It was a picture of Jason Wallis standing by a stretch limousine with several other young men. One he was sure was Stephen Ingham. He looked at the date on the back. This was taken just before Brook's camping holiday had come to an end, the day young Wallis had been released from White Oaks. In the pile were more pictures of Wallis and friends, which Brook examined carefully. He paused before picking up the next picture. The image showed Brook stepping out of his car at St Mary's Wharf.

And there were others – some taken at the crime scene with Grant and Hudson, some outside the Ottoman house, and several of Brook and Grant going door to door on the Drayfin. He sifted through and counted them. There were twenty-three pictures in total of Brook. The next one was taken at night and showed him walking away from the Midland Hotel towards Magnet House, chatting with Grant by his side. Judging by the angle, this photograph had been taken from the window of the flat. He turned these over and picked up the next batch, standing for several minutes examining them. He nodded. Grant walking her little circuit late at night, Grant looking up at the camera, a look of concentration on her face. He stared at the next one for a moment longer.

'You don't seem too surprised,' said a voice from the doorway.

Chapter Twenty-One

Drexler looked at Ashwell. The resemblance was clear. Then he looked at the girl.

'I don't understand. Who are you?' The girl set her jaw and looked away.

'It's Jacob Ashwell, Mike. What are we going to do?' said McQuarry.

'Why are you here?' Drexler pressed the girl.

The girl's eyes blazed back at him. 'That man was going to rape me. He raped my sister.'

Drexler's brow creased. 'You're English?'

'It's Jacob Ashwell, Mike. We have to do something.'

'You're English,' said Drexler again, staring at her. His eyes widened when the resemblance hit him. 'My God, you're Nicole Bailey. You're alive.'

'That man raped my sister. He murdered her. He would have raped me . . .'

'What did you do to him?' said Drexler, picking up the hypodermic with a handkerchief.

'I defended myself,' said the girl.

'But Sorenson said . . .' Drexler ran his hand through his hair.

'Can I get dressed?' asked the girl softly. Drexler nodded without thinking, just to let his brain work on the problem.

She stepped gingerly into a pair of jeans as though the whole of her right side was sore.

He looked up at McQuarry. 'Nicole Bailey. What the hell?'

'This is some kind of set-up, Mike. Has to be.'

Drexler nodded. 'It's that all right, but Sorenson didn't tell me about the girl . . .'

'What are you talking about, Mike?'

Drexler looked up at his partner. For a second he hesitated. 'Sorenson offered me a deal. In exchange for my father's whereabouts I was supposed to kill someone, someone who deserved it.'

'Who?'

'He didn't say. Just that it would be soon.'

McQuarry nodded and looked over at the prostrate night manager, spittle oozing from his uncontrolled bottom lip. 'And Sorenson led us right to him. Neat.' She paused and turned back to Drexler. 'What did you say?'

Drexler pulled the M9 from his jacket.

'Whose gun is that, Mike?'

'Sorenson's . . .'

'Mike!'

'Don't try and stop me, Ed.'

McQuarry held up her hands and backed away from him. 'Easy, Mike. You do what you gotta do. No one's gonna stop you, just take it slow . . .'

Drexler turned to her, eyes blazing. 'Don't talk me down like I'm a perp, Ed. Just shut up while I do this thing. We both know this piece of shit won't be missed.'

'Are you sure you want to do this, Mike?'

'Course I'm sure.'

'What are you waiting for?' said the girl from behind him.

'Shut up!'

Drexler raised the gun so that it was pointing at Jacob

Ashwell's temple. He took a deep breath and squeezed the trigger.

*

Brook turned and let the picture of Laura Grant waving to the camera fall to the floor. He stared into Grant's eyes, a sad smile deforming his face. 'Hello, Laura.'

'Damen. Why couldn't you have found out tomorrow?'

'When you'll be far away.'

'That's right.'

'You were coming here that night you saw me in the car, weren't you?'

She smiled. 'A minute later and I'd have been at the door. That would have saved you some time. How long have you known?'

Brook looked her over. She was dressed head to toe in figure-hugging black jeans and a sweater. No ski mask today. 'Before yesterday it was just a vague unease.'

'Caused by what?'

'Oh, the coincidence of Joshua being ill keeping you in Derby the night of the murders. That was a little too neat.'

Grant nodded. 'I didn't like it either, but I had to be in town for the Inghams. I'd had a couple of weeks off beforehand. We'd done so much preparation. Also, we figured if Josh was ill, you'd suspect him first.'

'I did. How did you pull that off?'

'A few nasty bacteria stirred into my curry when he was in the toilet. He always finishes my meals when we're on expenses. Is that all?'

Brook peeled off his gloves to cool his hands. 'Yesterday, inter-viewing Ottoman, you asked him why he didn't kill Jason, but you were actually looking at me, asking me.'

Grant smiled at him. 'It was the right question. Do you have an answer?' Brook said nothing. 'Anything else?'

373

'I suppose your uncanny ability to move the case forward rankled – that brainwave with the rope and the trapdoor for instance.'

Grant chuckled, her cold eyes boring into him. 'Maybe you couldn't accept that I was a better detective than you.'

Brook smiled. 'Actually, I think I had accepted it until our walk in the Peaks.'

'What did I say? I really tried to be careful.'

'You were, Laura. But you can't stifle muscle memory. You crossed that bridge to take the short cut to Alstonefield before me. Without a map, only a local would know that path.' Brook patted for his cigarettes and reached into a pocket. Grant produced a small revolver. It didn't seem natural in her hand.

She held his eyes but lowered the gun when Brook took out his cigarettes and lit up. Grant indicated the sofa with a dart of her eyes. Brook moved over and sat.

'Someone raised in Ashbourne, say.'

Grant's eyes widened and her hand seemed to stiffen around the gun. 'That was careless.'

'Hardly that, Laura. Or should I call you Nicole?'

She was wrong-footed for a second, then smiled faintly. 'Now I see why you're so highly rated. I'm impressed.'

'Don't be. Your partner gave me a copy of his book. It's all in there if you know how to read between the lines.'

Grant's smile faded. She looked towards the copy of Drexler's book on the bureau. 'Agent Drexler? Did he?'

Brook could see confusion in her face. Perhaps in giving him the book, Drexler had overstepped the mark. There were private things in there. Brook decided to press home this small advantage.

'I must say none of the pictures look like you.'

'It's not hard to alter your appearance in California, Damen.' She looked out of the window for a moment. 'My life as Nicole Bailey was over. Caleb and Billy Ashwell killed her.'

'And yet you're the body even the FBI couldn't find.'

Nicole smiled at that. 'Thank God Uncle Vic found me first.'

Uncle Vic. Brook flinched at the phrase he'd first heard uttered by Sorenson's niece, Vicky, two years earlier. Like it or not, Brook couldn't deny the unswerving loyalty and affection the professor inspired in others. He took a deep pull on his cigarette. It tasted bitter.

Nicole looked down at the floor then hard at Brook. 'He saved me, Damen. He saved me from those monsters and he saved countless future victims.'

Brook nodded. There it was. 'SAVED' – The Reaper's mantra buried deep inside her.

'I was half-dead and out of my mind in that cabin. Small windowless room. The smell. So hard to breathe. So claustrophobic. You can't imagine. I . . . we were in hell. Every time that door was unbolted I was ready for death. A few days earlier . . . my sister . . .' Her face crumpled for a moment but she blinked away the tears and stared back at Brook defiantly. 'But one night there was Uncle Vic, my dad's friend. Covered in the blood of Caleb Ashwell. The most beautiful sight I've ever seen.'

She laughed coldly. 'Funny, when he saw me from the door he didn't move at first – just stood there with a strange look on his face. He hadn't expected survivors. It threw him. I was too young to know, I couldn't realise what he was thinking, not until later. It's what I'm thinking now.'

Brook smiled. He was now a living witness. 'Trust.'

'The very word. Could he trust me with his life? He must have known he could never be sure, not for definite, I was just a kid. But he saved me anyway, risked everything he'd worked for, not knowing if one day I'd give him away. The professor was a great man. Instead of protecting himself he took me to his house and hired someone to nurse me back to health.

'You know what? If he'd killed me I would've understood. I could have died happily knowing my family's killers had been executed. But he took a leap of faith. I've spent the rest of my life repaying that faith, Damen.

'And later, when he explained how he'd found the Ashwells and how he found . . . other families, suddenly I knew how to make that payment. Ridding the world of those who prey on others.'

'Caleb and Billy got what they deserved,' replied Brook. 'No argument.'

'As did Sammy Elphick and Bobby Wallis. And of course Floyd Wrigley,' she added with a tilt of the head.

'Floyd Wrigley was a mistake. I've been trying to correct it ever since.'

'Have you?' Nicole shook her head. 'Uncle Vic said you were a moral man. That's why you were so right to be The Reaper. He never told me you were weak. In the early days, he'd tell me how he met you after Harlesden; how he knew you were the one, the one to take his work forward. He said you got so close that you were the only one who could've caught him; the only one capable of understanding what he was trying to do. He said you became friends.' Brook looked away. 'He was so happy to find Floyd Wrigley for you – to give you Laura Maples's killer.

'You were my hero, you know.' She smiled. 'I even think I had a crush on you. Then two years ago, after Uncle Vic left Jason Wallis for you to finish and you resisted, he wasn't so sure. But he said we owed you another chance to come to your senses, to recognise the value of The Reaper's work. It would've pained him to know that you failed him again.'

'You really did expect me to kill Wallis.'

'Why not? We killed Harvey-Ellis for you as a gift – to remind you. I trained for weeks to get in shape. It was quite difficult not to give it away, especially when I got back from sick leave. I had to play the delicate flower for a while.'

Brook smiled. 'The way you sprinted up that hill on the walk followed by all that fake panting – that was a nice touch. So it was you who ran Harvey-Ellis down and drugged him.' Grant nodded. 'How did it feel pushing him into the water?'

No answer. 'You wanted him dead, don't bother to deny it,' she said finally.

'It doesn't mean I would have killed him . . .'

'Because you couldn't, not after you'd assaulted him that time. We understood. So we did it for you. You owe us, Damen. And we made it easy for you. Was removing Jason Wallis so high a price to pay? You must know what a stain on the face of the earth he is.'

'Maybe. But he's not stupid. Wallis knew it was a trap.'

'He didn't know for sure, Damen. But you're right. He would have suspected. So we were careful. We were confident he wouldn't speak to the police, and if he didn't turn up it wasn't a problem. But he did turn up, Damen, because, thanks to John Ottoman, he thought he'd made a deal with The Reaper. I wish we'd known at the time. I'm willing to bet Jason would have held up his end and killed his friends if we'd just left him to it – maybe not the young boy or Mr and Mrs Dysfunctional, but the others, the ones who killed Annie Sewell. If we made it easy for him, he'd have done it. Just to get himself off the hook. He's a very dangerous young man.'

'Dangerous?'

'You saw him in hospital. He didn't give a shit that his friends were dead. And worse, thanks to you, he's survived a visit from The Reaper twice. Now he thinks he's untouchable.'

'He'll get what's coming to him.'

'Will he, Damen? I hope so, before others suffer. He's got a taste for killing.'

'And have you?'

Nicole's face hardened. 'Don't try that Lesson One psychology on me. What I do is valuable work. I take no pleasure. It's clinical, like removing a tumour.' Nicole, tired of standing, went to sit on the bed. Brook stood to stretch his legs. Nicole's gun was still raised.

'You know how to use that?'

'I wouldn't want you to test me.'

'The strong woman in a man's world?'

'I've had to be.'

'I'm sure . . . but stop waving it around, please. You won't kill me no matter how much I get in the way.'

She hesitated. 'Why so confident?'

'Because I'm just as exposed as you – Sorenson saw to that with Floyd. That's why you could afford to hang around and film me in the hope I'd slit Jason's throat.'

'Which you nearly did, apparently.'

'You weren't there?'

'I had to get back to the hotel.'

'On the remaining bike,' nodded Brook. 'How'd Mike get away?' Nicole stared hard at him. 'You can tell me. Mike and I have an understanding.'

Nicole narrowed her eyes. 'Do you?'

'We're the good guys, remember. We've served. So have you. That's *your* weakness. You call me weak but you sent me the film of Ottoman to clear him. Because he's a civilian. You can't stand by and watch him sink when he has no part in your war.'

Nicole nodded. '*Our* war, Damen. Don't forget Floyd.'

Brook pulled out another cigarette. 'I'll try not to. So what now?'

She looked at her watch, then went to the doorway to look out. 'We leave Derby tonight.'

'And if I try to stop you?'

'You won't.'

'A leap of faith?'

She smiled. It was a distant, hopeless smile. 'Far from it. Like you say, you're exposed. I think you just want us gone.' She checked her watch.

'Where are you going?'

Her lips tightened. 'A place The Reaper is needed.'

'And is this your life now, Nicole, planning the deaths of dysfunctional families?'

'That word. Makes it sound like a bowel disorder. Everybody

378

I held dear was killed by one of those families. Now Uncle Vic is dead. Even I'm dead. Nicole Bailey is dead. This work is all I have. But every day I question it, Damen, and every day I see my sister's face and hear her screams. I don't sleep at night, I have to walk. I have to keep moving like a shark. Maybe that's why I have to hunt. But when I see the relief after The Reaper has paid a visit I know it's all worthwhile. Those people on the Drayfin are just the first. Soon, on every estate, law-abiding residents will be thinking the same. In every school, teachers will . . .'

Brook laughed. 'Spare me. I heard this speech when you were still a carefree schoolkid.'

'Playing with my carefree sister Sally,' she responded bitterly.

Brook lit his cigarette. 'You can't keep avenging her death.'

'You think it's personal. It's not. After the first, it's not personal. You forgot that with Floyd – he died so you could sleep without seeing Laura Maples's rat-infested corpse. But after that your work is for others.'

'Is that why you mocked up her little squat in the Wallis house, as a reminder?'

'And why Victor chose to call me Laura. To remind you of what we do and why.'

'Damn it, I haven't forgotten, believe me, but it's futile. Nothing changes. All the deaths are meaningless because there's always someone else ready to step up. Don't you see? The death of the Wallis family allowed the Ingham family to flourish. Now the Ingham family are gone another will take their place and so it goes . . .'

'And somebody will come to remove them. It won't be me but there are others. We're not alone. The Reaper is not just an idea any more, Damen, it's an organisation. There are so many police officers like me and you around the world, biding their time, waiting for the chance to make the world a better place.' She smiled. 'You'll see that soon.'

Brook shook his head. 'It's madness. It'll destroy you like it destroyed Sorenson.'

'That's okay. Uncle Vic was a soldier. He gave his life right up to the end. What are you doing?'

Brook took a deep breath and ran his fingers through his hair. He looked up and fixed her in his sights. 'Then where's the beauty?'

'What?'

'You're the one who's forgotten. I knew Sorenson better than you. It's not just about wiping the scum off the earth. The professor had class. He gave them something before they died. He showed them beauty so they'd know what to look for if they ever found themselves in a better place. He made them see. What do you do? Destroy. What's the point? That's what your victims do, without thought for others, without the sensibility to know what they're doing, how it damages them. Don't you see? Victor showed them a better way, a shaft of light, of reason. A design for living that didn't involve instant gratification, didn't involve taking pleasure from the misery of others. Where was that for the Inghams? Where were the tears?'

Nicole stood now, unable to look at him. She checked her watch again. A noise from the other room focused her attention. 'In here,' she shouted over her shoulder. She raised her gun to Brook. 'Your phone please, Inspector.'

Brook stood up. 'I've told you. You won't kill me. Sorenson would spin in his grave.'

Nicole aimed the gun lower. 'How would he react to a kneecap, do you think?'

Brook held her gaze for a few seconds, then pulled out his phone. He took a huge pull on the last of his cigarette and threw the phone wide of her left hand. As she turned instinctively, he leapt for her gun hand and managed to knock the revolver up, then jammed the lit cigarette butt into her hand. She screamed and released the gun into Brook's hand. She glared at him, nursing her hand.

'Drop it, Damen!'

Brook and Nicole Bailey turned to the doorway together.

Brook's heart sank. Mike Drexler stood, face set, eyes like pebbles, looking at him down the barrel of a gun.

'Real careful.'

After a pause, Brook bent slowly to place the revolver on the floor. For some reason, Nicole didn't bolt over and pick it up. He looked over at her. She hadn't moved. Her eyes were glued onto Drexler, waiting while she massaged her burned hand.

'Good. Now kick it under the sofa.'

Brook backheeled the weapon under the sofa. 'Mike . . .'

'Shut up.'

'Agent Drexler. It's been a while. Let's see . . .'

'Fifteen years, Nicole – 1995. Think I'd forget?'

Nicole held his gaze, nodding in awe at the passing of time. 'As long as that?'

'Mike,' said Brook, looking from one to the other, unsure of what else he would say.

'Don't talk, Damen,' said Drexler insistently, a look of distaste on his face. 'Get on the bed, Nicole. No, not on your ass, on your knees. You can keep your clothes on this time.' Nicole slowly walked round the bed, then clambered onto the mattress.

'Mike,' tried Brook again. 'You've got to . . .'

Drexler trained the gun between Brook's eyes to halt him. 'Sorry to interrupt but I can't listen to you. I actually believed you, you're that good, Reaper man. Sorenson drilled you real well – and I ought to know.' He adopted a sneering, British accent. '"I was young and in a bad place." That was a good line. So imagine my surprise the next morning, looking out my window and seeing you with Nicole Bailey. All cosy – going for a walk and all. Now how careless is that, after all these years?' He speared a glance at Nicole. 'Did you think I wouldn't recognise you after all this time, kid? Think I wouldn't see past the hair colour and the cosmetic surgery?'

Nicole shrugged, adopting a pose. 'What do you think?'

Drexler broke into a smile. 'I think you look pretty damn good. For a dead girl.'

Nicole nodded. 'Better than my sister?' Drexler squirmed and rearranged the gun in his hand. 'Can you still see Sally's face, Mike? I carry it with me every day.'

'So do I,' he replied, through gritted teeth.

'Thank you for that, Mike. I appreciate it. I'm just glad you can't hear her screams like I do.'

Drexler lowered his gun and turned to Nicole, a haunted look in his eye. 'Cut it out.'

'Do you ever dream, Mike?'

'I said, cut it out.' Drexler aimed the gun at Nicole. 'Listen, kid, I dream about the things I've seen, sure, the things people do to other human beings. And I was on that estate after you took down that family.' Brook tried to speak but was halted by a wave of the gun. 'And no, they won't be missed. And yes, people are even glad they're gone. But Jesus, kid. A nine-year-old child?' Drexler took a deep breath and his tone became more measured. 'Look, I understand the impulse. And I'm not going to preach. You do whatever Sorenson wants; it's none of my business.' He lowered the gun. 'Killing a rapist is one thing but I couldn't shoot you any more than I could hang an unarmed kid. That's not why I've been all round the country looking for you.'

'Victor Sorenson is dead, Mike,' said Nicole with lowered head.

'So it's true.' Drexler looked at Brook.

'Mike. You have to know something,' began Brook.

'Damen, give it up,' said Nicole. 'We had a good run. But Mike's got us cold.'

'But, Mike, wait . . .'

'You heard. Give it up, Damen. I've been following you since I saw you together. See, you were my one link to Sorenson and The Reaper.'

'That's why you moved to Hartington.'

'And right next door too. How lucky was that? And boy, you were good. I was almost convinced but then you slipped up. And here I am in your secret lair. Your Aladdin's cave,' he chuckled, looking around the room. 'Sorenson was always so well organised. But like I said, I'm not trying to step on any toes. I'm here for one thing – to see my friend.' There was silence for a moment. 'Where is she?'

'Right behind you, Mike.'

*

A moment later Drexler's grip relaxed and the gun lowered. 'I can't.'

'Kill him,' screamed Nicole, tearing towards Drexler.

McQuarry stepped across her path and grabbed her flailing fists. She picked up the slight girl and threw her onto the bed where she stayed, sobbing into a pillow.

'Easy, honey.' She moved back to Drexler and patted him on the back. 'What's this?' She picked up an envelope from a side table. It had Drexler's name on it. She handed it to him.

Drexler took it from her and tore it open.

'What is it, Mike?'

'It's from Sorenson.' Drexler read the three lines of type quickly then let his hand fall and turned to stare at Jacob Ashwell moaning on the ground. He looked over at the girl, a bitter smile on his face. McQuarry took the note from him and read.

Your father's new name and address is overleaf.
You know what to do.
Remember . . .

'Go on, Ed. Finish the sentence.'

McQuarry smiled at her partner. 'Remember Sally Bailey's face.' She dropped the letter on the floor and walked over to the portable CD player and turned on the music. 'This is nice.' When she turned back to Drexler his weapon was raised again. 'Good, let's get this done, Mike.'

'You didn't speak to the nurse, did you, Ed?'

'This is a shock, Mike, I know . . .'

'Sorenson found the girl at Caleb's cabin – still alive.'

'Barely alive, Mike. The crash nearly killed her.'

'I wish it had,' squeaked the girl, tears still rolling down her face.

'All this time, trying to connect Sorenson to the Ashwells, and the girl was hidden away in his house. And the nurse . . . did you actually speak to her, Ed?'

McQuarry shook her head. 'No. But it stopped you talking to her.'

'And all that . . . stuff Sorenson knew about my father and Kerry. You?' McQuarry nodded. 'And Hunseth?' She nodded again. 'How could you?'

'I did what I had to do, Mike. Same as you will.'

Drexler nodded faintly. 'You think I'm going to shoot Ashwell for you and Sorenson?'

'Don't do it for either of us. Do it for her.' McQuarry nodded at Nicole Bailey. 'Do it for Sally.' Nicole covered her face with her hands, sobbing harder. 'You've no idea what she went through, Mike.'

'That doesn't justify . . .'

'Tell him, honey.'

'It doesn't matter, Ed. I can't just execute the guy . . .'

'You had no problem with Hunseth.'

'Hunseth could've killed you.'

McQuarry shook her head. 'I don't think so.'

'Every day I prayed those men would kill me, Agent Drexler,' said the girl softly. Both agents turned to her. 'I took a big hit in the crash, you see. Hurt my hip and my head. I was unconscious when that man and his brother and son killed Mum and Dad. I didn't wake up for days, though I could hear things sometimes. Hear what they did to Sally and the way they laughed when she begged them to stop.' The tears

384

continued to roll down her face. 'They were going to kill me, but the boy wanted to wait. Wait till I woke up. They wouldn't . . . hurt me unless they knew I could feel the pain. That's what they liked best. Towards the end I was conscious more and more, but you know what I did, Agent Drexler? I pretended. Every time they came in I pretended so they wouldn't touch me. But I had to listen when they hurt Sally. I had no choice – except one. I could have protected my little sister. I could've taken her place. I'm glad she's dead. She doesn't have to live with what happened to her. She doesn't have to hear the voices when she closes her eyes.'

'I'm sorry about your family, Nicole,' said Drexler.

'Then let's stop the hand-wringing, Mike and put an end to this,' urged McQuarry. 'Shoot the son of a bitch so we can get out of here. That's why you brought Sorenson's gun.'

Drexler looked down.

McQuarry looked at her watch. 'Come on, Mike. We haven't got all night.' She set off for the bathroom.

Drexler brandished the gun. 'Where the hell you going, Ed?'

'I've got to douse this baby in gasoline. We can't leave all this evidence around after you kill Ashwell.' She disappeared into the bathroom and returned with a canister and began to unscrew the top.

'Stop it, Ed.' She ignored him so Drexler braced to fire. 'Stop.'

McQuarry stopped unscrewing the top of the canister and stood upright. 'What are you going to do, Mike? Shoot me with a rogue gun, then ride off into the sunset with Ashwell? Think it through for once. That's always been your weakness. I know this is sudden, but I'm still your friend and always will be.'

Drexler stared coldly at her. 'I'm beginning to wonder if

you've ever been my friend. How long have you been planning this?'

'It doesn't matter, Mike. It doesn't change our friendship . . .'

'How long?'

McQuarry took a deep breath. 'The professor picked you out three years ago.'

'The professor?' snarled Drexler.

McQuarry looked down at her shoes. 'Then all we had to find was the right welcome gift.'

'My father,' nodded Drexler.

'It wasn't easy, Mike. He sure didn't want to be found. But we managed it.' She picked up the note. 'Put the address in your pocket. That's your introduction.'

'Introduction to what?'

'To our organisation. The Reaper. You figured it out. That's who the professor is. That's who I am now – a disciple. So will you be after your initiation.'

'Killing Ashwell?'

'He's already dead, Mike. You're just here to make it official.'

Drexler smiled grimly. Sorenson-speak. 'Why?'

'Because we're losing, Mike. Losing the war against the bad guys.'

'So we just execute them.'

'That's right. Like Hunseth was executed.'

Drexler nodded. 'That was no accident. You got too close, Ed. You got cut. Deliberate?'

'To do good, sacrifices have to be made. I told the professor you'd be useful to us but we had to be sure. I knew you'd take Hunseth down. He was a Doppelgänger for your father.' McQuarry took out a cigarette and her lighter. 'And now you're going to take down Caleb's brother.'

'Can I have a cigarette?'

McQuarry threw him the packet and the lighter after lighting her own. 'Remember Sally's face, partner.' She nodded at Jacob. 'He came in here to screw that little girl. He screwed her younger sister then stood around laughing while Caleb put a bullet in her head. It shouldn't be hard. You can do it. You'll be one of us.'

'Us?'

'Another disciple. The professor's recruiting all over the world.'

'Detective Sergeant Brook in England?'

'He's just one of many. Soon there'll be dozens, maybe even hundreds of us. Really making a difference.'

'He recruits traumatised little girls to help him?'

'Hell no. She volunteered.'

'That's right, Special Agent,' said Nicole. Drexler had almost forgotten she was in the room. 'I wanted to help. For Sally's sake. For Mum and Dad.'

'Can you even begin to imagine what she's been through in that hellhole of a room? The professor saved her life, Mike. If he hadn't gone there to kill Caleb and Billy, she'd be dead now.'

Drexler hung his head and remembered his own father torturing and abusing his sister, his mother.

'Of all people, Mike, you must understand. Remember that nothing is so difficult as not deceiving oneself.'

'Wittgenstein. Sorenson's got all the answers, hasn't he?'

McQuarry nodded. 'So shoot this piece of shit and avenge that little girl.'

'And if I don't? You kill me?'

'Jeez, Mike. Don't be so melodramatic. Think I could do that? That's not what we're about. You're one of us. One of the good guys. That's our oath to Sorenson. Go to the authorities, tell your story. We won't stop you. Not if it means killing one of our own. Chances are you'll be spilling to another disciple. Think about that. I'm your friend no matter what. We take out the lowlifes only when we're sure. If you won't do it, I'll have to.'

Drexler lit his cigarette and took a huge pull before picking up the note from Sorenson and holding the flame under it until the fire took hold. McQuarry pulled her weapon.

'Tell Sorenson I've made friends with my past.' He dropped the burning paper into a metal bin.

'He'll be as disappointed as I am,' said McQuarry, walking round the room now towards Ashwell.

Drexler levelled his gun at McQuarry. 'I can't let you do that, Ed.'

'You gonna stop me, Mike?' she said, pointing her weapon at Ashwell's head.

'Ed. I mean it.'

'Jacob Ashwell is going to die tonight. It's just a question of whether you kill me at the same time. That what you want?'

Drexler tossed the cigarette. 'I mean it, Ed. I will fire.'

McQuarry dropped her weapon to her side and turned to her partner. She looked him in the eye and moved towards him. 'You don't actually think Sorenson would give you a working gun before we were sure, do you?'

Drexler squirrelled a glance at his gun, but maintained firing position. McQuarry lifted her gun into her holster and clipped it home. 'Have it your way, Mike. Put that down. It's a dud.' She walked towards him and stood with her eyes an inch from the M9's barrel.

Drexler lifted the M9 to the ceiling and pulled the trigger. The gun made a dull clicking noise but didn't fire. He smiled into the break of tension then dropped the weapon to reach for his own gun in his ankle holster. But before he got close, a sharp pain in his neck made him

388

recoil and he turned to see Nicole Bailey pull away from him with an empty hypodermic in her fist.

Drexler began to feel his legs buckle but McQuarry held him upright. He could feel the skin of her face touching his and was vaguely aware that she was talking to him, but he couldn't take in what she was saying.

Then she dragged him to the bed and lowered him onto the mattress. She slapped his face and forced him into eye contact then extracted the keys to his Audi and threw them to Nicole.

'You blew it, Mike. All you had to do was make the world better. Gather up that sheet, hon.'

Nicole Bailey pulled the sheet to cover Drexler's feet and tied a knot in it. He followed her movements like a zombie, eyes only. McQuarry evidently did something similar behind his head, but he was unable to turn and see.

McQuarry extracted a camera from the case Sorenson had left behind, and took several photographs of the room and of Drexler and Jacob Ashwell, sitting helplessly against the wall. She returned the camera to the case and Nicole threw in the two hypodermics and unplugged the CD player and placed that inside also.

While Nicole trotted out to the car with the case, McQuarry rolled up Drexler's trouser leg and took out his back-up weapon. She checked the magazine and flicked off the safety. She aimed at Ashwell, who gazed up at her in mild interest.

'Welcome to hell, cockroach.' She fired twice to the head, causing blood and brain material to fan out around the wall. A last rasping breath bubbled through the blood in Ashwell's mouth and his chest stopped moving.

She put the gun in Drexler's hand, squeezed his fingers around the grip, then dropped it in an evidence bag peeled from another pocket.

'Insurance, Mike.' She tossed it to Nicole who departed to put it in Drexler's car.

Meanwhile McQuarry busied herself emptying gasoline around the room. When Nicole returned they each took an end of Drexler's sheet and lifted him onto the floor. They wrapped the sheet round him and McQuarry moved over him. His brain was on fire, his vision blurred and dotted with every colour in the rainbow and more. She slapped him playfully across the face to focus his eyes and grabbed his chin to hold his face to hers. He tried to speak and vaguely heard himself say, 'This gonna hurt?'

McQuarry smiled at him as he began to drift into a stupor. She slapped him softly again. 'No. It won't hurt. I'm going to miss you.' A tear sprang from the corner of her eye and landed on the sheet. 'Sleep now.' She bent down and kissed him on the forehead, then looked up at the girl. 'Okay, hon.' Between them they hoisted Drexler in the sheet and carried him to the Audi, squeezing him onto the back seat with some difficulty.

When they were ready to leave, McQuarry lit a cigarette, took a huge pull and threw the glowing butt into the cabin. A few moments later the hiss of the igniting accelerant was followed by the sizzle and crack of a fire starting. McQuarry jumped back into the Audi to watch the flames catch.

Nicole jumped into the passenger seat and turned to Drexler.

'I'm sorry. I know how it feels to be so powerless.' She bent down and picked something up from a bag and held it to her cheek. Drexler recognised the rag doll from the wrecked VW, before his eyes rolled up to his forehead and he fell into a black pit.

Chapter Twenty-Two

Drexler felt the cold steel of the gun by his ear and held his own weapon up to the ceiling. An arm grabbed it from him, then spun him round. Drexler looked at McQuarry and put his arms down. He broke into a grin.

'How you doing, Ed?'

McQuarry stepped into the light. She was below average height with medium-length grey hair; Brook could see the resemblance to the figure watching the Ingham house from Dottie North's bedroom. She turned her cold gaze to Brook, and gestured him to sit with a wave of her gun.

'You tell me,' she said with a touch more warmth in her eyes.

'You look great,' Drexler grinned. 'See you go to the same hair colourist as me.'

McQuarry laughed and her face softened around the rarely used laughter lines. She squinted down at Drexler's gun. 'Jeez, Mike. Is this Sorenson's M9?'

'Sure is. I knew you'd remember.'

'I hope you had the firing pin fixed.' She slid the M9 into her pocket and gestured across to Nicole, who got off the bed and searched Drexler's pockets. 'You,' she barked at Brook.

'Petra? Agent McQuarry? What do I call you?' asked Brook.

McQuarry smiled back at him. 'Well, I finally get to meet the great man without a lens between us. Tell a lie, we have met before.

391

I walked right past you, carrying that piece of fence outta the Ingham yard. That was a rush.'

'Wearing a forensic suit supplied by Nicole.' Brook nodded.

'That's right, Detective. You let me walk right by you. I coulda reached over and shook your hand – had to settle for a wink.' She grinned at Brook's face.

'And the other SOCOs thought you'd walked round the block to help them lift it.'

McQuarry continued to grin. Then she saw the computer. 'How long was he in here, hon?'

'Not long, Ed,' replied Nicole.

'He know about RAG?'

'No. He didn't know the password?'

Brook's eyes darted from one to the other. McQuarry grunted and stared at Brook, her grin long gone.

'On your knees, hands in front. Tie him, honey,' she said softly to Nicole. Nicole disappeared into the storage room. Drexler stared at Brook with a strange look on his face. Brook shrugged back at him.

'So you were telling the truth, Reaper man,' said Drexler.

'You two know each other?' asked McQuarry, her eyes narrowing.

'We're neighbours,' smiled Brook.

Nicole returned with a plastic tie. 'It's true,' she said. 'Agent Drexler saw me at his house. He's been following Brook.'

'Why?'

'To find you, Ed,' said Drexler. 'I nearly caught up with you in Brighton.'

'How did you know I was in England?'

'I didn't for sure. But Sorenson lived in England, Brook was here, Nicole was English. I just figured.'

Nicole held Brook's wrists together and pulled the plastic tie tight around them. Brook stared into her eyes while she worked and was finally rewarded with an almost embarrassed glance before she resumed her position behind McQuarry.

'Gotta hand it to you, Mike, you haven't lost your touch.' Her smile faded. 'What did you want to see me about?'

'You're my friend, Ed. Do I need a reason?'

McQuarry emitted a one-note chuckle. 'Yeah, after the Golden Nugget, you kinda do. Looking for some payback?'

'Payback? No. I just wanted to apologise . . .'

'Apologise?'

Drexler shrugged. 'I let you down in Tahoe. I shouldn't have got so moral on you. Jake Ashwell needed putting down. I know it's too late to make up for it, but there it is.'

'Mike, you're making me feel bad. I thought you'd still be pissed I sold you out to the professor.'

'You did what you thought was right.'

She fixed him with her cold blue eyes. 'And then there was your father.'

Drexler grinned. 'My father? I put that sorry-ass sonofabitch out of my mind from that moment on.'

'You didn't try to find him then?' asked McQuarry, her eyes piercing him.

'Nope. Far as I'm concerned, if the old fucker's still alive, whatever bar he's in right now and whatever woman he's beating up on, well, they're welcome to him. I started a new life that day and it's thanks to you. That's what I came to say.' He smiled at her.

There was silence while McQuarry looked at him. Finally she smiled. 'My pleasure. Well, if there's nothing else, Mike, we have a plane to catch.'

'What about Brook?' asked Nicole.

McQuarry turned her cold eyes back to him. '*This* sorry-ass sonofabitch is one major disappointment. I don't know what the professor ever saw in you. Just one cut and the world is saved from another scumbag. How many chances do you need to be a real man?'

Brook managed a chuckle. 'More than you I'm glad to say, Special Agent.'

McQuarry's face hardened. She looked again at the computer with its flashing prompt. 'Maybe we should just shoot him to be on the safe side.'

Brook continued to smile at McQuarry. 'Can I choose the music?'

McQuarry laughed. 'Keep it up, fella. With entertainment this good you just might live to see tomorrow. He comes with us,' she said to Nicole. 'We can drop him off on the way.'

'There's no need, Ed,' said Nicole. 'He can't do anything without giving himself away. Let's put him under for a day.'

'He comes with us, hon. Let's hustle.'

'What about me, Ed?' asked Drexler. 'Anything I can do?'

'Give us a hand with the luggage?'

*

Nicole marched Brook in front of her, a gun at his back, a coat thrown over his bound wrists. They went carefully down the stairs and, on reaching the entrance hall, continued down another flight to the basement.

'How's your hand?'

'It hurts.'

'I'm sorry.' Brook turned his head to her. 'She's going to kill me, Nicole. You know that, don't you? Mike too probably.'

'She's not like that, now stop talking.'

'People change.'

'That's not the way it works, Damen. Uncle Vic wouldn't allow it.'

'Sorenson's dead and I'll be joining him soon. She knows the area, right?'

'She's lived in Derby the last two years. I was in Brighton mostly.'

'Want to bet we'll make a detour down a deserted road on the way?'

'Give it a rest, Damen.' Nicole halted Brook next to a parking bay containing a sleek black Audi. She opened the side door, took out a roll of gaffer tape and stretched a piece over Brook's mouth before pushing him into the back seat. She sat behind the wheel and glanced up at Brook in the driver's mirror. His eyes were fixed on hers.

Two minutes later, Drexler and McQuarry emerged into the gloom carrying two bags. Each placed a bag in the boot before McQuarry closed it.

Drexler looked at her. 'Well, I guess this is it. What time's your plane?'

McQuarry smiled back. 'It's a private jet. Takeoff's when we get there.'

'Smooth.'

'Say, Mike. Come and see us off, would you? I'd appreciate it. You can drive the car back here.'

'You're coming back?'

'You never know.'

Drexler gazed into his former partner's eyes, a thin smile barely grazing his features.

'Don't worry. The satnav will get you back.'

Drexler's smile broadened. 'Sure, Ed. I'd like that. But no tears this time.'

McQuarry laughed. 'You sit in front with Nicky.'

'Why is Agent Drexler coming?' asked Nicole, starting the car.

'He's going to drive the car back,' McQuarry replied, not looking at her. She sat next to Brook in the back and when the car reached the security gate she waved a card at a sensor and it opened. She passed the security card forward to Drexler. 'You'll need this when you bring the car back, Mike.' He pocketed it with a nod. 'And you better have these, Inspector Damen Brook.' Nicole looked in the mirror as McQuarry took the keys to the flat and dropped them in Brook's jacket pocket. 'Just in case you come to your senses – it's a good location if you need to store supplies and there are plenty of resources already there.' Brook managed his best sceptical expression, despite his taped mouth. Thank God for eyebrows.

They set off through the deserted streets of Derby for the short trip to East Midlands Airport, past the Midland Hotel and the Indian restaurant in which Nicole/Laura had poisoned DCI Hudson. Within fifteen minutes they were on the A50 heading towards the motorway.

Brook used his bound hands to wind down the rear window a crack to suck in the cold, mulchy air. McQuarry looked over. 'The childlocks on, honey?' she asked Nicole.

'They're on.'

Ten minutes later they exited a roundabout. Nicole pulled on a baseball cap which made her look more anonymous, presumably for the upcoming airport cameras.

'Drive straight on,' said McQuarry.

Nicole looked sharply at Brook in the mirror. 'Why?' she asked a little too loudly.

'We can hardly drive into the airport with the inspector bound and gagged, honey. We'll just drop him in the middle of nowhere and he can walk back to civilisation. Okay with you, Inspector?'

Brook broke off his stare into the driver's mirror, but made no effort to acknowledge the question. Another five minutes and the streetlights disappeared and the roads started to narrow and meander.

Nicole was forced to drive much slower and Brook kept his gaze on her. When she wasn't looking at Brook, her eyes were darting from side to side.

'It's the middle of winter, Ed. What if the inspector turns an ankle and can't walk? He could die of hypothermia.'

McQuarry flashed back a private-joke smile. 'He'll be fine, honey. We'll wrap him up warm. Take the next left.'

Nicole turned left onto a one-car track, slowing the car to fifteen miles an hour. She had to put the headlights on full beam.

'Pull in here,' ordered McQuarry. The car halted next to a field covered in grass. Apart from those of the car and the moon and stars in the sky, there were no lights visible anywhere.

Nicole wouldn't look at Brook and he got the impression she was breathing heavily.

'Everybody out.' The gun had reappeared in McQuarry's hand and she dragged Brook from his seat. She pulled him round the car and walked him into the semi-gloom at the edge of the headlight beam before pushing him to his knees. Nicole and Drexler got out but didn't venture away from the vehicle. McQuarry tore off the gag and Brook exercised his jaw. He thought about shouting for help, but didn't want to hasten his end.

'If you've got any prayers, Brook, now's the time.' She tapped the back of his head with the nozzle of her gun.

Brook managed a bitter one-note chuckle. 'I'm British, Ed. We've abolished God.' The sight of one of his final breaths condensing in the air made him yearn for a last cigarette.

McQuarry turned to the car, a huge toothy grin on her mouth. 'This is a funny guy. What a waste.'

'This isn't right, Ed. Brook's a police officer. Uncle Vic wouldn't want this.' Nicole's voice was strained, her speech punctuated by sharp breaths visible in the cold.

'Uncle Vic is in the ground, honey, and times change. Only people don't. He's fucked up too many times. We can't trust him.'

'You can't kill him, Ed,' Nicole tried again. 'He's served. He's one of the good guys.'

'I'll make it quick, honey,' answered McQuarry. 'But we can't leave him. He knows too much. Now let's not drag this out.'

'Ed, please don't. He doesn't know anything.'

'RAG, Inspector Brook. It stands for Reaper Armageddon. On that day, the whole world will know the value of The Reaper's work.' McQuarry grinned at Nicole. 'See, honey, he knows too much.'

McQuarry turned to Drexler and beckoned him over. After a

brief hesitation Drexler walked across to Brook and McQuarry, his arms resolutely inside his coat.

'You said you wanted to make it right, Mike. Here.' McQuarry changed her own gun to her left hand and took out the M9. 'Use Sorenson's gun like you should've in Tahoe. It has a nice ring to it.'

Drexler looked at McQuarry's outstretched hand, then at Brook, then into McQuarry's cold eyes. He smiled suddenly then nodded and took the gun, examining it carefully before flicking off the safety. He pointed it at the back of Brook's head.

Brook saw the shadow of Drexler's outstretched arm in the glow of the headlights and closed his eyes. There would be no music tonight.

'The bad guys have guns,' he muttered, waiting for the explosion.

A second later Drexler swivelled, pointing the gun at McQuarry. 'Drop it, Ed.'

She grinned at him and nodded, but made no move to drop her gun. 'I knew it.'

'You have to answer for my father.'

McQuarry smiled faintly. 'You were always weak.' She held onto her revolver but made no move to raise it.

'Drop the gun, Ed.'

'So you didn't put him out of your mind.'

'I couldn't. I found him without your help. It was six months after the Golden Nugget. He was working in a soup kitchen in San Francisco. But then you already knew that.' McQuarry didn't reply. 'Did you also know he'd been sober for a year? No? Did you know he gave his time for free? No? Did you know he was doing the twelve steps?'

McQuarry shrugged.

'He sobbed when I found him, Ed. He begged me to try and forgive him for what he'd done. He said he'd understand if I couldn't, but he said he loved me and wanted me in his life.'

'And you believed him? What a schmuck.'

'No, I didn't believe him. And no, I didn't trust him. But guess what? I no longer wanted him dead. See, he was suffering for what he'd done. I saw that much. It was killing him inside. And if it took years to win back my trust he said he wanted to try. He needed at least that ray of hope. I was prepared to allow him that.'

'He was a wife-beating drunk, Mike.'

'Was? You heard he died then.'

'I heard, Mike,' smiled McQuarry.

'Did you hear someone waited for him in his fleapit hotel and cut his throat?'

'I didn't just hear it, Mike. I was there. He took it well. When I told your father you'd sent me, I think he wanted to die. He knew he didn't deserve to live.'

'People do change, Ed. My father had.'

'No, he hadn't. The first thing he did when I took out the blade was drop to his knees and start praying. That sound like he'd changed?'

'You've changed, Ed. You're crazy.'

McQuarry laughed. 'That's the thanks I get.'

'Drop the gun, Ed. It's not too late.'

McQuarry laughed again. 'Or what? You'll shoot me?'

'Before I let you kill a brother officer, yes.'

She shook her head. 'Like I said, people don't change.' She grinned. 'This is the second time you've put your faith in Sorenson's gun. Know how easy it is to disable the firing pin, Mike? I could do it with the gun in my pocket in the back of a dark car.'

Drexler glanced at the weapon then fired the M9 just above McQuarry's head. The trigger clicked but no bullet was discharged. Drexler nodded and wrenched out a resigned smile.

'See, Mike, you can't grift a grifter.'

'People do change,' said Drexler. 'The Edie McQuarry I knew wouldn't forget to check my ankle holster.'

McQuarry's grin froze on her face as Drexler raised his other hand a fraction before she could raise her own. Deafening explosions and a spray of orange were exchanged and both fell.

Nicole jumped out from behind the car and ran over to McQuarry. She was dead, her fish eyes glaring up at Pisces in the heavens. Drexler moaned and Nicole turned to him. Brook was on his feet by now, but kneeled again when he saw Drexler. He gestured with his hands to Nicole and she ran back to the car and returned with a scalpel. She severed his bonds and they both pulled Drexler up by the shoulders. He screamed in pain. The bullet had struck him just above the heart. The blood was flowing but he made to speak.

'The good guys too,' he whispered, then fell back.

'I'll get your phone,' sobbed Nicole.

'No, he won't last. Grab his legs.'

They grabbed each end of Drexler as delicately as they could manage and stretched him onto the back seat. Brook jumped into the driver's seat and started the engine. Nicole opened a door.

'Wait!' said Brook, looking over at McQuarry's twisted corpse. 'Empty her pockets.' Nicole looked at him. 'Hurry.'

She bolted over to the body. 'What about the guns?'

'Leave them.'

Nicole hurried back to the car and got in the back with Drexler.

'Hang on, Mike,' shouted Brook, spinning the wheels out of the field.

'Can you remember the way, Damen?' Nicole asked.

Brook caught her eyes in the driver's mirror. 'Every bloody inch.' She couldn't hold his look.

*

'Sal, Sal. It's okay. It's okay.'

Brook looked at his watch. It was 4.30 in the morning. He couldn't listen to the mumbled panic any more so he reached across to Nicole's chair and shook her awake. She shuddered, raised her sweat-flecked head from her arms and lifted a bleary eye to Brook.

'Any news?'

Brook shook his head. 'Still in surgery.'

She buried her head in her hands and screwed her face up. 'What have I done?'

Brook looked at her. 'What *have* you done?'

She looked at him and then at the floor. 'Tony was my first, the only one. It wasn't easy but it wasn't hard. He raped your daughter when she was only fifteen.'

Now it was Brook's turn to look at the floor. 'And the Inghams?'

Nicole looked at him and shook her head. 'If there's blood, Ed always . . .' she couldn't finish.

'The law won't make a distinction.'

'No.'

'And the boy?'

After a pause, 'I held his legs.' She started to cry. 'What have I done?'

'And you emptied McQuarry's pockets?'

'Completely,' she said. 'If you're worried about what I'll say about you and Sorenson . . .'

'I never worry about me. I have weaknesses. That's my strength.'

'Yes but—'

'You never lost that accent. Why?'

'What has that—?'

'Why?'

Nicole hesitated until her confusion gave way to resignation. 'Uncle Vic hired a private tutor. She was English.'

Brook smiled.

'Why is that funny? Why is it even significant?'

'And whose idea was it to become a police officer?'

'Uncle Vic thought . . .'

'Let me guess. He thought it would help his work.' Nicole looked away. 'It would give you access to deserving cases. To men like Caleb. Like Harvey-Ellis. Like me.'

After suitable reflection, Nicole answered with a barely audible, 'Yes.'

Brook threw her the car keys, then the keys to the flat in Magnet House. 'It's a gunshot. They have to inform the police. I showed them my warrant card so that buys you some time. We're in a different division so that buys you some more.'

'Where are we?'

'Queens Medical Centre in Nottingham – it was nearer.' She nodded.

'On your way out clean yourself up and keep that cap down low. Hospitals have cameras. Take the car back to Magnet House and put everything from McQuarry's pockets: the luggage, passports, everything, back in the flat.' He gave her the security card for the car park. 'Leave the car in the darkest bay and cover Mike's blood with a blanket, then get back to your room at the Midland. You're ill. You tell Joshua you have to go home. I assume you still have a home?' She nodded. 'No dramatic notes telling the world everything?' This time she shook her head. 'When you leave tomorrow put all the keys and the card in a padded envelope and leave it at the front desk for me. You're all over that flat so we can't risk it being discovered. When things die down, I'll sort things out.'

She looked at him. 'I don't understand.'

'You have to hurry.'

Nicole put a hand on his and sought his eyes. 'You don't have to risk everything for me.'

'Sorenson did.'

'But now I know what I've done. I have to pay for that.'

Brook looked up at her. 'You have paid. And if you're anything like me, you'll keep paying. That's why I have to help you.' Nicole was still perplexed. 'When you were asleep you kept mumbling

402

your sister's name. You suffered a trauma no child should have to go through. And you were fifteen when Sorenson got hold of you. You were easy meat. Don't you see? The private tutor, the career choice – Sorenson controlled you, groomed you.' Now it was Brook's turn to look away. 'I should know. He did the same to me. And no matter what he'd done to save you, you had a right to a normal life or at least a shot at one. Sorenson denied you that.'

Nicole stared at her hands unable to speak.

'You've lost half your life, Nicole. Some killers get out in ten years. You know what you've done? Well, that's the point. And you have a chance that most killers never get. You have another life to step into and a job that will allow you to spend the rest of that life making amends. What I can do, you can do. Now go.'

Finally she looked at him. 'What will you say?'

'I'll think of something. I've had a lot of practice.'

'But if Agent Drexler makes it—'

'He's been shot. If he makes it, he won't remember anything for a while.'

'I still don't—'

Brook got her to her feet. 'Call it a leap of faith.' Nicole moved into him and kissed him softly on the lips. He pulled her away. 'Goodbye, Nicole. Next time we meet you can tell me all about the Golden Nugget.'

'Call me Laura.' Her eyes lingered over his, then she hurried out, grabbing a white coat from a hook as she went.

Brook looked after her. 'Laura – beautiful name.'

Epilogue

Denise Ottoman had blinked in disbelief at the crowds outside the police station. There were journalists screaming questions at her, including that pushy one from the *Telegraph* with the yellow teeth. Then photographers and cameramen pointed bright lights in her face and shouted 'This way, Denise' or 'Over here, Mrs O'. She hadn't given a comment, not from choice but from sheer befuddlement. Even more bewildering were the dozens of people gathered outside the gates cheering, some carrying hastily produced placards with various slogans: 'Go JoDen. You got the X Factor.' 'Scum in fear, the Reaper's near' and the cryptic 'Sugar and spice, all throats sliced'.

Even at home there were well-wishers and back-clappers, though the two uniformed officers managed to get her inside unmolested. Hours later, she was sitting up in bed with a mug of cocoa, pulling her legs into her chest as hard as she could. It was nearing midnight – the telephone was off the hook and the freshening wind had dispersed the crowd who had gone to their own beds. Denise took a sip of lukewarm cocoa. No sleep without John.

She put her cup on the floor and just lay in the dark with her eyes closed. A creaking noise above opened them. A prolonged scrape followed a second later. She switched on the bedside lamp. It didn't come on. She peered at it in the gloom. The bulb was missing so she jumped out of bed and reached for the bedroom curtain, yanking it brusquely to let the moonlight in. A small column of dust falling from the ceiling sparkled in the lunar radiance and Denise followed it to its source. The trapdoor to the loft was shifting as though being lifted from above, and Denise Ottoman wondered if the wind had dislodged more roof tiles.

Then a foot in a black shoe dropped down, followed by a second. Denise shrank to the ground, wrapping the curtain around her, daring neither to look nor look away. Her scream of shock emerged as a mouse-like whimper and her heart skipped as black-clad legs, torso and head fell to the floor.

From the black ball a figure began to unravel like a newborn foal slowly clambering to its feet. Once upright, new lungs inflated with oxygen and new hands mimicked the sensation of first touch. Inch by tiny inch, the figure rotated the half circle to lay eyes on the squirming Denise, her bare feet pushing at the carpet, trying to force herself through the wall behind her.

A black-gloved palm was crossed with flashing steel and Jason's grinning teeth followed suit.

'I'm ready, bitch. Are you?'

In Conversation with Steven Dunne

If you were stranded on a desert island which book would you take with you?

This is a difficult question to answer because a desert island is exactly the place to catch up with all the books you've ever wanted to read but never had the time. To choose one is a terrible restriction, but as long as I had writing materials and sun block it probably wouldn't be too hard to bear.

The other consideration of course is whether to take a favourite book to re-read, or a novel you've always wanted to tackle but have never quite got round to. Although I write thrillers I have to admit I wouldn't take even a favourite one to the island. I'm not keen on reading books over and over because there are so many unread books on my shopping list and, once read, thrillers, no matter how satisfying, lose a large part of their allure when the plot is resolved.

For that reason I would select a novel that can deliver new pleasures with each reading. *The Corrections* by Jonathan Franzen would be a contender, as would Joseph Heller's *Catch 22*. *The Magus* by John Fowles is set on a Greek island so might be a more appropriate choice, as would *The Naked and the Dead* by Norman Mailer for similar reasons. And if I had to choose a novel that I haven't read but have always meant to – *Slaughterhouse Five* by Kurt Vonnegut.

Where does your inspiration come from?

The inspiration for *The Reaper* wasn't difficult. A regular look at the news will throw up stories reporting the kind of social problems that The Reaper thinks need addressing – young people killing one another in the streets, anti-social elements blighting run-down estates, living their lives without any consideration for the rest of society. These are the real issues that give The Reaper a reason for being. Despite the extremist solution to anti-social families, at least The Reaper kills quickly and takes no pleasure from the violence visited upon the victims. The only goal is their removal from the face of the earth because The Reaper believes that the victims have wasted their lives and do not deserve to live. In that sense my killer is disinterested and, it can even be argued, a moral force. Certainly readers have told me that they found it difficult at times to know who to root for and this ambiguity goes to the heart of *The Reaper* series and Inspector Brook's struggle with his conscience and inability to empathise with the victims.

Have you always wanted to be a writer?

Honestly, no. The creative urge hit me at Kent University when my great friend Giles Newington, who now writes for The Irish Times, persuaded me to act in a production of Pinter's *The Birthday Party*. From there it was a short journey to writing and performing with him. Being big fans of *Spitting Image* and other satirical fare, our chosen avenue was comedy, little realising how tough a nut it was to crack, especially when there was a conveyor belt of talent from the Footlights who usually had the contacts and the profile.

Writing a comedy pilot for a series was a good experience but at a certain point in the process it became necessary to seek the approval of others before going further. At that point, judgements are made by strangers that can kill a project cold. The novel appealed as a vehicle which required nothing but my own input to reach completion and, after a gap of several years in pursuit of a living in journalism and education, I turned to the form to create *Reaper: Coming Soon to a Family Near You*; the original title of *The Reaper*.

What is a typical working day for you? Have you ever had writer's block? If so, how do you cope with it?

My writing day is far from typical and I sometimes have to snatch time to get it done. I still work in education, though not full-time now that *The Reaper* series has taken off. But when I have got time to write, I'm happiest working a traditional day because eight hours is about my limit for sitting down. Besides, my wife – a head teacher – works long hours so I'm happy to do the domestic drudge of cleaning and cooking the evening meal while the work of the day percolates through my mind. Honestly, writer's block has never been a problem. From time to time I wrangle over a plot point, sometimes for weeks, especially if I feel the characters aren't comfortable with the path I've set them on, but that's usually not a problem as much of the joy of writing is the rewriting where such problems are smoothed out.

The hardest thing is coming up with a working synopsis for the next book because, although I have a vague idea of what's going to happen and where the story will end up, I know that things on the journey will not be set in stone. Once I start the actual work, things gradually drop into place.